STAY BURIED

NINA GRANT

ISBN-13: 979-8-3524-0636-6

Stay Buried

First edition 2022
Copyright © 2022 by Nina Grant

Cover design by Deranged Doctor Design
https://www.derangeddoctordesign.com/

All rights reserved. No part of this book may be reproduced in any form or by any electronic or mechanical means, including information storage and retrieval systems—except in the case of brief quotations embodied in critical articles or reviews—without permission from the publisher at ironwrenbooks@gmail.com.

This is a work of fiction. Names, characters, places and events are products of the author's imagination or are used fictitiously. Any resemblance to actual persons, places, or events is coincidental and unintended.

Printed in U.S.A.

For Pete, again and always.

CHAPTER 1
ROBIN

She's been in here plenty of times before. I've fixed her caramel lattes and iced mochas, scratched her name—Lisa—on the side of a cup with a dying Sharpie, slipped those drinks into her veiny hand without the hairs on my neck standing up or the shadowy spot at the corner of my mind, where Marina still lives, still craves truth and justice and an ounce of redemption, registering the slightest psychic tingle. But today is different. Today she orders a double espresso. Today it's raining, the kind of angry gray deluge that gripped us for days when we lost Marina and weeks (or so it seemed) when we found her.

I fill her cup, snap on the lid, take my time perfecting those four small letters—L-I-S-A—all the while weighing my options. The shop is busy. Classes have lurched back into gear at the university nearby, and this dimly lit hangout draws tortured poets and type-A ass kissers in droves. Only two of us are working the lunch rush, me and the manager, an uptight guy named Jeremy.

Jeremy hates me. Not that I care. He can complain all he wants about my unexcused absences and subpar customer-service skills. He can bash my faded tattoos and premature crow's feet—"You're only thirty-four?" he asked once, his face pinched like he'd tongued a lemon—until the cows come home. I didn't choose this life; it chose me.

Screw him, I think as I cap the marker and consider sliding Lisa's coffee across the counter without a word. Because what if I'm wrong?

What if she's not who I think she is? What if she never worked the streets? Never knew my sister? Doesn't have the smallest scrap of information about who killed Marina? Or worse: What if she says Marina overdosed, like the cops claimed? What if she saw the whole ugly thing? (There was evidence of two girls at the crime scene; soda cans with different lipstick prints were found near Marina's corpse.)

If Marina were still alive, she'd be forty now. Twenty-four years gone in the blink of an eye. Less than a blink. A flutter. She was only sixteen when she died. Sometimes I forget that. Back then, she was the sophisticated older sister, teasing her hair and wearing miniskirts and listening to Prince and Madonna LPs on our father's clunky old record player. I thought of her as a movie star—she had a dramatic streak and could've been Phoebe Cates's body double—or a ballerina or maybe a princess, like Grace Kelly or Lady Di.

Jeremy's breath hits my neck, hot and pulsing. He reaches past me for a plastic-wrapped muffin. "Let's hustle," he chirps, in a way that's meant to be encouraging but just pisses me off.

Beggars can't be choosers, I remind myself. I'm lucky to have this job—*any* job—with my spotty work history. The coffee gig is my third job this year, and I only got hired here because my cousin Peggy was the opening-shift supervisor.

I mumble something agreeable, hoping to keep Jeremy off my back for a few more seconds. Because I've made my choice. It wasn't a question, really. I have to know if this woman is Lisa Thompson, the doe-eyed teen who, in 1985, sold herself beside my sister for a crumpled handful of dollar bills, a fitful night of sleep on some perv's ratty couch, a few lines (if the sleazebag was feeling particularly generous) of cocaine.

What are the chances that I've found Lisa—*the* Lisa—after all these years? Slim, I'd say, except for those eyes. I've seen them thousands of times in a blotchy, peeling Polaroid from Marina's tattered purse. A flashing neon clue burrowed in my subconscious, watching and waiting, yearning to break free.

"Lisa?" I say, lifting my voice over the din of the crowd and the torrent of rain on the shop's metal roof. My fingers curl protectively around the cup, like it's a bargaining chip in an unspoken war.

Lisa looks better than you'd expect for a former prostitute. Clean. Wholesome. Soft pink makeup. Long straight ponytail. Chic black raincoat with voluminous pockets, maybe for holding Lisa Jr.'s ladybug barrettes or Teddy Grahams. She sidesteps a lumberjack-looking guy, who could be a student or a professor, and I loop around the counter to meet her. When she reaches for the coffee, I hold it back. "Lisa Thompson?" I say, pairing a familiar tone with a disarming smile.

Her gaze roams the shop as if another Lisa might be waiting in the wings. "Double espresso?" she asks, nodding at my frozen hand.

I don't budge. "You're Lisa Thompson, right?" The line has hit the door, and, without looking, I know Jeremy is hurling daggers at my back. "You used to live on the corner of March and Crimson, in the big yellow Victorian with the wraparound porch." This much police records and a long-ago night of drunk investigating have taught me.

Her head swings back and forth. "Sorry." A weak shrug. "Nope."

Something about the way she speaks—the evenness; the cool, slippery detachment—convinces me she's lying. But why? The obvious reason is guilt: She knows who killed Marina or maybe even did it herself.

I squeeze the coffee until its sides pucker. "Really?" I say, tamping down a tremor in my voice. "Are you sure? I never forget a face." *Especially one that might've been the last thing my sister saw*, I want to add. But I leave that out for now.

"Is that mine?" she asks, motioning at the coffee. "I'm late for class."

I wonder if she's one of those sad middle-aged women, trying to claw back her youth by invading the turf of the coeds she so desperately envies. But she's missing the messenger bag and the laptop. And her shiny new yoga pants say she's headed for a workout next door.

I stand my ground, ignoring the customers, who are jammed together by the cash register like disgruntled cattle. Somewhere behind me, Jeremy's voice reverberates in angry waves.

I give Lisa one last chance to tell the truth. "I remember you," I say, conjuring a lie of my own. "We hung out a few times, down by the river. You used to party with Alex Ross and Kim Forman and"—I squint for believability—"what was her name? That girl? The one who killed herself? Marie? Maria something?"

Deadpan, she says, "I don't know what you're talking about."

Liar.

"Oh, yeah," I say. "Marina. Marina Davis. You guys were like Siamese twins." I frown. "It must've been hard, when she—"

She pulls in a breath. "Listen, I've gotta go. Can I have the coffee?"

Sorry. My murdered sister trumps your yoga class. "I won't say anything," I lean in and whisper, "about, you know …" If she trusts me with her secrets, maybe she'll open up about Marina. About the pimps. The johns. The thefts. The beatings. The drugs. The loneliness. The cold concrete. The desperation. The inside jokes. The buddy system. The fleabag motels. The backseats. The rapes. The street lingo. The boredom. The regrets. The fire.

The fire.

When I think about Marina, that's what gets me the most: Two-thirds of her body was burnt beyond recognition. But how? She collapsed with a needle in her arm. (Supposedly.) So who set the fire?

My mind is raging about the shoddy investigation (if you can call it that), the prejudice (dead prostitutes, even *child* prostitutes, aren't exactly a top priority), the media blackout (not a single story on my sister's case in two decades), and on and on.

Lisa has had enough of my game. She grabs for the coffee.

I don't think; I just squeeze and push, and suddenly hot, dark liquid is streaming down her coat, rushing over her Spandexed thighs, splashing to a halt on her rainbow-colored sneakers (mostly) and the floor.

For some reason, I'm laughing—hysterically laughing—as she bats the coffee off her stomach, cursing and spitting, calling me a thousand shades of crazy and threatening to sue.

Let her try. You can't get blood from a stone, as they say. Not that she'd risk drawing attention to herself, anyway. Her kind of secrets stay buried at all costs.

The shop goes quiet. A sea of eyes digs into us. I compose myself enough to grind out an apology, which Lisa rebuffs with a snort. Before I can say anything else—a sarcastic "Have a nice day!" is itching to pop out of my mouth—Jeremy swoops in and calms things with some professional fawning and a fifty-dollar gift card on the house.

By the time Lisa melts back into the downpour, I'm behind the counter again, slogging through orders and plotting my next move. Because now that I've found her, I can't let her get away. Not without wringing every last drop of information out of her about Marina's murder—my pulse quickens at the thought of bringing my sister's killer to justice—and making her answer for what she's done.

CHAPTER 2
LISA

There's someone in every crowd who doesn't grasp how the world works, who's driven to buck the system at their own peril. Today that person is Sophie Gallagher, a spoiled housewife and mother of two preteen boys with nothing better to do than blather on about her superficial friendships and the political maneuverings of Roosevelt Junior High's PTA.

Unlike Sophie, most of my patients come in world-wise, through a loose underground referral network. Without a word from me, they know to check certain boxes on the intake forms to get the prescriptions they want (distractibility, forgetfulness, and lack of organizational skills for Adderall; irritability, restlessness, and uncontrollable worry for Xanax). It's a closed ecosystem, symbiotic—they get the pills; I get the cash—and in perfect, rational harmony. Except for the proverbial fly …

After twenty minutes of dissecting an encounter with a fellow Roosevelt parent that Sophie perceived as a snub ("She must've seen me! I was right outside the principal's office!"), she digs through her purse for a printout and confronts me about a "billing error."

I glance at the page just long enough to satisfy her. "I'll have my business manager look into it," I say, tucking the sheet into a stack of papers headed for the shredder.

"Good. Because there's a glitch or something. I've gotten the same bill three times."

She's right. There *is* a glitch: her. "Have you spoken to the insurance company?"

"Well, no."

"Don't bother," I say. "I'll handle it. You won't be seeing any more bills." Insurance is a double-edged sword: lucrative but risky. There's always a chance that some bean counter in Dubuque will catch on. Cash is king, of course, but an all-cash business draws unwanted attention. Accepting insurance and a few legitimate patients puts a respectable sheen on things. "Let's move on to Adam," I say. Adam is her pilot husband. She's convinced he's cheating on her with every flight attendant in the friendly skies. "Has he initiated sex this week?"

She rolls her neck, taps her foot, eyes the door like it's an escape hatch in a five-alarm fire. After a long pause, she says, "Not really."

I have her now. She's child's play: predictable, melodramatic, led easily—willingly—to the slaughter. "Do you think it's your weight?" I ask, fixing my face with a sympathetic frown. The woman is no bigger than I am, a svelte size six, but her anorexic frenemies have convinced her she's a beached whale.

Her tears are quick and violent. I withhold the tissues until her face is a blotchy, snot-soaked mess. Even then, I allow her only one and shift the box out of reach. At the height of her hysterics (she's devolved into a gasping rant about her father and cheerleading camp and a boy—a childhood crush, I assume—named Tom), I reach into my desk and retrieve my prescription pad. If memory serves, she's on a cocktail of antidepressants, plus something to help her sleep: Wellbutrin, Prozac, Xanax, and Ambien, maybe. Or Lunesta. Either way, it's a wonder she can walk. "Are you taking your medicines?" I ask in a concerned voice.

Between whimpering sobs, she assures me that she is.

"Excellent." Now I know what the authorities will find in her system after the fact. I'll just backdate some chart notes to show all but one of the prescriptions—the Prozac, probably—as discontinued. This will get me off the hook for overprescribing and paint her as an out-of-control addict. If anyone asks, I'll say she forged my signature. It'll be her word against mine if she survives to contradict me, but she won't.

As luck would have it, Sophie is the last patient of the day. And my receptionist, Jacquelyn, is champing at the bit to leave early for her granddaughter's recital.

I buzz Jacquelyn's extension and dismiss her. As for my business manager, she doesn't exist, unless you count a revolving door of temps I use for data entry and other menial tasks.

When I bought this building, I knew it would pay off. Instead of securing the anchor spot at a strip mall by the industrial park, I chose the quaint charm of an antique colonial, whose rooms I lease by ones and twos to accountants and lawyers, dentists and psychiatrists (my fellow shrink is a seventy-year-old sexist pig from India—Dr. Kapoor—whom I keep around as a mental sparring partner). My tenants come in late and leave early—the place is a ghost town by 3 P.M.—making it all but certain that, upon Jacquelyn's exit, Sophie and I will be alone.

As tempting as it is to rid myself of her here and now, I must think things through. Sloppy work is worse than a job undone. Maybe she'll turn a blind eye if I wield the right stick. Insurance fraud is nothing—who cares if I billed for nonexistent visits?—compared to her lesbian affair being revealed and her marriage, such as it is, being demolished.

I caress the prescription pad and mull over my options. Letting her live is too big a risk. She was fun while she lasted, but she's run her course. If she were better in bed, the math might be different—at least for a while longer. But perky breasts and an impish smile won't save her. "Do you need any refills?" I ask, tapping the pad. Prescribing something deadly—introducing a grenade into her bloodstream—would be easy, but also stupid. Traceably stupid. And beneath me.

She fidgets like a child in a timeout. "I'm all right."

It would be a pity to kill her without one last tryst, for old times' sake. I set the pad aside and make my way around the desk, my heels clicking as they move from carpet to hardwood. Behind Sophie's chair, I stop and lay my hands on her shoulders. Her muscles are putty, yielding to my every whim. I loosen her up to the point of tortured moaning before snaking my tongue down her neck. She protests weakly—this is part of our game, her pretending not to want it—and I ramp up the assault, falling over the chair in a tangle of lust and exploration. I pop the buttons of her blouse. Her hand slides under my skirt, skimming my thigh on its way to her personal Nirvana.

Ten minutes later, the damage is done. As I slip back into my heels, a thought occurs to me: Maybe I can seduce her into a suicide pact. She's gullible enough to believe we're star-crossed lovers. Might she kill herself and save me the trouble?

The problem with this idea is time. I don't doubt my sway over her, but the depth of control needed to bring someone to suicidal climax is immense. Practicality dictates another tack. Something blunt and brutal, over and done with. "Are you hungry?" I ask, a plan forming.

Instead of answering, she projects a stunned baby-bird look.

"I'm serious. We should grab a bite. I know the perfect place"—a dive too lowdown for video cameras, on the outskirts of town—"where we can be alone."

She bites her lip. "I'm supposed to help Caleb build a model of the human brain. I've still gotta get the clay."

"We won't be long," I promise, staring deep into her eyes. I squeeze her hand and smile. "Trust me."

CHAPTER 3
ROBIN

When the afternoon crew shows up—first the economics major named Drew, who should be running this place instead of Jeremy, and then Vickie, the retired art teacher and potter (some of her bowls are displayed around the shop, and they aren't half bad), and finally Emma, the mother of triplets who would do anything to get out of the house, including work here—Jeremy calls me into his office. "What the hell was that?" he asks, blowing out a tense breath.

I used to tell people the truth about Marina, before the eye rolling and whispering and crossing of streets. I learned the hard way that people don't care about your problems. Not when they're dark and deep and unrelenting. Not when they can't be solved in an hour by Dr. Phil.

I'm an army of one, I remind myself. The idea suits me. If this is what I have to do, who I have to become to avenge Marina, so be it. "It was an accident," I say and leave it at that. But by the way he's studying the calendar over my shoulder (I can see the wheels turning in his head, trying to replace my shifts), I know it's not enough.

If I had a speck of dignity left, I'd quit and save him the trouble of firing me. But job prospects are slim for someone in my boat. Quitting would take unemployment benefits off the table, and I can't afford the risk.

The office is stale and claustrophobic. I lean against a cluttered desk and wait for the axe to fall, which it does with swift mercy. I don't bother defending myself—there's no excuse for "assaulting a customer," as Jeremy put it—or groveling for another chance. I just shift out of the way of the filing cabinet so he can scrape together the two days' pay he owes me from petty cash. A hundred and thirty bucks to last until who knows when.

Jeremy instructs me to exit through the rear to "avoid further disruptions to business." But my car is on the street, and he's done telling me what to do. I swap my apron for my still-soggy hoodie on the hook by the bathroom. Tenting the garment over my head, I duck out the front door without a backward glance.

My battered Caprice is on the corner by Jenkins Funeral Home, where Marina's charred remains once sat in a shimmering gold coffin. I slip inside and root through a pile of junk on the passenger seat—notes and maps and photographs and printouts of internet searches, all adding up to zero progress in my sister's case—for my keys. They're under a spreadsheet of names, girls who ran in Marina's seedy social circles back in the day, all but three of which—Nancy Ellis, Carol Blake, and Lisa Thompson—are scratched out.

I twist the key in the ignition. It clicks softly—a weak, mechanical sort of noise—but the car doesn't start.

Son of a bitch. Dead battery. I must've left the lights on.

I rest my head on the steering wheel and think. The urge to cry explodes in my chest, but I squash it like a rogue beetle. With a sigh, I fish my phone out of my pocket and call Sam.

Three ... four ... five rings. My heart hammers more violently with each passing second. Samantha could be dead. My naïve fifteen-year-old daughter, whose otherworldly beauty has eclipsed even Marina's in recent months, could've been attacked on the street, muscled into a stranger's van, spirited away to God only knows where to suffer God only knows what kind of harm. They say lightning never strikes twice, but what if they're wrong?

I'm on the verge of punching the windshield when Sam picks up. "Yeah?"

My whole body exhales. I slam her with questions—where is she? who is she with? what took her so long to answer? does she want to be grounded for a week? a month? a year?—until my mind spirals back down to earth.

Sam is okay. Sam is not Marina. Nineteen eighty-five was a long time ago. I found Lisa Thompson. I got fired. (Again.) Marina didn't do drugs. She didn't kill herself. She wouldn't have killed herself, not even by accident.

I don't tell Sam about my being fired. She's got enough on her plate, with honors classes and her internet business (she sells hand-painted T-shirts out of Marina's old room).

"It's in the skinny drawer by the refrigerator," I say, guiding my daughter to my rainy-day fund. I bite back a laugh, realizing it's literally raining outside—pouring, actually—in my time of need.

Rattling noises fill Sam's end of the line. "Got it." I picture her peeling the envelope away from the back of the drawer, the same drawer that holds, among other useless things, six of her baby teeth and her grandfather's laminated obituary, which makes no mention of his gruesome death.

"There's a hundred dollars—"

The sound of ripping paper. "Mm-hmm."

"The Caprice needs a battery." If I thought a jumpstart would do the trick, I'd call in a favor. But the hunk of junk is two years past its life expectancy already. "Get Lewis"—the WWII vet who's lived next door since my parents bought the house in 1965—"to take you to the parts store. He can wait while you get the battery and then drive you over."

"He reeks."

"It's just cheap cologne," I say. "Don't argue with me."

"He's creepy. That's all I'm saying."

"He's eighty years old."

"So he can't be creepy?"

She knows I wouldn't let her near anyone dangerous, even if Marina had lived. "C'mon, Sam. Give it a rest. It's freezing out here."

"What kind of battery?" she groans.

"No idea. Ask the guy," I say, meaning the one at the parts store. "I'm going into the pharmacy to warm up."

Sam complains for a few more seconds before hanging up. She's a good girl, a straight-A student with dreams and goals—she wants to be a criminal profiler, of all things—and a wide-open future. A future as big as—or maybe even bigger than—the one dancing on Marina's horizon when she …

Suddenly, I'm lost in a swirl of nostalgia and emotion, my mind pulsing like a strobe light through memories of lazy summer days at the lake, Marina pushing me off the dock in a fit of laughter and then heroically catapulting to my rescue, saving me at the last possible moment—she was a graceful swimmer; I sank like a brick—before my lungs betrayed me and inhaled.

It was a glittering time. Excitement crackled in the air. Smells were sharper, visions clearer. We could taste possibilities in the raindrops on our tongues, sense the power of the universe in our sunburnt skin.

The dashboard is a map of split vinyl and coffee stains. I trace a finger along a particular crack, my mind circling a song Marina and I used to sing in our bunks at camp, until a semitruck roars by, spraying a wave of filthy water at my window.

The spell is broken. Leaving the keys in the ignition, I make a run for the pharmacy. A cluster of bells jangles as I burst inside.

Jumpy fluorescent lights assault my eyes. I power through a bout of lightheadedness, gripping the edge of a shelf as I make my way to the cough syrup. I can't afford the good stuff, so I grab the biggest bottle of the generic nighttime stuff I can find—thoughts of that fake cherry flavor coating my mouth and that warm sleepiness flooding my veins give me a palpable high—and then round the corner for the snack section. I feel like I haven't eaten in a day. A week. More.

"Good afternoon," says the pharmacist, a rotund man in his fifties with a wispy halo of salt-and-pepper hair, as he straightens a cardboard display of allergy pills.

I nod vaguely, loading my arms with Pepperidge Farm cookies and Bugles (I'd forgotten they make these corny, cone-shaped things, which Marina and I—and our big brother, Scott—would jam on our fingers and devour like they were ripe flesh and we were ravenous zombies).

"Can I help you find anything?" asks the pharmacist, cutting a glance at my neck. From my collarbone unfurls an ominous web, in which a spider has ensnared a helpless moth. I'm told that people find the image frightening. But to me, when I think of it at all, it's strange comfort: The moth is trapped, but the spider is trapped, too. Frozen in ink just far enough away to be harmless ...

The pharmacist must think I'm about to rob the place. I try for a smile but fall short. "Just these," I say, clutching the snacks to my chest as I head for the checkout.

Behind the counter is the pharmacist's daughter. She's perpetually bored-looking. Huge gold hoop earrings overwhelm her face. She's not much for chitchat, so the transaction is quick and painless.

I'm feeding the change into my pocket when another employee—she's older, around forty, with a strangely familiar face (her dimpled cheeks are ringing alarm bells in my mind)—snags my eye. She's framed from the chest up by a pane of glass as she concentrates on an unseen task—counting pills, maybe—oblivious to my fascination. "Who's that?" I ask, nodding in the woman's direction.

The pharmacist's daughter—Julie, according to her little brass nametag—purses her lips. She throws a glance over her shoulder. "Carol, you mean?"

I nod aggressively. Somehow I know this is Carol Blake, another former prostitute and potential witness to Marina's murder, one of three such specimens left on earth. (It's no surprise that eight of the women on my list died young of predictable causes like suicide and domestic violence and unpredictable ones like car accidents and cancer. Two overdosed, a fact that squirms in my gut like a pool of maggots.)

Julie shrugs. "She's the new tech. Been here a week. Seems to know her stuff."

"I think I know her," I say, trying to sound casual. Finding Carol might be even better than finding Lisa. Of all the girls who were ruined on those streets, Carol Blake had the best shot (other than Marina, of course) of making a comeback, of digging herself out of that deep, dark hole. "Is she one of the Blakes from Eastman Street?"

A baffled squint. "No idea."

Big help, Julie, I want to say. *Someone was killed here. Murdered. Can you wrap your self-absorbed pea-brain around that? Can you get off your spoiled-little-daddy's-girl high horse and give a damn about someone else for a change?*

I thread my fingers through the handles of the shopping bag and lend my voice a note of camaraderie. "Can you find out? I'd really like to talk to her, if she's the one—"

Julie shuts me down with a line about privacy laws and confidentiality. I feign understanding. There's no point causing a scene. I know where Carol is, and that's enough for now. I can bide my time.

CHAPTER 4
LISA

Sophie's following me in the BMW her husband bought as penance for standing her up on Valentine's Day, as we twist and turn over patchwork roads, away from curious eyes, the setting sun squarely in our faces.

The diner I'm luring her to is a trucker hangout known for drugs (half the pills I prescribe filter through here), prostitution, and gritty corned-beef hash. The police gave up patrolling the place long ago—it's a den of uncooperative witnesses at the edge of their jurisdiction—making it an ideal spot for a quickie murder. Sophie won't be the first to die in the dusty parking lot among the flatbeds and tanker trucks, spent condoms and rusty needles.

I check the rearview mirror. The BMW is still in sight. With only a few miles to go, it's time to decide: Should I smash her skull with a socket wrench, plunge a screwdriver through her throat, or pulp her under my Hummer's knobby tires?

The wrench is too messy. Ditto the screwdriver. And I've seen enough CSI to know that even with the most careful cleaning, a speck of blood on the oil pan or a hair on the drive axle could sink me. Not to mention the tire tracks. How many H2s would the cops have to check before finding a link between Sophie and me?

A gun would be best: simple, easy, clean. A brain-dead circus monkey could kill someone with a snub-nosed revolver and get away with it. But my .38 Special went missing three housekeepers ago (my husband has a habit of hiring hot, young things with sticky fingers to scrub our toilets and fold our underwear).

An accident is the only way. And on a road like this—rolling hills; sharp, winding curves; a never-ending caravan of big rigs—the idea is kismet. I'll slam on the brakes at an opportune moment (if necessary, I'll later claim that a deer darted across the road), forcing Sophie's BMW into the trees or, better yet, the path of an oncoming semi. The worst-case scenario is that she rear-ends me. It'd be a shame to sacrifice the Hummer's custom gold-fleck paintjob, but sometimes you have to give something to get something.

Hopefully the airbag snaps her neck.

Trucks tick by like numbers on a roulette wheel. Which one is lucky? This one? No. (Too slow.) That one? No. (Too fast.) Car, car, SUV? No, no, no. Finally, an opening appears. As we start into a curve, a logging truck crests the hill ahead. It's traveling roughly our speed—fifty miles an hour—and will parallel us in a matter of seconds, beside a particularly dense patch of woods. The logs are a wild card and make me think twice. If I don't time the maneuver perfectly, I could get tangled in the wreckage. And even the Hummer is no match for an airborne oak tree.

I keep my foot steady on the gas as the collision nears, shafts of amber light skipping across the road and marking time. *Whoosh, whoosh, whoosh*: one, two, three. *Whoosh, whoosh, whoosh*: four, five, six.

The truck bears down on us. A heartbeat before the eight-second mark, a window of action flashes open like a portal to another dimension, a blinding tunnel of bright white.

Slowly, deliberately, I move my foot off the gas.

The brakes shudder as I stomp down, a chatter rippling up my leg. If the tires screech, I don't hear them, my every atom braced for impact. I should check the mirrors—has Sophie catapulted toward the semi or the woods?—but my senses are mesmerized by a swirl of scenery.

A sharp breath steadies me. I venture a look around. The news is good: I'm free and clear, stopped safely (though cockeyed) on the shoulder of the road, without a hint of damage to the Hummer's pricey paintjob or anything else of value. As for the BMW and the logging truck, neither is visible in the rearview mirror. There are no signs of wreckage, either.

Disbelief erupts within me. Could Sophie have survived? Did the semi miss her?

The flow of traffic slowly dawns on me. Something must've gone wrong if vehicles are moving freely in both directions. A jackknifed big rig would've crippled things for hours.

I'm sorting through possible outcomes—did Sophie steer around me and continue on ahead? is she stopped farther back, on the leading edge of the curve?—when a car horn blares. Then another.

The rear of the Hummer is jutting into the road. I straighten it and creep backward along the shoulder. Hanging around is a risk, especially in such an identifiable vehicle. But I have protections, too, like my money—technically my husband's multimillion-dollar surgical-device empire—and my unassailable professional reputation. If all else fails, there are lawyers for days. Good luck getting a word out of me without a grand-jury subpoena. Even then, I'll lie.

At first I don't see anything of note, except some light tire marks on my side of the road. The other side, where the logging truck should've smashed Sophie's BMW to jagged bits, is untouched, as far as I can tell in the dusky twilight.

I reverse another twenty feet. Thirty. Fifty. All the way back to the start of that fateful curve. Everything looks normal. Irrationally normal. For a moment, I doubt myself—my judgment, my memory, my vision, my thoughts, everything. But then I ease forward again, sweeping the woods with the high beams, scouring for any trace of the destruction that should've been.

There's still nothing—no twisted metal or fragmented plastic, no glittering shards of glass—until I've progressed two-thirds of the way through the turn to the site of those nearly nonexistent tire marks.

It's getting dark. I squint at the headlights' hazy fan of illumination, stopping at the sight of two—no, *three*—paint-scarred trees. It's black paint, the color of Sophie's BMW. The closer I look, some branches are snapped, too. Not many and not in a pattern suggesting a catastrophic crash. Just enough to prove that luck has indeed shone upon me.

Like a two-ton javelin, Sophie's car shot through the woods, her resting place the epitome of occult perfection.

A laugh bubbles up in my throat at the thought of poor, sappy Adam (there was never any evidence of his cheating, but I stoked Sophie's fears for the challenge, to see how far I could push her fragile ego before it broke) buzzing her phone over and over again to no avail. Per my instructions, under the guise of concealing our affair, the phone is switched off. Steve Jobs himself couldn't locate it—or Sophie—now.

I wonder if she's dead. Or dying. It doesn't matter, either way. She'll meet her end soon enough from shock or exposure or starvation. Time is on my side. Fortune is mine, too, the logging truck having disappeared without its driver so much as tapping the brakes.

There *will* be questions, though, since I'm Sophie's psychiatrist—especially once the medical examiner autopsies the body. The benzos alone, due to their sedative properties, could provoke a knock at my office door. But I'll cross that bridge when I come to it. Something tells me that a call to the upper echelons of the police department, accompanied, if necessary, by a suitcase full of hundred-dollar bills, will grant me safe passage.

For now, though, it's time to go.

I draw a satisfied breath, check my makeup in the vanity mirror—it could use a touch-up—activate the turn signal, and glide back onto the road.

CHAPTER 5
ROBIN

I kill forty minutes staring at the foggy windshield, memorizing its fingerprint smudges and road rash, shuddering from the damp chill that has crept into my bones. I'm clearing the side mirror with my sleeve when Lewis's van arrives.

The rain intensifies as I crank the window back up. Lewis double parks inches from the Caprice, forcing me to contort, snakelike, into the narrow space between the vehicles.

Samantha's in the van, gazing past me like I'm a ghost. I slap my palm on the window, rattling her back to life. She joins me on the street, shivering and hugging herself. Between the two of us—Lewis is recovering from knee surgery and is no help—we raise the hood, exhume the dead battery (my talent for hoarding garbage pays off when I find a screwdriver in the wheel well), and fasten the new one into place without electrocuting ourselves. As payment for the favor, I give Lewis the old battery. He can return it to the store and get back a few bucks, which is more than I can offer him.

My daughter and I hop in the car. The van's taillights ease into traffic up ahead. As Sam reaches for the radio, a necklace spills out of the V of her shirt. It dangles there for a second, suspended like a fly in amber, then starts swaying back and forth like a hypnotist's watch. The teardrop pendant is a translucent shade of yellowish green—peridot, I think it's called—bordered by a row of diamonds. The chain is a lattice of rosy gold that, once upon a time, glowed like the sun itself against Marina's tawny skin.

My hand moves ahead of my mind, clutching the pendant and drawing it closer. "Where did you get this?" I ask.

"What're you doing?" yelps Sam, her neck wrenched toward my shoulder, her face a mask of confusion and pain.

I keep up the pressure. "Answer me."

My daughter wriggles around, trying to free herself. "Stop!" she cries, clawing at her neck. She finds the clasp and releases the necklace. It goes limp in my palm.

"Samantha," I say, my heart pounding in my ears, "where did you get this?"

She rubs at an ugly red mark on her throat.

Half of me feels sorry for Sam; the other half is trapped in a nightmare that never ends. "Tell me where you found this," I insist, thumbing the pendant like it's a talisman, a touchstone, a gateway to another dimension where Marina still lives.

Sam's eyes are wet and narrow. "Uncle Scott's back," she announces venomously.

The news hits me like a bulldozer. First one of Marina's favorite necklaces, the one she lent me on special occasions, like the elementary school awards banquet where I won ribbons in English and math, is resurrected—the more I think about it, it must've been in the junk drawer all along—and then my brother gets out of prison? Already? After killing that girl? "Back where?"

Brooding silence.

"Back where?" I repeat, my voice climbing with panic. I haven't seen Scott since he slaughtered an innocent teenager named Amy Lawrence in a drunk-driving accident. (Like Marina, Amy is frozen in time at sweet sixteen.) Amy was on her way to work at her family's sandwich shop; she was partially decapitated. Scott claimed the sun was in his eyes; he had a blood alcohol level of .22 and limped into a police cruiser with a sprained ankle.

My daughter shrugs defiantly.

I nail the gas, revving the engine, my palm electric with the feel of Marina's misplaced treasure. "Is he at the house?"

"Don't ask me." Sam's gaze is fixed on the downpour, which has transformed the street into a dismal impressionist painting.

Spite seizes me. "I got fired," I say, glad for the twitch of worry that crosses my daughter's face. When I'm sure she's subdued—better to squelch her fire now than watch her burn like Marina—I pocket the necklace and, with a tremor in my stomach, aim for home.

Our house is in what used to be a middle-class neighborhood of ranches and Capes, their lawns clipped in matching crew cuts, their driveways awash in family sedans and station wagons, a gang of housewives like my mother keeping watch over a block of children at a time, swapping in and out like stuntwomen on a movie set.

Our lives weren't as idyllic as all that, though. Behind closed doors there were beatings (we were blessed that our father only had a taste for belts and electrical cords), affairs, drug abuse—uppers, downers, liquor (our mother had an unquenchable thirst for Caribbean rum), pot, cocaine....

Now the neighborhood has gone to hell, as they say, every fifth house boarded up and sprayed with vulgar, illiterate graffiti—misshaped penises and misspelled racial slurs rule the day—or hanging on by a thread, the Great Recession having forced an army of homeowners to the brink of foreclosure and beyond.

I check the driveway, whose surface was once as smooth as a still pond but now resembles chunky asphalt vomit, for cars (negative) before swinging in and cutting the engine.

If Scott were here, he wouldn't have a car, anyway, would he?

Asking Sam is no use; she hasn't said a word since I tore that necklace off her throat. I didn't mean to hurt her—I never do—but the damage is done.

Finally, the rain is receding. I repay my daughter's silence as I make my way inside, breathing shallow and squinting for fear of what I'll see. Somewhere behind me, the passenger door squeaks open.

The kitchen is clear. The living room, too. In the distance, the screen door slaps shut, making me jump. It's Sam; it has to be. But what if it's not?

With effort, I force my chest to expand. I'm being paranoid, hysterical. So what if Scott turns up? Would that be so bad? It's not like he killed that girl on purpose. He's never killed anyone on purpose, has he?

Out of the corner of my eye, I glimpse Marina's ghost floating down the hall. But when I blink, it's Samantha, coiled tight as a viper, glaring at me from beneath hooded eyes.

An apology blooms in my mouth. I can taste the words—salty, bitter, a wisp of hope—but before I can spit them out, she's gone.

The house is clear, including the basement and the closets and under the beds. I check twice, three times. Nothing. Scott could still be in the yard, though, waiting for us. Plotting something. But what? He's my brother. Marina's and my brother, who chased off jackasses like Bobby Nason and Mike Pitts at the bus stop every morning for months—years—to keep Marina and me safe.

"They tease you because they like you," my mother once said, when I told her about Bobby pinching my chest until it bled.

Sam has sought refuge in the bathroom. I rap on the door quietly at first and then louder and louder, until I'm pounding like an enraged gorilla. She won't answer. My hands hurt. My wrists. My shoulders. It feels good to do some damage—to myself, the door, my daughter's hearing, anything. Sometimes pain is the only proof that I'm alive.

I collapse against the wall and sink to the floor. The truth is, I'm half a person if that. A breathing corpse. God knows I tried faking it for a while, getting my degree and teaching for a year (third grade at the elementary school Scott, Marina, and I attended in what seems like another life) and even dragging Sam from playdates to karate classes to reading hour at the library. But none of it stuck. It was superficial and phony and irrelevant. When someone you love is murdered and the killer roams free—unpunished, unaccountable—nothing else matters until the scales of justice are balanced.

A jab at my hip reminds me of the necklace. I curl my fingers into my pants and tug it loose. In my memory, the pendant is a brighter shade of green, almost emerald, its shape closer to oval than teardrop. I hunch on the shag carpet, which itself used to be avocado-colored but has now assumed the hue of roadside sludge, pressing the pendant to my lips and whispering promises to whatever faint essence of my sister remains:

We'll get the bastard. He'll pay for what he's done. I'll put a bullet between his eyes with a giddy grin. Yes, I've got a gun. A pretty little .38-caliber pistol with a rosewood grip. It cost me Dad's decrepit tin of Nazi memorabilia and a 2 A.M. meeting with a cross-eyed, oily-haired kid off Armslist. But I've got it. Now I just have to find the son of a bitch.

My mind swings from the gun to the day Marina brought this necklace and its cousin, a square citrine pendant that resembled golden rust, home from Berman's Jewelry Store. She'd been hiring herself out around the neighborhood all summer, washing cars—the men, fathers of our friends and classmates, made an occupation of guzzling beer and leering at her from behind their Ray-Bans—running errands for a flock of old ladies, and even babysitting, despite the fact that she found children boring. You'd never have guessed her true feelings, though, and neither did the lucky kids. (Marina was an entertainer and kept her charges busy with imaginative games and stories.)

As Marina toiled through June, July, and August, she refused to reveal what she was saving her earnings for (she got a kick out of having a secret and dangling it just far enough out of reach to drive you mad), only that the object of her desire was spectacular and exquisite and would provoke jealousy among the girls at school and adoration from any boy who mattered—and they all mattered to Marina.

When Marina floated down the front steps that blistering Sunday afternoon, I assumed she was headed to another gig—weeding the Palmers' flower beds, maybe—and then for a butterscotch sundae (her favorite) or an Italian ice (she liked the lemon; I always picked cherry) at the corner store. She didn't see me tucked under a shade tree, reading my Judy Blume book and watching her slip inside Lewis and

Georgette's house next door. Georgette must've hired Marina to scrub the floors while she and Lewis caught the early-bird special.

Whatever Georgette had hired Marina to do hadn't taken long. As I was holding the garden hose to my mouth, waiting for the hot water to clear so I could steal a cool drink, Marina eased the neighbors' screen door shut and, on cat feet, vanished down the sidewalk. An hour later, she blew into our house like a manic tornado, cooing and singing, clutching the two gemstone pendants—the peridot and the citrine—in her fist, her cheeks aglow like they were lit from within.

In the hallway, in my crouched position, which has become almost fetal, I let the memories wash over me and wait for the tears to come. Sometimes they do; sometimes they don't. It doesn't matter, either way. What I crave is the anger, which wraps around me like a cocoon, smothering the hurt that grips my stomach day after day, even now, all these years later.

In the bathroom, Sam is stirring. I can hear her rummaging around. Maybe she's gotten her period and needs a tampon.

I collect myself and rise to my feet. But before I can knock again, this time gentler and with understanding—why should Sam pay for what some soulless demon has done?—the door creaks open. There stands my daughter, her chestnut hair mussed and stringy, like she's been dragging her fingers through it to calm her nerves. Her cheeks are streaked with the feathery tracks of mascara-laced tears, her eyes cracked with rivers of red. She looks dazed, like a mental patient whose brain has been shocked one too many times. "You can't do this anymore," she drones, staring at my forehead. "You have to stop."

I don't want to do any of this; I *never* wanted to do any of this. But what choice do I have? Let Marina's killer go free? What if he kills someone else? What if he's *already* killed someone else?

Sam shifts sideways, and I see what she's done. On the toilet and vanity are, huddled together like frightened children, bottles upon bottles of four-dollar wine and ten-dollar vodka. Empty, dusty bottles I've stashed in the back of the closet and never bothered cleaning out, because I was blind drunk and no one would notice them, anyway, including me when I sobered up.

I swallow hard, but the rock in my throat refuses to dislodge. "I'll try," I say, knowing it's a lie. I can no more give up on Marina than I can stop my heart from beating. The alcohol is fuel for the fight, collateral damage in my wasted life. It won't be wasted if I find him, though. If I take down the beast that has destroyed Marina and now me.

I summon a reassuring smile and hold it until my daughter's eyes soften.

CHAPTER 6
LISA

Three nights in a row, Sophie Gallagher's beaming face leads the evening news, amid feverish conjecture over her whereabouts. Her husband looks like a guilty fool, fidgeting and stammering and groveling for the cameras.

She must be dead, medically speaking. I'd like to be sure, but I won't make the mistake some killers do, returning to the scene of the crime. No amount of temptation will reduce me to that level of stupidity.

"What do you think happened there?" asks my husband, Edward, gesturing at the kitchen TV with a steak knife. He saws off another chunk of his filet, which he's warmed to room temperature in a frying pan, and scrapes the flesh off the fork with his teeth.

Edward disgusts me. He always has, even since college, when he was at the peak of his sexual and intellectual powers. There's something diseased about him, a feral twitch known only to me, caught in flashes that grow more frequent as the years bleed by.

I was right about him, though. He was a good investment. From the moment he schooled our physics professor on a little-known aspect of Einstein's theory of relativity, I knew I could mold him into a financial powerhouse. Back then, I'd thought he'd become a biomedical researcher, inventing cures for things like diabetes and hepatitis. Instead, thanks to my keen instincts and expert guidance, he turned out to be an inventor and entrepreneur (eighty-two patents and counting!). The surgical tools he devised are used in operating rooms worldwide.

You don't have to look far for the fruits of our labor. Our eight-bedroom, ten-bathroom, custom-built chateau on a hundred pristine acres adjacent to a nature reserve is a rebuttal of my humble beginnings.

Feigning disinterest in the story of Sophie Gallagher, I say, "Probably a car crash." This way I'll have bragging rights when the authorities exhume her BMW from its wooded grave.

My husband drags the back of his hand across his mouth. "She's sexy. Could be a kidnapping."

I laugh. "You think everything's foul play."

"Isn't it?" His stubbled face cracks a grin.

I don't like where this is going. One wrong turn with him and I could end up with a big mess. "When are the girls getting back?" I ask, carrying his plate to the sink. A finger of gristle slides off the plate and lands in the basin with a slap. I jam it down the garbage disposal and hit the power switch. The disposal was supposed to be whisper quiet, but it bucks and brays like a dying donkey.

Over the racket, Edward shouts, "An hour, at least. Ashley took them to that new animated thing."

Ashley is the perky blond collegiate nanny to our eight-year-old twin daughters, Darian and Mae (short for Mavis, in honor of Edward's grandmother). She lives in a suite downstairs, drives our spare Mercedes, and plans her classes around the girls' schedules. She's a twelve-year-old boy's wet dream, romping around in her satin baby-doll pajamas, her ass cheeks winking like horny crescent moons. My husband would like to plant his flag in her fertile valley—who wouldn't?—but she's one of those robotic, airheaded, virginity-pledging Evangelicals. Even with the amount of cash wafting through here, his chances are low.

I value Ashley for her fastidiousness and blind devotion. She does what's asked of her the first time around. Her suite is in military order, always, and she keeps the girls on pins and needles, poised and polished as if a beauty contest might break out. I bet she took them for mani-pedis and got their hair blown out before the movie today. For that kind of service, she can ride my husband to Timbuktu if the urge should arise.

Edward lumbers around the Pyrolave island—our countertops are volcanic lava stone, imported from overseas—his thick velour robe yawning open. Underneath, he's wearing a pair of basketball shorts and a wifebeater, his uniform of choice for enhanced productivity.

He stalks up behind me, grabs my waist, scuffs his beard across my neck. My skin lights up with fire as his lips land on my ear. A lick. A bite. A pornographic phrase dropped like an atomic bomb. He's lustful in a roiling, visceral sort of way that can only mean one thing: He's made an inventive breakthrough. One that'll catapult us to new heights of wealth, adulation, and power. One whose perks will include our names on buildings at esteemed universities and invitations to inaugural balls. There's nothing the rich value more than cleverness, except maybe loyalty.

Edward's brilliant output is enough to make me overlook the broken blood vessels under his eyes and his paunchy gut.

"You're a god," I say in a smoky voice, twisting around and reaching for his crotch. If rabid, videotaped kitchen sex is what he wants—a security camera is trained on us, its cyclops eye engorged with desire—he'll have it.

We end up on the floor. I'm on my knees, my forearms flattened to the cool marble. Edward plays the rutting dog.

He lasts six minutes, give or take. A predictable performance. Predictable but unifying—that's the important part. He must believe in his mitochondria that we're a team, a unit of singular mind and purpose. The hormonal explosion from a good fuck will go a long way toward cementing that impression.

Our daughters are another arrow in my quiver. It's not long before they're floating into the great room—rough-hewn beams, a soaring cobblestone fireplace, and a sweeping wall of windows help the space live up to its name—where I'm curled on a sofa, researching potential board openings. With Edward's company—*our* company—poised to make a quantum leap, I may give up the petty charade of psychiatry altogether (the drug money's nice, but it's about to become chicken feed) and remake myself as a socialite, filling my days with committee meetings and luncheons and standing appointments at the spa.

Edward has retired for the evening. When Ashley bounces along a few steps behind the girls, her face droops at the sight of me. My husband showers her with compliments and thinly veiled innuendoes; I'm more business than pleasure. "Sorry we're late," she says, snatching up a scrap of paper that's fallen from Darian's coat to the immaculate Brazilian walnut floor. "Route 9 was closed. We had to detour through, well, not the best neighborhoods."

Our sweet, pious Ashley is turning snobbish. It was bound to happen with the luxuries we allow her. "Route 9?" I ask, keeping my voice steady. This is where I took Sophie to die.

"Mm-hmm. There were a bunch of police cars and news cameras. Do you think they found that missing woman?"

My gaze wanders from Ashley to my daughters' intertwined fingers. Their nails are clean and trimmed, polished pink with multi-colored glitter. I swallow hard, a reflex in need of excision, and say, "Yes, I do."

CHAPTER 7
ROBIN

My brother left a note on the door, a few bleary sentences scratched on the back of a McDonald's receipt in the hand (and the grammar) of a sixth grader. Prison has made him dumb, a fact that strikes me as vulgar. One thing all of us kids—not just Marina, who was gilded in the womb, but every one of Dr. Paul Davis Jr.'s offspring—had was God-given potential, which our father held over us like an iron club. When, five years after Marina's murder, he leaned forward in his easy chair, propped a shotgun under his chin and stretched for the trigger, the house shook and those claustrophobic expectations shattered, once and for all.

I wasn't sorry to see him go, his contempt for me and Scott and, especially, our mother, who was lost in a rummy haze by then, having crescendoed in the weeks before his death. He left a big bank balance, most of which went to caring for our mother after her stroke, and this house. From where I sit at the kitchen table, going over Scott's note with the eye of a jaded detective, I can't quite see the spot where our father's recliner once sat, where his brains painted the wall in a grotesque sort of abstraction.

The gist of Scott's note is that he wants money, an idea so laughable, so *ridiculous*, that I snort in anger. Who does he think he is, spouting demands after he abandoned us in the wake of Marina's murder? A chunk of what took our mother down was his absence, a sin I'll never forgive.

Scott left an address for a halfway house in the same six-block purgatory that claimed Marina, a crime-ridden, drug-infested island of flophouses, pawnshops, and neon-signed hole-in-the-wall stores that deal in beef jerky and cigars.

Since Sam left for school, I've been defacing Scott's note with hatch marks. They've formed a rough cross and are bleeding through to the table. If I had any spare cash—fifty bucks, say—it might be worthwhile to visit my brother and make peace for Marina's sake. Scott's in the perfect spot, imbedded with the filth and vermin who stole our sister, to shine a light on her murder and inflict justice on the guilty.

I tap the pen on the table, thinking. The battery took all of my emergency fund but sixteen dollars. Of the hundred and thirty bucks Jeremy coughed up, I've got a hundred and eleven left. But Sam and I have to eat, and the electric bill is overdue. If I don't make a payment soon—something inconsequential, to show I'm still trying—we'll never get service back once they cut it off.

I wander the house, surveying objects and coming up empty on something to sell. Over the years, I've shed every valuable my parents once owned to keep a roof over our heads. And here we are again—still—staring at a bottomless hole.

If Marina were alive, she'd know how to fix things. How to turn our lives around on a dime. How to squeeze lemons and make it rain gold.

The only thing left worth a damn is Marina's forgotten pendant. And even that won't bring much at the junk dealers that've sprung up like weeds to suck the value out of whatever the addicts can steal from unlocked cars and unsuspecting riders on the city bus. From late-night infomercials, I'm aware of a jewelry store an hour north that buys and sells, but the drive is too far and I don't want to part with the last trace of my sister, anyway. The day her body was found, on my father's orders and in a storm of rage and denial, we—my mother, my father, and I (Scott was on a road trip three states away)—stuffed garbage bags with Marina's U2 posters and leather boots and even the pink angora blanket our French-Canadian grandmother brought to the hospital when Marina was born. A distant cousin I'd never met and haven't seen since showed up with a monstrous truck and hauled the scraps of Marina's existence to the dump before we could reckon with what we'd done.

The idea of seeing my brother after all these years puts me in need of a drink. I'm not like him, though. I drink and drive carefully or not at all.

I lean over the kitchen sink and gulp a triple dose of the sickly sweet cough syrup straight from the bottle. While the medicine travels through my veins, I watch Lewis hobble around the yard next door, leaning on a cane. He's not doing much—checking his rain gutters and scowling at a clump of garbage at the foot of his driveway—or I might offer to help, considering all he's done for us over the years. (In the time between our father's suicide and our mother's stroke, Lewis was our chauffeur, gardener, personal shopper, financial advisor, and more, even while Georgette was dying of leukemia.)

From the fuzzy depths of my mind, an unsettling memory surfaces. It's a vision of Lewis and Marina on the sidewalk out front, arguing wordlessly. Their mouths are moving, but I'm too far away—frozen in an altered, dreamlike state—to hear what they're saying. Marina looks fifteen or sixteen, around the age she was when she disappeared. Despite his graying sideburns and distinct potbelly, Lewis appears shockingly young and strong, his sleeves stretched tight over muscled biceps, his skin a glowing bronze that rivals even Marina's dewy, sun-kissed radiance. As the two go back and forth, posturing and gesturing and practically spitting in each other's faces, a sick thought hits me: What if Marina was already selling herself before she ran off? What if Lewis was one of her customers—her *first* customer, even? What if Marina was doing more than mop Georgette's floors? That would give Lewis a motive to kill her, wouldn't it?

In the vision, which has a strange, unreal quality (the houses look like cardboard cutouts; Marina and Lewis could be puppets on strings),

Marina shouts hysterically and spins around for home. Like a steel claw, Lewis's hand clamps around her arm and drags her toward him. As she stands there wobbling, trying to get her footing on those spongy marionette legs, Lewis's claw-hand goes for her throat....

A swell of rage eclipses my senses. I flail for the counter and grab hold, fighting an onslaught of dizziness. Over my shoulder, the shadowy outline of the table seems miles away. *What if Lewis killed Marina?* The thought is a wrecking ball to my chest—icy, dense, obliterating. When I slam against the linoleum, it's a welcome reprieve.

The gun is holstered to my ribcage under an innocent flannel shirt. But before I can pay my brother a visit, I have to stop at the library. The clock is ticking on my unemployment claim. The sooner I file it the better. And the library computers are my least painful option.

As I scrawl my name on the sign-in sheet beside number six, the only vacant machine, the pistol shifts in its holster. Inside me, something pathological smiles. There's strange power—raw, exhilarating power—in carrying a concealed weapon, much like harboring the secret of a long-ago murder, coddling it and protecting it and shielding it from the light.

The library is in a dank brick building by the railroad tracks, a squat rectangle on the verge of closure from the same forces that've savaged our neighbors and disintegrated our neighborhoods. I claim my spot on a folding chair between a tween girl and a leathery man in a tracksuit.

The unemployment website is a relic, a dysfunctional maze of red tape, minutia, and intrusion. It takes three tries—and most of my allotted time—to input the information, tick the right boxes, and submit. I check the computer's tiny desktop clock. Only five of my thirty minutes remain. Should I Google Marina's name? It's probably a lost cause. But what if it's not?

My fingers decide for me, punching M-A-R before fate intervenes. At the edge of my vision, drifting by like an ominous thunderhead, is the unmistakable form of Carol Blake. If I hadn't just seen her at the pharmacy, I might not have recognized her, despite the yearbook headshot that's been stuck to my bedroom mirror for decades.

I whip out of my chair and chase her down the hall, into the reading room, where various magazines and newspapers are on display. Carol picks something frivolous, one of those glossy celebrity rags, and settles into a red vinyl chair with slashes of silver duct tape. I grab the nearest thing—a nature magazine with a snarling grizzly on the cover—and land in the chair across from her.

My hands are jittering along with my pulse. I swallow repeatedly to clear my throat. "Hey," I say, propelling my voice in Carol's direction. I mine the cover of her magazine for conversational material. "Do you like Tom Cruise?"

She glances up. "Huh?"

"Tom Cruise. Do you like him?"

She licks her finger and flips the page. "He's all right."

I dig deep for the name of a movie Marina let me watch once, even though I was eight and it was rated R. "He was good in that one, you know, a long time ago. What was it called?"

"*Rain Man*?" mumbles Carol.

"No." I furrow my brow. "Not that one. He was younger, I think."

"*Top Gun*?"

I shake my head. "The one where he slides around in his underwear."

She cracks a smile. "*Risky Business*."

"That's right." I lay my magazine facedown on the table. "Did you see it?"

"I can't remember. The commercials were on a lot."

"My sister loved that movie. It was the last thing we saw together"—a purposeful lie—"before she died."

The magazine falls into Carol's lap. "I'm sorry. That's so …" She frowns. "Sorry for your loss."

Anger fuses with euphoria in my gut. With the right kind of arm twisting, Carol could end the void of Marina's murder and send the dominoes of justice tumbling. "She was great," I say. "I miss her, still."

A tense, silent beat. "Are you from around here? Maybe you knew her."

"Sort of. I grew up in Springdale. But my husband's from Jackman. We've been here, oh, twenty-nine years, I guess. Our oldest, Levi, is twenty-eight. He's in the Army. We bought our house when I was seven months pregnant with him."

Marina has only been dead for twenty-four years. Carol Blake can't have a twenty-eight-year-old son. "Do you have a picture?" I ask, hoping to force her hand.

Carol drags her purse out from under the chair. "Sure do. And a bunch of my grandson, too." She rummages for her wallet, flopping it open and revealing a plastic accordion of photographs. First she shows off her grandson, a chipmunk-cheeked platinum blond with the same cavernous dimples that are carved into her own face.

Next comes a candid shot of her younger son, Jacob—"He's a hoot," she tells me in an excited whisper—who looks sixteen or seventeen, wearing a stocking cap and mugging for the camera.

Finally, Levi appears, dressed in camo fatigues and brandishing a rifle. With his buzzed hair and soft, doughy features, he could be as young as eighteen. And the grandkid looks nothing like him.

"Can I?" I reach for the wallet, pretending to admire her family. The only way to prove she's lying—about her age, her past, her identity—is to check her ID.

She hesitates, but I don't take no for an answer. I coax the wallet away from her and riffle through the pictures—half are of a three-legged dog named Geronimo—pretending to fawn over every detail while I secretly feel for her driver's license. It's not in any of the obvious places, like the windowed pocket or the credit card slots.

Damn you, Carol. Don't make me get ugly.

"What about you?" she asks. "Are you married?"

I keep probing the wallet. "Nope."

"Kids?"

Wedged behind a crinkly receipt is a plastic card that feels like an ID. I thumb it loose, careful not to draw her eye. "Guilty," I say, laughing. "Her name's Samantha. She's fifteen." I palm the card and slide it up my sleeve.

We trade pained looks that only mothers of teenagers understand. I close the wallet and hand it back.

"Well, um ..." says Carol. She scans the wall for a nonexistent clock. "I should get going. Allison—that's my daughter-in-law—is probably waiting." She stands up and swings her purse over her shoulder. "Nice meeting you."

I smile. "Nice to meet you, too."

CHAPTER 8
LISA

Sophie Gallagher is dead, a fact that solves one problem—she won't be bringing any fraudulent insurance claims to light—but opens the door to other nuisances, like my psychiatric colleague, Dr. Kapoor. I'm between patients, a rare occurrence the way we churn bodies through here, and Jacquelyn's off fetching lunch (a defunct gas station around the corner has been reborn as a trendy café) when the doctor lets himself into my office.

"May I help you?" I ask, fixing him with a cold stare. He licks his shriveled lips and continues marching wordlessly toward me. I rise from my chair, lean forward, flex my hands on the desk. "Hmm?"

His mustache trembles in a foul, rodentlike way. "Have you seen the news?" he asks, his black eyes glinting.

He's referring to Sophie, I assume.

"It's a shame," I say. "She was very young." There's no use denying my knowledge of Sophie Gallagher. The trick is controlling the narrative of our relationship. We were doctor and patient, nothing more. I was helping the poor, troubled woman cope with crippling depression and a cheating spouse. If the police should look anywhere, it's at that ridiculous fop of a husband. He had hundreds of thousands of reasons—"Was there life insurance?" I'll whisper innocently in a detective's ear—to want her dead. As they say, follow the money.

"I hope they don't arrest you," remarks Dr. Kapoor.

So far, my name has stayed out of things, thanks to an unreliable witness. How anyone could mistake a Hummer for a Jeep is beyond me, but the gift horse is welcome. As far as I know, Sophie's and my exploits were known to no one, and even our therapy sessions were a guarded secret.

What *could* sink me are the toxicology results, though only professionally. If I'm guilty of overprescribing, they can't prove malice. At worst, I've been sloppy. Negligent. They could take my medical license. But they won't, because everything has a price. And Edward will pay.

"Your imagination is running wild," I say. "Sophie Gallagher died in a tragic accident. What does that have to do with me?"

The doctor stands there studying me in his plaid bowtie and rumpled linen shirt, his forehead needled with sweat. "I came back to the office that day to drop off a filing cabinet. The door was unlocked. I was quiet."

He could be lying. "So?"

His mustache rat twitches again. "I saw you. The two of you."

"I'm sure you did." I steel my spine. "She was a patient. We had a session."

"You won't mind my telling the police, then?" he asks, grinning like a mad sheep.

I can't believe my ears. Is he going to make me kill him, too? I can only stack up so many bodies before the dots start connecting themselves.

I step out from behind the desk. "What do you want?"

He shuffles his feet. "A hundred thousand dollars."

He's so small and frail and pathetic that I almost pity him. "No," I say, undoing the top button of my blouse. "Something else."

The creep can't help eyeing my cleavage. "N—no. The money."

I pop another button, revealing my lacy red bra. "Impossible," I say, though the pittance he's demanded is a joke. I could pay five times as much—ten times—without flinching. But I won't. And he's not about to make me.

I slip around him, lock the door, twirl the little wand that closes the blinds. "Is this what you saw?" I ask, undoing a third button. When I release the front clasp of my bra, my breasts spill out.

For human shoe leather, he's unexpectedly responsive, his pupils dilating and his mouth falling open. A gurgled response—no doubt an enthusiastic affirmation—dies in his throat.

I guide his fingers to my nipple and swirl them around. His eyes glaze over. "This is better than watching, isn't it?" I say, wondering if the fossil can even get an erection. Not that I'd let him use it on me. But a quick hand job would produce the seminal fluid I need.

I'm winning him over one lewd caress at a time—is there anything on earth more powerful than the female body?—when the outer office door groans open, announcing Jacquelyn's return. I move the doctor's hand away from my breast and press a finger to my lips. We have a secret now, he and I.

The sandwiches from the gas station are going downhill fast, an annoyance I might overlook. But the baguette on my smoked salmon and lox is soggy.

I stride out to the reception area, a tidy room with soothing earth-tone paint (the color is *sienna sand*; I picked it myself to calm the addicts and the crazies) and a dozen hard-backed office chairs, arranged along the walls in an L-shaped pattern.

Jacquelyn is at her desk, three-quarters of the way through a predictable ham and cheese croissant. With a sigh, I plop my lunch, the whole gooey, wax-paper-wrapped mess of it, in her inbox. She covers her mouth with a napkin, her gunmetal-gray hair spiraling wildly about her face.

"Get rid of this," I say, gesturing at the sad excuse for a sandwich. "I want a roast beef from Angelo's"—the Italian deli across town—"with horseradish mustard. And a newspaper." Details of Sophie's death have vanished from the evening news, but the print media will bring me up to speed. I can't poke around the internet, in case someone's watching.

"What about—?" She scans a crooked finger down the scheduling book. "You've got twenty appointments this afternoon."

The woman is full of herself, isn't she? Her employment is a matter of my convenience. If I felt like absorbing her trivial duties, I would. But my time is too valuable. "I'll handle it. You'll only be gone thirty minutes."

She glances at the clock and frowns. "I'll try," she says, stuffing the last of the croissant in her mouth. As soon as she scuttles off, my next client comes stumbling along. I usher her into my office and post a note on Jacquelyn's desk, instructing the afternoon horde to stand by. At hundreds of tax-free dollars apiece, depending on what kind of pills they want, I'll be grinding through all of my appointments today.

My waiting client, Belinda, a knobby-kneed fiftysomething with harsh bangs and a ghoulish smile, is a holdover from my previous practice. Her skin is splotchy and eroded, probably from methamphetamine. A few years ago, she came to me for grief counseling after her son died in an industrial accident or a plane crash. I steered her toward a lawyer cousin of Edward's for a wrongful-death lawsuit. On the eve of trial, the case settled for $9.8 million. Once the lawyers took their cut, Belinda netted roughly $6 million. It's fair to say I've siphoned off most of that money by now.

Better mine than hers.

Usually I make small talk, but I'm not in the mood. And Belinda's fidgety. "Let's see," I say, pulling her file from the mound on my desk. I flip it open. "Xanax, Prozac, Ambien ..."

"I was thinking," says Belinda, "about dropping one of those. I don't know if ... I don't think I need ..." She picks at a loose thread on her shirt, averting my eye.

Her money must be running out. Or she found Jesus. Believe it or not, churches are my fiercest competitor for the almighty buck. "I don't think that's wise," I say. "Remember how devastated you were when your son died? You don't want to go back to that dark place, do you? We've got things under control. Let's not rock the boat."

"It's just that, um, my boyfriend, Leroy, says this stuff, the drugs, has too many side effects. It can kill your liver and kidneys and—"

"Is Leroy a doctor?"

She shakes her head. "He's a mechanic. At Raymore's. My car got towed over there from the Target by the mall. It needed a belt—an alternator belt, I think it was."

I slide my prescription pad across the desk and start writing. "Discontinuing your medicine is unwise." I tear off the first script and jot down the second and third. "You don't want to find out the hard way, okay? You don't want to end up hanging like a ragdoll in your closet. Trust me. I know what's best. Leroy can stick to fixing cars."

She crumbles like dry cornbread. As I take the stack of twenties, I make a mental note to scrub her from my records—she's another nuisance I don't need—and maybe even stop by Raymore's and slash Leroy's tires. No good deed goes unpunished, as they say—especially those done at my expense.

CHAPTER 9
ROBIN

I make it all the way to the car without checking the ID. If I'm right and this woman is Carol Blake—Marina's street sister and confidante, a victim of the same wretched vice that stole my best friend, my idol, the person I aspired to be—then I'm a heartbeat away from knowing, finally, what evil has made me.

The air outside is thick with the dying smells of autumn. Slumping in the driver's seat, I remove the card from my sleeve. It's not a license, like I'd suspected, but a blood-donor card in the name of Carolyn Price-James. Carolyn's blood type is O negative. She was born in 1961, eight years before Marina. There's no picture, so I can't be sure the person from the library is even the owner of the card, let alone that she's Carolyn Price-James and not Carol Blake. And even if she is—technically, legally—Carolyn Price-James, she could've changed her name. Her identity. With her criminal past, she would've been stupid not to.

It's obvious now: I should've gone for the jugular, pounded her with questions about Marina's murder, threatened her with the pistol if that's what it took to shake the truth out of her—or, hell, shot her somewhere non-vital (a foot, maybe) to get what I need. Playing nice is for Sunday-school teachers and soccer moms, suckers and fools. I won't make that mistake twice.

With the tip of a chewed pen, I gouge out Carolyn's name and hurl the card out the window onto a patch of brown grass.

The Caprice blends right in at the crumbling curb of New Life, the hopefully—and obviously—named halfway house charged with transforming my brother from prison inmate to contributing member of society.

I shut down the car and ponder my gun. Ten or twelve jobs ago, I sold appliance warranties over the phone in a drafty warehouse of makeshift cubicles, alongside an ex-con named Albert who resided in a sober-living house. Firearms were prohibited there, a fact that pissed off Al to no end.

The gun will stay in the car. There's no sense getting Scott kicked out of the program and locked up again. He's worth more to me on the outside, where he can do my bidding.

The glove box is full of cheese-smudged burger wrappers, greasy french-fry sleeves, and clumps of ketchup packets, one of which has burst open, smearing the compartment like a bloody crime scene. I mutter obscenities as I wipe away the sticky mess and pile up the dirty napkins on the floor. Then I undo my holster and relieve myself of the gun.

New Life is what you'd expect of supervised, transitional housing for criminals: a bare-bones hulk with sharp angles and rough yellow paint, a futile attempt at making the place cheerful.

I exit the car and glance up the block. It's 10 A.M. and a knot of kids is kicking a half-deflated basketball around the sidewalk, taking turns darting into traffic when the thing veers off course. They range in age from roughly four to thirteen and are distinguished by gangly limbs, hollow cheeks, and a zealous disregard for their safety.

The flophouse where my sister was murdered, in a squalid, dirt-floored basement, is a block and a half away. As I climb the weathered halfway house porch, I shake off the image of Marina's lifeless body, lying alone in the dark with a syringe plunged in its arm, helpless against those hungry flames.

I'm reaching for the entry door when a grainy shadow appears on the other side. I tense up, the absence of my gun palpable. Before I can jump out of the way, the door flies open, nearly slicing off my nose. "Jesus!" I howl, stumbling backward into the railing.

My brother is bulkier than I remember, his face sallow, jaundiced, his eyes racooned in a sickly shade of purple. He stuffs his hands in his pockets and cuts suspicious glances up and down the street. "C'mon," he mumbles, striding agitatedly toward the car.

So much for a Lifetime-movie reunion—not that I was expecting anything sentimental. Scott has always been hard-edged, aloof, brooding. He stuck up for Marina and me out of blood alone. Otherwise, he would've been one of our tormentors.

"Yeah, okay." I rush after him. Based on our three-minute phone call this morning—a surreal walk down memory lane, made possible by the chipper halfway house manager, Robert—I was prepared for an uncomfortable, claustrophobic, mostly silent meeting in New Life's common room with a bunch of ex-cons staring at us.

Apparently not.

Scott yanks the Caprice's door handle. "You lock this piece of shit?"

"Look around." Most of the buildings have bars on their windows. I let him in and then reclaim my spot behind the wheel. The car starts with a growl, thanks to the new battery. "So?" I say.

"Talk and drive."

"Where?"

"Doyle's."

"The beer joint by the high school?"

"That's O'Doherty's." He scratches his ear. "Doyle's Lumberyard. On Church Street."

"What for?"

"Just go. I'm gonna be late."

The obvious question is: Late for what? But I don't ask. I just pull onto the road, make a quick left, and aim for Church Street via Temple. One sixty-two Temple, to be exact—the scene of Marina's murder. In a matter of seconds, we're crawling by the dilapidated house.

I check Scott for a reaction: an eye twitch, a pulsing vein in his forehead, the beginning of a frown—something. But the site of our sister's murder elicits no change in him, a fact that sparks rage in my soul.

I can't help myself. I pull over to the side of the road.

"What're you doing?" he asks.

I gesture at the crime scene. "Recognize anything?"

He holds firm. Ignorantly firm. Laughably puzzled.

"Marina," I simply say.

"Not this again. You're gonna get my ass fired."

"Our sister's dead and you just want to pretend it never happened? Do you even remember her? Do you remember how beautiful she was? How special? How she glowed like—?"

"You don't know what you're talking about."

"She was the favorite. You hated that, didn't you? Once Marina started getting straight A's and riding in homecoming parades, Mom and Dad weren't impressed by your third-place track-and-field medals or your lawn-mowing business anymore. Her picture was in the newspaper—what?—eight or nine times?"

"Dad was a prick; Mom was a drunk." He shakes his head. "And Marina overdosed. Can we get the fuck out of here?" His leg starts jittering, a sign that I'm on to something. But was he jealous enough to kill her?

Suddenly, I remember the pistol. If Scott killed Marina, he could kill me, too. I can't take any chances. I lean across him and grab the gun. When he sees it, the blood drains from his face.

"Fuck, Robin. What're you—?" His eyes are glued to the .38.

"Tell me what you did to her." The gun shakes in my hand. "I know you hurt her. That's why you took off, right? That's why you weren't around when they found her. That's why you weren't around when Dad blew his brains out or when Mom—"

"She wasn't ... she wasn't like you thought she was."

Blood thunders in my ears. "Just tell me everything—everything you know."

"You were too young. It's nothing for a kid to hear."

"What happened, Scott? I've waited twenty-four years. I'm not waiting anymore." I level the gun.

"Marina was messed up, okay? She was messed up in the head. Something was wrong with her."

Here we go again. Blame the victim. Marina overdosed because she was a street whore—an addict (as if!)—who didn't know when to quit. She sealed her own fate. What did she expect, running around with the scum of the earth? She got what she deserved. "Bullshit."

"You know what? You're as bad as her. Put the gun down."

"Is that how you talked to her? Like she was a piece of trash?"

"She's gone. Forget it. Forget *her*."

"You're good at forgetting, aren't you? I bet you never even thought of Amy Lawrence while you were in prison. She's buried in Franklin Hills, you know, near Mom and Dad and Marina. They've got her picture on the gravestone. Sweet, innocent, pretty Amy L—"

"Shut up." He yanks the gun away from me. I try fighting him, but his muscles—even the tiny ones in his hands—are like rocks. I'm no match. All I can do is claw at his neck, but even this is pathetic and useless. "Crazy bitch," he says, shaking his head. He tucks the pistol between the passenger seat and the door. "Start driving."

For now, I'll do as I'm told. I'll choose my battles. But if he thinks he's won, if he thinks I'll forgive and forget—something tells me he was hurting Marina, probably sexually (I caught him once in the backyard, peeking through the window while she was in the shower), long before she ended up dead—he'll soon learn different.

CHAPTER 10
LISA

My last client of the day, a retired high-school principal with a silver afro and sleek, womanish hands, is off and running with prescriptions for Adderall and Klonopin. And Jacquelyn has skipped out early again, this time to meet with a low-level bureaucrat about her mother's nursing home stay.

I'm poring over the latest newspaper article on Sophie Gallagher, looking for clues as to whether I've been found out. The short answer is no. While the accident is still under investigation, there's not the faintest whiff of suspicion around me or anyone else. As usual, the authorities will do the bare minimum to close the case, unless they're handed my head on a platter by a buffoon like Dr. Kapoor. The more I think about it, the more I'm convinced the good doctor must go. I can kill two birds with one stone, so to speak, by framing him as Sophie's stalker/rapist/murderer and staging his guilt-induced suicide. The police will wet themselves when they see all those loose ends tied up in a nice, neat bow. I can hear them toasting me at the corner bar already.

Unfortunately, though, my plans must wait. Tonight I'm playing Cecily Cardew in *The Importance of Being Earnest* at our country club's theater for a few hundred bluebloods, diplomats, and CEOs—and their United Colors of Benetton arm candy (exotic wives have surpassed Ferraris as the import of choice among the powerful, the bloated, the balding). Tickets to the show sold out in twenty minutes—a club record!—thanks to my performance as Isabelle in last year's production of *The School for Husbands*, a show I selected, directed, and, according to anyone worth asking, perfected.

I consider clipping the article from the newspaper, but it's not worth the bother. What would I do with it, anyway? Hide it in a dusty book and sneak off to read it when no one was looking?

The newspaper goes in the trash. There have been Sophie Gallaghers before, like Edward's college sweetheart (Kayla? Katie? Kelly?), who had the nerve to return from her year abroad in Australia—Australia!—and try to pick up where she and Edward had left off. A fall from a third-floor balcony cured her of any romantic notions (pro tip: never open your apartment to a mousy nerd—those lopsided braids and librarian glasses made me unrecognizable!—feigning car trouble). Of course, I was a rock for Edward as he grieved, accompanying him from the florist to the funeral parlor to the church and the gravesite.

The thought is easy comfort. In a few months, I won't remember Sophie Gallagher's name.

On my way to the country club, I stop at the post office. I've been renting a box in my sister-in-law Ellen's name—Edward is the only male in a brood of six, all of whom, except my dear husband, are suburbanites with soul-sucking nine-to-fives and relentless money woes—since before the twins were born, back when Ellen Campbell was still Ellen Hayes.

Anything I don't want showing up at home gets routed here and, if need be, transferred to a safe-deposit box two towns over. My trove includes dirt on a number of individuals, from clients to employees to Edward's professional rivals; incriminating financial records; and select personal items.

The parking lot is jammed, so I take a handicapped spot. As I exit the Hummer, a dark-haired woman in the adjacent car shoots me a scornful look—people get so hysterical over petty social infractions—and starts furiously rolling down her window.

I proceed inside without sparing Miss Self-Righteous a backward glance.

Ellen Hayes's post office box is number 914. I thumb through my keys for a slim bronze one and let myself in. As expected, a small bubble envelope awaits. I extract it and check the return address—Women's Reproductive Rights Company of America—before slipping the envelope in my bag and relocking the box.

When I get back to the Hummer, the dark-haired woman is gone, but not without leaving what I assume is a chastising note (I won't be reading it) under my windshield wiper.

I toss the note on the ground and climb into my vehicle, setting the package on the passenger seat. I've ordered this medication before, a combo of mifepristone and misoprostol to flush away an unwanted pregnancy. In fact, this will be Ellen Hayes's eighth spin around the abortion track. By now, I know how to sift through the dubious websites for meds that'll get the job done. Someone less knowledgeable might end up swallowing crushed glass or rat poison or concrete dust, none of which will expel a mass of embryonic tissue. At best, one could hope to miscarry from a violent near-death experience.

I'm secure enough in my purchase that I don't bother opening the envelope. Soon all traces of this little mistake will be gone—odds are four to one against Edward being the daddy—and the issue will be moot. But between now and then, I've got wardrobe and makeup and faux jitters to contend with (people aren't happy unless you have a nervous breakdown before a performance). And I'm running late. They'll hold the curtain—I *am* the show, after all—but I don't want to play that card quite yet. I'm saving my influence for something bigger. Something more dramatic. Something worthy of causing a stir.

CHAPTER 11
ROBIN

The drive to the lumberyard is tense. My brother exits the car without a word, slamming the door behind him. Part of me wishes our relationship was as simple as one of those old black-and-white sitcoms, where the worst problem anyone has is whether their pie will win first prize at the county fair. There are no parallel universes, though. No do-overs. No wishes upon a star. Life is cold and lonely. The only choices are to keep moving or die.

I'm forging ahead with the cheapest case of beer at the distributor and a big bag of potato chips. The chips are on sale and I have a nasty salt craving. I just hope my unemployment benefits come through soon, or I'll have to hit up Samantha for a loan. Last I knew, she had a couple hundred bucks saved from her T-shirt business.

The clerk, a confused old man who can't seem to work the register, is grumbling at the lady in front of me when my cell phone starts ringing.

My hands are full. I couldn't wrestle the phone out of my jeans if I wanted to. The call goes to voicemail. The lady ahead of me counts out a stack of bills as my phone beeps with a text message.

I get a sudden shiver.

Finally, it's my turn. I slam the beer down on the counter with a thud. My phone beeps again.

Shiver, shiver, shiver.

Has the temperature dropped thirty degrees? Or is the air conditioning on this time of year?

The clerk rings up my order. I don't feel bad about paying with a five-dollar bill and a handful of change.

By the time the third message comes rolling in, I've made it to the garbage-strewn parking lot. "Dammit," I mutter, heaving the beer onto the hood of the Caprice. "What's so damn important?" I wiggle the phone out of my pocket and flip it open. Right away, I recognize the number. It belongs to my ex-boyfriend, Nate, an adjunct professor (in other words, he's paid as much as the janitors) at the university by my old job.

Before I can wonder about Nate's motives for calling—I let things cool off with him a few weeks ago, and he took it in stride—I scan the texts and find my worst nightmare since Marina's murder.

Samantha is at Nate's condo. She's hurt. (He doesn't say how.) I'm urged to get there as soon as possible.

My pulse spikes. I drop the chips on the sticky, wet ground and hop in the car. My hands are shaking, but somehow I manage to dial Nate. With the phone shouldered to my ear, I zip backward out of the parking spot. The beer skids down the hood and impacts the pavement somewhere to my left.

The phone rings three or four times and then goes to voicemail. Why isn't he answering? It must be worse than I thought. What if Samantha is dead?

Not my baby girl. She can't leave me. She's all I have.

Nate won't pick up, no matter how many times I call. I hurl the phone into the backseat and focus on banking turns at top speed and blowing through red lights with inches to spare before colliding with oncoming traffic.

I'm getting woozy, hyperventilating. The symptoms are familiar. When I learned of Marina's death, I fainted straight out. Someone (looking back, it must've been a police officer) moved me to the couch, where I came around to our mother's choked whimpering.

For my daughter's sake, I must keep a level head. I force a deep breath and the moment passes. A wall forms in my mind around those ice-pick memories.

Even at this pace, I'm still a mile from Nate's condo. (Actually, Nate's parents' condo; he's something of a squatter.) The roads seem to be stretching out in ways that defy physics. To make matters worse, my brain has switched to autopilot. Instead of taking the shortcut ahead of the university, I've driven two blocks out of the way by my old stomping ground at the café.

Son of a bitch.

I nail the gas, weaving in and out of traffic and crisscrossing the double-yellow line. Every second could be the difference between life and death for Samantha. What has happened to her? How is Nate involved? If he did anything to hurt my daughter—the idea is beyond belief, Nate being one of those dorky, tree-hugging, granola-crunching, save-the-whales types—I'll kill him. And I have the pistol to make it happen.

The last few minutes of the drive are an excruciating blur. Soon I'm ramming to a stop at the curb in front of Nate's building. His Honda is tucked in its spot by the retaining wall.

I charge ahead for Nate's unit, a townhouse with direct entry via a small patio. When I reach the door, it's unlocked. I don't bother knocking; I just push my way inside.

I should've grabbed the gun. What if Nate and Samantha are *both* dead? The idea ricochets around in my brain for a moment before Nate's voice finds my ears. "Robin? Is that you? We're in here."

The living room is straight ahead. Six steps and I'm there. My legs go weak when I see my daughter's bruised and battered face, her blue-gold iris encased in a blood-red eye. "God—Jesus—what happened?" I fall onto the couch beside her. "Are you okay?" I want to drown her in kisses—I've envisioned this kind of reunion with Marina countless times—but the pain might do her in. She's cringing from my proximity alone.

Samantha clutches her knees to her chest and buries her chin in her neck. She rocks gently, rhythmically, emitting the strangled cry of a dying animal.

Nate's wearing a hole in the carpet, pacing from window to window, peering guardedly outside. "We should get her to a hospital," he says. "I tried to convince her—"

I can't look at my daughter head-on. The destruction is too severe. "What happened?" The only thing I can think of is a car wreck, but Nate's Honda looked fine. So how did Samantha end up here? Like this?

Nate circles back to the couch and pats Samantha's shoulder. "Your mother will understand. Go ahead and tell her."

My mind goes to a dark place: Are Nate and Samantha having an affair? He *is* only twenty-eight. And he looks all of twenty-one, with those whiskered jeans and scuffed tennis shoes and tousled boy-band hair. "I love you, Samantha," I say, eyeing Nate with suspicion. "Whatever's going on, we'll fix it, okay?" It hits me that my daughter might not be able to speak. "Can you talk? Is anything broken? Your teeth? How are your teeth?" Nate's suggestion of a doctor is admirable, but who would pay? Sam and I get by on hydrogen peroxide and Tylenol, ice packs and elastic bandages and prayers.

Samantha is locked in place, silent and emotionless, every drop of life drained from her. I've been there before—cold, hollow, laid low. A sucking vacuum of inhumanity.

Nate gestures at the hallway. I rub Sam's leg and tell her to stay put, then follow him to the kitchen. It's a narrow space—a galley—with a cutout looking back on the living room. At a certain angle, I can keep watch over my shattered child.

I don't give Nate a chance to explain. "What the fuck?" I hiss, just above a whisper. "What's going on?"

He looks like a schoolboy in trouble, staring at the peeling laminate floor. "She showed up an hour ago," he tells me, running a hand through his hair. "I was correcting exams in my office." (It's a second bedroom, actually, with a bare mattress on the floor and a hand-me-down desk in the corner.) "All of a sudden, there was this crazy banging. I had my phone out. I was going to call the cops. There have been junkies in the parking lot, shooting up and ... I'd had enough.

"But then I saw her through the window. She was a mess—*is* a mess. I brought her inside, gave her a towel to clean up with. Her face was bloody—bloodier than it is now."

The bruises are so deep and dark that I hadn't noticed any blood.

"Someone beat her up, Robin. A boyfriend. I couldn't get his name. She made me promise not to call the police. She didn't want me to call you, either."

It's happening again. Marina was the canary in the coalmine. Now they've come for my baby. "She doesn't have a boyfriend."

"Apparently, she does." He sighs. "Listen, I'm just the messenger, okay? She needed help and she came here. I don't want to get in the middle of this, between the two of you."

"Sorry," I say, leaning sideways to check Samantha's wellbeing. "You're already involved. I need to know who he is. Tell me everything she said."

"Where's the thirty-eight?" he asks, reading my mind. "I'm not going to let you make this worse. Do you want Samantha feeling responsible for—?"

He must have a lead on the scumbag "boyfriend," or the location of my gun wouldn't matter. "This is no time for Boy Scouts, Nate. A real man would take a baseball bat up one side of that prick's pathetic carcass and down the other. But maybe you don't have it in you."

There. I've picked his fatal scab, unleashed his Kryptonite. He'll give me what I need now to prove his masculinity, to counter the echoes of his father's criticisms, branding him forever soft, weak, helpless.

His father is wrong. Nate's as tough as anyone—tougher—when it matters. But he's also steadfast, trustworthy, kind. My daughter was no fool coming to him.

He grabs my hand. "This is between me and you"—his eyes search mine for a promise—"okay?"

I give a shallow nod.

"No vigilante stuff. If we find out who did this, we go to the police."

"I know, okay? Just tell me—"

"I saw a car. A small green sports car. Maybe a Miata or a Civic del Sol. A junker with a primer-gray front fender. It was circling the parking lot after Samantha showed up. A skinny guy with a blond ponytail was behind the wheel. He was looking for something—some*one*. When he spotted me in the window, he smoked the tires and took off."

"How old was he?"

"My age? I don't know. I only saw him for a few seconds."

So the thug is a pedophile, too? How did my daughter get hooked by such a piece of garbage? "Was he alone?"

Nate shrugs. "It was shadowy out there."

It's too much to hope for, but I have to ask. "Did you get a license plate?"

"There wasn't one—on the back, anyway. I didn't see the front." Thick silence falls over us. "We should get back in there, right?"

I pump his fingers. "Thank you. If you hadn't—"

A soft kiss lands on my forehead. "Go take care of your girl."

CHAPTER 12
LISA

The show goes off without a hitch, thanks to my brilliant casting. Oscar Wilde himself would've wept with pride. And this after the club president's wife, a fat, old shrew named Penelope Anne, insisted that her daughter—a former Russian orphan and underwear model—play The Honourable Gwendolen Fairfax, threatening to torpedo the whole production. I mean, who would've believed a gaunt, unibrowed Amazonian—the girl is six feet tall, for Pete's sake!—with a nasally accent as a member of the British nobility? As luck would have it, the girl tripped over a rug or a cord or her own gigantic feet and was sidelined by a ruptured Achilles tendon. She's seated in the front row with her leg in a medical boot and a sulky look on her face.

As the cast converges onstage for its final bow, with me as its glimmering centerpiece (I'm aglow not only from the stage lights, but from the invigorating force of pregnancy blood), I grab the understudy's hand and hoist it triumphantly in the air, making sure to catch Penelope Anne's humbled eye.

Cheers pulse through the audience, our standing ovation lasting a full five minutes. All but the Russian and a few geriatrics are on their feet, including my husband, an enhanced version of himself in his best Armani tuxedo, our girls in matching scarlet ball gowns, and our goody two-shoes nanny, Ashley, in the sort of boring black shift dress one might wear to an undertakers' convention. Her saving grace is the bundle of roses draped across her lap.

When the applause trickles off, I'm taken by the urge to announce my pregnancy. It would be the crowning moment of a wildly successful night. It would put a point—a sharp, *final* point—on my superiority to Penelope Anne. She couldn't pull off a children's puppet show, let alone a full production of a comic masterpiece worthy of Broadway. Reaching such heights while battling fatigue and hormones and morning sickness—not to mention running a thriving medical practice and serving as my husband's muse—well, *that* would be superhuman. The only way Penelope Anne could top me would be to commit suicide onstage by Romeo's dagger.

There's little downside to the revelation. In fact, making the pregnancy known will boost my standing with club wives once news of the miscarriage spreads through the gossip-clotted grapevine. Condolence baskets and flowers and invitations to catered lunches will flow my way like a river of undammed sympathy.

The happy announcement should come from Edward, though. Men are the best tragic figures, with their toughness and bravado, their swallowed feelings and stiff upper lips. Let my husband break the good news. Then, when the sad news hits, it'll be that much sweeter.

Edward must be reading my mind. Before the other spouses react—again, my husband is a maverick, a leader—he struts up to the stage with the roses. "For you, darling!" he says, heaving the flowers at my feet. I bend down and scoop them up—they're fragrant and waterlogged—and then summon him into the limelight.

Soon we're embracing—I hold him long and tight for dramatic effect—for everyone to see, the roses bruising as they flatten between us. With my head resting on his shoulder, I peer back at the audience. Ashley—solid, dependable Ashley—is brushing Darian's bangs away from her forehead and smoothing Mae's skirt into a wrinkle-free dream.

Our daughters are the envy of every mother and father around and not just for their twinness—though their mirror-image looks *can* be quite mesmerizing—but for their poise and grace. They're china dolls come to life, the stuff of magic wands and enchanted forests, fairy stories whispered in the dark.

I turn my mouth to Edward's ear. "I'm pregnant," I say, my belly hiccupping. It's too soon for the baby—the fetus, the embryo—to be kicking. That won't happen for weeks. That won't happen at all, once I take the pills.

Must be indigestion.

Edward grabs my pinched waist—these Victorian costumes are murder!—and leans back to look at me. "Really?"

I beam a girlish grin.

Edward's eyes dance with joy. He's wanted another baby for years. A boy, preferably, to mold into the next Hank Aaron or Babe Ruth. But I have my heir and a spare, as they say. (One can never be too careful about locking down a fortune.) And I have no intention of submitting to his whims. Not in this arena, anyway.

"You're serious?" says my husband, his voice brimming with awe. "A baby?" His gaze falls to my abdomen, the upper half of which is impossibly corseted. The lower half, where the pregnancy exerts itself, is obscured by the folds of Cecily Cardew's lavish skirt.

I nod and smile, pushing tears into my eyes to match his. Nothing wins him over like mimicking his facial expressions and reflecting his body language. If he caresses my cheek, I'll caress his. Such actions build immediate, primal trust. An unbreakable bond.

The theater is buzzing with congratulatory noise. Even the stodgy old-timers are raising their voices and whistling and adding to the commotion. "It's wonderful news, isn't it?" I say. "Why don't you get the girls? I'd like to have our pictures taken to remember this moment. Ashley brought the good camera, didn't she?"

My husband is suddenly distracted. "Um, yes," he mutters, scanning the theater. "Of course she did."

"What's the matter?"

"Nothing." A sigh. "Nothing at all, sweetheart." He refocuses on me. "I'm just *so happy*."

"Should we make an announcement, then? It might be nice to include everyone." Nudge nudge.

"See," he says, his clean-shaven face beaming from ear to ear. "That's why I married you. You're the Empress of Great Ideas." He holds up a finger. "Just give me a minute to—" He backs down the stairs and vanishes into the crowd.

I seize the opportunity to shower praise on a few of my actors and deride a few others. I've just brought a ruddy-faced blonde—Melissa? Melody? an M name fit for a sex worker—to the verge of tears with a scathing critique of her accent ("Your Lady Augusta Bracknell sounded like a hyena giving birth to a porcupine"), when my daughters come floating up the stairs.

Miss What's Her Name slinks off as Edward materializes beside me. By the fermented stench oozing off him, I assume he's slipped away for a drink of the oatmeal stout he's been brewing in his laboratory bunker. (Between work sessions, he plays master brewer. And who am I to argue? As long as those patents and the money they bring keep rolling in …) "I was about to send the National Guard out looking for you," I say, an edge to my voice.

In my ear, he slurs, "Shall we tell the girls first? Or surprise them?"

Our daughters have flanked us. They're old-fashioned, speak-only-when-spoken-to children. Reserved. Demure. Some might say repressed. It's for the best, though, with the state of society today. An emphasis on manners would go a long way toward righting the ship. "Oh, a surprise!" I coo. Imagine the looks on their faces when they learn of their (brief) status as big sisters. You'll be able to knock them over with a feather.

Edward spins around. "Is there a microphone?"

I shake my head. "We're miked individually." Mine is sewn into the collar of Cecily Cardew's dress. "Just be loud about it."

He sweeps the girls under one arm and me under the other and elbows his way to the front of the stage. "Excuse me!" he bellows, piercing the ongoing twitter of voices. "Excuse me! May I have everyone's attention?"

The house is slow to quiet. Penelope Anne, leaning on one of her daughter's crutches, shifts her floral girth our way. Our faithful Ashley has snaked into prime photo-shooting territory with the top-of-the-line Nikon I gifted Edward for his thirty-ninth birthday.

Edward cups his hands around his mouth and, once again, calls for all eyes. It's a bold move—club members don't like being ordered around—but one he gets away with, thanks to his reputation as an eccentric and his Old Hollywood charm.

Eventually, the ruckus settles. Edward requests a round of applause for my acting, my directing, my producing. The crowd obliges.

I'm still flushed from the performance, eliminating the need for faux modesty. My slapped-cheek appearance speaks for itself. I do, however, smile and wave like a beauty queen until the ovation ends.

"Thank you!" shouts my husband. He peers out over the audience, his dark eyes glittering. "That was wonderful! And we have something else wonderful to share with you, too!" He tosses me a mischievous look. "Right, darling?"

I manufacture a nervous shrug.

Our daughters stare raptly up at their father, who to them must look like a hulking statue. A monolith of ambiguity. A colossus or a god.

He continues: "Lisa and I want you all to be the first to know"—a swollen pause—"that we're expecting our third child."

Darian's chirpy voice: "Really?"

Mae tugs on my skirt. "Nuh-uh."

The crowd erupts in gasps and cheers. Still clutching the roses, I'm spun from person to person in a chain reaction of hugs, until I'm deposited, dizzy and nauseated, at the opposite end of the stage. As I get my sea legs again, I realize that the roses have punched through the sleeve of Cecily Cardew's dress and drawn blood.

Flash bulbs explode in my peripheral vision.

I press a finger to a splotch on the fabric. It comes away damp and runny, pinkish orange and suggestive of menstruation. I examine the blood and then suck the metallic taste away.

CHAPTER 13
ROBIN

Samantha and I get home after dark. I make her wait in the car while I comb the house for intruders, my pistol gripped with both hands.

The place is clean.

I double check every window. A latch is broken in Samantha's room, of all places, so I scour the basement for a two-by-four and jam it in the window frame. The basement itself is an intruder's dream with that rickety bulkhead. Its rusty doors don't line up and the bicycle chain looped around the handles is more decoration than anything. We'd be better off hanging a BEWARE OF DOG sign. I can't do anything about that particular risk, though, except brace the interior door—it leads from the basement to the kitchen—with a chair and cross my fingers. It won't stop anyone from getting in, especially if he's determined. But it might slow him down.

I get all the lights blazing before whisking Sam inside. Once the deadbolt clunks shut, I breathe a sigh of relief.

The cupboards are almost bare. I used to steal meals at the café and Sam eats breakfast and lunch at school and picks up extra calories at friends' houses. I prefer my nourishment from a bottle, anyway. "I can make peanut butter and jelly sandwiches," I say, trying to sound hopeful. "Are you hungry?"

Samantha doesn't want a sandwich. She just wants to be left alone in the bathroom. I put up meager resistance—she won't be allowed to lock the door, for instance—but ultimately, I give in. I can only imagine that a hot shower will help those bruises heal.

Still, I'm a nervous wreck. What if she wants a shower for another reason? What if the scumbag who did that to her did something else, too? Something perverse? Something my daughter must cleanse herself of, body and soul? And if the scalding water doesn't work, what will she try next? Marijuana? Pills? A needle in the arm, like Marina?

I couldn't save my sister, but I'll protect my daughter with my life.

My fingers skim my ribcage, checking the gun. It's ready and able. Let the fucker show his face here and I'll blow him away.

The pipes clunk and groan, settling at a squeaky hiss as Sam starts the shower. I should stop her from destroying evidence. Maybe this "boyfriend" left behind his DNA in a droplet of blood or, God forbid, a smear of semen. Samantha's been on the pill since the age of fourteen, a fact that is a supreme blessing today.

I should get her checked for STDs.

I don't have the will to interrupt her, to invade the safety she's carved out from the world. Instead, I dose myself with cough syrup—a single, measured cup to keep my head clear—and then get on the phone to my brother. I need someone watching Samantha—preferably someone muscular with a chip on his shoulder—while I hit the streets looking for green sports cars with mismatched fenders.

My brother is still mad at me, so it's a surprise when he answers. "Yeah?"

"It's me," I say.

"I know."

"Listen, um, sorry about before, okay?" Dead air. "Okay?"

"Whatever."

My throat is dry and sticky. I swallow hard. "Someone hurt Samantha. I need you to come over."

"So you can shoot me?"

I plop down in a kitchen chair and pinch the bridge of my nose. "She's in bad shape. Someone—some dirtbag—got to her. She might need stitches." The blood Nate helped her wash away must've come from somewhere. She probably has a scalp wound that should be closed up.

"I can't."

"Your medical kit's still in the garage." I've thought about throwing out the box labeled SCOTT'S STUFF a hundred times but never got around to it. "Remember when you used to read those survivalist magazines? You made Dad order that kit in case of, like, World War III."

"I bought that myself."

"Who cares? Just come help Sam. I'll owe you."

My brother says he's on the equivalent of house arrest, per his parole. New Life only lets him off the premises for work and medical appointments (he leveraged this rule to leave a note on my door en route to getting a tooth pulled). His good behavior has earned him an overnight pass, but the outing must be approved a week in advance.

"Can't you sneak out?"

"Probably could. Ain't gonna chance it, though. Find out who hurt Sam and I'll take care of him."

At least we're on the same page. "I'll call you when I know something." Without waiting for his reply, I hang up.

The light under Samantha's door tells me she can't sleep. I suppress the urge to stalk her and instead stake out a spot on the couch with a view of the front door and several vulnerable windows. If an intruder were to attack, this area would be a prime target. The porch light has been busted for years and the nearest streetlight is half a block away. The floodlight on Lewis's garage gives only a dim crescent of illumination to the side yard. And with four or five vacant houses on the street, there's a good chance that any late-night drive-bys would go unnoticed.

I can't shake the feeling that my daughter and I are sitting ducks.

The TV is muted. I flip the channels, bouncing shadows off the torn blue-floral wallpaper as I cradle the pistol in a nest of blankets on my lap. With glazed eyes, I watch a cop drama bleed into the evening news and the evening news bleed into a talk show. Around 3 A.M., when the infomercials are in full swing, Sam comes wandering out of her room. The good side of her face—the right side, where only a nick on her lip and an odd, square-shaped scratch on her temple give away her suffering—looks calm, almost peaceful.

Peaceful. I don't like the word. It makes me think of dead people. *May she rest in peace*, everyone kept saying at Marina's funeral. But how was she supposed to do that when no one was hunting for her killer? When no one even believed she'd been murdered in the first place?

Samantha curls up on the other end of the couch. I shift the gun to the coffee table and cover her with blankets. Through force of will, I keep vigil until morning light filters through the curtains, a stray beam highlighting an unseen world of floating dust.

I wonder what else is lurking around us that we cannot see.

At seven thirty, Samantha stirs. Her stomach has been howling all night. I convince her to eat some toast. As she pads off to the kitchen, I crawl into the warm spot she's left behind and collapse thoughtlessly into sleep.

CHAPTER 14
LISA

I suffer the pregnancy for a few more days, long enough to pay a visit to my ob-gyn. Getting a blood test on record could be useful, should I need to play the mommy-to-be card during, say, a police investigation into Sophie Gallagher's demise. The hardest part is working up enough enthusiasm for Edward, who's determined to tag along to the appointment.

I pull off the performance in spades. By the time my husband and I zigzag back through the waiting room, cooing at random babies and petting toddlers like they're zoo animals, I've not only bowled over Edward with my prenatal zest, but the two of us have won the hearts of every doctor and nurse and expectant mother in the building. The receptionist even asks to photograph us for the Wall of Fame (the practice has a bulletin board devoted to round, pink mommies and stiff, nervous daddies).

After signing a release form, we're told in hushed tones that our images will grace the homepage of their website ("You're both so photogenic!") and our glowing grins will appear on the cover of their highly anticipated Christmas calendar. ("Would you like extra copies? We'd be happy to send three dozen!") Of course, some of the fawning may be due to Edward's status in the medical community—he's famous for ingenious tweaks to surgical instruments, which, in hindsight, every doctor on earth thinks he or she could've devised—but the attention is welcome, nonetheless. It draws Edward and me closer in this little charade.

My husband is bent over, helping a small, dark-haired boy tie his shoe, while the receptionist scans my doctor's schedule for appointments. "How about the nineteenth? At two o'clock?"

"Do you have anything earlier in the day?" I ask. The appointment will be canceled once I "miscarry," but for now I must play the harried mother-to-be.

We settle on the twenty-second at 8 A.M. As the receptionist slides a reminder card across the counter, Edward's hand finds my belly and gives "the bambino" a series of gentle pats.

I should feel guilty over Edward's attachment to the pregnancy, given my plans. I've seen enough after-school specials to know what I'm doing is "wrong." But guilt is useless and I don't care about *should*s.

People are riddles. If I do X, will he do Y? Or will the result be E, F, or G? What if I start with G? Can I get him to do X and Y? I enjoy experimenting, testing theories—if only people were as predictable as litmus paper and hydrochloric acid!—and cataloguing the results for future use.

Edward holds the door. We step into the autumn light. The low angle of the sun burnishes everything around, from the pavement to the rows of luxury vehicles to the stand of evergreens by the roadside.

As insurance—never get complacent, even with the wind at your back on a cloudless day—I lace my fingers with my husband's. "I hope it's a boy," I say, aiming for the kind of beatific smile one might find on the Virgin Mary's radiant face.

Edward's reply is tried and true: "As long as it's healthy."

"Yes," I say with conviction. "That's what matters. As long as it's healthy."

It's 2 A.M. and I can't sleep. Not because of anything I've done. (I'm one of the lucky few blessed with an immunity to regret.) My body just doesn't need as much rest as the average person's.

At times like these, I appreciate the keenness Edward and I displayed designing this house, especially our installing an indoor swimming pool. The only thing we could've done better—and I blame the architect here—was locate the pool closer to our master suite. As it is, the natatorium is clear across the house, on the other side of the great room. I may wear myself out getting there, never mind the sedating effects of a few leisurely laps.

At least I won't have to explain my late-night wanderings to Edward. He's crashed in his downstairs office. When I checked on him at midnight, he was out cold on the chaise lounge, his moth-eaten University of Virginia T-shirt pushed up over his belly. Gone is the dapper, tuxedo-clad charmer of a few days ago. In his place is an older, fatter version of the guy who let me cheat off his statistics homework and carried my tray in the UVA cafeteria.

That husband of mine is a chameleon, isn't he?

I strip naked in front of an antique mirror with elaborate curves, shell motifs, and botanical renderings. Some might call it gaudy. *Decadent* is my word of choice.

From a similarly styled pet bed nearby, my Yorkshire terrier, Magnum, watches.

My discarded blouse and skirt pool on the floor. I sweep them aside with my foot for the housekeeper to collect. When I pass Magnum's bed on my way to the armoire, he rises to greet me. "Hey, boy," I chirp over my shoulder. Despite how people cling to their Labrador retrievers and German shepherds, their French bulldogs and standard poodles, the Yorkshire terrier packs more loyalty per pound than any dog on earth.

My bikinis are missing. I wonder if the former housekeeper—she's one of those pasty-skinned Czechoslovakian sluts my husband is so fond of—misplaced them when she swapped my wardrobe at the change of season. Or maybe she stole them.

I could grab a towel from the master bath (it's stocked with crisp whites, like a five-star hotel) or throw on a negligee. But the cool air feels good on my skin—the pregnancy, even at this early stage, is ramping up my body temperature—and no one's awake but me. Plus, as the mirror confirms, I'm as toned as ever. Maybe more so. And I haven't broken a sweat in weeks. If Edward stumbles out of his office or catches my Lady Godiva routine later on the security cameras, he'll count himself lucky.

On a whim, I scoop up Magnum and tuck him under my arm. He enjoys being toted around the house—twenty thousand square feet is a lot to ask of his stubby legs—and I don't mind the company. His hair is like silk against my bare breast, delicate and ticklish.

I'm not an exhibitionist, per se. I get no special thrill from flaunting my body. Like everything in life, though, nudity has its purposes. I use it to my advantage when possible and otherwise remain indifferent.

The house is what some might call eerily quiet. It's lit by moonlight, courtesy of the skyscraper windows. As I pad around, I sense that I'm tracing a burglar's route. On the flip side, though, I'm a fish in a barrel. If anyone were skulking around outside—doubtful with our extensive security—I'd be easy prey.

When I cross into the kitchen, a craving for peanut butter grips me. I drop Magnum on the island and round the corner for the pantry. The new housekeeper is older than most we've had—fortyish with enormous, globe-shaped breasts (definite implants; they have their own field of gravity), long, raven hair (from a bottle, not that I'm one to talk; my natural color is closer to Belgian chocolate than honeyed wheat), and something like twelve kids. Her name is Ricki. She keeps the pantry bursting at the seams. Maybe we'll keep *her* longer than six months, if she doesn't turn out to be a common thief or a gold-digging whore.

I can't be bothered to get a spoon. I just slide a finger into the jar and suck it clean. Any traces I've missed are lapped away by Magnum as we continue on toward the natatorium.

A swim is sounding better by the minute. My body stirs at the memory of cool water licking my bare flesh. Sometimes I skinny dip when Ashley has the girls busy with a game or a movie. On such occasions, Edward leers at me from his perch in the Jacuzzi (my husband is more delicate than I am and prefers a cocoon of warmth).

I'm nearing the natatorium, gliding down the wainscoted hallway with Magnum's doggie heart fluttering against my ribs, when I hear the first suspicious sounds. I stop in my tracks ten feet from the door, which is uncharacteristically open.

The noises could be someone—or multiple someones, judging by the symphonic grunts—straining to lift something. If our safes were nearby, I'd think we were being robbed. But there's nothing to steal in the natatorium but flotation devices, beach towels, and maybe a pitcher of whiskey sours Ricki hasn't purged from the refrigerator. Plus, the alarms haven't so much as chirped, and Magnum is a bundle of relaxation. And he turns into a snarling wolf pup around strangers.

I venture a few more soundless steps. Finally, I get a line of sight—albeit a choppy, obstructed one—on the pool deck (we settled on some kind of Spanish marble, the name of which escapes me). Still, I can't see anyone, but the noises are more pronounced.

Sex. A man and a woman. Possibly a third person, but I can't be sure.

Has Ricki snuck in one of her many paramours—you don't get twelve kids without a little bed hopping!—for a clandestine tryst?

I consider turning around, but this is my house. I should get something for walking all the way down here. (I won't ruin Ricki's fun; I'm not a monster!) Some live-action porn might put me in the mood to masturbate. And masturbating makes me sleepy. I've got to log a few hours of rest before morning. The thought of Ricki's gravity-defying breasts juddering around is already sparking a twitch between my legs that would be easy to satisfy in my exposed state.

Another two feet and I'm leaning through the doorway. The natatorium is as dim as the rest of the house, despite the shimmering reflections of the pool lights. I trace the carnal echoes—boy, that Ricki and her man-beast are laying it on thick!—to the far end of the room, behind a row of teak lounge chairs.

Flashes of skin undulate like waves on a beach. Heads and faces—*any* identifiable features, really—are lost in the shadows or just plain hidden, until ...

Magnum wriggles loose, making a leap for that Spanish marble. He lands with a slap and skids a few inches before bouncing back onto his feet and scrambling toward the noise.

I hold my position. Prick my ears. Squint. The robust sex continues, despite Magnum's invasion. When my neck starts cramping from straining too long, someone comes up for air.

It's Ashley, the virtuous nanny. She's on top—on top of whom I can't say, but the possibilities are few—her wavy butterscotch hair tossed in a storm of lust.

The swim is out. I abandon Magnum and chart a course for Edward's subterranean lair. But my husband's office is empty.

Son of a bitch.

I hadn't planned on taking the abortion pills just yet, since I don't know where my best interests lie. The pregnancy—and any resultant child—could be a valuable bargaining chip, depending on the course of future events. But back in the master bathroom, swaddled in my plush, leopard-print robe, I seethe, thinking of Edward fucking the nanny. It's not the act itself that offends me—I can get better sex off a G.I. Joe or a gym rat—but the ludicrous betrayal, the being made a fool of. How dare he? My allegiance comes at a price. He should know that by now.

The bubble envelope is tucked behind a baby-blue perfume atomizer in the drawer of my Louis XV vanity. I remove it, take out the pills—they're in blister packs with little sticky labels—and break the mifepristone free. A stream of cool water flows from the sparkling chrome faucet into a crystal tumbler.

Gulp, gulp, gulp. The medicine goes down like hot buttered rum. The process is underway. Forty-eight hours from now, I'll ingest the misoprostol and my uterus will eject the fetal tissue in violent, erratic waves.

Check mate, dear husband.

When I catch my reflection in the mirror, I can't help but smile.

CHAPTER 15
ROBIN

I wait at the lumberyard for an hour before my brother gets his lunch break. "Where to?" I ask as he drops into the passenger seat.

"Fast Frankie's," he says, referring to an old-school burger joint that our parents, especially our father, used to love. "I'll buy."

And I'll let him. This morning, I learned that my unemployment claim was denied. I can appeal the decision, but I don't like my odds. "No argument here," I say, chuckling morbidly. Let Scott shoulder some responsibility for once, even if it's just a ten-dollar lunch tab. He's been missing in action for so much pain, when I could've used someone to lean on.

It's a dreary day, borderline drizzly—the precipitation is sputtering like a waterlogged engine—but on the warm side at sixty degrees. I've got the window cracked and the defroster going to keep the windshield from fogging up. After a quiet stretch, Scott asks, "How's Sam?"

"I called her in sick to school."

"You said she needed stitches."

"Nah. The bleeding stopped."

"Did you get a name?"

"I tried. She's not talking—about that, anyway. She ate something, though. And took a shower." Actually, two showers and a bath. "Lewis came over to sit with her. I doubt she'll get out of bed. She's in a lot of pain."

"I know people," Scott says ominously. "Just say the word."

I relay the scant information about the scumbag: "He drives a small green sports car. A junky old Mazda or Honda with a primed front fender. Nate said it—he, the guy, I mean—was a skinny dude with long blond hair."

"Nate?"

I downplay my and Nate's relationship. Half a block past the restaurant, the Caprice's last hubcap scrapes the curb. We trek back in silence. The restaurant is spotlessly clean, clogged with construction workers, lawyers, and elderly couples in matching outfits.

Scott orders three single patties with chopped onions and yellow mustard. I get one with American cheese, ketchup, and relish. He wants to spring for Cokes, but I just steal a watery sip of his once the ice has melted. Every dollar counts to someone in my situation and in my brother's, too.

Money is still on my mind when we get back in the car. "Hey, uh, I was wondering if you could do me a favor."

His gaze is stuck on my neck. For a second, I can't figure out why. Then it dawns on me: the tattoo. Sometimes I forget about that helpless moth in the web, that spider in relentless pursuit. "When are you gonna get that thing removed?" he asks.

There's no sense answering. Tattoo removal won't be in my budget for a long time. And I'd miss the thing, anyway.

I reach into my jeans for Marina's necklace. Selling it is a last resort, but I'm at the end of my rope, financially speaking. I could hit up a food pantry—and I will, for Samantha's sake—but winter's coming and we can't afford oil. Even my daughter's life savings, a couple hundred bucks squirreled away for some teenage fun, won't do much to pull us out of this hole. "I need to sell this," I say, holding out the necklace. It's both delicate and stunning, like our murdered sister. "I thought you might know where I could get the best price."

Scott strangles the door handle. "Where'd you get *that*? Wasn't it buried with *her*?"

"Our sister has a name." I can feel him willing me not to say it.

"I'm not talking about this. About *her*. Didn't you learn anything from what Dad did? Or what happened to Mom?"

What is he implying? That Marina caused our father's suicide and our mother's alcoholic stroke? "You're confused," I say, thumbing the glassy green pendant, which still crackles with Marina's vitality. "Whoever did it—whoever killed her—is to blame. It wasn't her fault."

"How would you know? I could tell you stories that'd—"

"Go ahead." What's the worst he could say? That Marina was confident? That she trusted herself? That she was comfortable in her own skin? That kind of cockiness might've gotten her in trouble a time or two—I vaguely remember her being hauled home in the middle of the night by the cops from a party gone wild—but so what? That's every teenager. She would've grown out of her restlessness if she'd gotten the chance.

Scott grinds his teeth and stares across the street at a dance studio with silhouettes of pirouetting girls on the windows. "It's fucked up. You wouldn't believe it, anyways."

"Try me."

"I don't want to do this, okay? Or see *that thing*." The necklace.

"Why? Did you kill her?" I've wanted to ask the question for a long time.

"Nope." A heavy pause. "But if someone did—and I ain't sayin' he did; there's no proof—she probably provoked him."

Lying bastard. I steady my voice. "How would she have provoked him?" Provoked *you*, I want to say, but I bite my tongue. Does he think I'm stupid? I'm not the naïve ten-year-old he remembers.

"She did things, okay? She tricked people. She got off on it."

Not the Marina I knew. She was playful, maybe. Pulled a harmless joke once in a while. But never maliciously. "Yeah?" I study my brother's hands. They're rough and calloused, with dirt jammed in the cracks and crevices. "Like how?"

"You really want to know?" His shoulders kick up. "Fine. She showed up at this Halloween party once, dressed as Catwoman. She was covered from head to toe, with a mask and everything. No one knew who she was. She was thirteen, probably. A bunch of teenagers were there, mostly kids a few grades above her. She wasn't even invited."

"She crashed a party? Big deal." So much for our dead sister's bad-girl streak.

"She did a lot more than crash it. Believe me." He stiffens. "What time is it?"

"I don't know." I start the car. The dashboard clock reads 1:40.

"I gotta go," says Scott. "They'll be lookin' for me. I'm not supposed to leave."

It's a short drive back to the lumberyard. As we pull away from the curb, I coax him to finish the story. I like hearing about Marina. There's no one left to remember her but Scott and me.

Reluctantly, he obliges. "So, uh, yeah … she came to this party, disguised and everything. The kid—the kid whose house it was—his parents were in the Bahamas. There were like, I don't know, fifty or sixty kids there. A few of 'em were in costumes, but everyone else was just normal.

"Anyways, there was booze—wine coolers and tall boys. Most of us were hammered."

"Mm-hmm."

"Marina started hanging around this guy. She pretended to be his girlfriend, who wasn't supposed to show up because her grandfather died. The guy was too drunk to know the difference. He was glad his girlfriend came. He made out with Marina for a while in the kitchen. Then she took him into a bedroom—a baby's room, with a crib and shit—and gave him a blowjob. He couldn't believe it. He was a virgin, and his girlfriend was a priss. Wouldn't even let him feel her up over her clothes. But then all of a sudden, she was …"

"She was thirteen," I say. I would've been seven. Scott would've been fifteen.

"So?"

We're closing in on the lumberyard. "Nothing. Go ahead."

"The guy already couldn't believe his luck. It was like he'd won the lottery. But then Marina, who still wouldn't take off the mask, who was hazy because of the dark and the booze, whispered, 'I wanna fuck you' or 'Wanna fuck?' and the guy … it was all he could do to rip off his clothes without …

"Marina wiggled out of the catsuit and got down on the rug. The guy was blasted, didn't know what he was doing. After trying for months to cop a feel off this girl, he was about to get laid. It was so easy. It was *too* easy, but he couldn't stop and think."

We're creeping down a long dirt drive, nearing the spot where I picked him up. Machinery clicks and buzzes in the distance. I pull over in the grass, away from traffic. I can't decide whether to order him out of the car—what he's saying about Marina isn't true; she wasn't that kind of girl, not yet, anyway—or prod him to continue.

My brother needs no encouragement. A dam has burst in his brain and the twisted wreckage is spilling out of his mouth. "The guy was nervous and awkward, you know, because he'd never done it before. But he crawled in between her legs—and, remember, he still thought she was this other girl, his girlfriend for six months that he felt things for.

"Once they got going, he could only take it for a few minutes. When it was over, they layed there for a while. As Marina got up, the guy noticed the necklace. She was wearing it under the catsuit."

"*This* necklace?"

He sniffs. "He didn't get the best look at it. Like I said, it was dark. Once Marina got the catsuit back on, she thanked the guy and then leaned in and said, 'Say hi to Jennie for me.' Jennie was the guy's girlfriend.

"Later on, the guy saw Marina somewhere. At the mall or wherever. She was wearing the necklace. He put two and two together. He was pretty messed up after that. It was like he was raped or something. But it was also like *he* raped *her*."

It was also like he *raped* her. Of everything my brother has said, these words curl in my ear and hiss like a snake. There was no other guy. No masquerade. No bad-girl version of Marina. There was just Scott, a sick kid with an even sicker lust for his beautiful sister. Maybe he protected Marina and me from bus-stop tormentors with ulterior motives, to keep us for himself (was I next on his list?), to control us. And when he'd done what he'd done to Marina, when he couldn't manipulate her anymore—she was too bold to be kept under anyone's thumb for long—maybe he killed her.

CHAPTER 16
LISA

Our not-so-innocent Ashley will pay a price for her infidelity. Something short of firing—despite her betrayal, she'll continue minding the girls (who else would keep my daughters so poised and primped?)—but with enough sting to teach her a lesson. If she'd asked permission to fuck my husband, I might've obliged. But sneaking around behind my back? Under my roof? And then flashing that coy smile when we crossed paths at the microwave? With Edward right there, hunched over the counter, slurping his soggy raisin bran? Sorry, dear. Such insolence will not stand. The cliché alone—the nanny? really?—is enough to warrant retribution.

First things first, though. With the mifepristone doing its job, cutting off the flow of pregnancy hormones—in all likelihood, the embryo has already detached from the uterine wall—I've double-booked my office hours, aiming to squeeze every last drop of cash out of my schedule before the contractions kick in. Normally, I have superhuman pain tolerance—I once extracted my own tooth with a bottle of Polish vodka and a pair of pliers—but the misoprostol tests my mettle every time.

I plan to take the next few days off work, which I'll spend receiving therapeutic massage—Edward and I have a rangy Bulgarian masseuse named Lyubo on permanent retainer—and, when the bleeding dies down, soaking in the Jacuzzi. My husband will be away on business, making the process that much easier. I'll call him when all is said and done and break the devastating news.

It's only eleven o'clock and I've buzzed through thirty-one clients. An average day is forty-five and a minimum of ten thousand dollars in my pocket. If I keep up this pace, I'll triple my take today.

"Jacquelyn, hold my next appointment," I say into the phone as an elderly widow scuffs out of my office with a handful of prescriptions. Her husband died six months ago of lymphoma or Lou Gehrig's disease or some other L-named malady that dragged on for years. She said she'd quit the pills once he was gone, but here she is. Still. The only difference now is that she doesn't talk about "weaning off" the drugs anymore.

I don't wait for Jacquelyn's reply. She feels the need to respond to my every order when she should be doing something productive. My next assistant will be ex-military. Those folks know how to execute and obey.

My heels clack satisfyingly as I stride to my private bathroom. (Two more reasons to expunge this pregnancy: swollen feet and the inevitability of sensible shoes.) By the time I put myself back together—it's shocking how severely one's makeup can wilt in a few short hours!—a strange man is wandering through my office. He's a cop. A junior detective, maybe. I have a nose for these things.

I flip through a mental Rolodex of personalities, deciding which one to put on. A smile works its way from the center of my face outward. I give it a bump into my eyes. "May I help you?" I ask, my voice lilting.

The cop—the detective, if that's what he is—turns slowly toward me. He's disarmingly handsome: mossy green eyes, square jaw, a wavy sweep of black hair. He should be selling boxer briefs on a billboard in Times Square.

I will not be disarmed. If anything, I'll be *more* vigilant.

"Yes, um"—he extends a hand—"hello, ma'am. I'm Luke Jones, with the Jackman PD." A badge on his belt catches the light from the window. "I was hoping to ask you a few questions about a patient."

I slip my hand into his and squeeze firmly but gently. A solid, girlish grip. "About Sophie Gallagher?" I say, beating him to the punch. I purse my lips and frown. "It's just awful what happened—"

His head bobs up and down. A funeral nod. "This won't take long," he assures me. "Routine stuff. We just need to check all the boxes before we close the file." He eyes a chair. "May I?"

"Make yourself comfortable. Anything I can do to help."

He settles in. I offer him a bottle of water. He declines.

As I'm claiming my spot behind the desk, he flips open a folder. I crane my neck, but he holds the folder close, foiling me. "So, um, let's see what we've got already."

My chair squeaks as I lean back.

He runs through some basic information, which he's gleaned from the husband et al. (Sophie's and my sessions were less of a secret than I'd imagined. Or the pills gave me away. If Sophie leaked the torrid details of our relationship—to her hairdresser, say, or the checkout girl at the A&P—I'll dismiss them as lesbian fantasy.)

I confirm that Sophie Gallagher was a patient. That I'd been counseling her for nineteen months. Beyond that, I can't say much—or so I tell him, anyway—due to doctor-patient confidentiality. "Ethics," I say with an apologetic shrug. "I'm bound to protect the patient's privacy, even after death. I'd be glad to turn over, well, everything"—I motion at the filing cabinet—"if you have ... if you've got some kind of legal paperwork."

If he had a warrant, he would've led with it. He's either ticking off boxes, like he said, or feeling me out for possible charges. Overprescribing, maybe. But not murder. The idea probably hasn't even crossed his mind, unless he's spoken to that shriveled old turd, Dr. Kapoor.

It's way past time to subtract that variable.

The detective—*Luke*, I remind myself, pondering how the name fits—studies me opaquely. "No problem. We don't want you breaking any rules. We just want to cover our bases before signing off on this."

I nod my agreement.

Again, he checks the file. Is he stealing repeat glances to rattle me? Nice try, sir. My pulse is as reliable as an atomic clock.

"Let's forget about the therapy," he says. "That's confidential, obviously. But can you tell me if you noticed Mrs. Gallagher interacting with anyone the day of the incident? As far as we know, you were the last one to see her alive."

Thorny, thorny, thorny. I could spin my answer a hundred ways. And that phrase: *the last one to see her alive*. It sounds like they suspect foul play. I furrow my brow. "No. Not really." A gentle sigh. "Unless you mean my receptionist, Jacquelyn. She checks everyone in. You must've met her." Fat, flaky, thick-skulled Jacquelyn.

"Mm. Yes. We'll be talking to her, too."

We? How many cops are working this case?

"She was here—Jacquelyn, I mean—for that last appointment. She checked in Sophie—Mrs. Gallagher—and then, a little while into the session, she left. Her granddaughter had a recital. She plays the clarinet."

"So the receptionist was gone when Mrs. Gallagher left?"

"That's right."

Without asking, he plucks a pen from a cup on my desk and scribbles sideways in the file. I resist the urge to blather—guilty people can't keep their mouths shut—and wait for him to finish.

"Did Mrs. Gallagher speak to anyone else the day of the incident?"

What is he getting at? "Gee, I don't think so. Why?"

He taps the pen on his knee. "Just following up on some information we've received."

"You don't think someone tampered with her car, do you?" I bring my hand to my mouth. "I can't imagine anyone around *here* doing *that*. Except ..." There. I've set the hook. Now I just have to reel him in.

His jaw twitches. "Except?"

"Oh, nothing," I say, waving him off.

"Are you sure?" He sits up straighter. "If you've remembered something—"

"It's nothing," I say. "Nothing important."

"Even small details, things that seem irrelevant, can make a big difference."

"She didn't kill herself, did she? She wouldn't have crashed on purpose."

"We haven't reached any conclusions. If you have information that could help us—help the family—we'd appreciate—"

"It's just that ..."

"Yes?"

"There *is* one thing."

He moves to the edge of his seat. Just then, Jacquelyn lumbers into the office. "Will you be much longer?" she asks, bursting the bubble of anticipation I've created. "We're getting backed up out here." She grimaces.

What an idiot. I'd take her down a peg, but I don't want to tip my hand. "This is important," I say, lightly chastising. "Clear my schedule for an hour. We'll have to work everyone in next week."

Jacquelyn groans. "You're the boss."

Damn right. As she swings around for the door, I say, "Oh, and Luke would like to speak with you, too. When we're done, I'll buzz you." My skin crawls ahead of what I'm about to say. "Thank you, Jacquelyn."

She does a double take. It must be the first time I've thanked her. Personally, I don't see the point. I pay her to do a job; the money is her reward. Would she rather work for empty praise? Because that can be arranged. "N—no problem." She rushes off like she's seen a ghost.

I refocus on the detective. "Where were we?"

Luke and I dance, conversationally speaking, awhile longer. I make him work for the seed of disinformation I'm trying to sow. If he thinks he's pulling clues out of me, he'll feel like he's done his job. He'll pat himself on the back. He'll hold the lie sacred, like a shard of ruby sea glass plucked from the tide.

"It's just that," I finally say, "something unusual *did* happen that day. One of my tenants—a colleague, actually—another psychiatrist with a practice down the hall—"

"Mm."

"His name is Aarush—Dr. Aarush Kapoor. He showed up after hours, around the time Mrs. Gallagher's session was ending. He'd never done that before. It seemed odd. He's a creature of habit, I guess you could say. Anyway, he was lurking around in the hallway. It made the hairs on my neck stand up."

"Did he talk to Mrs. Gallagher?"

"Not that I saw. Not directly. But—" I shake my head, as if questioning what I'm about to say.

The detective's hand roams my desk, fondling random objects: a paperclip, a highlighter, a blank prescription pad.

I hadn't decided how to focus suspicion on Dr. Kapoor, but an idea quickly forms. "I overheard Sophie—Mrs. Gallagher—on the phone about a month ago. She'd arrived early for a session, during our lunch hour. Jacquelyn had—well, I can't remember where she'd gone, but she wasn't around. I was in my office, right here, eating a salad—bleu cheese, walnuts, and cranberries—from the grocery store.

"Anyway, Mrs. Gallagher was in the waiting room, killing time until one o'clock. I wasn't eavesdropping. In fact, I was reading an intriguing article in *Psychology Today* about ... oh, never mind." I flap a hand through the air. "The point is, she was agitated. I can't say to whom she was speaking, but she was—gee, this is concerning, given what's happened—she was saying she'd been followed. After her previous session—not that day; that day was beautiful and sunny—but after her prior session, she felt like she'd been stalked. In the rain, in the dark, by someone hiding in the back of the parking lot. He'd followed her home. She was going to call the police, call *you*, if it happened again."

While I've been talking, the detective has been scribbling. Without looking up, he asks, "And you think this psychiatrist"—he checks his notes—"this Dr. Kapoor could've been the one following her?"

"I wouldn't have thought so, no. Not in a million years. He's a harmless older gentleman. He's got a family. He pays his rent on time. And his patients love him. Plus, he drives a Lexus."

The detective's eyes narrow.

"The guy—the stalker—drove a pickup truck. Sophie was adamant about that: a red Toyota with a bunch of rakes and shovels in the back. I didn't think much of it until I saw a similar truck beside me at a stoplight. It was a landscaping truck, with a picture of a pig riding a tractor on the door.

"When you asked about Sophie—about her interactions at the office—it jogged my memory about the stalker. About the pickup truck. And then I remembered that Dr. Kapoor's son runs a landscaping business. He even has a red truck. I'm not sure it's a Toyota, though." This part of the story is true. A quick check of motor-vehicle records will show the young Mr. Kapoor (there can't be many men of that surname around) owning a red pickup. The logical inference is that the doctor borrowed his son's vehicle to conceal his identity while committing a crime—the stalking of pretty, young Sophie Gallagher. And if he stalked her, it's a hop, skip, and a jump to rape and murder. Once I concoct a suicide note and dispatch the doctor, the pieces will fall into place.

Case closed.

With a glint in his eye, the detective thanks me for my candor. He actually uses that word: *candor*. He must be a college boy. I suppose most detectives are nowadays.

As the interview winds down, he asks about security cameras. I tell him I haven't felt the need. The building is in a safe area. He arches an eyebrow, a suggestion to reconsider.

"Shall I get Jacquelyn?" I ask, sensing he has enough to chew on—maybe even more than he expected—from me.

"Please," he says.

I rise from my chair. "Certainly."

CHAPTER 17
ROBIN

Samantha misses nine days of school. I write a note saying we're in Disney World—if I'm going to lie, I might as well lie big—so the school won't ask for a doctor's excuse. "Are you sure you're okay?" I ask as Sam slings her backpack over her shoulder. "I can call and say we got a flat tire. Or our plane was delayed."

She rolls her eyes. "I'm fine, Mom. You can't even see anything anymore."

She's right. The bruises have faded. And some strategically placed concealer goes a long way. But I *can* still see them—they're *all* I see, actually—every time I look at her beautiful face.

"Hold on!" I blurt as she angles for the door. "No bus. I'm driving." The problem isn't the bus itself. Samantha's attacker isn't a high school kid who'll stick gum on her seat or blow spitballs in her hair (as if such childish pranks are all high school kids are capable of). The problem is the bus stop. It's too exposed.

Her fingers are on the deadbolt. "Since when?" *Thunk.*

My pulse jumps. "I said, wait!"

"Jeez." She raises her hands. "Chill."

I jam my foot into a sneaker. "You've lost all rights to tell me to 'chill.'" It's a hurtful comment, one I should've holstered. But when it comes to my daughter's safety, I'm on a hair trigger. I always have been, because of Marina. Being a single mother didn't help, either.

Samantha's father—assuming he's still alive—is a self-centered jerk with more money than class. We got stoned together a few times when I was drowning in grief. He denied the pregnancy, tried to buy his way out of fatherhood, and conveniently disappeared. I made up a fake name and told Samantha he died of a brain tumor.

"Are you almost done? We're gonna be late." She huffs.

"Yup," I say, grabbing my keys off the counter. "Let's go."

The bus stop is deserted and not just because the neighborhood is turning into a ghost town. We *are* running late. Still, as I drive, I scan for beat-up old sports cars. But like every other day, on every other road I've checked—and I've checked lots, when Sam was curled up on Lewis's couch next door, watching reruns of old sitcoms—the effort is fruitless.

Samantha's attacker is a phantom. I *will* find him, though, one way or another. If it's the last thing I do.

The high school is across town. As soon as the car stops, Sam jumps out and blends into the sea of bodies. I should be happy that she's coping so well. But I know from experience that repressed emotions will carve an exit sooner or later. They'll find a way to make you bleed.

I track Sam's movements until her hoodie is swallowed by a collage of motorcycle jackets and skinny jeans.

Something tells me to park and go inside, register at the office with a made-up excuse—in an embarrassed whisper, I could tell the secretary that Sam has forgotten her maxi pads—and lay eyes on my daughter. For all I know, the bastard boyfriend is an upperclassman (from a shadowy glimpse, Nate thought the guy was older, but he could be wrong) or a student-teacher or a punk brother of one of Sam's friends. Whoever the piece of garbage is, he probably targeted my daughter here or somewhere nearby.

I should go in.

I should.

I should.

A contrary voice rises within me, telling me to relax, calm down, insisting I'm overreacting. Samantha is safe inside Jackman High, with plenty of teachers keeping an eye out. Whatever happened to my daughter did not happen here, could not.

My foot is like iron, unable to move off the brake, nerve signals hitting dead ends. I stare past a tree—a maple, judging by the crimson leaves twisting in the wind—for another twenty minutes until I'm alone, even the burnouts having surrendered to the day.

When a cop makes a second loop around the block, I take the hint and leave. I've got things to do, anyway. Problems to solve. Money to snatch from the cloudy gray sky.

Between hawk-eyeing Samantha and scouring the streets for the green junker, I've barely had time for the job hunt. But Sam's back in school. It's time to get serious.

As usual, the library comes to my rescue. I use their internet to throw together a list of potential employers—I'd like to get out of the food-service biz, but I'm not holding my breath—and print copies of my doctored résumé. Where others embellish their accomplishments, I delete them. College degree? Gone. Teaching job? Replaced by a stint selling car stereos at Circuit City, a claim impossible to verify since the company is out of business. Too much education or experience—especially *professional* experience—is a hindrance in the jobs I target now. Better to be a sheep with a spotless attendance record—I'll fudge this in the interview—a strong back, and a pocketful of synonyms for the word *yes*.

Despite the recession, a few places have advertised for help online. I hit them first—an office-supply store, a pet groomer, a bakery, an auto-repair shop (they need someone to answer the phone and do "light filing"), a strip club (they want a morning cleaner/prep person), a liquor store, etcetera. Mostly, I'm met with dumb stares from managers half my age who are oblivious to the fact that their establishments have job vacancies. On the occasions I'm able to speak with someone knowledgeable, the position is already filled. Or so I'm told. The nicer people—a chubby, middle-aged man at the liquor store, for example—take my résumé, offering to keep it on file in case a job opens up.

By noon, I'm down to six résumés left. I feel like chucking them out the window, watching them scatter like dandelion seeds on the wind. Or maybe I should shove a few down that pompous ass Jeremy's throat. If he hadn't fired me, I'd still be grinding away at the café for a hair over minimum wage.

My next move is the most humiliating yet: the food court at the mall. I run the gauntlet, forcing my leprous credentials into the disposable-gloved hands of anyone with a pulse, including the owner of the sketchy Chinese place that's been cited twice recently for food-safety violations (the news has a segment devoted to such horrors) and the stoner kid at the pizza shop whose dense, chewy slices could double as roof shingles.

A strange calm comes over me—when you've done all you can, the rest is up to fate—as I drop back into the driver's seat and grope around for my phone. It's one of those shitty pay-as-you-go deals, but even at ten bucks a month, it's a luxury I may soon do without.

Samantha was supposed to text me on her lunch break. Although she made the promise grudgingly, I expected her to keep it. But she hasn't. I choose to believe she's swept up in a tornado of back-to-school excitement and can't tear herself away to ease my worried mind.

In place of Samantha's missing text is one from Nate. Or should I say *another one* from Nate? He's been needling me for updates on Sam's condition. I appreciate what he did for my daughter, but he's not her father. What I share with him—*if* I share anything at all—will be minimal. Surface. Vague. Enough to keep him off my case and not a word more. Between the lines of his messages are veiled invitations to meet. Always. He's like a sixth-grade boy who hangs around your locker, dropping playful comments but never working up the nerve to ask you out.

I've had my fill of tender men. They're preferable to loudmouth jackasses, I suppose, but give me a rough-and-tumble man's man—one who'll slaughter a pig and slap a mound of bloody, quivering flesh on the counter before fucking me senseless—or give me no one.

No one's sounding pretty good. Who's left to put up with my damage, anyway? I inhabit a thimble of ugliness and regret, a dark umbilicus tugging me back through time to Marina's murder, our father's gruesome suicide (I found the splattered mess of his body), our mother's descent into an alcoholic hell (I drink to numb; she was out to kill), and now another painful signpost on my journey: my only child's purple-bruised face.

I need an escape, a distraction. From myself, my thoughts. Sometimes they wind too tight and I can't catch my breath. "Hey," I say when Nate answers. "Where are you?"

CHAPTER 18
LISA

The abortion goes off like clockwork. It feels good to be empty. Clean. Free. Now I wait for the right time to phone Edward and pull the pin on the miscarriage grenade. He has the shock coming, I'm not afraid to say. The baby probably wasn't his, but he'll suffer its loss just the same.

Or maybe he won't, I think, reconsidering. With pretty, young, empty-headed Ashley in the wings, ovulating like it's an Olympic sport, I must consider every angle. It's possible that my husband could become despondent over the loss of our child and impregnate the nanny on the rebound to salve his emotional wounds. He *is* that reckless. He has to be to stay on top in the business world. (You don't make millions by playing it safe!)

The miscarriage will keep. In fact, it'll pack a bigger punch a month or two down the road, when I've dealt with Ashley—her punishment is yet to be determined—and sewn up the Sophie Gallagher matter. On that note, I'm at the office on a Sunday (Lyubo's magic fingers make all things possible!), setting a snare for Dr. Kapoor.

The building is vacant except for a mousy young secretary who, no matter the weather, wears cardigan sweaters and elastic-waist polyester pants. Greasy bangs zigzag across her forehead above chronically pink eyes. "Excuse me," I say, rapping on the door of the CPA who employs her. She's bent over a stack of binders and file folders, her face puckered. "Excuse me," I repeat, striding into the fishbowl of a room. "No one's supposed to be here. The exterminator's coming."

She dazedly lifts her head. "Oh. Sorry." She slams the binder shut. A stack of papers flutters off the desk. She scrambles to her feet (orthopedic shoes, too? really?) and snatches up the slips. "I'm almost done." Her gaze dances around my shoulder, unable to meet mine.

"Good," I say. "Hurry up."

She flails around, trying to straighten her work area, then searches in vain for the office keys.

I grab her arm and squeeze. "Never mind. He'll be spraying in here, anyway." I usher her out of the office, out of the building. On the front steps, she asks in a helium voice—the voice of a laryngitic wood nymph—what the exterminator is spraying for. I consider saying something simple like ants (the best lies are boring and forgettable), but they're out of season. So I tell her cockroaches. In five seconds flat, she's jumping into a tiny, disgusting car and peeling away.

Good riddance.

In the back corner of my office, hidden in the false bottom of a china-cabinet drawer, is a camisole—cream satin with bubblegum-pink lace—that once belonged to Sophie Gallagher. After our first liaison, I took it as a memento. A trophy. When Sophie prepared to leave that day, flush and satisfied, her head swimming with fantasies of our next tryst, her nipples bobbing luxuriously against the fabric of her blouse, I grinned coyly and denied knowledge of the camisole's whereabouts. ("Maybe it grew legs and walked away, ha-ha.") Little did I know that my future would hang on this small, slippery garment.

With a flathead screwdriver, I pry open the false bottom of the drawer and reach inside, my hands shrouded by rubber gloves. I've touched the camisole before, leaving behind my genetic fingerprint. If I'm lucky, the DNA has degraded. If my material *is* retrievable, I'm counting on the lab technicians' incompetence. They'll have an uphill battle linking me to the camisole, anyway, once it's smeared with Dr. Kapoor's semen. Just in case, though, I'll be the one to "discover" the crucial evidence, turning any DNA of mine into inadvertent contamination.

The body is another matter. I'll arrive late to work tomorrow, after someone has phoned the police to report the doctor's suicide.

The camisole is in good shape, despite having been secreted in a musty compartment for months. As I look it over, I note only a couple of hopscotching snags. But then something else dawns on me: The camisole is pink (more flamingo than bubblegum) with white lace, instead of the other way around. Funny how the memory works...

I shrug off the inconsistency and refocus on the task at hand. Dr. Kapoor will be arriving soon, thanks to the hour I spent tailing him this morning, waiting to deliver my invitation. Technology being what it is, I couldn't risk something as simple as a phone call.

To say the doctor was happy to see me when I leaned out the driver's window with a lewd proposition (odds are he's been wet-dreaming about me since that ridiculous extortion attempt) would be an understatement. The man was giddy—as giddy as an old lecher gets without keeling over, that is.

The doctor is coming at noon, which gives me forty minutes to lay the trap. As far as he knows, we'll be fucking every which way to Sunday as payment for his silence in the Sophie Gallagher affair. If I trusted him, I might consider the deal. Murder is a messy business. But then who would take the fall on my behalf? Who would put that mossy-eyed detective off my trail?

I go into my desk for the jangly loop of master keys, find the one to Dr. Kapoor's office, and let myself in. The place is stuffy, disheveled. It smells faintly of garlic and sesame. A tufted cobalt-blue sofa (this would fit snugly in an alcove in Edward's and my master suite, I note) distracts from the teetering mounds of paperwork and books and unopened mail.

Behind the sofa is a carved rosewood table with a single drawer. Like every other surface, it's cluttered and dusty. I clear a spot on the table—the doctor won't live long enough to notice the rejiggering—for my tools: a pair of fuzzy pink handcuffs (these will end up in a dumpster somewhere, after the fact), a bottle of cherry lube (the quicker I extract the semen the better), and a couple of neckties Edward received as gifts (who gives a powerhouse like my husband a tie with baby pandas splotched all over it or one with bug-eyed frogs?).

Then there's the rope—the rope the good doctor will be hanging himself with. I couldn't exactly pick up a length at The Home Depot. ("Excuse me, sir, what kind of rope do you recommend for staging a suicide? Oh, nylon's best for fake hangings? Three-quarters of an inch in diameter? You don't say.") So I dropped by my sister-in-law Ellen's house and prowled through her garage, supposedly looking for an old yearbook of Edward's. Neither Ellen nor her husband, Bart, was home. They both work weekends. He's a carwash manager; she does something or other at the crappy, outdated hospital three towns over. Thankfully, twelve-year-old Jane was around to fix Auntie Lisa a tall glass of iced tea while she dug through those moldy boxes.

I left Ellen's house empty-handed ("Shucks! Where has that yearbook gone?") with a spool of rope in my purse. Black. Three-quarters of an inch, like my friend at The Home Depot would've recommended.

I'm down to thirty minutes, assuming the doctor isn't champing at the bit to ravish me. (Who am I kidding? Of course he is!) I unspool the rope—phew, it's long enough to suspend a septuagenarian from a ceiling fan!—and tie a quick but deadly noose. The rosewood table is the obvious place to hide it, but the drawer, which barely looks big enough to start with, is crammed with empty food wrappers (the doctor has an affinity for Nutter Butters, Raisinets, Gummi Bears). I jiggle the drawer loose and dump its contents between a filing cabinet and the window. After rearranging the curtains, the trash is invisible. But I've lost another six minutes. In my mind's eye, the doctor is at a traffic light, drumming his fingers on the steering wheel.

The only thing left to do is scoop my hair into a ballerina bun—or a dominatrix knot, if I'm staying in character. (I am!) I can explain away a hair or two to the police—I own the building, after all—but a handful of strands where they don't belong might put me in choppy waters. The last thing I want to do is cast doubt on the doctor's suicide.

My hair, my makeup, my clothes—I'm going full vamp, with patent leather stilettos and a studded bustier (might as well give the doctor a memorable sendoff!)—are all in place when the front door scrapes open.

Showtime.

CHAPTER 19
ROBIN

Nate teaches three sections of biology a week to a mostly disinterested lecture hall of hundreds. His class just let out. He wants to meet for lunch somewhere. My choice.

"Sorry," I say, already regretting the call. "I've got to run an errand." It's now or never for Marina's necklace. Sell or get off the pot.

"After, then," he says. In the background, a chirpy girl's voice wishes him a good afternoon. His response: "You, too, Emily."

Must be a student. An attention-paying sort. Nate prizes those rare gems. They make the drudgery worth it. "All right," I say, yielding to a vein of jealousy. "Come in an hour. I'll be home by then."

"*Your* place?"

My mind is scattered. I'm not thinking clearly. Not thinking, period. "You know where it is, right?" Like I said, things with Nate were casual. His condo was the hookup spot, since I have a kid. The only reason my daughter knows he exists—knows where he lives—is because of a mishap at the café. I tripped over an out-of-place box (on top of being a prick, Jeremy's sloppy, too) and torqued my knee. Nate had to rescue me from work—I couldn't put enough pressure on the gas pedal to drive—and, together, we collected Samantha from school. She and Nate bonded over takeout Chinese at his "cool, retro" (Sam's words) Formica dining table.

"I think I can find it." He chuckles. "An hour?"

"Yup."

"See you then."

It's a cold, bleak day. A harbinger of winter. I start the Caprice and crank up the heater. At top function, it warms the air to just above Eskimo level. Which is more than I can ask of a twenty-six-year-old car.

Still, I need to take the edge off. A slug of something would do me good. But what? I'm out of cough syrup. My stash of cheap wine is depleted. Maybe a tiny bottle of ...

I'm leaning over, feeling around under the passenger seat—if I'm lucky, a nip of vodka has gotten away from me, only to reappear now—when the rumble of a car exhaust assaults my ears. I don't look up. I'm too focused. My fingers have brushed something smooth. Glasslike. Promising. I pry the object loose. It's a nail polish bottle Samantha must've lost five or six years ago, based on the color. (She went through a pinky-pink, girly-girl phase starting at nine that was dead and buried by twelve.)

The car is clean—of alcohol, anyway. I hold my hand in front of the heater, warming it up. In a second, I'll summon the nerve to sell the last trace of my murdered sister, other than a few photos—our father never got around to scrubbing Marina from the albums—and the grimy purse found with her charred remains.

The exhaust noise has been fading, but now it comes roaring back. My head snaps around. Racing through the parking lot is a junky little sports car. A dark-colored—blue? gray? green?—Porsche or Beemer or Nissan 300ZX.

My heart spasms. Is this Samantha's attacker?

The car is too far gone to tell. Luckily I'm driving an aggressive V8. Say what you will about the Caprice, but it hauls ass.

The junker is peppy, but I've got raw, angry power on my side—under the hood and in my blood. If this is my chance to catch the bastard who hurt my daughter, I'll grab it with both hands.

I bully my way through a four-way stop, slip out a side exit, and narrowly miss cutting off the suspect vehicle. It's exited via a major intersection and ended up on the same road I'm impatiently merging onto. I nail the gas. The horn. Erratically change lanes, all to catch a glimpse of the driver. If nothing else, I must see if he fits the description of Samantha's attacker. Or if the car has that telltale mismatched fender. Once those boxes are checked off, my pistol is fair game.

Fate is against me. I'm in the passing lane like my target, but each time I gain on him, something—a left-turning SUV full of kids, a bicyclist shooting across the road—stymies me. Soon I lose track of my target altogether. He could've cut down any number of side streets—we're in a busy retail area—or fled onto the highway, whose entrance was a block back.

In a last-ditch effort, I roll down the window. I can't *see* the bastard anymore, but maybe I can *hear* him.

The cabin floods with cold air and the dull hum of traffic. Regular, normal-pitched traffic. I roll up the window. I've been disappointed for twenty-four years about Marina. The feeling is familiar. I wonder what I'll do if I ever manage to put my sister's killer or my daughter's attacker in my sights.

Part of me, a part I don't want to admit exists, is relieved to have lost the trail. Because I've got to finally sell Marina's necklace and get home to meet Nate. On a deeper level, I'm not sure I want to know what I'm capable of at my worst. Not yet, anyway.

I park in a thirty-minute zone, zip my hoodie up to my neck, and hustle past a barbershop, a Thai restaurant, a vacant storefront, a bank—in this neighborhood, I'm amazed a bank dares to operate—and a Depression-era bridal boutique. A cloud of cigarette smoke and piss hits me as I shove by a disheveled couple on the stoop of the pawnshop and slip inside.

It flashes through my mind that maybe Marina did overdose, like everyone thinks. Being here, on the edge of humanity, makes drug abuse seem natural. Necessary.

I shrug off the idea. Marina had too much going for her—beauty, charisma, popularity. She never would've given that up. Not willingly.

An accident is out of the question, too. My sister was smart. Careful. And what about the fire?

The pawnshop is less of a store than a musty closet of glass display cabinets and rickety metal shelving. For sale are such varied objects as an acoustic guitar; an antique baking tin; and an assortment of daguerreotypes, their subjects as humorless as the average nineteenth-century portrait sitter. The west wall is devoted to DVDs. The north wall houses a collection of video games, gaming systems, and relevant paraphernalia.

In and out. That's my goal. I have a rough idea what Marina's necklace will bring. Modern versions sell online for six hundred to three thousand dollars apiece, depending on the size of the stones. I'll get a fraction of that here, of course. Still, I'm hoping for three hundred, minimum. The piece has a spark of intangible charm, much like its previous owner.

Behind the counter is the sort of grizzled biker (sleeveless T-shirt, do-rag, a week of stubble) you'd expect to be running a shady establishment on the wrong side of town. He's bullshitting with a pale, lanky guy with muttonchops and a curved spine.

I sidle up to the jewelry case, which is stuffed with turquoise bracelets and vintage cigarette lighters. After a failed attempt to bump gazes with the clerk, I have no choice but to interrupt. "Hey," I say, clenching the necklace in my fist. "Wanna make a deal?"

The lanky guy backs up. I step into his shadow.

Biker Man tilts his head and grins. A mouthful of rotten corn. "We'll see about that," he says, thrusting out his hand.

I drop the necklace in his filthy palm and hold my breath.

CHAPTER 20
LISA

I'm soaking in the Jacuzzi, nude, my eyes shut, a rolled towel behind my neck, perspiration glazing my cheeks, my chin, my forehead. The natatorium's sound system, which is elaborate enough for a live band, plinks out a children's song in colloquial French. My husband wants our daughters to learn multiple languages, an outcome he's tasked his little blond piece of ass with bringing to fruition. Hence, Ashley has loaded foreign-language discs in the CD players house-wide.

Fine by me, as long as she doesn't drag me into her shenanigans. I have enough on my plate already. In fact, I can't seem to get a moment's peace, which I sorely need after such a grueling showdown yesterday. Disposing of the doctor was more of a challenge than I'd anticipated, and I have the rope burns to prove it.

Footsteps punch through my consciousness, through the jingly, upbeat tune, growing louder with each tap on that Spanish marble. "Excuse me, Mrs. Hayes," says our housekeeper, Ricki.

At least it's not Ashley. I can only take her in small doses nowadays. "Turn down the music," I say without opening my eyes. "I can barely hear you."

Ricki clops away. The music quiets to a murmur. She clops back. "Sorry, ma'am, but you've got a phone call. It's an emergency."

I wonder who'd contact me on the landline. Surely not Edward, the coveter of all things technological and forward-thinking. He'd sooner leap into the Grand Canyon, a plausible idea since he's tumbleweeding through Vegas right now, hammering out the details of a patent-infringement settlement.

My eyes flip open. Ricki's arm is outstretched. She's gripping a cordless phone like her life depends on it. "Get me a towel," I say, ignoring her urgent body language. I'm not about to take the call, whoever it is—a jab at the base of my skull says the emergency is about Dr. Kapoor—in the Jacuzzi.

She spins around for the laundry closet. By the time she returns, I'm standing on the pool deck, glistening from head to toe, awaiting the towel's embrace. She wraps me gingerly, her gaze flitting over my taut nipples, lingering on my belly (a slight "baby bump" remains, despite my otherwise phenomenal shape), and trailing over a tuft of pubic hair before breaking free.

"Hello?" I bark into the receiver, drawing the towel tight around me.

Ricki slips off.

Sad to say, but I recognize the voice immediately: Jacquelyn. "Dr. Hayes? Thank God. I've been trying to reach you for hours. I finally thought to … finally found the number for …"

"What is it?" As if I don't already know.

"There's been"—*sniffle, sniffle*—"something awful … I just don't …"

What is she so broken up about? The woman has exchanged all of ten words with Dr. Kapoor in her life. She must be angling for bereavement pay. "Please, Jacquelyn, get to the point. I'm ill, remember?" The morning-sickness excuse has served me well. I recommend it. In fact, it was the pretext for canceling all of my appointments today.

"It's one of the tenants—Dr. Kapoor," she says, her voice quaking. "He's killed himself."

"That's too bad. His rent was always on time. Do we have next month's check? Or do we"—meaning her; she's my receptionist/property manager—"need to post an ad?" My inquiry is met with yawning silence. "Jacquelyn? Are you there? Hello?"

She comes back harder, stiffer. "He did it here, in the building. He hung himself."

"How unfortunate." I start meandering down the hall, bound for the kitchen. I skipped breakfast and now I'm famished. I'm thinking that a banana split—or maybe some salted butterscotch gelato between a couple of soft molasses cookies—will hit the spot. "Is it cleaned up?"

"Fr—from the suicide?"

"What else?"

"They want to talk to you."

"They?"

"The police. The medical examiner." An exasperated sigh. "As the owner of the building—"

From nowhere, Magnum starts barking. Soon he's zigzagging around my feet. Silently, I shoo him off. "I don't know anything," I say. "Stand in for me. You have access to the records and whatever else—"

"They didn't say anything about records."

I knew I was right to hold off on the miscarriage. "I can't. I'm bleeding." The flow has nearly dried up, but that's irrelevant. "I'm on my way to the hospital. Handle this, okay? I'll make it worth your while." Above all, the police can't see me until the rope burns heal.

She has no choice. What is she going to do, argue with me?

In a fluster, she agrees. I tell her to reschedule the entire week's appointments (I'll have to pretend to recover from the miscarriage for that long) and then abruptly hang up. That should do the trick. Now she's concerned and confused, off-kilter and buried in work. The authorities will get honest but minimal cooperation.

Odds are, in a few days, the suicide note will have resolved things in my favor. I took extreme care composing it (wearing gloves, of course), with the doctor's own paper and ink, on his whirring old desktop computer. I even went so far as to borrow his phrasing (his chart notes helped here) and reproduce his errors (*conscious* instead of *conscience*, for example) for added authenticity.

The note can't miss. It's a masterpiece of fiction. Good thing, too, since it'll be doing the heavy lifting, convincing the police to look no further for Sophie Gallagher's killer. (Have they even ruled her death a homicide? If not, they soon will, once they read about Dr. Kapoor running her off the road.) Without the semen-stained camisole—long story short, the doctor couldn't perform—things are a bit more tenuous; the case against him is thinner. But with the stalking seed I planted in Detective Luke's mind and the intimate details I revealed about Sophie in the suicide note (things only a sex partner or her rapist would know), I'm still on solid ground.

The vanilla ice cream is gone. Ashley must be spoiling the girls to make up for their father's absence. No matter. We have a fresh half gallon of strawberry and the gelato. I split a banana lengthwise, arrange it in a lace-edged dish Edward inherited from his spinster aunt, and plop three scoops—two gelato and a strawberry—between the severed halves. A drizzle of chocolate syrup, a spray of whipped cream, a scattering of rainbow sprinkles, and the all-important cherry top things off.

When I'm done serving myself, the kitchen is a mess. But my creation is delicious. I settle on a barstool and scarf it down, sucking the spoon clean.

My belly is full, a good thing since I'll be spending the rest of the day hunched in a dirty, smelly, rocklike chair in the emergency-department waiting room.

But first I must call Edward. He should be in this with me every terrible, horrible, gut-wrenching step of the way.

I have to think for a minute about where I've left my phone. The master suite is the most obvious place. My personal effects stay as far away from the sticky-fingered help as possible. But then I remember: the library. I was in there last night, looking for a book of herbal remedies—one of the few med-school texts I've held on to and the only one with alternative treatments (they're less traceable by the police)—to heal these ridiculous abrasions.

Why couldn't the geezer just go down peacefully?

Alas, the herbal-remedy book was nowhere to be found. (These domestics will steal anything that isn't bolted down.) I did, however, stumble across a juicy murder mystery that kept me turning pages into the wee hours.

The book is where I left it, on a leather-inlaid table with intricate gold embossing. With a bit more work—I have to get down on my hands and knees and grope around under the sofa, the towel shrugging loose in the process—I find my phone, which, it dawns on me, must've been knocked aside when I tossed the book down in a sleepy haze.

I select Edward's name from my contacts and press the phone icon. The call rings through, but he doesn't answer. I smother a flame of anger. Now is not the time to alienate the man who'll shield me from the police, from anyone who casts a suspicious eye my way. "Hi," I say, keeping my tone neutral. "It's me." As if he needs a reminder. Even with his adulterous romping—if I know him, Ashley is a momentary distraction—I'm in a league of my own, atop an ivory pedestal.

I continue with the message: "Don't panic, okay? I just wanted you to know that I'm going to the hospital. It's probably nothing. I'm sure the baby's fine. I woke up with some bleeding is all. I thought I'd play it safe and get it checked.

"That's it, really. Just a minor hiccup. I'll call back when everything's sorted out. Have a wonderful day. I love you." That last bit, the warm and fuzzy, lovey-dovey part, isn't me. Edward will know. He respects the hell out of me for a reason, his recent escapades notwithstanding. My sweetness will tie his stomach in knots. Five to one, he's on a plane, on his way home, before I ever set foot in an examining room.

CHAPTER 21
ROBIN

I exit the pawnshop with a hundred bucks in my pocket and a writhing pit of snakes in my stomach over having sold out my sister for such a temporary reprieve. The cash is a Band-Aid on a gaping wound. If I don't find a reliable source of income soon, the sacrifice will be for nothing. Samantha and I will be in the same predicament two weeks down the road.

Either the temperature has shot up twenty degrees or my nerves have gotten the best of me. Or maybe it's hormones. I've heard of women as young as me—younger, even, if they have diseased ovaries—getting hot flashes. Whatever the cause, I'm suddenly sweating out of every pore. My flesh is a coal furnace, my skin a popping, hissing radiator. I strip off my hoodie and tie it around my waist. I'm passing the vacant storefront—from left-behind window decals ("GOT JESUS?" "IT'S ALL GOD"), I gather that the place was a fly-by-night church or a religious gift store—when I spot Lewis's van creeping toward me.

I'm not up for small talk. And I'm late. Actually, I'd hoped Lewis was at my house right now, keeping Nate company.

I hang my head and pick up my pace. Soon the barbershop slides into my peripheral vision. Then the Caprice. I duck into the passenger seat and shimmy over, taking my place behind the wheel.

Lewis noses into a spot up ahead. If I had the spare brain cells, I'd wonder what he's doing in this sketchy part of town. But all I can think of is the money in my pocket (a fiendish slice of me wants to blow it all on liquor) and my poor, murdered sister. I feel like I've slaughtered the last of her, like I'm complicit in wiping her from the earth.

I force a knot of guilt out of my chest—there's nothing I can do to bring back Marina, to give her story a happy ending—and steer for home.

The radio is stuck on a country station, thanks to a broken knob. What I can hear of the music is scratchy and distant-sounding. I'd give anything for some hard rock, a thumping beat to own me.

Obliterate. Obliterate. The word rolls around in my head like a loose marble. Someone should pry open my skull and tweeze out the things that don't belong. They'd fill a bucket, I think.

The radio is on full blast, but it's not enough. Tears pulse to the surface of my eyes and spill down my face.

I hate this. This is bullshit. I need a drink.

I'm a heartbeat away from ditching Nate and heading to a bar—*any* bar. A hundred bucks isn't going to put a dent in what I owe, anyway. (Did I mention the credit card bills and property tax liens and student loans the government was foolish enough to float me?) Only one thing is stopping me: Samantha. I'm all she has.

By the time I coast into the driveway at home, I've pulled myself together. Gone are the puffy eyes and intermittent sniffling. I'm done feeling sorry for myself.

Nate is parked across the street, in front of the foreclosed house that's drowning in weeds. If the bank doesn't liquidate the thing soon, the ground will finish choking it down. In a way, I hope it rots, despite what it'll do to my property value. There's beauty in destruction. Hope. Renewal. A fresh start. Or so I keep telling myself.

In the rearview mirror, Nate strides toward me. His nerdy exterior hides an undercurrent of raw masculinity. He's equal parts Clark Kent and Superman—except, today, Superman is winning. "Hey," I say, emerging to greet him, "sorry I'm late. What happened to your glasses?"

His thumbs are hooked in his jeans. "Dumb story," he says, shaking his head. "I'm going commando."

I appraise him sideways. He looks ... *different*. "I don't think that means what you think it means." I wave a hand in front of his face. "Can you even see?"

Suddenly, his mouth is on mine. He kisses deep, probing. "You tell me."

His aim is spectacular. There's no denying that. But what is he doing? We're not a thing anymore, and he knows it. Then again, sex is what we do best. "We've only got an hour," I blurt, pivoting for the house. "Come on."

We don't bother lying around after, stroking each other's hair and cooing promises we won't keep. It's too indulgent. Too juvenile. Wham-bam is our style, something that hasn't changed with the scenery.

One barrier *has* been broken, though. Nate is the first man to seduce me in my own bed since Samantha learned her times tables. I had a boyfriend back then. A landscaper named Connor. He drank more than I did. It lasted two years. Now my daughter's taking precalculus.

Marina was taking precalculus when she disappeared.

Nate's jeans are back on, but he's barefoot and bare-chested, wandering around my bedroom, examining objects with an archeologist's eye. "*Shopaholic and Baby?*" he says, lifting a dusty book off a shelf by the window. "Doesn't seem like you."

Dig a little deeper, I want to say. *You'll find the stories that haunt me.* "It was a gift," I lie, "for a friend. I just never got around to ..." The truth is that light, frothy fiction makes me feel safe. Gives me a sense that at least somewhere—even if that place sprang whole from the author's mind—is immune to the cruelties of life.

I hold out Nate's shirt. He slips it on. Bit by bit, I herd him toward the door. Just when I think he might go—not from the house but from my private space, which has grown claustrophobic—he pauses. "What's that?" he asks, gesturing past the doorway.

I can't do this; I can't dredge up every ruined thing. Nate knows I had a sister. That she died when I was small. The circumstances have been left vague. He probably imagines a car accident or one of those vicious childhood cancers. Not prostitution. Drugs. Murder. "It's nothing," I say, grabbing his hand. Three more steps and he'll be face-to-face with an altar. A shrine. An investigation that's led nowhere in twenty-odd years.

I should take it down, all of it—the snapshots and newspaper clippings (Marina's case never made it to print, but there have been other dead bodies, tragedies that cast similar shadows); the spreadsheets and index cards; the background checks and work schedules; the neighborhood maps and death notices. I can almost see the scattering of thumbtack holes that would be left behind if I could bring myself to purge.

Nate has fallen under a spell, under Marina's spell. He veers toward the altar, which is just my beat-up childhood dresser and the nook around it. "Is this …?" he murmurs, his fingers skimming a candid shot of Marina in her teenage glory: wind-tossed hair and sun-kissed skin, her toes dug into the sand, her dark eyes sparkling like the lake behind her.

I swallow hard. "My sister?" I say. "Yeah, that's her." We stand there for a few silent beats, absorbing.

"Pretty," says Nate.

There's so much more to say about Marina, about how her personality could fill a room, about how she'd sweep you off your feet with a secret wink meant just for you, about her voice—it was gentle and warm, making even the worst news bearable. (When our cat, Barnaby, got mauled by a loose dog and had to be put down, Marina was the one to tell me. We walked two miles to the vet's office and left a trail of food all the way home, so Barnaby's soul could find its way back to us.)

"She looks like Sam." Nate tilts his head and squints. "And you. She looks like both of you."

"Powerful genes," I say, trying to lighten the mood. But my words fall flat. A change of subject, instead: "Are you hungry?"

Nate is perceptive. He pushes me only as far as I can go. "Sure."

We settle at the kitchen table with a block of cheese and a sleeve of stale saltines. He asks about my day, about what I've been up to. He knows I was fired from that bigmouth Jeremy and my absence at the café.

I wasn't keeping secrets, I assure him. I've been busy with Sam. And the job hunt. What I do is none of his business, but I can't say that when I can still feel him inside me.

"You know," he says, stuffing a cracker-and-cheese sandwich in his mouth, "if you're looking for quick cash, under the table, my cousin's wife needs help on her catering crew. It's a last-minute thing, day by day. I can give her your number."

"Under the table?" The idea would've been even more appealing had I gotten the unemployment. Then I could've double-dipped. Still, not paying taxes would be a godsend.

"As far as I know, yeah. For the replacement crew, it's all cash. The regulars are on the books."

It's a stop-gap measure. I'll need something more reliable, ASAP. But it's better than nothing. And it's the only offer on the table right now. "Have her call me," I say.

Relief washes over Nate's face. "Good," he says, squeezing my knee. "Good."

CHAPTER 22
LISA

I offer Ricki double time to drive me to the hospital and stay until my husband arrives, which, I have full faith, will be very soon. She agrees, even packing an overnight bag in case the doctors keep me.

They will; I'll make sure of it.

We're nestled in the Hummer, preparing to back out of the garage, when Ashley rolls into the bay beside us—Edward's bay—at the wheel of our Mercedes.

She's sleeping with my husband *and* parking in his spot? Since when? Edward's Jag is at the airport, but that doesn't give her the right to break protocol, to insert herself where she doesn't belong. I bet she's got visions of dethroning me dancing in her head.

Think again.

It may take a while, but I'll find another Mary Poppins. A burly one with chipped teeth and a unibrow. Disposing of Ashley will be the easy part.

"Hold on," I say, catching Ricki as she's about to shift into reverse. She's nervous behind the wheel. Twitchy. And who could blame her, driving a vehicle worth triple her yearly salary? "Change of plans." I climb down and head for Ashley, who's exited the Mercedes with a trove of shopping bags. The pink-on-pink Victoria's Secret bag grabs my eye.

The Hummer is huge. Ashley doesn't see me coming. "Oh, God!" she gasps as I pop up in her path. "You scared me!" She spots Ricki behind the wheel. "What's going on?"

I could ask her the same. And maybe I will, once I've raked her over the coals. Once she's good and burnt, her skin flaking off like charred coconut flesh. Once she's begging for mercy that will not come. "Leave the bags," I say, gesturing at the polished concrete floor. "We're going to the hospital."

She pulls the pathetic, confused face of a child sent to bed early. This is what attracts my husband?

Ricki has abandoned her post and turned up at my side like a henchman of sorts. My protector. I can't swear to it (I've got more important things to concern myself with than the relations of the help), but I don't think she likes Ashley. Maybe she knows about Edward and the tramp. Maybe she's had to clean up after them.

I'm off on a tangent. I must rein myself in.

In the panicked hiss of a woman about to miscarry, I order Ashley into the Hummer and Ricki back to the house. For today, they're swapping places. Ricki can mind the girls—she's raised a baseball team already—while Ashley gets a front-row seat to the drama about to unfold between my husband and me. A tragedy that will irrevocably bind us.

Ashley is reluctant, but I don't give her a choice. I threaten to fire her. If she were more confident of Edward's loyalty, of her position with him, she'd challenge me. But she doesn't.

Ricki would do anything for double time, a fact I file away for future use.

Our estate is fifteen minutes from the hospital. I tell Ashley to hurry: forty miles an hour in a twenty-five, seventy in a fifty. I have to push her to go faster, faster. It's not imperative to arrive so quickly—the abortion pills have already worked their magic—but I'm playing a part. I'm also hoping to get her pulled over, hoping to embarrass her, hoping to leave a black mark on her snow-white record.

She won't feel so high and mighty when I'm done with her. Maybe she won't feel anything at all.

Sadly, the speeding ticket is not to be. "Drop me at the emergency room," I say as we swing the last turn before the hospital campus. "You can park and then find me afterward. Oh, and put my car on the top level of the garage, away from everyone else. I don't want to come out to any nicks in my paint." Bonus: She'll have to walk a lot farther to the elevators.

The emergency room is heralded by a sign reading AMBULANCES ONLY. Ashley brakes to a crawl. "Um, I don't think we're supposed to—"

"Forget it," I say, losing patience. "Just pull over. Here." I poke a finger at the windshield. "Right here."

"But—"

"Do it."

She sucks in a sharp breath. "Okay." Instead of stopping in front of the automatic doors, she overshoots by a car length. This is a hedge, I assume. Proof she's followed the rules, at least to a degree, should the parking police appear to confront her.

What little respect I had for the woman is dwindling fast. I don't bother giving her any more direction. She's proven that in matters other than fastidiousness and childcare, she's as useless as a mink coat in Zimbabwe.

With a sigh—you'd think she'd offer to help me, given my supposed condition—I climb out of the vehicle and make my way inside, hunching over and moaning softly.

The reception desk is straight ahead. I line up behind an obese woman with a toothache (I know this from a squawking cell phone conversation she's having) and an old guy with a severe, almost comically fake limp.

Five minutes tick by without the line moving. The old guy is doing everything—providing his medical insurance, explaining his complaint, etcetera—with excessive detail, at a snail's pace. When Toothache

Woman turns around and rolls her eyes, I shrug and offer a weak smile.

Behind me, the line is extending: a screeching toddler with flaming cheeks and a thread of snot squiggling into its mouth (and its disheveled, unequipped father); a middle-aged woman with some sort of equilibrium problem (she's swaying back and forth and grabbing hold of her companion, a younger woman with the same prominent Roman nose); a guy with ripped, blood-splotched jeans who might've fallen off a skateboard, judging by his cockeyed baseball cap and flat-bottomed shoes.

Still, no Ashley. But the old guy's clearing out, courtesy of a wheelchair that unfolded from nowhere and an orderly pushing him to Phase Two, the triage holding pen.

One down, one to go. Toothache Woman lumbers up to the counter. I groan and cinch my face, rubbing circles around my belly. I hadn't planned this drama, but sometimes you have to improvise. If miscarrying here—now, on the record—keeps me out of the crosshairs of the police, so be it. It's past time to teach my husband a lesson on fidelity, too. Let's see how he feels about his mistress once our baby's life is snuffed out. Who'll pick up the pieces with him then?

Me. It'll *always* be me—unless I decide otherwise.

Toothache Woman has her facts in order. In no time, she's rubbing elbows with Wheelchair Guy, while they await their turns with the triage nurse.

Just as I'm stepping forward, the receptionist springs out of her chair. "Be right back!" she squeaks, then dashes around the corner, flashing her ID badge at a card reader on the wall. A set of double doors drifts open and she disappears inside.

Good thing nobody's dying out here. Can't the employees use the restroom on their own time?

While the receptionist is MIA, Ashley arrives. She loiters in the wings, but I beckon her with a stiff wave. If she thinks she's going to escape without getting her hands dirty, she's mistaken. "Take this," I say, shoving my purse at her, "and find my credit card." The insurance card would be better, but I forget where I've left it. For now, the charges will hit my American Express. Jacquelyn will have the pleasure of sorting out the bill later.

The receptionist reappears, collects my data, and, thanks to a well-placed remark ("I'd hate to be stuck waiting and lose my baby *in such a preventable way*"), leapfrogs me to the triage room, where a nurse checks my vitals and asks a few basic questions. I give all the right answers about cramping and blood and labored breathing.

Soon Ashley and I find ourselves in an exam room (if anyone asks, she'll be posing as my sister). Again, she tries to worm out of helping me, this time under the guise of modesty. "Wouldn't you be more comfortable with a professional?" she asks, when I tell her to slip the hospital gown up over my arms (I've been instructed to take off everything, including my underwear) and tie it loosely in the back, where no normal-jointed human could reach.

I'm barely situated in bed when the nurse returns. She writes her name—Kaylee—in huge, loopy cursive on a whiteboard nearby. "All right," she says, clicking through computer screens, "let's see."

Ashley's eyes dart at the door. "I should go, right?" Her voice adds *please, please, please*.

"No," I say firmly. "Until Edward arrives, I need you." And even then, she'll remain. Nothing will drive home the commitment between my husband and me like witnessing our sorrow.

Kaylee reviews the information in my chart and inquires about medications. "I'm taking B6 for morning sickness," I tell her. (A lie.) "Ten milligrams. And prenatal vitamins. That's it. I'm keeping things very natural. Which is why this is all so ..." My voice quivers. I stare wistfully into the distance.

"Nothing for high blood pressure? Or diabetes?"

"No. Why?"

She shrugs. "A lot of women your age ... when they're pregnant, they need"—she scans the computer—"but your blood pressure's good. One eighteen over sixty-seven."

"I make a point of staying fit. I'm a doctor, you know. Well, a psychiatrist, but I went to medical school." You raging nitwit.

Kaylee's cheeks flush. She stumbles over an apology, then heads for the hall, promising to send in a doctor, ASAP. Once she's gone, Ashley musters, "That's good, isn't it? Your blood pressure being normal?" She's leaning against the wall—there's no bedside chair, only a stumpy, wheeled stool—twirling a length of hair.

"Yes," I say. "But it doesn't mean anything. I'm losing the baby. I can feel it."

Her hand goes to her mouth. "Don't say that." She's on the verge of tears. "They can do something. They can stop it. I'm sure—"

I'm sinking into the bed and my pillow needs adjusting. I take a moment to compose myself. "They can't fix it," I say, smoothing the covers across my lap. "It's already happening. And it's your fault. Yours and Edward's." I pin her with an insect's stare. "Did you think I wouldn't find out?" My lips curl into a sneer. "I've known for a while now. Nothing stays secret in that house. Remember that."

She's dumbstruck (a step up from just plain dumb!), which sends a thrill of delight pulsing through me. I let her flap on the hook like a dying fish. Her face is trembling, her eyes locked on a floor tile a few feet away. She swallows repetitively, her throat emitting a sticky, slurpy, gurgling sound.

I've made my point—as much as possible for the moment, anyway. "Get your phone," I say, meaning the seven-hundred-dollar iPhone Edward and I supply. My husband hasn't seen fit to answer me (I assume he's sleeping off a hangover), but maybe he'll respond to her. "I need you to make a call."

"Me?"

"Get Edward on the line. Tell him it's time to come home."

CHAPTER 23
ROBIN

Once Nate is gone, I call Samantha. In the rush this morning, I forgot to nail down our plans for this afternoon. School has only been out for a few minutes, though. She can't have gotten far.

Five rings, then to voicemail. "Sam, it's me. Why aren't you picking up?" I let a few seconds pass, as if she might answer. "I'm heading over. Stay there, okay? In front of the school, where I can find you." My voice betrays me: high-pitched, shaky, desperate. "Do not leave, Samantha. I'll be there in fifteen minutes."

A twitch in my mind—I imagine whole sections of my brain cordoned off with crime-scene tape and NO TRESPASSING signs—tells me to go, go, go, before it's too late.

I take a few steadying breaths and head for the car. It doesn't dawn on me until I grab the door handle that I've left the keys in the house.

Dammit. The house is locked up tight (force of habit, given what happened to Marina and, especially, what's stalking my daughter).

Ironically, the Caprice is open, which does me no good. I'm not exactly a hot-wiring phenom.

Blood rushes through my ears. I throw darting glances around the yard, hoping for a miracle. My salvation is a loose brick on the front porch. I could jiggle it free—it's only wedged in, the mortar having disintegrated ages ago—and smash it through a window. The one in the corner of the living room looks promising.

The brick slides out easily, bringing with it a powdery cloud of debris. I wipe my hands on my jeans, leaving ghostly prints across my thighs.

Am I really going to vandalize my own property? Hurl a brick through the window my mother so carefully cleaned with crumpled newspapers and diluted vinegar, even when her hands shook from alcohol withdrawal?

Time is ticking. My daughter is waiting. I tramp across the lawn—it's overgrown and despairing, anticipating its winter coating of snow—and stop several feet from the window.

I should've paid more attention in physics class. Will glass come flying back at me when the window breaks? I'm about to test the theory when a gentle squeaking noise catches my ear. The sound is faraway. Faint. Imagined?

I concentrate harder, focusing on the sound of Lewis's van. I've heard its telltale squeaking hundreds of times. Thousands. It's nothing serious if it hasn't taken the van out of commission. (Lewis isn't one to part with a buck prematurely.) I'm so accustomed to the noise that it doesn't usually register. It's like living by a busy airport or railroad tracks. The roars and shakes become the background music of your life.

Not today, though. Today I hear that whiny squeak with every molecule of my being. Which means I won't have to smash the window, after all.

I drop the brick at the base of the steps. My phone is in my back pocket. I tug it out and text Sam: Delayed. Stay put. Lewis is driving. Text me back.

The squeaking grows louder. At the end of Lewis's driveway, I pace. What's taking him so long?

My whole body buzzes with anxiety. I might lift off the ground and float away, vanish in an explosive shimmer.

My daughter needs me. I can feel it. Something's wrong. And the universe—I would say God, but I stopped believing in Him when Marina died—is laughing at me, throwing roadblocks in my path and watching me flounder time and again.

The warmth from earlier has receded, leaving behind a nibbling chill. I wish briefly for a coat—or at least my hoodie, which is crumpled by my bed, where Nate left it in a heated rush.

I could call him. Nate. I could, but I won't. He's done enough already, rescuing Samantha and helping me find a job. (The catering gig will be a life raft if it comes through.)

Illogically, I start walking down the street, toward the main road. Where do I think I'm going? The high school is miles away. It would take hours to walk there.

Our house is at the back of the neighborhood, hemmed in by a grid of similar homes. By the time I reach the first crossroad—Blueberry Street—I can't hear the squeaking anymore. I think about turning around and smashing the window like I'd planned. A sheet of plywood would cover the hole. The house wouldn't look any different, any worse, than a bunch of others around here. But something inside me—vestigial pride? a sentimental desire to protect the place that holds my memories of Marina?—won't let me do it.

I press on: Apple Court, Raspberry Lane, Peach Place. The sidewalks are pockmarked, degraded, dangerous. Every step is a risk. I keep my eyes on my feet until the asphalt evens out.

If Lewis had a cell phone, I'd call him. But he's stuck in the past, clinging to a way of life that never really existed. The bits and pieces that *are* tangible—his dependable, old rotary phone, for example—will be wiped from the collective memory sooner rather than later.

I flip open my phone and check again. Still no reply from Samantha. I shouldn't have let her go back to school. It's too soon. She hasn't had any counseling, hasn't figured out how she got into such a mess, hasn't dealt with the blind spot that let her become some loser's punching bag. As devastating as Marina's murder was—*is*—it taught me to self-protect, to be wary, to assume ulterior (and nefarious) motives until proven wrong.

Fifty yards ahead, traffic hums along the main road. I'm weighing my options—I could call a cab (not my first choice with my financial situation) or trudge another half mile to the nearest bus stop—when my phone starts ringing.

The number is local. I don't recognize it. "Hello?" I answer, my voice flashing with irritation.

"Mom?"

"Samantha? Sam?" I stop in my tracks. "Where are you? What's going on?" Please let her be okay. I'll give anything.

"My phone died."

"I've been trying to call you for—"

"I'm at Quinn's. We're gonna work on a history project—like research online and stuff—and make tacos. She's babysitting her little brother. Her mom will give me a ride home later, okay?"

"Quinn? Do I know her?"

"Do you know *any* of my friends? I don't hang out with the same kids from kindergarten anymore."

Is she trying to bait me? If so, it's working. "Who else is there?"

A dramatic huff. "I *told* you. Quinn and her little brother." To Quinn: "What's your brother's name?" A muffled reply. "Liam. His name's Liam."

"No one else is going to be there? No boys?" I come right out and ask.

"Don't do this, Mom." I imagine her gritting her teeth. "Just don't. I'm with Quinn, eating tacos and doing homework. That's all."

"What's the address?"

"You're not coming over."

"The address," I repeat.

"First, promise you're not gonna show up and go ballistic."

"Why would I do that?" Go crazy, I mean.

"I don't know. Because you overreact to everything."

I struggle to hold my tongue. She's given me plenty to react to lately. And I'm not sure the damage is done. "I don't want to argue with you, Samantha. Give me the address. Then you can go back to studying. I'll wait for you at home."

"Fine." She gets the address from Quinn and passes it along. I recognize the location. It's in a leafy subdivision a few blocks from the high school with wide streets and spotless sidewalks.

Samantha is anxious to be rid of me. I oblige, flipping the phone shut and disconnecting the call. The trek home takes longer than the walk in the other direction—or so it seems. I'm a block and a half away—how I'm going to get inside is still a mystery—when Lewis's van comes squeaking up behind me.

He slows to a crawl and rolls down the window. "Your car break down again?" he asks, shaking his head. "Hop in. I'll give you a lift. You're headed home, I assume." The van jerks to a stop.

There's no sense arguing with an old man trying to do a good deed. I shrug inwardly and take the passenger seat, which is slick with some sort of vinyl protectant.

"Thanks. I'm locked out. I was trying to …" What was I trying to do, exactly? Rescue my daughter from tacos and homework? "Never mind."

Lewis asks about the lockout. I tell him I flaked and left the keys inside. He says he has lock-picking tools we can use to get in.

I'm relieved but curious: Why does he have locksmith tools? As far as I know, he spent forty years pushing numbers around a ledger for the school district.

Before I can inquire, something unexpected catches my eye. In the spotless ashtray, which is stuck open like a screaming mouth, is a delicate, rosy-gold chain. I recognize it in my blood: Marina's necklace.

As we pull into Lewis's driveway, my head is swimming. I blink a few times, in case I'm imagining things. But the necklace is still there.

I must be staring, because Lewis scoops the necklace out of the ashtray and holds it up. "Beautiful, isn't it?" he says, tears glistening in his eyes.

He doesn't seem to expect an answer. Which is good, because my tongue feels like an engorged cactus. "Um … yeah," is the best I can produce.

"I can't believe"—his voice cracks—"I can't believe I found it, after all these years. Georgette must be smiling down from Heaven."

"What? I mean, sorry, but—" I grimace. "What about Georgette?"

"This was hers. Her favorite." Even his smile is sad. "It was stolen back in the eighties, along with another one. Another necklace, I mean. She had two good pieces of jewelry in her life. I wanted to bury her with one of them. Then when your sister … well, I thought maybe …"

"Marina?"

He nods.

My eyebrows pull together. What is he saying? "Marina?" I repeat. "You think that … you think she …"

"She was a spitfire, your sister. Georgette liked her somethin' fierce. She was the daughter we never had, I guess you could say. No offense." He clears his throat. "But she could raise hell, too, like a wild mustang. Didn't quite know her limits."

Is he calling my sister a thief?

"Marina got those necklaces"—the peridot, which is curled around his hand, and the citrine, which vanished with my sister when she ran away—"from Berman's Jewelry Store. With her own money. She worked all summer saving up."

"I wish that were true."

"She did. I saw her."

"It's a long time ago." He shrugs. "Maybe you're right. I'm just glad to have it back. Call me a sentimental old fool, but it's like a part of Georgie is here with us again."

I stare at his wilted morning glories, whose tendrils have choked their way to the top of his rain gutters. If he doesn't chop them down soon, they'll be a perfect base for the inevitable ice dams. "She is," I say about Georgette. "Of course she is."

CHAPTER 24
LISA

I'm only mildly surprised when Edward answers Ashley's call. I let him sweet talk her for a minute, a situation she endures with discomfort, before motioning for the phone. When my voice hits my husband's ears, he stumbles over himself, trying to explain his disloyalty.

Oh, how the mighty have fallen.

Edward's declarations of fatherly concern—"When I saw her number, I thought something had happened to the girls"—are believable enough to the average fool. But I'm neither average nor foolish.

"Forget it," I say as he apologizes for the umpteenth time. "Where are you?"

"The hotel." Vegas. He hasn't even left yet.

"Didn't you get my message?" If he has an ounce of perceptiveness—not to mention self-preservation (he's safe only if he remains valuable, only if he serves a purpose)—he'll sense the impatience in my voice.

"Norm had my phone. He was checking for a text from …" (Norman Frankel is his lawyer-cum-sidekick.) "We got the patent, by the way. For a fraction of—"

This is good news. We'll make untold millions off the doohickey he's laid claim to. "I need you back here, as soon as possible. There's a problem with the baby. I'm—*we're*—in the hospital." He stops cold. The air hisses out of him. "Edward? Are you there?"

"I'm on my way. Make them do everything they can, okay? *Everything*. Offer to donate. We'll build a new wing. Whatever it takes."

As much as I'd like to see our names emblazoned over, say, a spruced up emergency observation unit—this place is in dire need of an upgrade, starting with the lumpy beds!—shedding that kind of cash is out of the question. "I will. Just hurry."

In the background on Edward's end of the line, elevators chime, proving he's taking me seriously, taking the threat to our unborn child for the cataclysm it is—or would've been, had I not brought matters into my own hands.

I'm satisfied and hang up. Ashley's phone goes in the bedside stand, where I can keep an eye on it. She won't be sneaking off to text my husband from a bathroom stall—or anywhere else, for that matter. Those days are done.

Speaking of bathrooms, I don't see one in this third-world excuse for a hospital room. "Find out what's taking so long," I tell Ashley. "The doctor should've been here by now. And look for a restroom. I need to go." Preferably before they start poking around *down there*.

The twit assumes a deer-in-the-headlights look. How could you, Edward? How could you fuck this dopey, skittish girl? "Who … um … what do I … ?"

"The nurses' station," I say with a sigh. "We passed it on the way in. Tell them who I am. Who Edward is. Remind them."

She heads for the door with the zeal of a garden slug. She's destined to fail; her body language demands it. If she doesn't get pegged as an interloper—an apt characterization in multiple regards—and tossed out on her ear, I'll be amazed.

A minute later, I follow in her tracks, my bladder aching for release. Across the hall is a unisex facility. I use it and then wander down the corridor—it's abandoned, like in a low-budget horror film—in the opposite direction of the nurses' station, glancing into rooms as I go. Except for a small boy reclining on a mountain of pillows, a splint strapped to his forearm and a wedge of gauze stuck to his temple, no one notices my foray.

I'm about to turn around—I've hit a dead end, unless I'm aiming to slither off to another section of the hospital—when an unattended purse catches my eye. It's plopped in a chair, just inside the doorway of a darkened room. I don't need the money. And the purse is cheap. Hideous. (Who in their right mind totes around something made of purple faux croc?) But when opportunity knocks …

My gaze sweeps the area. It's clear. I pretend to lean against the wall for support—excruciating cramps again!—and unzip the purse. I rummage around inside until I encounter a wallet.

Jackpot.

I tuck the wallet under my arm, high up by my armpit, where the folds of the gown shield it from view. Then I race back to my room, where Ashley has left *her* purse unguarded.

Piece of cake, as they say. I stuff the stolen wallet in the nanny's purse—a time bomb of sorts—and hop back into bed, a twitter of voices heading my way.

Enter the doctor. He's young. Sexy. Like James Spader in *Pretty in Pink*, minus the feathered hair. He gets down to business, ordering tests—blood and urine and an ultrasound—and offering to feel around inside me for pregnancy-related evidence, good or bad.

"I'd prefer you didn't," I tell him, though I'm tempted to take him up on the offer and make Ashley watch. It'd be payback for the images of her and Edward that are stamped in my mind. "I'm in too much pain. I might be sick."

He exerts himself—his authority—but I hold my ground, mainly because the bleeding has all but died off. I don't want him monkeying around with the timeline of my story, putting a bug in Edward's ear about the miscarriage being a few days old.

Nurse Kaylee retrieves a kidney-shaped bowl and lingers by my side, waiting for the doctor to finish. He does, without so much as ordering pain meds—a shot of Demerol sure would hit the spot!—or patting my shoulder in reassurance.

The doctor moves on to another patient. Nurse Kaylee checks my vitals—all good—and leaves me with the vomit bowl and a carafe of water. I pour a cup and drink it down, watching Ashley out of the corner of my eye. She hasn't gone near the purse. Good. Hopefully she'll be caught in the act—forget the speeding ticket; a theft charge will send her reeling!—at any moment.

In the meantime, we watch TV in bitter silence. One of those nature shows where the lion takes down the zebra by its throat. I almost feel bad for Ashley; she's in over her head. Then again, she put herself here. She asked for what comes next.

Soon the phlebotomist shows up to draw my blood. She's a human beach ball with frizzy orange hair. No matter. She's magic with a needle, a skill I appreciate. Hitting a vein with such ease on the first try is a high art. I should know.

Three tubes of black-cherry syrup later—my blood is thicker and darker than most—the needle retreats, leaving behind only the faintest prick mark. The bandage is overkill, but I let her apply it. A reward for a job well done.

Ashley has been shifting around, crossing and uncrossing her arms, eyeing the stool like it's an oasis in the Sahara. No one's stopping her from sitting. Hell, I'd welcome the pluck. At least she'd be showing initiative in something other than adultery.

It's only midafternoon and I'm exhausted. I hitch the blanket up to my chest and shut my eyes, intending to doze briefly. Just long enough to recharge for the rollercoaster ahead. Because once the diagnosis is made and my husband arrives (preferably in the reverse order), I'll be called upon to enact all sorts of exotic emotions—fear, disbelief, regret, sadness—to preserve my marriage and firewall myself against the investigation into Dr. Kapoor's death.

Suicide, I tell myself as my mind starts to drift. *The doctor killed himself. That's all you know. And you heard that secondhand, from Jacquelyn, over the phone. That's it. That's everything....*

CHAPTER 25
ROBIN

I can't stop thinking about the necklace. What does it mean?

The most likely explanation is that Lewis is confused. He found that pendant—Marina's pendant, the one she worked her fingers to the bone to get—by chance on the day I sold it and mistook it for one that once belonged to his wife. Marina probably admired Georgette's necklace while she was cleaning next door and resolved to earn herself something equally dazzling by summer's end. That was the Marina I knew: diligent, hardworking, determined. Never met a problem she couldn't solve with a little patience and some elbow grease.

Of course, there's the smallest chance that Lewis is right. I can't see how, though. Even if Marina did something impulsive, she would've known better than to flaunt the proof around. My sister was smarter than that by far.

I place my coffee mug in the sink and call for Samantha. It's Saturday and she's agreed to help me pick out work clothes for the catering job. Nate's cousin's wife—I don't know her name, but she's hired me by text to waitress at a wedding tonight—specified NEW (yes, all caps) black pants and a CRISP white shirt. Unfortunately, I possess neither. Good thing I've got a few bucks left from the pawnshop. I hate to spend even a cent, but the investment should pay off.

"Sam! C'mon!" I have roughly three hours to shop, shower, and drive to the venue—a repurposed warehouse in a revitalized section of downtown, a pocket of privilege not unlike the university district where I last worked.

The bathroom door is shut. I rap gently. "Are you all right?"

No answer.

I try the knob. It's unlocked. "Samantha?" When no reply comes, I push open the door.

The bathroom is empty. Sam's dirty clothes are bunched up on the floor. I grab them and toss them in the hamper.

I'm on a schedule; I don't have time for hide and seek. Sighing, I traipse to Samantha's room. But it, too, is vacant. A tic of laughter rises in my throat. Have I lost my daughter in a twelve hundred square foot house?

Or . . .

My heart starts hammering. I dart across the hall for Marina's old room—Samantha's T-shirt workshop. The door is ajar. I burst in like a runaway train.

Crouched over a periwinkle V-neck shirt, which is spread out on the floor in front of her, is my daughter, her hair in a tangled knot, a yellow-tipped paintbrush poised in midair as she considers her next dab.

I pull up short. "Jesus, Samantha, what're you doing? I've been trying to—"

She tugs an earbud out of her ear. It falls listlessly against her chest. "Huh?"

"Shopping," I say. "Remember?" I motion at my ripped jeans and threadbare flannel shirt. "For work clothes. You were supposed to come with me."

She gives a half shrug. "Yeah, I know. Just let me—"

"No," I say. "It's too late. I'll have Lewis come over." I pause to take in her latest creation. It's both abstract and familiar. An echo of an echo. A certain kind of déjà vu.

"Do you like it?" she asks, her voice swollen with anticipation.

"It's good." The shirt is splashed with vibrant colors—lime, teal, fuchsia, canary—that remind me of . . . *something*.

Samantha plops the brush in a cup of sludge-colored water. She riffles through layers of newsprint—a condition of using this room was protecting the carpet—and comes out with a photograph pinched between her fingers.

Before the image crystallizes, I recognize it in my mind's eye. It's a picture of me and Marina, snapped by our mother with one of those boxy little 110 cameras, within three feet of where I'm now standing. In the photo, I'm barefoot and bare-legged, lounging at Marina's desk—she was generous with her things, letting me use whatever I wanted—doodling with her scented markers and feeling like a hotshot for having been invited into my teenage sister's room. Marina is behind me, her arms slung loosely around my neck, a Broadway grin smeared across her face. Our heads are tipped toward the camera, toward our mother's coaxing voice—"Okay, girls, smile!"—toward a puzzle-piece view of the hall, where Scott is lurking in our mother's blind spot, doing his best jackass impression: a double-middle-fingered salute, capped off by a flurry of air kisses.

I start to ask Sam where she got the photo—there's only one choice, really: a duct-taped tote in the basement, where the old albums have gone to die—but then, in the upper right corner of the image, I spot the posters on the wall. I'm not sure Marina even liked Jimi Hendrix, Pink Floyd, or the Grateful Dead, but she loved the vibrant colors and optical illusions their ads contained. One lazy Sunday afternoon, she painstakingly adhered the posters to the wall, groaning and muttering when the edge of one glossy sheet wouldn't line up just right with the next. If I squint, I can still see her wobbling on her tiptoes on the bed (replaced now by a scuffed futon), stretching for the ceiling, putting one last flappy corner in its place.

Sam hoists herself up. "Ow," she says, thumping her heel on the floor. "Freakin' pins and needles." She hops from leg to leg, urging the blood to flow.

I'm still holding the photo, gripping it tighter than I mean to. "What're you doing? You're painting—"

"Memories," she says. "I've never seen that picture of you and Aunt Marina. It's a good one. You look happy." The nostalgia in my daughter's voice defies explanation. She's never known the hopeful, open-hearted girl I was before Marina disappeared. Marina herself has the depth of a movie character in my daughter's mind. *Dearly Departed Aunt* she might be called in the screenplay of Samantha's life. "Plus," Sam continues, "the colors are awesome. I'm just, sort of, using them for inspiration. It'll look better when it's done."

"I'm sure they'll love it." My daughter has a slew of repeat customers, kids her age who want cool, unique clothes to distinguish themselves from the herd. I set the photo on a wicker stand. "I've gotta go, okay? Don't stop what you're doing. It's coming out great." I pat her arm. "Stay in the groove and I'll check it out when I get back from work." The thought of jumping headfirst into something new, especially a job tied to Nate's family, is nauseating. But what choice do I have?

"Lewis is gone. Just so you know. I'll be fine, though."

"What?"

"He left an hour ago with two suitcases." She tilts her head at the window. "I saw him rolling them to the van."

Since Georgette died, Lewis hasn't taken one vacation. "Did he say where he was going?" The idea of his running off without notifying anyone—who's going to pick up his newspapers and check his mail?—is peculiar, to say the least.

Samantha shrugs.

Maybe he's sick. Maybe he went to the hospital. Maybe he doesn't want anyone to know.

I don't have time to mull over the possibilities. "Lock up behind me," I say, pivoting for the door. "Where's your phone?"

She taps her pocket.

"Good. Keep it on you. Call 911 if anything happens."

"Nothing's gonna happen." She rolls her eyes.

"I'll be back in an hour. Or sooner," I threaten. Then I tear myself away.

By the time I get to Walmart, the roads are drenched with rain. It's a nasty storm, and it's showing no signs of letting up, the wind swirling clouds of water at my face as I exit the car.

A lake greets me as I approach the store. I tromp through it and head for the women's clothing. Five minutes later, I'm in line with a small white dress shirt and a pair of black pants.

The line is moving at a glacial pace. I tap my foot, glance desperately around, move to another register. Success. Soon I'm behind the wheel of the Caprice again, praying to make it home safely and then downtown for my shift. The first thing I should buy when money picks up is a new set of tires. The car is all over the road, and winter hasn't even begun yet.

When I get home, I check Lewis's driveway. Still empty. Samantha was right. The old man is AWOL.

In the shower, I turn up the hot water as far as it'll go. The cold has eaten into my bones. If I don't knock it back, I'll be useless for my first shift. God knows I've got more than my fair share of aches and pains—physical and otherwise—for someone my age.

The steam settles in layers, making the bathroom feel like a balmy corner of heaven. As I towel off, I wonder where Marina is now. Is she with our mother and father, tucked away on a silky cloud, feasting off endless golden platters?

My intuition says no. While the idea of a charmed afterlife has its appeal—for one thing, Marina's scorched remains would rise again in their stunning, earthly form—there's no evidence that such a place exists. Not in my experience, anyway.

Wherever my sister is, one thing is sure: She's the star of the show. It's a happy, comforting thought. One I cling to for lack of alternatives.

Samantha catches me in the hall while I'm still wrapped in the towel. "I cooked some food," she says. "You can't go on an empty stomach."

My heart swells. Whatever mistakes I've made, whatever bad judgment my daughter has exercised—in the near future, I'll discover who's harmed her and balance the scales—we're each other's safe place. I should track down that asshole sperm donor and thank him.

Leaning against the kitchen counter, Sam and I gobble down a whole box of mac and cheese straight from the pan. It's the cheap, powdery stuff, but it satisfies something deep inside me.

The jitters I had about the catering job evaporate. Suddenly, I know everything will work out. I'll use this experience as a springboard to bigger and better things. I have to, for Samantha's sake. And in honor of Marina. To make the most of a life she never got to live.

CHAPTER 26
LISA

The ultrasound proves what I already know: The fetus is gone. I can tell by the way the technician withdraws the equipment, avoiding my eye.

"Is everything okay?" I ask. "What did you see?"

She wastes no time tugging the machinery toward the door. "I only perform the test," she says, pausing briefly. "The doctor will interpret it." She puts on a brave smile, one I must mimic later for Edward. "Try to relax. Someone will be in soon to speak with you."

I bite my lip and nod.

Off the technician goes, into the hall, the machinery creaking and groaning every inch of the way.

Ashley is sitting on the floor, her back to the wall, hugging her knees. "Do you think he'll be here tonight?" she asks about Edward. "Did he say anything about . . . ?"

If she expects my husband to play the white knight to her damsel in distress, she's delusional. *I'm* the one miscarrying his child. "He'll be here," I say. Edward has either chartered a private plane or paid some lucky fool a hundred times the face value of their airline ticket. The worst-case scenario is that he had to fly coach.

In a squeaky voice, Ashley asks, "Can I go to the cafeteria? I haven't eaten all day. I can get you something, too."

She *is* looking a little pasty around the edges. I can't have her passing out before the main event. "Yes. Go." I shoo her off. "But come right back. And bring me a lemon fizz." Her eyebrows pucker. Can she really be so dumb? "It's a carbonated beverage," I explain with a sigh. "Made in Italy. Comes in a can with a little foil wrapper on top. Ask someone if you can't find it."

"Okay," she says, hauling herself up off the floor and grabbing her purse. She takes a couple of steps toward the stand where I've stashed her phone before thinking better of the idea and retreating.

I've just shut my eyes when Nurse Kaylee comes poking around for my vitals. As the automatic blood pressure cuff inflates, constricting my circulation, the clunky hospital phone begins ringing.

Kaylee picks up the call and hands me the receiver. It's Edward. He's on a plane. He pulled some strings with a friend of a friend who owns a logistics venture—the man's company flies excess cargo around for the big package-delivery services—and just so happened to have an aircraft in the area.

My husband will arrive in five hours, give or take. Time I'll spend keeping the medical folks at bay. Because I can't summon such raw emotions twice in one day, and I'm saving myself—my performance—for Edward.

Kaylee assures me that my test results are on the way. We'll have an answer, one way or the other, about the pregnancy. She asks if I need anything else—she's already refilled my water carafe and fetched an extra blanket—and I tell her, "Just peace and quiet to rest."

She takes the hint and slinks away.

A good bit of time passes. Forty minutes? An hour? Longer than it should take to track down a lemon fizz. I glue my eyelids shut—twice I feel someone loitering in the doorway, but the lurker leaves without disturbing me—and drift through a veiled dreamscape, revisiting, of all places, the slums I haunted as a teenager.

Why these flashbacks are rearing their heads now is beyond me. For twenty years, I've had not so much as a whispering thought about that girl. That fire. My part in it. But suddenly I'm back in that dim, musty basement, flicking that lighter, watching that puff of sparks give way to a bouncy little flame.

The girl was dead already, of course—at least I couldn't find a pulse. She'd overdosed on ketamine, a powerful anesthetic and horse tranquilizer I'd injected her with after she'd popped a handful of muscle relaxants I'd lifted off a bodybuilder john. The ketamine came from a fourteen-year-old suburban kid with a surfer name—Dax or Brody—whose uncle was a veterinarian. The kid would've gotten any drug imaginable for the right sexual favor.

I see myself reflected in the girl's vacant, surprised eyes, the light going out of her from within. One version of events has her reaching out for me, calling my name, making a last desperate clutch at vitality. But this is an alternate history, my mind playing tricks, a confused retelling. The truth is that she fell into a rapturous sleep and never woke up. It was an easy death. Pleasant, even.

For the third time, I sense a lingering presence. If I didn't know better, I'd think the girl—she was a runaway who'd gotten mixed up with the wrong crowd (not unlike me at the time) and sunk to prostitution to turn a quick buck—was resurfacing, clawing her way out of the grave to thank me for putting her out of her misery.

The sound of a throat clearing snaps me awake. It's Ashley. She's returned with a bottle of Orangina. The lemon fizz was too much to ask, I guess.

I straighten up and reach for the drink. "What took you so long?" I crack the seal of the little blue cap and take a sip. I'd never tell her this, but the Orangina is even better than the lemon fizz.

She stares at the water rings on the overbed table. "They were searching people's bags—the security guards. A lady's wallet ..." She's speaking in a monotone, as if drugged or hypnotized.

"And?"

Her eyes are teary. Bloodshot. "I didn't think ..." A mechanical shrug. "Why would I?"

"You never let anyone search you—search anything of yours—without a lawyer's say-so, without probable cause," I remark. "Or a warrant. You didn't *do* anything, right? You'd never do something *like that*. You'd never steal." I take a long gulp of the drink. "Except husbands."

Her whole being recoils. She knows I've set her up, but she can't call me on it. She has no proof, and the power differential is too great. With a snap of my fingers, I could do a lot worse than hang a petty crime on her. From the looks of things, she got away unscathed, anyway. (That blond bimbo routine works for things other than home-wrecking, I see.)

"There was nothing missing," she says, still droning. "The cash, the credit cards—it was all there. The woman said it must've been a mistake. A mix-up. She didn't want to do anything about it."

She rode to freedom on the kindness of strangers? On the victim's willingness to let things go? (The guards' aversion to paperwork probably broke in her favor, too.)

I should've flushed the cash down the toilet. Then Miss Goody Two-Shoes would've gotten her comeuppance.

Lesson learned.

"Come here." I pat the bed.

She eyes me with deep suspicion.

"Oh, relax." My mouth can't help curling into a grin. "I won't bite." Not hard, anyway.

She moves closer. Hesitates. I shift over, making space. Reluctantly, she edges onto the mattress, assuming a perched, catty-corner position. Good enough for my purposes.

For a few moments, I behold her neutrally, forgetting that she's played with my toys uninvited. From a strictly sexual viewpoint, there *is* something appealing about her. It's the lips, mostly. They're raw, meaty, a hue of purplish red like a fresh bruise.

I trail a finger across the inside of her wrist. Her skin is soft, tender, vulnerable. No wonder my husband is bewitched. "You know," I whisper, "it was my choice to hire you. I thought you'd be good with the girls. And I was right."

Her dainty little Adam's apple bobs up and down. "Thanks."

"Did Edward say it was his idea? I bet he did."

She shakes her head. "I don't ..."

"I saw something in you. Something special." I frown. "I trusted you and you betrayed me."

She makes no effort at a response.

"What should we do about that, Ashley? About you and Edward? About your going behind my back?"

Still, nothing.

"A good place to start would be a confession. From the beginning. Who did what—that kind of thing. Spare no detail. The only way we'll get past this is to put everything on the table."

The blood drains from her face, making those lips pop even more against her milky skin. I have a naughty urge to snake my tongue across them, but I won't. Not here. Not with God knows who watching. "If you want to fire me, it's okay. I can find another job. I didn't do anything, though," she claims. "I didn't do anything with Mr. Hayes. He'd never—"

How disappointing. Just when I thought she was growing a spine. "I saw you with my own eyes. Do you call him 'Mr. Hayes' while he's fucking you?"

The moron gasps, as if I've said something vulgar. As if *I'm* the villain for shining a light on *her* crimes.

"You're not the first," I inform her. "My husband has had many liaisons with the help. He has an affinity for bony Eastern Europeans and black girls from the Caribbean. Oh, and we had a Chinese girl once, just for the summer. What was her name? Liu? Ling?" I shrug. "Anyway, she was a tiny thing. Would've made a great gymnast. She gave the best blowjobs, from what I hear.

"Honestly, you're not Edward's type. You're too apple-cheeked, too all-American, too squeaky clean. That holier-than-thou attitude rubs him the wrong way." I tap my fingers on my chin. "He talks about you. I bet you didn't know that." I pause to let the information sink in. "He tells me your deepest, darkest secrets. Like how—"

She coughs a frog out of her throat. "He talks about you, too," she mumbles, a crack forming in her subdued demeanor.

"Really?" I say, feeling a jolt of delight. "Tell me all about it, before Edward arrives. It'll be easier that way, don't you think? Easier than dragging everything out in front of him?" My goal isn't so much to reduce her agony as to divide and conquer. The more I know about her—especially about her relationship with my husband—the more power I'll wield in my interactions with Edward.

Once the nanny starts talking, she can't stop. She claims the affair was Edward's idea, that he plied her with cash and jewelry. Pearl earrings are mentioned, among other trifles. She waxes on about my husband's personality—this is muddier water; it suggests an emotional connection, one I must eradicate swiftly—about how he's "so nice" and says "the most wonderful things" to her. About how he makes her feel "like the only woman on earth" and "totally safe and protected."

She was on a roll until that last bit. Like I said, Edward's a known philanderer. He's rained cash on a parade of domestics to entice them to perform. Those sluts were little more than dancing bears. Fucking everything in sight is good for him. It frees his brain for bigger and better things.

My husband's facility with a compliment is also an open secret, a cornerstone of his manly charm. But that bleeding-heart stuff—that eye-of-the-hurricane, soul-mate drivel—is a malignancy I can't abide.

"This has to stop," I say, looping my fingers around her wrist. "What you're doing is wrong. It's a sin. What would your parents say if—?"

She becomes instantly weepy—psychologically shattered—the way only young girls can. She rushes to assure me, to contain me. "Yes, yes. I'm sorry. I will. We will. I mean, we won't. Just promise … please, don't …"

I knew from the day her clergyman father ushered that U-Haul onto our estate and his demure wife spent hours helping Ashley arrange her suite that these two were the nanny's Achilles' heel. She'd do anything to impress them, to stay in their good graces.

I'm preparing to swear Ashley to a blood oath—religious fanatics are big on superstition—when the doctor reappears to deliver the sad news.

CHAPTER 27
ROBIN

The universe has a twisted sense of humor. I've braved slick roads with balding tires and trudged over sloppy, rain-soaked sidewalks, only to find that I've arrived at the wrong converted warehouse. The yuppie tower of bricks I'm looking for is two blocks west. And I've already fed the meter enough quarters to last past six o'clock, when parking enforcement ends.

I throw a glance at the Caprice, deciding whether to move it or just walk. The weather is shit, but there's no guarantee that I'll find a spot near the venue with all the wedding hoopla going on.

In my pocket is the torn edge of a credit card bill. I pull it out and study the directions. My mistake is glaring: I took Andrew Johnson Road instead of Lyndon B. Johnson Way.

I start the walk, striding quickly and ducking under awnings to keep my hair as dry as possible. The venue is tucked down an alley of colorful wrought-iron bistro tables. I enter through the front and find a clean-cut guy wearing black pants, a starched white shirt, and a black apron. He's setting up a gift table with a photo of the bride and groom. "Excuse me," I say, surprising him from behind. He's the only one in the vast space, a loft-style ballroom with exposed beams, linen-draped tables, and soft, twinkling lights. "I'm supposed to be working here. It's my first day, and I don't know who to …"

The guy is stiff, hurried. "That'd be Lisa." He gestures vaguely to the left, where the main room opens up to a rustic bar. "She runs everything. She's in the kitchen."

"Over there?" I ask, tilting my head at the shadowy hallway.

He looks me over. "C'mon. I'll show you." His steps are twice as big as mine; I struggle to keep up. Something tells me that the pace for a ritzy, once-in-a-lifetime event is going to be faster than the predictable hum of the café.

I hope I'm up to the challenge. Disappointing Nate would be painful, not to mention the hurt such a failure would put on my wallet and my self-esteem.

The kitchen is huge. Industrial. A mosaic of slate tiles and stainless steel. It's also stifling hot and smells of chocolate, potatoes, and … roasted chicken? Workers toil away at various stations, prepping dishes for the imminent horde. I scan for a female who looks authoritative but come up empty. It crosses my mind to search for someone who resembles Nate, but then I remember that the woman in charge, this Lisa, is only related by marriage. A cousin's wife.

Hmm.

My guide winds effortlessly through the maze of activity, stopping by a table of cupcakes. Two women are on either side, hollowing out the cakes. My coworker signals the darker-haired one. Before I can thank him, he's gone.

The woman he's pointed out finishes coring a cupcake and sets it aside. Then she fixes on me. "Hell, no. Not *you*."

I'm mystified for a second, but then it dawns on me: the café. The coffee. I threw it at her when she wouldn't answer my questions about Marina, when she denied being that teenage prostitute—Marina's friend, Lisa Thompson—when she denied knowing anything about Marina's murder.

Shit.

Even if I knew what to say, I doubt my mouth would make the words. Instead, I just stand there, rooted to the floor, cursing my luck. Because here, now, in this upscale kitchen, with that pointy knife in her hand and that shock of hair eclipsing her eye, she's too young—by ten years, at least—to have had anything to do with Marina. She was probably organizing My Little Pony races and playing Care Bear school ("Remember to raise your hand, Cheer Bear!") while Marina was running off in search of... what? Freedom? Adventure? A place to belong?

The only place my sister didn't belong was in a coffin in the cold, hard ground.

I shake off the gnarled fingers of the past. "Um, hi," I say, pulling out my phone and scrolling through the texts. "I'm Nate's friend. I'm supposed to be working tonight." As proof, I brandish the text in which she's hired me. I'd like nothing more than to spin around and storm out—I have the tiniest shred of pride left—but what would that solve? Better to take my lumps and apologize, in hopes of digging myself out of this financial hole.

The rumble of activity quiets. "Seriously?" says Lisa—*a* Lisa, not *the* Lisa. She purses her lips and shakes her head. "I should put you out there?" She slashes the knife through the air, in the direction of the dining room. "Waiting on people? So you can give my company a huge black eye?"

"I wouldn't—"

"This is a reputation-based business," she practically spits. "Why don't I just flush my sales—my future—down the toilet?" She scans the frozen faces around us. "And what about them? Are you going to explain to their kids why they don't have jobs tomorrow?"

"I'm sorry. I thought you were someone else. It's no excuse. It's just that... my sister..."

"Yeah, right."

"My sister was killed. It was a long time ago. The police wouldn't even investigate. When I saw you, I just... I got confused. You look... *looked* so much like this girl, Lisa. *Her name is Lisa*," I repeat. "She has information—at least I think she does—about my sister's murder."

"So you burned her—burned *me*—with hot coffee?" She snorts. "Makes sense."

I've groveled past my limits already. My options are dwindling. "It won't happen again. That wasn't me. I don't hurt people."

She sets down the knife. "Whatever," she says, rubbing her temple. "We're buried. I don't have time for this. Two people have no-showed already." Her head rocks back and forth. "So help me God, when I see Nate …"

"What can I do?" I ask, sensing an opening. "Just point me in the right direction. You won't be sorry."

She stares right through me. "I'd better not be."

CHAPTER 28
LISA

Edward arrives late. Nearly midnight. I'm curled in the fetal position, clutching the blankets to my chest, whimpering every now and then to drive home my angst at losing the baby. The doctor wanted to release me with a handful of antibiotics and benzos, but I'm playing destroyed—catatonic, almost—to string Edward along. He deserves to suffer.

One painstaking blink at a time, I open my eyes and drag myself out of a pit of grief. My husband loiters by the bed, a look of cautious optimism creasing his face. No one has pulled him aside and broken the news. I meet his gaze and start slowly—wordlessly—shaking my head.

He grips the bedrail for support. "No," he mutters. "No. It can't—"

I just keep shaking my head, my eyes glistening with tears, my face folding in on itself. I've practiced this expression in the mirror countless times. It's a toned-down version of the ugly cry. It comes in handy for melodramatic plays, like Douglas Jerrold's *Black-Eyed Susan*, which I'm considering for next year's big show at the club.

Anyway ...

Edward glances around, searching for somewhere to sit—there's still nowhere—not even registering the pile of exhausted flesh that is his mistress. (Ashley is hunched in the corner, sleeping with her head against the wall.) I'd hoped for some sparks between them, but this is even better. He's indifferent to her. Funny how things change ...

I give my husband's hand a mournful squeeze. My tongue goes to my lips, wetting them. "I'm sorry," I say in a cracked whisper. "So sorry."

Edward can't bear looking at me, at anything. His eyes are unfocused, bouncy, like a drug addict's. He opens his mouth—probably to speak words of comfort—but only a gasping sob comes out. Before long, he's on his knees on the filthy hospital floor, his chest buckling and his shoulders heaving. He vomits somewhere behind the bed and wipes his mouth on his sleeve.

The room is silent except for the faint buzz of the muted TV and the *swoosh-swoosh* of footsteps down the hall. Edward grazes his thumb across my cheek, erasing the single tear I've managed to squeeze out. "We can try again," he says, forcing a smile. "There's still time." Beneath that signature five o'clock shadow, his face is the color of brick.

The stench of vomit wafts into my nostrils; nonetheless, I put on a brave face. "I just worry about the girls. Those poor girls. They'll be crushed."

Edward swallows hard. "Are *you* all right? Are they taking good care of you?"

I give a hurt shrug. This puts my husband into action. It'll be good for him to do something, to feel useful, to get his mind off the baby.

Ten minutes later, the powers that be find a spare room and transfer me for observation. It's a step up from the ER: soft green paint, landscape art, a private bathroom. Once I'm settled in, Edward coos platitudes in my ear while Ashley mopes around like a disheveled handmaid, still lugging her purse and everything of mine. My husband hasn't said two words to her since he arrived.

Good.

I motion at the wardrobe. "My clothes will go in there," I tell Ashley. "Please hang them neatly." She's too worn down to respond. "After that you can leave. Don't say anything to the girls, though. I don't want them being upset. Edward and I will handle things tomorrow." I stare expectantly into my husband's eyes. "Right?"

"Yes. That's best, I think. We'll have more perspective once we've gotten some sleep."

The wardrobe groans open and Ashley gets to work.

I shove over in bed. "Stay with me," I tell Edward, patting the sheets. His gaze flits over Ashley. "I need you."

It's no contest. He'll pick me over her a thousand times, especially now.

He crawls into bed. I pull him to me, cradling him like an injured child. I stroke his hair, his face, kiss him gently on the forehead. By the time Ashley finishes arranging my things, my husband's hot tears are staining my chest. I rub his back and, simultaneously, gesture for Ashley to go. I'm done with her for now.

But…

She mimes a telephone, a panicked look crossing her face. Does she think I'm stupid? Does she think I'd lose track of that expensive paperweight? And then what? We'd just buy her a new one?

Not a chance.

I retrieve the phone, which is tucked behind my hip, and set it on the bedside stand. I should keep it and dig around for more dirt on the nanny, but she's not worth the bother. I'll see to it that Edward discards her like a used tissue very soon. I doubt I'll even have to mention the idea; his conscience will get the best of him.

Edward has started breathing rhythmically, as if falling asleep. Ashley grabs the phone and heads for the door.

"Wait," I stage whisper.

Her body tenses up. "Yes?"

"Leave the keys to the Hummer."

"But how am I gonna …?"

"A taxi. Edward and I need a way home tomorrow."

She digs around in her purse and holds out the key ring.

I nod at a nearby recliner. "Over there."

She drops the keys in the lap of the chair and, once again, sets her sights on the door. This time I let her go.

CHAPTER 29
ROBIN

The wedding reception runs until ten o'clock and then there's the cleanup. I end up working eight hours at twelve bucks an hour, which Lisa rounds to a solid hundred. In cash. Once the waitstaff and bartenders divvy up the tips (the father of the groom has been sprinkling around twenties like confetti), my total take is $185. Which makes the trek back to the car worth the trouble.

On the way home, I stop at a bar and buy two cans of beer to go with the tray of leftovers I've been allowed to take. I deserve a treat, I figure. And two cans barely count as drinking.

Speaking of treats, Samantha's going to love the chicken-parm sliders I scoffed up. And the pistachio cannoli. That kid has weird taste buds she definitely didn't get from me.

As I roll past Lewis's house, I note with muted interest that his van is still missing. It's none of my business where he went. And with the accusations he made about Marina—is he serious, suggesting my sister was a thief?—I'm not keen on hunting him down, calling the numbers in my mother's old notebook until I hit on someone who remembers the guy.

I grab the crumpled paper bag off the passenger seat and head inside, my spirit hopeful for the first time in a long while. After a bumpy start, things went better than expected at the catering job. I could've had wings on my feet, the way I flew from table to table, making every last guest feel like the Queen of England. It wasn't hard, either, with the adrenaline pounding through my veins. Lisa even thanked me, somewhat grudgingly, and promised to call soon with another gig.

For some reason, I expect Sam to be waiting like a loyal dog. I've been stealing away all night to text her, so she knows when I'll be getting home. But there's no sign of her in the kitchen. Or the living room.

I double back and set the food on the counter. "Sam?"

Down the hall, the door of Marina's room groans open. Time flickers—jolts back and forth and back again, leaving me dizzy, whirling—for a fraction of a second, images of my murdered sister and my precious daughter mingling in my mind.

If I close my left eye, the shadow moving across the carpet is Samantha. If I close my right eye, Marina.

The shadow grows bigger. *Too* big. A man, not a girl. I reach for my holster, but I don't have it on me. Ditto the gun. I've got time to grab a knife from the dish drainer, maybe, depending on how fast the intruder moves.

My hand's in midair, reaching for the utensil cup, when my brother appears in the hall. "Fuck, Scott," I gasp, my heart pulsing in my throat. "What're you doing?"

He grins. An inside joke I don't understand. "You sure are jumpy."

I lean against the counter and watch him. He's dangerous in a hard-to-pin-down way. Prison will do that to you, I guess—make you impenetrable.

He peels back the foil and gives the leftovers a sniff. "What's this?"

"Help yourself," I say distractedly. "Where's Samantha?"

He reaches past me for a spoon and pokes at a clump of baked ziti.

A moment later, Sam comes shuffling out of Marina's room. I'd assumed she'd fallen asleep—and maybe she had, given her disheveled clothes and hair. But what was Scott doing in there with her? There's nothing left in Marina's room but that battered futon and Sam's art supplies.

My stomach turns over. A wave of heat rushes from the top of my head to the tips of my toes. Maybe my brother is doing to my daughter what he did to Marina. Maybe he's been plotting—fantasizing—for years, watching the clock tick down in prison until he got the chance to …

"Hey, Mom," says Sam. She gives me a sideways hug and a peck on the cheek. "How'd it go?"

Suddenly, all I can think about is the beer. Something to settle my nerves. "Good," I say, unfurling the bag and taking out a can. I crack it open and gulp down the skunky liquid. "What've you guys been up to?" To Scott: "I thought you were under house arrest."

He shoots a glance at Samantha. "I'm checked out overnight."

Chug, chug, chug.

Two-thirds of the beer is gone. I come up for air. I want to grill Scott further about his sudden appearance, but I decide not to push it. He can stay the night in my room in an old sleeping bag, where I'll hear every move he makes.

Samantha is ravenous. She goes at the leftovers with both hands, eating out of the tray—two bites of chicken parm to one bite of cannoli—while Scott finishes the ziti and laps the spoon. I *do* feel bad for him, seeing him eat. It's obvious that he hasn't had a solid meal in years. Not that Sam and I have fared much better.

I drop the empty can in the sink and move on to beer number two. My brother eyes me covetously, but he doesn't ask for a swig.

Once Sam and Scott have scraped the tray clean (I grazed on everything from stuffed olives to chicken cordon bleu to Neapolitan wedding cake throughout the night), Sam heads to bed.

Scott flicks on the TV, turns out the lights, and plants himself on the couch. His face looks ghoulish, like a human jack-o'-lantern, in the blue-white glow of a cop show. I wonder how he can watch that law-and-order stuff after spending so much time in the justice system. Then again, maybe these shows are comforting. Familiar. Maybe they remind him of home.

It's a sick idea. I push it out of my mind. What would that say about me, Marina, and our parents if my brother's true self found expression—fulfillment—behind bars?

"Hey, uh ..." I say, taking the other side of the couch. "Thanks for coming over. I'm sure Sam was happy to have company."

He stares straight ahead. "Uh-huh."

"It must be good to be out of there."

His shoulders kick up. "Yeah."

"You can sleep in my room," I say. Forget the sleeping bag. He can have my bed, as long as he stays away from my daughter.

"You mean Mom and Dad's room? No thanks." He pats the couch. "This'll do."

It dawns on me that he probably still thinks of Sam's room as his. I feel like I've made a mistake, putting her in there. My old room would've been better, except none of the electrical outlets work and there's a draft no amount of window caulking can cure.

I don't know how to make small talk with my brother. He's a stranger in every way but genetically. Yet I'm compelled to try. "You've been out for a while now. Have you talked to anyone?"

"Like who?"

I rack my brain for the name of the girl he was dating when he went to prison, but it dances away from me. I *do* recall his childhood best friend, though. "What about Peter?" I say. "Pete Dunlow?"

He shakes his head. "You don't have to do this."

"Do what?"

"Pretend to be interested. You didn't give two shits while I was locked up. What's so different now?"

"That's not fair. I was alone. I had Samantha. I couldn't just ... What was I supposed to do, bring her in there? With all those ...?" I rub my forehead. "My car has a hundred and fifty thousand miles on it." The prison is ninety miles away. He can do the math.

"You couldn't get a babysitter? For one visit?" He sneers. "Or pick up the phone?"

It's not my fault that Marina was murdered. That our father blew his brains out. That our mother absorbed the family nest egg with her slow, agonizing death. That Scott drank himself stupid and got behind the wheel of a car, slaughtering a bright, innocent child. Still, I bear some guilt for abandoning him, even though he abandoned me first. "You're right. I should've done something. I should've called."

We sit silently, staring at the TV. We're our own separate islands in our own separate worlds. I'm not really watching—the show could've switched to a NASCAR race midstream and I wouldn't have noticed—the images bubbling over my brain like water over a bed of stones.

Eventually, Scott's hand slides across the couch, palm up, fingers curled. I expect him to punch my thigh—a sign he's gotten over our tiff?—but then his fingers bloom, revealing something small, white, papery.

It looks like garbage. An inside-out gum wrapper, maybe. It could also be a packet of drugs. My brother has a penchant for self-destruction, and, God knows, he has no shortage of suppliers in that halfway house. Random drug tests are nothing but a challenge to some people. And even if they don't use, they can always sell.

"Take it," he says, the tips of his fingers touching my leg.

Curiosity gets the best of me. I pinch the object out of his hand. It's a scrap of paper folded into a crooked square. I unfold it and flip it around, looking for an explanation of why he's forced it on me.

At first I can't see anything. The light is too dim. But with some focused squinting, I make out a few faint lines of pencil writing. They're illegible scribbles, until I reach for the lamp over my shoulder. "What's this?" I ask, studying the text, which is developing into an address before my eyes. A few seconds later, my brain catches up. "Is this Samantha's?" The writing sure looks like hers.

"You tell me."

"I think so. Where'd you—?"

"There's a hidden drawer in the desk. When she was in the bathroom, I searched it. She's got other stuff in there, too, by the way."

Of course, he'd remember the hiding spots in Samantha's room. The furniture hasn't changed in ages. He probably stored his porn in there once upon a time. "Like what?" I say, still studying the address. I've lived in this town my whole life, and Gleason Street isn't ringing a bell. Wherever it is, I'm sure of one thing: Sam has no business there.

He holds up his hands. "The ball's in your court. You're her mother."

"Why did you take this? You think it means something?"

"Don't you?"

"The asshole? You think he lives here?" The paper seems to vibrate in my hand.

"Either that or her dealer does."

"Don't even joke about that," I say, whacking his arm.

His mouth is a straight line. "Check the drawer."

CHAPTER 30
LISA

Before we arrive home, the condolences start rolling in. I let the outpouring of support go to voicemail and the gift baskets pile up in an unused corner of the dining room. A merry-go-round of casseroles finds me in bed—a gold star for Ricki for being so attentive!—where I examine the handiwork of our friends' personal chefs, occasionally finding something worthy of tasting. But no matter how delectable the food is—that cow Penelope Anne sent over a pan of Brazilian steak that's to die for—I must make queasy faces and feign a diminished appetite to stay in step with my shattered husband.

Speaking of Edward, he's taken a leave of absence from his company, as I have from mine. We're conjoined, spending every waking moment together until the tsunami of grief subsides. We doze. We cuddle. We stare silently out the window for long stretches, overlooking our sprawling estate, which is as gray and desolate as a Longfellow poem.

When the angst becomes too much to bear, Edward offers to draw me a bath—this kind of loving practicality helps him cope—and I let him. As he tenderly washes my back, I recount stories from the twins' preschool years, like the time Darian sheared off Mae's hair with an unattended electric shaver (*that* nanny was out the door before lunch) and how Mae refused to eat eggs for a whole year, because a boy at the park said he found a bloody chick in one.

Our children are treasures. Blessings. This is what I'm reinforcing with my husband. They're here; they're ours. We love them and they're enough. Another baby just wasn't meant to be.

It's nearing dark, the days melting into one another, boredom ascending. As my husband and I weave from room to claustrophobic room, choreographed like ballet dancers, the air thrums with the ticking of clocks. If something doesn't break soon, I may go mad.

We end up in the kitchen. Edward opens the refrigerator and peers inside. "Where's that steak?"

Hallelujah. His appetite's returning, which means mine can return, too. I slip under his arm and shuffle around containers. "Here," I say, exhuming the tub of soft, spicy meat. "Shall I get the girls?" It's not quite dinnertime, but it would do us good to sit down as a family, to strengthen our bonds so nothing can tear us apart. Not that there's any real threat. The drama with Ashley has receded (like I thought, she was a temporary fascination) and the investigations into the deaths of Sophie Gallagher and Dr. Kapoor have stalled, thanks to Edward's shrewd handling of that pretty-boy detective, Luke Jones.

I chuckle, recalling the conversation between the two men a few days ago. Edward and I had just returned from a stroll around the grounds, bundled in our parkas and cashmere scarves. We'd barely kicked off our sheepskin boots when my phone began ringing.

Edward was invigorated from the outdoors. And he was nearest the credenza. He spotted the detective's name on the caller ID and answered out of a sense of husbandly duty.

In light of the miscarriage, I should've known he'd be spoiling for a fight, itching to prove himself relevant. Which he did with a lecture on decorum and some not-so-veiled references to our law-enforcement philanthropy. Who does the detective think pays for those drunken police outings (team-building exercises, my ass!) to Atlantic City, anyway?

Questions about Sophie Gallagher and Dr. Kapoor will wait weeks—months—before finding their way to my door. And even then, they'll come in writing. (Edward is a savant for seizing on this idea;

now I'll be able to plot my answers to the smallest detail.) If Edward's instructions aren't followed to the letter, the Jackman PD will be met with a never-ending column of lawyers, paperwork, and red tape.

While Edward empties the refrigerator, I slip away and retrieve our children. Like their parents, our girls have been holed up in the house, watching videos from their vast library, mourning the brother or sister who's no longer to be. The school offered to send over a tutor—the headmaster should do the work himself for the money we've poured into that historic (read: old, musty, falling down), ivy-covered campus—but Edward declined, citing the girls' advanced academic standing. He's right, too. Our little DNA legacies are precocious, even by elite-prep-school standards.

The four of us are huddled around the island, spooning bits of this and clumps of that—a broccoli au gratin is particularly congealed—onto plates and zapping them in the microwave.

"I was thinking," says Edward, after polishing off a third plateful and patting his belly, "that we should have a party." His mouth twitches into a grin.

Mae's eyes widen. Of the twins, she's the more social. Just the mention of a party—especially one planned by Edward, who'll spare no expense (chocolate fountains and ice castles will no doubt be on the agenda)—will send her swirling.

I set down my fork. "What kind of party?"

Darian pricks her ears.

"It's early, I know," he says, making prolonged eye contact with me, "but our anniversary is coming up."

He's never suggested such a thing before. He must be extra contrite over his slipup with the nanny. "Ten years already?" I ask, my throat tightening. I'd planned on disposing of him by now, but he turned out to be a cash cow. No amount of life insurance could top his earning power. Not without getting me locked up for a very long time.

So here I am. Still. Playing the trophy wife. I'm much more than that, of course. But in Edward's mind, I must remain the high-class, supremely fuckable commodity he signed on for. (Ashley's big mistake was going up against me in bed—or, well, on the pool deck, ha-ha. I've done things sexually that would curl her soul. Things my husband appreciates. Things he'd kill for.)

Edward studies me, awaiting an answer. "So?"

"Please, Mommy?" says Mae.

I shrug playfully. "I don't know," I say, turning to Darian. "What do you think?" But I've made up my mind. The party is a no-brainer. Let our friends come and pay tribute to our unflinching marriage, our triumph in the face of tragedy. It'll be good for them to see us holding strong. It'll humanize us. Hell, I might even invite Detective Luke—keep your enemies closer, as they say—if I can find a way of doing so without triggering any extra scrutiny.

Darian gives a quiet thumbs-up—she's one to watch, that girl, with her clever, under-the-radar ways—and a soft smile.

Edward: "It's settled, then. Two weeks from Saturday. Do you want to call Alonzo"—the party planner he uses for corporate events—"or should I?"

I reach across the island and squeeze his hand. "Let me," I say.

He's more than happy to oblige.

CHAPTER 31
ROBIN

I refrain from searching Samantha's room while she sleeps, but as soon as my brother is in a taxi, on his way to the lumberyard, I drop Sam at the mall. Once she's sauntering through the doors of the food court with her friend, Glory, I race home, dread and excitement mingling in my gut.

I'm on the verge of finding out something about my daughter, something I don't want to know. Yet I must know it. Maybe this information will help me nail her attacker.

Sam's room is in its usual state of disarray. I kick a pile of clothes against her bed to clear a walking path and then plop down on the metal folding chair in front of her desk.

Scott's desk, I think. *Or maybe our father's.* For all I know, the oak relic once belonged to George Washington.

If the desk were a simpler style, it would be obvious where to start searching. But I'm dealing with a hutched banker's desk with enough drawers and cubbies to confuse a postal inspector.

I start in the upper left corner, where a row of tiny drawers, each big enough for an egg, spans the width of the hutch. There are ten of these. Most are empty. Which makes sense, because what would fit in there, anyway?

I remove the drawers and set them aside, preserving their order so I can restore them to their original places. If Samantha goes looking for that cotton ball or that mood ring later, I want it to be at her fingertips, like nothing ever happened.

On the left side of the hutch, under the row of tiny drawers, is a stack of larger drawers, each the size of a hardback book. Four in all. They're crammed with everything from old homework to stale candy—cracked butterscotch discs are a recurring theme, along with pulverized peppermints—to brittle paintbrushes and loose pastels. But nothing incriminating, nothing secret.

It crosses my mind that Scott might be bullshitting. But I keep going, extracting the five remaining drawers—two side by side in the middle of the hutch; three in a column on the right—and picking through half a dozen vertical slots.

The hutch looks like a witch's mouth—gaping and toothless. And I feel like a fool. Either Scott has played me, or I'm stupid. Blind.

I think about cutting my losses. I could be doing something productive, like sifting through clues in Marina's case. You never know when a lead might jump out of the ashes. But I've come this far. I might as well drive for the finish.

I shove the chair backward and get on my knees. There are more drawers in the lower half of the desk and a cupboard, too. I check everywhere, but all I find is more of the same: art supplies and school junk and smuggled snacks.

I put the desk back together and then, just for kicks, crawl underneath and bang around, listening for hollow spots and looking for breaks in the wood. The underside checks out, but when I reach the back outside corner, where the desk meets the wall, my fingers skim an unexpected joint. What looks like a strip of molding is oddly raised for an eight-inch stretch. I have a hunch that if I jiggle this section, it may come away from the desk at that strange joint.

I slip my fingers under the molding and wiggle it back and forth. When I pull on it, it slides out, bringing with it a small tray, like a crumb catcher under a toaster. On the tray are two condoms. They look abused, like they've been banging around in the bottom of a messy backpack, their foil wrappers imprinted with a ring of grime.

The condoms are enough. I don't want to see anything else. But like Scott implied, there's also evidence of drug use: a pack of rolling papers and an inside-out plastic baggie, flecked with bits of greenish brown plant material. It reeks of weed, though no usable quantity remains.

I hate thinking like this—a responsible parent would haul Sam off to drug rehab, ASAP—but it's only pot. It could be worse. She's probably only done it a few times. I mean, wouldn't I have smelled it on her? And she's still making straight A's in school, as far as I know.

The last object hits me like a nuclear bomb: a switchblade. I recognize the stubby handle from childhood, when Scott was into that survivalist crap. He had a collection of the things—junky ones he'd milked out of his friends' fathers and "found" on the streets. He sat at the picnic table out back for hours, flicking the knives open and closed, staring at the blades until his eyes crossed. The only time he let me near one—it was a mini model, perfect for my girly hand, he said—I immediately understood the attraction. When I pressed the button and that blade shot out, my blood sizzled.

Fear and power. Those were the emotions I felt. Hot and raw and alive.

I stare at the handle, considering everything I know about my daughter. Everything I *knew* until recently. The pot, the condoms, the knife, the beating ... none of it adds up with the happy, resourceful, whip-smart girl I've raised.

Why does Samantha need a knife?

Something tells me that Scott's involved. Either he gave Sam the knife as some sort of inappropriate bonding attempt or he planted it. He could be trying to drive a wedge between my daughter and me to get her where he wants her.

I roll the switchblade around in my hand, feeling the same charge I did twenty years ago. I study the handle. It's powder-coated metal and molded to fit snuggly in a clenched palm. On its back is a long, slender clip. The front has a grooved switch that steps up to a crown, like a staircase landing, and then back down again.

I curl my fingers around the handle and rest my thumb on the switch. I conjure thoughts of Samantha's battered face; Marina's lifeless body, splayed in the dirt, twisting with flames; shards of our father's skull stuck to the wall like road rash to a skinned knee.

My thumb glides forward. In a fraction of a second, the blade shoots out and locks in place. The steel itself is curved on both sides, like a dagger, and tapers to a fine point. If I'd had it pressed to some dirtbag's throat—angled over his pulsing carotid artery, say—it would've sliced him dead.

Enough fantasizing.

I retract the blade and slip the knife into my pocket. When I'm done replacing the tray and fitting the drawers back into place, I gulp a glass of lukewarm water, grab my keys out of my hoodie, and lock the house.

Samantha's expecting me in an hour. Plenty of time for a detour to Gleason Street.

CHAPTER 32
LISA

The girls go back to school on Monday. Edward and I use the day to relax (our masseuse, Lyubo, brings three assistants with him; between them, they dissolve every knot and kink in Edward's and my bodies), sip champagne, and make love. It's the first time my husband has touched me since the miscarriage; he insists on doing it bareback, in hopes of impregnating me again.

On Tuesday, Edward returns to work.

I call Jacquelyn on Thursday. The addicts are antsy, she tells me. She implores me to get the office back up and running, ASAP. I don't know what she's worried about. She's being paid to sit around and babysit things until I'm emotionally sound enough to pick up where I left off.

If it weren't for the boredom, I might take another week to myself, invite a couple of club wives or, God forbid, one of Edward's downtrodden sisters, on a getaway to Saint Lucia or the British Virgin Islands. But the thought of five more minutes treading water nauseates me, let alone five more days. I've been out of circulation too long already.

After lunch, the itch becomes too much to bear. I have to get out of this house. It's turning into a gilded cage.

I take the long way to work, indulging my need for a change of scenery. As I approach the turn for Route 9, where Sophie Gallagher met her end, something—curiosity? nostalgia? pride?—urges me to take it, to revisit what I've done.

What could be the harm?

I'm slowing down, preparing to engage the blinker, when a dissenting voice—an overwhelming gut feeling, you could call it—decides otherwise. I hit the gas and keep going.

When I reach the office, I find Jacquelyn on the computer, playing mahjong and slurping from a barrel of soda. She's in yoga pants—a disturbing choice for someone of her age, in her condition—and a sequined tunic. "Oh, hi," she blurts, bouncing to her feet and sending the chair flying backward. "I didn't know you were coming in today."

I look her up and down. "No, you didn't."

"You're not seeing patients, are you? I haven't got anyone scheduled for—"

With a wave of my hand, I silence her. "Never mind about that. What's going on with the police?"

Her face wrinkles. "The police?"

Just the reaction I was hoping for. "Are they done with Dr. Kapoor's office? You need to get a new tenant in there, pronto."

Instead of replying to my query, she asks, "Is everything okay? Should you be back already?"

"Correct me if I'm wrong, but haven't you been pestering me to get this place back in business?"

"It's just that ... you look ..." Whatever she's trying to say gets stuck in her throat.

"I'm fine. Nothing a little sunshine and fresh air won't cure."

"Did you get my card?" She must mean one of the hundreds of condolences we received. "We all signed it. Everyone in the building. Except for, well, obviously ..."

"I'm sure we did. Now come on." I motion at the hallway. "Let's get started."

Her mouth flaps open and shut again.

"Dr. Kapoor's office. You don't expect me to clean it out on my own, do you?"

"I forgot to tell you," she says, biting her lip.

"Tell me what?"

"The family came in. They've been taking stuff away, little by little."

"You gave them a key?" I shake my head. "Who told you to do that?"

"No," she says. "I only opened the office a couple of times. They wanted some personal items, things the police didn't take for—"

An investigation? This is unsettling news. Even if the police have released the office back to me, they must have suspicions. I start marching down the hall, Jacquelyn trailing me like a wounded dog. At the locked door, she hurls herself past me with a huff. "Sorry," she says, jamming the key in the lock and grinding it around.

Before the door is halfway open, I see that the authorities have had their fun. Or Dr. Kapoor's widow has looted everything. All of the good furniture is gone, including the tufted cobalt-blue sofa I had my eye on and the carved rosewood table.

I stare at the scattered books and empty filing cabinets. "This is all that's left?"

Jacquelyn shrugs. "I thought there was more. Maybe there was an extra key we didn't know about. The police only labeled stuff and took pictures and—"

"Labels? What kind of labels?"

"You know, those little yellow numbers." She gives a bumpy laugh. "Like they show on TV at a murder," she says, crossing herself. "God rest his soul."

"Yes," I respond. "God rest his soul."

I instruct Jacquelyn to brave the cobwebbed basement for empty boxes. She'll need them to finish packing. While she's gone, I wrestle with the windows—they're stuck shut from eons of paint buildup—freeing one just enough to let in a splash of cold air.

Once I can breathe again—it's strange being back in this room, where I put an end to Dr. Kapoor's ill-conceived extortion attempt—I wander around, using a stray pencil to pick through the remainder of the doctor's belongings. I assume the authorities took the computer and paper files out of an abundance of caution, in case any foul play cropped up. But I've been meticulous. There's no way this death can boomerang back at me.

Still, I have a niggling feeling that something's left undone, that the Kapoors must be silenced, that if anyone were to egg on the police it would be the grieving widow or that grubby blue-collar son of hers.

By the time Jacquelyn returns with three small boxes—she claims the rest are laden with rat droppings—I've formulated a plan to tie up the loose ends of the doctor's suicide. "Leave those here," I say, "and come with me. I've got a job for you."

As we stride back down the hall, the girl with the zigzag bangs stumbles out of the CPA's office, clutching a coffee mug. Over the lip of the mug hangs a limp string with a paper tab attached.

Tea time. How quaint.

"Excuse me," says the girl, pressing against the wall to let us pass. The kitchen is just beyond my office, on the east side of the building, adjacent to the foyer. If the girl had kept walking—assuming she moved at a normal human pace, which she does not—she would've been out of our way before we crossed paths. Instead, she'll wait.

Fine by me.

Jacquelyn pulls ahead, beating me back to home base. I instruct her to get on the phone and start booking appointments—the addicts will be doing cartwheels for those slots—while I fetch a checkbook from a hollow dictionary (one of many secret accounts Edward knows nothing about) and, in perfect cursive, write a twenty thousand dollar payout to Mrs. Aarush Kapoor. It's a fraction of the hundred grand her husband was trying to extort, but it should hush her for the time being, especially once I pen a heartfelt condolence letter equating her husband with Vishnu himself.

Once the check and letter are complete, I seal them in an envelope and trot out to Jacquelyn's desk. "Send this to Dr. Kapoor's widow, right away."

She makes a confused face. "Is this the security deposit? Because—"

"It's personal. Take it straight to the post office." *And mind your own business*, I want to add. But I temper myself. Jacquelyn could be an important ally, depending on how things unfold.

"Sure," she says, swallowing her pride and whatever inane thing she was about to say. Does she really think a few thousand dollars matters to me, in the scheme of things? She knows Edward's reputation. And she must have a vague idea how much money flows through this practice (one thing she doesn't have her fingers in is the finances). The phrase *chump change* springs to mind.

I tap my foot thoughtfully. "I'm going to need some addresses," I say, mulling over invitees to Edward's and my anniversary party. "Make a list of tenants. Go back three years." I squint. "On second thought, make it five." Our estate can handle hundreds of guests. I want the place packed.

"May I ask what for?"

I give her an inch and she takes a mile. "If you must know, there will be a celebration a week from Saturday for Edward's and my tenth anniversary."

Her face is a mix of pity (she's still hung up on the miscarriage), jealousy (she'd give both lungs for my luck with men), and hurt feelings (she pretends to dislike me, but nothing would make her happier than being invited to my soiree). "I didn't realize …" She puts on a jolly face. "Congratulations. That's a big milestone."

"Yes, it is." A familiar clenched feeling grips my throat. "Do you have a pen?" Her desk is littered with garbage. "I'll give you the party planner's information."

She swats through some papers and holds up a blue Bic. "Go ahead."

I rattle off Alonzo's number and then innocently say, "Oh, and add that nice detective, would you? He and Edward would get along famously." Little does she know that my husband and the detective have been sparring over the phone.

"Which one?" She laughs. "Things around here lately …"

"Luke," I say. "Detective Luke Jones."

CHAPTER 33
ROBIN

If the library ever shuts down, I'm doomed. Where else am I going to file unemployment claims, chase clues in my sister's murder, and get directions to mysterious addresses my daughter has hidden with her condoms and weed?

I catch a lucky break and slip inside, five minutes before closing. The librarian shoots me a frosty glare when I forgo the signup sheet and head straight for a vacant computer. The staff has seen me in here enough times, printing résumés and scrounging for change to pay for copies, to know I'm perpetually desperate, on edge, a breath away from unraveling.

They cut me a wide berth.

I settle in a chair, which is strangely warm as if someone has just gotten up, and launch a web browser. If I had time, I'd plumb the depths of the internet for information on Lisa Thompson. Since mistaking Nate's cousin-in-law for Marina's old friend, Lisa has moved to the front of my mind. I'm sure she knows something about Marina's killer, something I could tease out of her with the right kind of interrogation. But my questions will have to wait. Twenty-four years and counting...

As it turns out, Gleason Street is only eight blocks from Scott's temporary home at New Life and slightly farther from the shabby tenement where Marina took her last breath. According to MapQuest, it's a short connector road with a few houses and a stretch of vacant lots.

I've committed the location to memory when the computer-lab guy clears his throat.

I get on my feet. "It's all yours."

The building I'm looking for is on the corner of Gleason and Reid. I park on the Reid side, in front of an updated duplex, and begin surveillance. Samantha's still at the mall, so she won't be wandering out of the house—number eight, a two-story rectangle with a pitched roof and a clumsy side dormer that makes it look lopsided. It's a clean building, though, with vinyl siding and a couple of freshly painted porches.

I wonder who Sam was visiting here. It sure doesn't look like a drug dealer. But I could be wrong. And there's always the chance that I've found her attacker.

The temperature has dipped down into the forties. Only a couple of people are on the streets. In fact, I'm probably suspicious, lurking in my car, staring at everything but doing nothing.

Still, I gawk awhile longer, my gaze drawn to the driveway of the building in question—a black SUV is parked tandem with an old babyblue Cadillac—and on to the garage, which is closed up tight.

Sitting around is doing me no good. I wait for a willowy woman to lug the last of her groceries into the building beside me and then get out of the car with only a vague idea what I might do next.

At times like these, I wish I had Marina's ingenuity or Scott's self-assuredness or a bottle of our mother's Caribbean rum. Because I can't just walk up to the house and knock on the door, can I? Which door, anyway? And what would I say?

Whatever I'm going to do—or say—I'd better think of it fast. Samantha will be expecting me soon, and I can't risk being late, hanging her out to dry for some scumbag (they seem to be everywhere now) to zero in on.

I cross the road and follow the sidewalk as it hooks for Gleason Street. If I could invent a ruse—maybe I could pretend to be looking for a long-lost relative?—the rest would follow.

As I approach the building, my stomach starts grinding. Coming at me on the sidewalk is a young guy, a thug type with saggy pants and a hoodie pulled tight around his face.

I can't turn for the house now in case he lives there, in case he's Samantha's piece-of-shit boyfriend.

Please, God, let Nate be wrong. Let my daughter know better than to hitch her star to someone who'd hurt her.

The creep and I jockey for position. I cast a leery look at him—are you the one who hurt my baby?—holding my ground as we come abreast of each other. He stares at his feet and keeps going—past the house, around the corner, out of sight, away from me.

I should've brought my gun. What was I thinking, coming here unarmed? *I do have the knife*, I remind myself. *Sam's knife*.

In the next yard, a young girl is trying to corral a cat. The animal is crouched, hissing, torn between accepting the girl's offer of food and tearing away into the bushes.

"Hey," I say. "Need some help?"

The wind blows a length of golden hair into the girl's eyes. She moves it aside with her fist. "He's scared," she says. "He came to me last time, but now he's just ... he's being mean." She looks me over. "He doesn't trust people, ya know."

I can't help but smile. The girl is smart. Spunky. She reminds me of Samantha. "I think you're right," I say. "Why don't we put the food by the driveway"—I point at the spot I have in mind—"and then go this way?" I motion across the lawn. "We can still watch him, and he'll feel safe enough to eat."

"I'm gonna pat him. That's why I got this." She shakes around the fistful of food.

"He'll be a lot friendlier after he eats," I reason. "I bet he'll let you pet him then."

She makes a face. "He'll prob'ly just run off."

"Is he your kitty?"

Her head swings back and forth. "We're not allowed to get a cat. Maybe next year, when I'm seven. That's what Mom said."

I wonder where she got the cat food, if she doesn't have a cat. Maybe the parents bought it to humor her?

The cat slashes its skinny gray body back and forth, its tail cracking like an angry whip. I hold out my hand to the girl. "Let me see. I'll get him to come over."

Grudgingly, she relinquishes the grainy bits. They're clammy from being clenched in her palm. I crouch down and approach the cat. It arches its back and hisses, but it doesn't run away. It must be starving. I pile up the food a few feet from the mangy beast and back off again.

The cat moves in, growling low in its throat. Even as it eats, the rumbling continues. While the girl and I quietly observe, I glance at her house. Shouldn't someone be watching her? Shouldn't the curtains be drawing back? Shouldn't a head be popping into the window to check that she's still alive, at the very least?

Not everyone has a Marina in their life, I remind myself. *Not everyone is conditioned to expect the worst.*

"How long have you lived here?" I ask.

"Ever since I was born."

I stifle a laugh. "Wow. That long?"

"Mm-hmm."

"Do you know who lives on this street?"

She shrugs. "Who?"

"No, I mean … the neighbors. Do you know their names? Like over there," I say, pointing at number eight. "Who lives in that house? Who drives that pretty blue car?"

Her face lights up. "Joe. He brings me chocolate donuts from the donut store. The ones with the powder sugar on 'em."

"Those are good," I agree. "Is Joe young or old?"

"Old," she says. But I take it with a grain of salt. She'd probably say the same about me.

"Who else lives with Joe? Does he have a wife?"

Her brow furrows. "Why?"

I glance up and down the street. "I like it here. I'm thinking of moving into one of these houses."

"You can't!" she howls, spooking the cat, which bolts around the building. "Uh-oh." She covers her mouth, her eyes watering.

I lean over to console her, but our friendship comes to an abrupt end when the cat starts mewling and she goes chasing after it.

It's just as well. I'm running late. I rush back to my car, crank it up, and head out. I'm easing past 8 Gleason Street when, out of the corner of my eye, I spot a flicker of movement. Instinctively, I step on the brake.

The garage door hums open.

I pull over and wait. A car—small, sporty, dark-colored—reverses onto the road. My mouth goes dry. This must be the vehicle Nate was talking about. I'm on the verge of discovering Samantha's attacker. Just another second or two ...

As the car pulls level with me, heading in the same direction, I stare dead at it, expecting the scumbag with the blond ponytail. But the driver is a woman in her twenties with flat, stringy hair and thick glasses. She's wearing a chunky gray cardigan and focusing straight ahead. I can't help noticing that the fenders on the passenger side are a perfect match.

For a moment, I'm thrown. But then I get into gear—literally—and follow her through the neighborhood and out onto the main road. Who is this woman? How is she connected to Samantha?

I'm running scenarios through my mind—does the scumbag have a girlfriend? a wife? a frumpy roommate?—when my phone starts ringing. It's Sam. "What's up?" I answer breathlessly.

"Where are you?"

"On my way." In truth, I'm traveling in the opposite direction of the mall.

Her voice breaks. "Can you hurry?"

"Why? What's going on? Are you all right?" *Thud, thud, thud* goes my pulse.

"I'm sick."

"What kind of sick?" It flashes through my mind that she could be pregnant, but I don't see how, unless she hasn't been taking her pills.

"We ate lunch at the Jade Palace." That fucking biohazard from the news. "It might be food poisoning." She groans. "*Please hurry up.*"

"Have Glory take you to the bathroom—she's not sick, is she?—and splash water on your face." I shake my head and prepare to do a U-turn. "Then wait on the bench outside. The cold air will help you feel better."

"Just get here soon."

"I will." The moment traffic clears—actually, I cut it close, whipping around in front of a sleek black Mercedes—I zing back in the other direction, letting my prey go.

CHAPTER 34
LISA

The addicts haven't strayed far. As soon as I open up shop again, there they are, like maggots on a corpse, ready to feed. I churn them through at a dizzying pace, barely slowing down to catch my breath, making back nearly all of the money I lost to the miscarriage in a few short days.

Things are settling back into a rhythm. Normally, I bore easily, but the heat from these murders has been nerve-rattling, even for me. The calm is welcome.

Pulling into the garage at home, I run last-minute party details through my mind, tasks various entities must complete in the next thirty-six hours. Alonzo is fine for throwing together Edward's company picnics, but this anniversary bash must blow everyone away, a tall order with our crème-de-la-crème guest list.

Never fear, though. I have things well in hand. Six catering crews are poised to keep every plate overflowing with bourbon-glazed beef tenderloin and every glass topped off with Veuve Clicquot. Without a doubt, the party will be a smashing success.

The kitchen is vacant when I arrive. Edward and the girls have long since eaten. Feeling hungry, I check the refrigerator for one of Ricki's chicken pot pies. Technically, she's the housekeeper, but she can cook circles around every professional chef we've had. I thought I could smell the tang of that homemade crust in the air, and I was right.

After a brief spin in the microwave, my dinner is ready. I kick off my heels, grab a fork, and go padding for the great room, intending to unwind in front of the fire with my phone. There are messages to attend to—a disaster in South America is threatening our floral delivery, for example—most of which I'll dump in Alonzo's lap. Let him rent a van and drive a hundred miles in every direction, buying up roses and peonies for our big event.

I nibble as I walk, savoring the crust as it flakes away in my mouth, leaving the salt and fat of the gravy behind. Just shy of the great room, my phone slips out from under my arm and crashes to the floor. I mutter obscenities and pick it up—it's no worse for wear—making sure to protect it until I claim the chocolate suede armchair by the fireplace. But upon my arrival, the chair is occupied.

Ashley. That no-good whore. With my sweet little pup cradled in her lap.

She's done it now, crossed an uncrossable line, set fate turning. Her escapades with my husband were one thing, but going behind my back with Magnum, seducing him into whatever sort of relationship this is (imagine how confused my darling boy must be!) is the last straw. She'll get what she has coming.

I edge my phone onto the fireplace mantel and scoop Magnum into the crook of my arm, jostling Ashley deeper into the chair. "Where are the children?" I ask, setting Magnum on the coffee table and placing the pie in front of him. He wastes no time sinking his face into the dish. I spoil him something awful already, but with God knows what going on behind my back, I might have to ratchet up the treats.

Ashley blinks repeatedly. "Mr. Hayes took them for dessert."

"What kind of dessert?" And why didn't I notice the Jag missing from the garage? I pride myself on being observant.

A clueless shrug.

"You didn't go? Why not?"

"I wasn't hungry," she says, the words carrying a double meaning: *I'm not hungry for him anymore.*

Like hell she isn't. I'm going to use that lust to bring her down. And maybe him, too—at least temporarily.

Moving on ...

"Has Ricki spoken to you about the party?"

She nods. "The dresses are in. We've got a fitting tomorrow with Cleo."

"She can do the alterations that fast?"

"Mm-hmm."

"What about hair, makeup, shoes?"

"The salon's sending over a team. Is that okay? I thought they were doing yours, too."

"Yes, they will."

"Do you want new shoes—for the girls, I mean. They have so many already."

"Absolutely," I trill. "Make them very sparkly, like the ruby slippers from *The Wizard of Oz*."

She pulls out her phone and starts typing. "Anything else?"

"As a matter of fact, yes." A deliberate pause. "I'd like you to attend the party. Buy the most beautiful dress you can find. Put it on the card with everything else. You can keep it afterward," I say to sweeten the deal.

Her eyebrows knit together. "But ... why?"

"I'll be too busy to watch the children. I'm the guest of honor, after all. You understand."

"Won't Mr. Hayes be—?"

Mad? Excited? Confused? What reaction does she expect her presence to elicit from my husband? "It's fine," I insist. "Parties are my territory. He'll play along." I swallow a tendril of acid that has crept up my throat. "We're going to have a great time. All of us."

She regards me uncertainly. "If you're sure."

I've never been surer of anything. "I am."

Her face yields to an undercurrent of excitement (what girl wouldn't welcome the chance to play Cinderella on someone else's dime?). "I should go, then," she says, glancing at the clock. "I'm running out of time."

I bite back a grin. "Yes, you are. You'd better hurry."

CHAPTER 35
ROBIN

Samantha is the sickest I've ever seen her, including when a case of strep throat morphed into a 106-degree fever, nearly cooking her brain. Whatever's wrong with her—I still suspect the food, but Glory's fine after eating the same meal—is twisting her inside out, turning her into a husk of the daughter I know and love.

With Glory's help, I managed to get Sam into bed, where she's tangled in a flannel sheet, her hair sweaty, matted, clinging to her face like seaweed to a rock. Every so often she moans and whimpers, flails blindly for the mop bucket, hurls herself over the side of the bed and vomits. She's bringing up foam, mostly, which I dump down the toilet between fruitless attempts to make her drink. Just a little water is all I'm asking, but it's still too much.

If Lewis were next door, I'd send him for Gatorade and Tylenol. A box of saltines and a bottle of ginger ale. Whatever might give my sick child a shred of relief. But there's been no sign of him in what seems like a month, and his newspapers and mail have stopped coming.

Maybe he's gone for good. Maybe he's dead. Maybe a khakied dweeb from the city is going to show up and slap an auction sign on the door, letting the place go for back taxes.

I have few choices if I'm going to call someone for help. Over the years, I've lost every friend I've had to my undying focus on Marina, my bloodlust for her killer. I'm a human black cloud, warning people away, urging them to seek shelter lest they be ravaged by my storm.

Scott's unreliable and he doesn't have a car.

Nate will come through for me, as always, but I don't want to rack up any more debts with him. I already feel obligated to keep seeing him out of guilt and gratitude and other things.

I should've asked Glory's father to go to the store when he picked up his daughter. I would've paid him for his trouble.

Too late.

I pace the hall, gnawing on my fingernails. When I peek in on Samantha, her eyes are glassy and she's breathing erratically—jagged gasps strung together with drawn-out wheezes.

A ball of panic grows in my chest. I consider dashing to the store myself. It would only take ten minutes. But what if something happens? What if I have an accident and I'm delayed? What if Sam gets worse? *Much* worse?

Life has trained me to be paranoid. If Marina could end up how she did, what hope is there for the rest of us?

I was dumb to think I had a choice. With Lewis gone, Nate's my rock. I need him more now than ever. I head back to the kitchen, slump in a chair, and call him. When he answers, I make small talk for a minute before an awkward silence falls over us.

Nate breaks the tension. "Is everything all right? I heard the wedding went well."

I draw a blank. What wedding? But then I realize he's talking about the catering job. His cousin is reporting back to him. "Yeah," I say. "It was good." I wonder briefly if anyone ratted me out for the coffee incident. Not that it matters. "Um, listen, are you busy?"

"No. Why?" He's probably imagining an invitation for sex. I never should've let him into my personal sphere.

A defeated sigh. "The thing is …"

"What's wrong? Is it Sam?"

My emotions tip over the edge. "She's sick. Really bad. Can you come …? Can you get …? I'd go to the store myself, but—"

"Just tell me what you need. I'll stop on the way."

A weight lifts off me. I rattle off a list of supplies that might help Sam feel better—or so I hope. Nate pledges to be here in thirty minutes. We hang up and I force a couple of deep breaths. Then I check on Sam again. She's dazed—not just sleepy, but plain out of it.

I dampen a cloth and dab at her forehead, hoping to quell the fever—it's a mild one, unlike the monster she had before—and soothe away the nausea. She hasn't thrown up in twenty minutes, which gives me hope that she'll come out of this sickness, sooner rather than later.

Please, God.

The minutes crawl by until, finally, a knock at the door. When I see Nate on the porch with a bag curled in his arm, I lurch outside and hug him. He runs a hand over my hair. "Don't worry," he says in my ear. "We've got this."

He has more confidence than I do. Still, I find myself smiling optimistically. "Come in."

Nate sets the bag on the counter by the stove. "Where's the patient?" he asks, looking around. He's never been here while Samantha was home. It's weirder—more intimate somehow—with the three of us under one roof like a family.

I can't afford such stupid thoughts. What is a family, anyway, but a gang of people genetically engineered to destroy you? Maybe if Marina had lived, things would be different. *I'd* be different. But I decided long ago that it's me and Sam against the world. That isn't about to change.

I wave Nate toward the living room. "Do you mind? I don't think she'd want anyone seeing her like this."

He plops down on the couch, grabs the remote, kicks up his feet. "Don't worry about me."

"Be right back," I say.

This time when I check on Samantha, she's showing signs of improvement. Her color has returned to normal and her breathing is quiet and even. And the bucket's still empty. I nudge her shoulder and offer the ginger ale.

"Bathroom," she says in a hoarse whisper.

I set the ginger ale on the nightstand and peel her out of bed. She bristles slightly as I lean her against me and hobble us down the hall. When I try to follow her into the bathroom, she slams the door in my face. It's such a good sign that I almost burst out laughing—or crying. It's hard to tell which.

Sam is steady enough on her feet to make it back to bed on her own. I sort through the medications Nate has brought—Tylenol, antihistamine, cough syrup, a flu remedy—bringing all but the cough syrup to Sam's bedside. She's not much for pills, but the antihistamines are small. And they'll help her sleep. I get her to take one with the ginger ale, a double victory. She gives in to the flu medicine, too, chasing it with what's left of the soda and then collapsing into bed with a groan. But it's a familiar, frustrated groan, and I know she'll be okay ... eventually.

On my way back to the living room, I stop and open the cough syrup, being quiet so Nate doesn't hear. I gulp down two solid cups of the green, medicine-y stuff and rejoin him. He has the TV tuned to a western that went off the air before he was born. "So?" he says, raising an eyebrow.

"She's doing better," I report, snuggling up beside him.

He kisses my temple. "Good."

"Thanks for rescuing us," I say, my words drifting into a yawn. I'm suddenly exhausted.

He says something forthright and charming—he's one of the few solid, ethical guys left on earth—but the words just slide through my brain. Before I can answer, I'm bent into the hollow of his neck, falling fast asleep.

CHAPTER 36
LISA

It's 3 A.M. on the day of the party, and I can't sleep. I roll Edward onto his side and slip out of bed. Of all nights to have insomnia, tonight is most inconvenient. I must be rested and refreshed, looking and feeling my best, glowing at Edward's side when the guests arrive to get tongues wagging at the club.

What's the sense of hosting a lavish gala if it doesn't make people talk?

The house is bathed in moonlight. I carve a familiar path to the natatorium. At least this time I won't catch my husband fornicating with the nanny.

The pool is tranquil. Dazzling. The water swallows my nude form with ease. I float weightlessly along on my back, staring at the vaulted canopy of timber until I reach the far end of the pool, then turn onto my stomach and begin freestyle laps. There's nothing quite like the feel of crisp, cool liquid rushing against your skin to let you know you're alive.

I don't tire easily, even in the wee hours. It takes twenty laps to put a dent in my energy reserves. I could go longer—*much* longer, with the fire crackling in my veins—but enough is enough. The workers will be arriving soon (I insisted on a predawn start time) and it's only just hit me that I haven't chosen my jewelry. I'm thinking of wearing an eye-catching statement piece, like the Harry Winston sunflower necklace that cups my throat like a wreath of glittering stars. Or the Hope Diamond-inspired pendant Edward commissioned from a reclusive old lapidary in the Swiss Alps—or was it the *French* Alps?—when I gave birth to the twins.

Choices, choices.

I wring out my hair and snatch my negligee off the deck, slipping it over my head and shimmying it into place. I usually run hot, but I've caught a chill. Despite myself, I shiver.

The master suite is a long way off. I wrap my arms around my chest and hurry, bypassing the kitchen, even though I'm hungry. Food will have to wait. I don't want an extra ounce on my body when I slip into that designer gown. There will be plenty to eat later, once the curtain goes up on our Decade of Love.

As usual, Edward is snoring like a deranged mule. I poke him hard in the stomach (he quiets down temporarily) on my way to the bathroom, where my jewelry armoire is tucked in beside my vanity. I sink into the cushioned vanity chair and spread the wings of the armoire, revealing a selection of everyday necklaces—ones I bought by the dozen at chain jewelry stores (gasp!) and the Macy's at the mall. Each one is pretty in its own right, but none has that special something—that mixture of pixie dust and opulence—that'll make the club wives drool.

Still, it's fun to try on a few and imagine how they'd look with the dress, a form-fitting masterpiece of gold lace that covers as much skin as a wetsuit, which I might as well be wearing the way that dress clings to me. Nothing will be left to the imagination, yet everything will be.

I start at the beginning of the rainbow, lifting red-stoned necklaces off their hooks—I have a stash of ruby chokers and pendants, along with some strands of imperial topaz and fire opal—and holding them up to my neck, watching them blaze against my skin in the mirror.

Unfortunately, none are worthy of the dress. I replace them and move on to orange gems, of which I have few. There's a round sapphire pendant (yes, an *orange* sapphire!), wrapped in a triple loop of diamonds. And a collar of orangish yellow stones I vaguely recollect being called beryl (an ugly name for a sparkling little gem!). But these, too, come up lacking.

I fan my fingers through the gold and platinum chains, searching for something yellow. A lemon quartz, perhaps. But before I find anything that fits the bill, I spot another orange pendant that's escaped my eye. A square citrine that sparks a pleasurable memory, a visceral feeling of satisfaction.

I pull the necklace loose and coil it around my hand, trying to divine its meaning, decode its history. For the life of me, I can't remember where I got it (probably from a smitten boyfriend) or why it has such a magnetic pull.

My mind is running away with me, a fact I blame on the late—or should I say early?—hour.

I'm re-hanging the citrine pendant when my mind jolts back to that slummy basement (it was a crawlspace, truth be told), to *that girl*.

Suddenly, I know where the necklace came from. She was wearing it when the needle pierced her arm, when the ketamine conspired with the muscle relaxants to finish her off, to push her over the edge of oblivion. I checked her flat, blank eyes one last time—not a glimmer of life left, not the slightest chance she'd survive to implicate me—before unclasping the chain and making it mine.

I caress the stone, remembering how good it felt—how fulfilling it was—seeing my plan come to fruition. It was my first time going that far, my first time killing someone. There had been other opportunities, other nobodies who'd wronged me—what hooker hasn't been roughed up by an unruly john or stepped on by a wannabe pimp?—but my nerve hadn't yet solidified. I got back at those trolls in my own way, though. Trust me.

The girl had it coming, of course. She was a no-good thief with an ego the size of Montana. She babbled on and on about her family—if they were so great, why was she turning tricks on the street?—especially a little sister she squealed over like it was her own child. And then there were her delusions. It squirmed in her brain like a toxic worm that she could be famous, that she was the next Brooke Shields or Rebecca De Mornay.

Give me a break. If anyone had that kind of potential, it was me. I mean, look at me now. This kind of success doesn't just happen.

With a contented sigh, I close the armoire and make my way to bed. My first instincts were correct: Mr. Winston's glittering sunflowers will adorn my neck. They're timeless and elegant—not to mention expensive. When Edward rises, I'll have him retrieve the necklace from one of our many safes. While he's at it, he can rustle up some antique pearls—if he hasn't squandered them all on his mistress, that is—for Darian and Mae. Our daughters should look every bit as stunning as their mother on this special day.

CHAPTER 37
ROBIN

Against my better judgment, I let Nate stay the night. He's a calming force, and I need a rational voice right now, a steady heartbeat pressed against me in the dark, keeping me tethered to facts, to reality.

Samantha is going to be fine. Nate thinks so, and so do I. If I can't trust myself because of what happened to Marina, because of the paranoia her murder (overdose?) instilled in me, then at least I can trust him. He's earned that much.

In the morning, Nate tells me to sleep in. I resist—what if Sam needs something?—but he's already checked on her. "She's hungry," he says with a laugh. "I'm going to get breakfast from that new bakery."

I squint through bleary eyes. "What bakery?"

"The one by the library," he says, slipping on his shoes.

"There's a bakery by the library?"

He pats my head. "Go back to sleep. I won't be long."

My eyelids feel heavier than normal, as if I've been blackout drunk. But all I had was the cough syrup and not even much of that. I guess a solid night's sleep hangs on with a vengeance.

I drift off again. Soon Sam is poking her head into my room. Once I've rubbed the gunk out of my eyes, I'm shocked to see that she's showered and dressed. "If you want a bagel, get out here," she says. "They're really good. We're gonna eat all of 'em without you." She goes to my dresser and starts fumbling around.

Yawning, I sit up. "What're you doing?"

"Getting ready for school." She holds up a makeup brush. "I'm taking this, okay?"

"Yeah, okay," I respond, feeling like I've awoken from a bad dream, like my daughter's sickness was a figment of my warped mind. Am I really seeing things so differently, so *wrongly*, from how they are? Can my reactions—my suspicions, my assumptions, my uncanny ability to expect the worst—be boiled down to The Marina Effect?

I'm unconvinced that a change of outlook, that calibrating my vision for rainbows and butterflies, will set my life on a different course.

I follow Sam to the bathroom. She ducks inside to finish putting on her face. Since the attack, she's been vigilant about covering every blemish to perfection. She doesn't want her friends seeing the trauma she's undergone. Which makes me think that the son of a bitch who beat her up is an outsider, someone from a tougher crowd. Or maybe a stranger. No matter what Nate says, I can't bring myself to believe that Sam is dating a thug, a criminal, an animal.

I push the reset button in my brain and join Nate for breakfast. He's too young for me, too good for me, but I don't care. The bagels are delicious—crusty and chewy and still a bit warm—and the way he smiles at me with those crinkly hazel eyes makes the rest of the world disappear.

The day after Sam's miraculous recovery, my phone rings. It's Lisa from the catering company. She's offering me five days' work—today through Saturday—for a VIP event at a private estate. The pay is a thousand dollars. "Are you in?" she asks. "I could use you in an hour."

"For a thousand bucks?" A stunned pause. "Uh, yeah."

"Good. What kind of car do you have?"

"An old one," I reply, chuckling.

"Can you fit a couple of boxes from the butcher shop? They're already paid for. I just need someone to pick them up."

I'm distracted, looking for a pen to leave Sam a note. "In the backseat, probably," I mutter, realizing I can text Sam once I hang up.

She gives me the name and address of the butcher shop. Thankfully, I recognize it. "It's under Class Act Catering. They'll have it ready."

I feel like an idiot for asking this, but ... "And then what? I mean, where do I take it?"

"To me. Here," she says, sounding flustered. "We're working around the clock to pull this thing off. This is a big client. The biggest. Nothing can go wrong."

"My internet's down," I lie. "Tell me where you're located, and I'll be there in less than an hour."

She describes the building, which is in the business district, a few blocks from the café. No wonder she was always popping in for those mochas and lattes.

"Got it," I say. "See you soon."

She hangs up.

On my way to the car, I text Sam. She'll have to fix her own dinner. It's a small price to pay for the chunk of change I'm about to earn. I can't remember the last time I had a thousand dollars to my name.

I back out of the driveway and head down the street, my mind swirling with things I'll be able to buy—those new tires are a sudden reality—in a few short days. As I turn onto Raspberry Lane, a squeaking sound pierces my dreamy bubble. Moving toward me in the opposite direction is Lewis's van. I squint into the harsh autumn sun, trying to make out who's behind the wheel. But instead of Lewis's geometric white haircut, I glimpse a cascade of black curls flowing over the shoulders of a fuchsia jacket. The face of the driver is a smudge. If anyone's in the passenger seat, they're consumed by a dark shadow.

I'm almost at a dead stop. The van rolls by without its driver hitting the brakes. My curiosity is piqued, but there's no time to investigate. Lisa will fire me if I'm even a minute late.

Tomorrow, I promise myself. *I'll find out what's going on with Lewis when I can spare a moment to think.*

CHAPTER 38
LISA

Turnout for the party is phenomenal, easily surpassing the two hundred warm bodies I'd set my sights on. Edward's family alone makes up a quarter of the guest list. All of his sisters—Ellen, Eve, Esther, Alice, and Fawn—are here, along with their significant others and their offspring. Most of his cousins have made the trip, too. Even his employees have carved out time from their busy schedules (as if they had a choice!) to celebrate the shining example—the twinkling North Star—that is Edward's and my blessed union.

Being an only child of deceased only-child parents—a convenient cover story to keep Edward from digging through my past—I have no family in attendance. But I *have* pulled in dozens of business contacts and a horde of club wives. The prize for Most Interesting Guest, however, goes to Detective Luke Jones. I added him to the list on a lark, hoping to get on his good side, to find out what he knows about Sophie Gallagher and Dr. Kapoor, to inoculate myself against any accusations. Once he sees the lifestyle Edward and I lead, can he really suspect me of murder? Money doesn't get its hands dirty; money doesn't take the fall. If he's any kind of detective, he'll know that.

Along with Detective Luke has come a leggy brunette with a fake tan and overbleached teeth. She's wearing some kind of bedazzled monstrosity—a jumpsuit or palazzo pants with a matching top—and hanging on the poor detective like a pair of limp pantyhose on a shower rod.

The only thing more ridiculous than the detective and his floozy of a date are the club geezers who've come with a parade of arm candy young enough to be their granddaughters. I have half a mind to show them the door—this is an anniversary celebration, not a third-rate beauty pageant—but it's not worth the effort. And the May-Decembers are good gossip fodder, if nothing else. More than a few drunken giggles will be had at their expense.

I'm gliding through the natatorium like a great white shark, never far from my husband. I pull him close and whisper, "Do your cheeks hurt?" We've posed for umpteen photographs with eager guests, shot mostly on cell phones. The professional photographers are less obtrusive and more skilled. We'll have a sea of top-notch images to choose from to commemorate this glorious event. Not a moment too soon, either. The life-size oil painting Edward commissioned for our fifth anniversary has worn out its welcome. The girls look like porcelain ghouls and Edward and I are inbred mountain folk. From day one, it gave me the creeps.

Edward chuckles. "Only a little," he says, flashing a smile for yet another snapshot. He tips back a glass of brandy—he's on hard liquor, which will work in my favor—emptying it and depositing it on a passing waiter's tray. He kisses me high on the cheekbone. "You are"—*kiss, kiss*—"delectable, Mrs. Hayes." A gentle sigh. "Did anyone ever tell you that?"

I grin wickedly. "Loads of people."

He feigns outrage. "Who? I'll kill 'em right now. Tell me their names."

We continue our repartee for a pop-up audience, including two of Edward's brothers-in-law, who can only dream of being married to someone as feisty as me, until a platter of hors d'oeuvres floats by. I hold up a finger. "Excuse me," I say. And then I'm gone, camouflaged by a mass of tuxedo- and taffeta-wrapped flesh. Knowing that everyone has gone out of their way primping and polishing gives me a secret shiver.

I pinch a nibble off a tray that someone has abandoned on a stereo speaker. It's a pillow of pastry filled with spicy meat. Even at room temperature, it sets off explosions of delight in my mouth. *Orgasmic* would be an appropriate word.

The flood of feel-good hormones sends me to one of the bar carts, which are strategically posted around the house so no one goes more than ten steps without a drink. Until now, I've been avoiding booze, trying to keep my head clear. I have things to accomplish, first among them a closer look at that hottie detective, Luke Jones. Sophie Gallagher and Dr. Kapoor have drifted to the back of my mind—and hopefully everyone else's. And I intend to keep it that way.

One little drink can't hurt, can it? "Give me a Malibu Sunset," I tell the woman behind the cart, a scraggly middle-aged thing with a life of victimhood etched on her face. She fumbles the bottles, looking confused. "One part Malibu rum, three parts pineapple juice, three parts orange juice, and a splash of cranberry," I say, shaking my head. "You *do* have those, don't you?" I tap my fingers on the cart, awaiting her reply.

Her response evaporates in a twitter of voices and the smooth grooves of our jazz band. (The live music is in the natatorium; other realms of the house have DJs, face painters, mimes, magicians, caricaturists, palm readers, etcetera.) She stares straight down, her hands trembling as she makes the drink. Alonzo must've scraped the bottom of the barrel staffing our big event.

The drink is weak. I should dress her down, but I won't. Not with so many eyes on me. Tonight is for practicing restraint. Once the last tipsy club member is folded into their luxury SUV—my money's on Penelope Anne, who's been inhaling crab cakes and piña coladas with equal verve, hanging on the longest—I'll let my hair down.

I'm cutting my way back to Edward, stopping here and there for air kisses and side hugs with everyone from Ellen (Edward's eldest sister and my alter ego) to the understudy who played The Honourable

Gwendolen Fairfax, when Ashley is turned out of a clot of dirty old men.

We come abruptly face-to-face, close enough to kiss. She gasps lightly.

My husband's mistress has made good use of our credit card, I see. She's an ethereal vision—a celestial goddess—in an off-the-shoulder cream-silk gown. All that bare skin—from behind her ear, down her neck, to those French-manicured fingernails—is intoxicating.

"Just the person I was looking for," I say, running my tongue over my lips. I hold out the Malibu Sunset. "I got you something."

Her nose does a charming little twitch. "Sorry. I don't drink."

Of course not. How could she maintain that delusional religious façade otherwise? I press the drink into her hand. "It's just juice and syrup. Nothing naughty."

"Really?"

"Try it," I insist.

She takes a sip. "Mmm," she says, a dimple piercing her cheek. "It's good."

I stare over her shoulder at the detective. "You're welcome." Once she's gotten the first drink down, her lowered inhibitions will allow a second and a third, each more potent than the last. By the time my plan gets going, she'll barely know her name.

I excuse myself, intending to happen upon the detective. "Gee, I don't know how you got on the guest list," I'll say, if he finds the invitation suspicious, "but I'm sure glad you did!" As I'm closing the last few steps between us—his date's tan is even more grotesque up close, a hue between squash and marmalade—an unexpected voice catches my ear. A woman's voice with a distinctly Indian accent.

Before I know it, someone is grasping my wrist. "Dr. Hayes," the woman says, "may I speak with you for a moment?" I stop short, no small feat on this Spanish marble in these spike-heeled Jimmy Choos.

The woman is older, dark skinned with heavy cat's-eye makeup. She's wearing a color-blocked dress—scarlet bodice and charcoal-gray skirt—that's too informal for the occasion. I smile warmly. "You must be Mrs. Kapoor," I say, taking her hands into mine. A sympathetic frown. "I'm so sorry about ..."

"That is for another time," she answers. "I only want to thank you for the kind words about my husband. And also for the generous gift. It was far too generous, though." She reaches into the neckline of her dress and pulls out my check, which is neatly folded and stuck through with a pin. "The arrangements were only half of this. You've gone above and beyond."

How exactly did the doctor's widow end up here? I told Jacquelyn to make a list of tenants, excluding—obviously!—those who are dead. Do I have to spell everything out for that woman? "Please," I say, pushing her hand away, "it's our honor. When my husband learned of *the tragedy*, he insisted on doing our part." (Actually, Edward has no idea that I've paid off the widow of the most recent thorn in my side.) I lower my voice. "We've suffered a loss, too. A baby." I glance wistfully down at my abdomen.

Her face crumples. "My condolences."

"Thank you." I gesture at the check, which she's holding uncertainly in the air. "You have grandchildren, don't you?" I vaguely remember seeing a snapshot on the doctor's desk.

She nods. "A girl and a boy."

"Put the rest toward their college funds, in memory of our little angel." I bite the inside of my cheek, making my eyes water. If this doesn't convince her, nothing will.

"You're sure?"

I pat her shoulder. "Absolutely."

With no further argument, she tucks the check back into its hiding spot.

A moment later, Darian comes prancing along. One of the caricaturists has drawn Magnum in a tuxedo and top hat, which I must see at once. Apologetically, I take my leave.

CHAPTER 39
ROBIN

It turns out that Lewis was gone for the most obvious reason on earth: love. He's been dating a woman online for two years. Her name is Wanda. She's a nursing assistant from Lubbock, Texas. He drove fifteen hundred miles each way in that beat-up old van to meet her. Now Wanda's testing the waters here, seeing if she can bear a Northeast winter before the lovebirds take the next step.

Will he marry her after all these years? After grieving so long for Georgette?

I should bring over a welcome gift—a tin of cookies or a bag of coffee—but the pressure has been building at Class Act to get things just right for the Big Event, an anniversary party for a rich inventor and his wife, which kicks off in two hours.

Lewis and Wanda will have to wait.

Most of the catering team is already on-site, but those of us who drew the short straws and will be "interfacing" (Lisa's new favorite word) with the guests are taking the late bus, so we'll be in top form.

I say a quick prayer as the catering van rolls through the gates at the foot of the estate and begins its slow, winding climb. From my second-row seat (there are seven of us in this vehicle and six in the one following along behind), I watch the view unfurl like a bleak painting. The expanse of land is parklike, breathtaking, but also cold and dark. It reeks of death.

The girl next to me has been smacking a wad of gum for the twenty-minute ride. When the compound comes into view—a series of interconnected buildings of glass, stone, and timber with multiple peaked roofs, chimneys, and balconies—she says, "Cool," and then promptly starts choking.

My maternal instincts kick in. I whack her on the back. "Are you all right?"

Her eyes are watering. "Yeah," she croaks between coughs. She spits the gum into her hand. "Thanks."

"Crisis averted," I say, laughing. Her mishap makes me feel like the bad mojo has passed. Everything will be tulips and waterfalls from now on.

Our driver circles around to the back of the estate and parks in the withered grass at the end of a long row of trucks, vans, and SUVs. There must be a hundred people working this event. Another kink in my stomach relaxes.

We grab the supplies—random stuff Lisa remembered at the eleventh hour and requested in a frantic group text—and play follow-the-leader to what would normally be called a basement, though this underground area is five times the size of my house and a hundred times as nice. There are so many rooms, each a hive of activity, that my head is spinning.

Our crew chief is a Jamaican guy named Griffin. He directs us to our own little corner—a crude sign taped to the wall reads CLASS ACT CATERING—which our coworkers have claimed as a staging area. Boxes and bags and coolers and warming trays and handcarts are strewn everywhere, giving the impression of mass chaos.

"Okay, so ..." I search the faces of my fellow waiters and waitresses for a clue about what to do next.

"It's hotter than hell in here," says Gum Girl, whose name I have yet to learn. She digs a package of napkins out of a bag and starts fanning herself.

She's right; it *is* roasting. Which is strange with the temperature outside bobbing around freezing. Then again, there are so many bodies in here.

Griffin's thumbs fly over his phone. "Lisa's on her way down with the party planner," he says. "They'll give us the tour and then divide everyone into zones. She has to stay up top—front of house, on call—in case the client gets a hangnail. I'm the point person. If you need anything, just ask. It goes without saying that we're bending over backwards here. Whatever the guests want, they get. No questions asked. Extra cheesecake, babysitting, help with their makeup ... all fair game, okay?"

We wouldn't be here if we weren't willing to sell our souls for cold, hard cash.

A few minutes later, Lisa sails in. She's wearing a peacock-blue strapless gown that matches her companion's necktie. Quickly, she introduces the man—Alonzo—but just as quickly, she orders us not to bother him. He's the head honcho, Lisa's liaison to the client, and has too many balls in the air to be bothered with the likes of us.

Fair enough.

The tour of the main level is an episode of *Lifestyles of the Rich and Famous*. Everything is big, new, immaculate. My eyes don't know where to look. As we zing from room to room, dodging our counterparts from other catering crews, I count five bathrooms (that I know of), a kitchen fit for a Saudi prince, and a colossal room with a swimming pool inside.

A pool? In the house? Only an ice rink or a Starbucks would stun me more.

Even though the house is huge, its layout is intuitive. Navigating will be a breeze, except for all of the human traffic.

The last hour vanishes in a flurry of preparations. I'm sweating through my shirt when the guests start arriving. Everyone's lavishly turned out, as if attending a royal supper. The spectacle makes me laugh: grown-ups playing make believe. If these people had real jobs, they'd know how ridiculous—how self-serving, how arrogant, how wasteful—such extravagance is.

I've been clinging to the bottom rung of society long enough to know when to shut my mouth, when to fetch water and aspirin and tissues with a plastic smile. Later, alone in my bed at night, I'll feel the sting of my father's judging gaze, asking why I couldn't crawl out from under Marina's shadow, why I couldn't pull myself up by the bootstraps and achieve.

I shake off the negative thoughts and take a tray of appetizers to the library, where a group of children is amassed around a woman in an overstuffed chair. She's wearing a splotched smock and gripping a palette of paints. The line is fifteen kids long for the chance to be transformed into a lion or a mouse—a pair of dark-eyed twins are sporting these contrary faces, along with their pearl necklaces and sparkly shoes—or a bear, like the boy who's just spun around and roared at the waiting crowd.

The tray wobbles in my hand, threatening to rain mini quiches on the future rulers of America. I suck in a breath and steady myself. "Who's hungry?" I ask, flashing back to lunchroom duty at the school where I once taught.

My heart clenches. Part of me knows our father was right. I could've done—could've *been*—so much more, if I'd just kept trying.

Focus.

Mouse Girl points at the tray. "What are those?" she asks, scrunching up her nose.

"Quiche," I say, bending down so she can inspect them. "They're little egg pies. I think these ones have bacon in them." At the risk of overselling, I add, "They're yummy."

Lion Girl grabs one of the quiches and pops it in her mouth. "She hates eggs," she mumbles, elbowing her sister. "She thinks they're made of bloody chickens." A big grin. "Right, Mavis."

Mavis stares at the floor and shrugs; meanwhile, a barrage of chubby hands—they come fast and furious, closing over the food like Hungry Hungry Hippos—empties the tray.

I head back to the kitchen for a refill, but the quiches are gone. Griffin's wearing a groove in the floor, pinballing from station to station. "Take these," he says when I hesitate over the appetizers, thrusting a platter of cocktail meatballs at me. They look like ordinary beef, but they're probably something exotic like moose or elk or bison. "They're for the great room."

"Will do," I say.

The meatballs are harder to unload. The older crowd must be watching their cholesterol. But eventually they succumb, clustering around the gigantic fireplace—the fire itself gives me chills; all I can see is Marina's melting face—and scraping the meatballs off brightly colored toothpicks with their teeth.

"Excuse me, excuse me, excuse me," I say, slicing through the packed hallway with the empty platter tucked under my arm.

I'm gearing up to reload from the never-ending conveyor belt of food when an unfamiliar woman interrupts me. "You're Class Act, right?" she says, her pointy-nailed fingers balanced on her voluptuous hips. She's wearing a black knee-length fitted dress that shines like her long dark hair. Her fake breasts give the vibe of an ex-porn star.

Something about her makes me nervous. I glance searchingly around for Griffin, but he's vanished. "Yeah," I say. "One of them." Why has she singled me out? This is only my second gig and I don't want to blow it.

"Your girl is sick."

For a moment, I think she's talking about Samantha. But then I realize she means one of my fellow waitresses. "Who? I mean, who is it? I don't really know—" Shouldn't she be telling Griffin? Or Lisa? Anyone but me?

"The young one with the kinky hair. She passed out and hit her head. That guy—what's his name?—Greg or Gareth ... he's taking her home."

I'm not sure what this has to do with me. "Okay."

"You've gotta sub," she informs me, "in the natatorium. We're a bartender short. I'd do it myself, but Mrs. Hayes wants me available at all times. I can't get tied down to anything. You know what you're doing, right? Everything you'll need is already there."

"As a matter of fact, yes," I say, glad for once about my checkered work history. There aren't too many jobs in the service sector I haven't performed. "But … where …?" The location she's rattled off sounds like a murder site in the game of Clue.

"Follow me," she says, swirling a hand through the air. She wobbles ahead. I wonder if she's drunk, but her speech is clear. And she's not giving off any telltale odors. Must be the heels; she's not used to wearing them.

We end up in the pool room, which is swinging with jazz music and shimmering with thousands—maybe *tens of thousands*—of tiny white lights. I'm speechless, mesmerized. Everyone is so beautiful, so happy, so perfect it breaks my heart.

Why couldn't Marina have lived? She would've slipped easily into this posh world. She would've shone among the stars.

My guide has been talking while I've been wallowing. "… under here." She indicates a shelf on the back of the cart. "Any questions?"

"I'm good," I say.

She wishes me luck and teeters back into the thicket of bodies. Thirty seconds later, a line starts forming. I rummage through the supplies and make a margarita, a daiquiri, a Tom Collins, another daiquiri, a Mai Tai, a few drinks on the rocks, another daiquiri, and so on.

Finally, a lull appears. I wipe down the cart, allowing my gaze to roam. I have yet to spot the anniversary couple, but now, in a particularly dense gathering, contenders emerge. The man is a ringer for the young Marlon Brando, except he's darker haired—black instead of brown. The woman is a regal beauty with stark, engrossing features. Everything about her is symmetrical, proportionate. She's graceful, flawless. She floats instead of walks.

I've been holding my breath without realizing it. I remind myself to inhale. I'd like to continue watching the couple—they're hypnotic, like white lines on a dark highway—but customers are trickling in. I turn my attention back to the bar.

Martini.

Gin and tonic.

Sex on the beach. (Should I be checking IDs? This girl looks Sam's age. I let her slide.)

Daiquiri.

Daiquiri.

Mai Tai.

I'm tucking an empty rum bottle away as the next customer comes forward. When I straighten up, it's *her*—the owner, I'm now convinced, of this formidable mansion.

She asks for a Malibu Sunset. My mind blanks. She helps me, listing out the ingredients. When I make the drink, my hands shake. It isn't until she's gone, mingling and laughing, basking in the glow of her admirers, that I realize she reminds me of someone. At first I think it's Marina; the two share an indefinable charisma. A magnetic dynamism. But no. It's someone else. Someone I can't quite pin down.

I shrug off the thought. The drinks won't make themselves. And I'm probably imagining things, anyway.

Halfway through a group order—three mother-daughter pairs have descended on me at once—my phone buzzes. I pour the last cosmopolitan before discreetly checking the call history.

The caller was Samantha. She's left a message. I can't listen to it here, in front of all these people. Lisa will kill me.

The opportunity to slip away is now. I bypass the nearest bathroom—the one by the pool has a loosely formed line—and head down the hall. The bathroom by the library is vacant. I duck inside and lock the door. As I access my voicemail, my heart crashes against my ribs. I try talking myself down, making sense of Sam's disturbing me at work—maybe she's locked herself out of the house; maybe the toilet overflowed—but it's no use. My daughter is smarter than that, more self-reliant. And Lewis is back. She would've gone next door before calling me.

I play the message. It's agony from word one. Sam is hysterical, begging me to come home. I can't call her back fast enough.

C'mon, dammit. Pick up the phone.

On the fifth ring, she does. "Mom?" Her voice is scratchy, ragged.

I stare at myself in the ornate gold mirror. My mouth is moving, but I can't hear the words. Everything is slow, distant. A soft buzzing sound envelops my head. Through the fog, my daughter tells me that she's scared. She needs me. Everything has gone wrong.

She's hurt again. I know it in my bones. Maybe worse than before.

The tension in my head breaks. "Call the police. Call Scott. Call Lewis. But don't go out. Don't you dare leave the house!" I gasp. "I'm on my way."

As I exit the bathroom, my mind is tumbling. I lurch toward the pool room but then abruptly change course for the kitchen. There's no easy way out of here—off this gated estate—without a car. I'm going to need the catering van.

My eyes fill with tears. The hallway is a funhouse of gaping mouths and grotesque, twisted faces. When I reach the kitchen, Lisa's in Griffin's place, overseeing preparations for the main course. "I've gotta go," I announce. "It's an emergency." This will spell the end of my employment and the loss of that thousand-dollar payday, but I don't care. Sam is my top priority. My *only* priority.

Lisa snorts. "Good luck."

"I'm serious," I say, grabbing her arm. "Where are the keys?"

She pulls against me. Soon we're in a tug-of-war over nothing. The keys are nowhere in sight, and I doubt she has them hidden in that silky gown.

Curious onlookers converge. I tell myself to give up, to find another way home. But images of Marina's dead body tangle with memories of Samantha's battered face and I can't stop. I claw at the air, trying to hurt her, trying to make her give me what I want, what I need, what Samantha needs.

A voice cuts through the commotion. "Is everything all right? May I be of assistance?"

Lisa lets go. I stumble backward, getting my footing just short of crashing into the wall. "We're fine," says Lisa in a cool voice. "Just a small misunderstanding."

When I gather myself, I'm surprised to see *her*—the woman of the house, the guest of honor—slumming with the hired help. She's even more bewitching the second time around. Her warm eyes and serene disposition temporarily erase thoughts of Samantha from my mind. "I need a ride," I blurt, knowing it's useless. This rich, glamorous woman has no reason to help a pathetic fool like me.

She takes my hand—a jolt of electricity sparks between us—and guides me around the corner to a quiet, out-of-the-way spot. "Wait here," she says, motioning at a granite workstation. "I'll have my housekeeper take you home." She searches my face for understanding. "Okay?"

The energy drains from my body. What good will I be to Sam when I finally reach her? "Yes," I say. "Please." I pull out the chair and drop into it.

Her hand flutters by my head, landing on something behind me. She draws the object into my peripheral vision. "Here," she says, offering the item to me. "I'm a psychiatrist. I can help with whatever's going on."

I hesitate, but she presses the object—a pink business card, identifying her as Dr. L.A. Hayes—into my palm. "Thank you," I say, though I won't be dialing her up for any overpriced head shrinking.

Like she's reading my mind (really, she just knows a hard-luck case when she sees one), she says, "First five sessions free. What do you have to lose?"

I slip the card into my pocket and promise to call. And who knows, maybe I will.

CHAPTER 40
LISA

I'm poised to handle the Ashley situation when a whole new problem crops up: the original dead girl's sister. She has a teardrop-shaped mole on her jaw that has stood the test of time. I haven't seen it since that girl's funeral (I attended, disguised as a male classmate with mud-caked work boots, baggy carpenter jeans, dark glasses, and a bushy black wig), but it's stuck in my mind ever since, the irony of a permanent tearstain on such a sorry creature.

Robin Davis. I never thought *she'd* surface again. Isn't fate full of surprises?

I could take my chances and assume she didn't recognize me—why would she? I'm nothing like I was back then, even if she could put two and two together—but I don't want to be caught unawares. The last thing I need is the ghost of that murder coiling around my ankle and dragging me down.

I can't let Robin go without probing what she knows. But that's for tomorrow, when the celebratory buzz has worn off. The more I think about it, the more I realize that my plans for Ashley can proceed. If anything, getting rid of the nanny will open up a world of possibilities I can capitalize on with the dead girl's sister.

I stand arm in arm with my husband, our sleepy daughters barefoot beside us in their fancy dresses, waving goodbye to the last of our guests as they disappear in a squall of snow.

The house is still bustling with activity as the cleanup continues. But the band has packed up its basses and horns and drums; the DJs have unplugged their computers and turntables and mixers; and a certain kind of rustling calm has fallen over us.

Edward tousles Mae's hair—she's his favorite; he sees something of himself in her—and dismisses the girls for bed. They're on their own tonight, Ricki having clocked out after bringing Robin home. Ashley is passed out in the master suite. I helped her there myself, held her hair while she vomited in the sink, encouraged her to brush her teeth—Edward will appreciate my forethought—and peeled her out of that heart-stopping dress.

The girls scamper off.

"I have a surprise for you," I whisper in Edward's ear.

"I've been dying to get my hands on you all night," he replies, his voice husky with liquor. He leans into me and massages my hips, the gown riding up as he kneads deeper, deeper.

I feel his erection at my waist. "Not here," I say. I lead him to the master suite. It's dark. The bathroom door is ajar. A thin stream of light sparks across the floor.

It's a big room. I steer him toward the tufted cobalt-blue sofa I bought online after the doctor's widow stole the original out from under me. He doesn't notice Ashley on the bed.

Perfect.

I only hope the tramp isn't dead. (It's hard to know how much these liquor virgins can drink before their organs shut down. The waiter I tipped five hundred bucks to keep her supplied with strawberry margaritas didn't report back with an exact count, either.) In the best-case scenario, she's groggy and pliable when we get around to her.

Edward lost his tuxedo jacket an hour into the party and his vest shortly thereafter. He's down to a sloppily tucked shirt and a pair of trousers.

I sink to the floor, my gown stretching across my thighs. Slowly, I unbutton his pants. His fingers tangle in my hair. He pulls me—my face, my mouth—toward his crotch. "Not yet," I say, giggling. I press him against the sofa. He falls back, taking me with him. My strappy heels slide out from under me. I land on his chest, knocking the wind out of us.

We kiss feverishly. I'm playing up my desire—panting, moaning, gasping. While I fumble with the buttons on his shirt, he dry humps my leg, so much so that I'm afraid he'll complete the act. Which would ruin everything. There's a naked, blacked out, wet dream of a girl in our bed. It'd be a shame to waste her.

I strip off his shirt and boxers. My dress is another matter. I could let him shove it up over my waist and force my underwear aside—he likes pretending the brute, roughing me up a little—but that might be too much. When he's drunk like this, when his walls are down, his orgasm could tip at any moment. I need him to last long enough to get inside the nanny. The video of them—of all of us—will be solid gold. Maybe even good enough to upload to one of those amateur porn websites.

"Just ... hold on ..." I twist around, so he can reach the zipper of my dress. "Undo me."

He's too anxious, too hurried. He snags the zipper, swears at himself, yanks it back up and then down again. It catches a second time. He's breathing hot and heavy on my neck.

"Good enough." I shrug the sleeves down over my shoulders, exposing my breasts. The fabric bunches at my waist. I shimmy it past my hips and gravity does the rest. I step out of the oval of lace and nudge it aside.

I'm wearing only those gladiator stilettos and a pair of thong underwear. Edward lets out a sigh of appreciation. (Why wouldn't he? Even with that porcelain temptress sprawled out on our bed, I'm perfection personified.)

My husband can't wait any longer. He pinches the thong and seesaws it down around my knees. I let him have me in a veritable *Kama Sutra* of positions (pressed face-first to the window while he works me from behind is particularly risqué, since the help is still clearing out and will likely see), but never for more than a few seconds. I know his rhythms—his tolerance—and I'm focused on turning him blue. His need for release must override any qualms he might have about playing with the nanny in front of me, *with* me.

The moment is near. I jerk off his lap, almost foiling my plans. It's been years since he could go two rounds; the main event is more than enough with me. Then again, maybe a second act *would* be possible with the infusion of fresh blood.

It's not worth finding out. When he starts up again, this time zeroing in on my nipples, I take him to bed.

"What's this?" he asks, finally recognizing the situation, the opportunity. He doesn't bother pretending shock at the sight of her. Maybe he's been shooting for the three of us together all along.

Attaboy.

If I could read his mind, it would be triple sevens, a row of cherries, dollar signs all around. But money can't buy what I'm about to deliver.

With a lurid grin, I say, "Happy anniversary, sweetheart."

He raises an eyebrow. "Is she ...?"

Breathing? Yes. Her pert breasts are rising and falling on cue. "She had a little too much fun, I'm afraid." A mock frown. "She wanted this to be special. She wanted you to enjoy it. It's sweet, really, when you think about it."

He grabs my hips and bends me over the bed. We rock back and forth a few times—he's still set to go off—before I crawl up onto the duvet. He moves on her slowly, taking the time to bring her around. At first I think it's a lost cause, but then her eyes flutter open—she recognizes him! hallelujah!—and her hand goes to his chest, rubbing soft circles. When he kisses her, she moans and kisses back.

I wait until they're in the thick of it to join in. She's far enough gone that my presence doesn't register. Whose lips and fingers go where is a fuzzy dream. She won't know the truth until I confront her with the video, until I threaten to expose her as the lying, cheating whore she is.

How will Mommy and Daddy digest them apples? She'll be banished from the family, the church, her entire world ... unless she disappears and never returns. Unless she forgets she ever knew Edward Hayes.

Could the justice be any sweeter? I think not. Still, I bring Edward back to me for the grand finale, because the only thing that could wreck my plan would be a rogue pregnancy. (Leave it to the ditz to be ovulating.) And I have no intention of getting sloppy now.

CHAPTER 41
ROBIN

The ride home is a blur. I jump out of the car without thanking the woman who drove me. She backs out of the driveway, headlights casting slithering shadows as I wrestle with my keys at the door. After a couple of misfires, I jam the key in the lock and get inside.

The house is dark. "Samantha?" I shout, groping the wall for the light switch. I flick it and the bulb sputters on. "Sam?" I rush through the kitchen and down the hall, yelling into rooms as I go, the glow from that bulb getting fainter with every step.

My daughter doesn't answer. In the pit of my stomach, I know she's gone, kidnapped, never to return again. If losing Marina wounded me, losing Sam would carve out my heart—bloody and beating—from my willing chest.

I turn on the bathroom light. Used tissues are bunched up on the vanity and strewn across the floor, but still no Sam. My nerves are frayed, twitchy. As I pivot for my bedroom, the last place to check before the basement, I hear a soft rustling.

She's alive. I cling to the thought as I maneuver from doorway to doorway. I press my shoulder into the door. It creaks open. I scan the darkness (there's no overhead light, only a lamp—currently off—in the corner by the window) for signs of movement, forms out of place. I know this room in my blood. Deeper.

When my gaze hits a lumpy shadow on the carpet, I know I've found her. And when my fingers touch her skin, it's warm. "My God, Sam." I exhale hard. "What happened?"

She doesn't answer, doesn't move. She must be badly hurt.

"Stay there." I have a sinking feeling that my daughter needs an ambulance.

I work my way around the bed and turn on the lamp. The light shocks my eyes. I squint in Sam's direction. She's curled on her side in front of Marina's altar.

I should've guzzled some top-shelf liquor while I had the chance.

I get on my knees and examine her. To my relief, she's mostly whole, with the exception of some knotted clumps of hair and a scratch on her cheek. Her face is blotchy, but there's no trace of the bludgeoning she took last time around.

Then why is she comatose? I can't get her to acknowledge me or even open her eyes. It's about time I found out who did this to her. The bastard needs to pay. Boyfriend or not (definitely *not*, from here on out, if I have to chain myself to Samantha night and day), his number is up. He won't lay another finger on my daughter as long as he lives.

"C'mon, Sam." I nudge her shoulder. "Wake up."

She just lies there, breathing shallow, pretending not to exist. I get the sense that she wants to disappear, that she's a suicide risk, that there's more at play than an altercation with some shady boyfriend. But before I can explore the idea further, footsteps echo through the house.

I lunge for my dresser and scramble through the drawers. Where the hell is my gun?

I kick the door shut and continue frantically searching. "Get out!" I scream. "I have a gun! The police are coming!"

What on earth has Samantha gotten us into?

I'm yanking my phone out—the .38 is MIA—and struggling to dial 911 with trembling fingers, when …

"Robin," calls a familiar voice, "it's me." My brain stumbles, trying to place the intruder. "Do you hear me? Say something." The footsteps stop. "I'm here; I'm here for Sam."

Nate.

I fold the phone back into my pocket and concentrate on regulating my pulse. For a few dark seconds, I thought I was going to have to kill someone.

Samantha is still unresponsive. I leave her and meet Nate in the kitchen. Something tells me to keep the lights off, but I override the impulse and reach for the switch beside the sink, illuminating a patch of countertop.

"What was that about?" asks Nate when he finally gets a look at me. He studies my work clothes, probably surmising that I've blown my chances; I've embarrassed him with his family; I'm the sort of radioactive person who should be avoided at all costs.

"How did you …?" I rub my head. "I mean, why are you here? Did Sam call you?" It's the only thing that makes sense.

"She sounded pretty scared." He peeks around my shoulder. "Where is she?"

I explain about Samantha's hysterical voicemail, about ditching the catering job—he was going to find out soon enough, anyway—about my daughter's inward retreat. He offers to talk to her; he thinks he can get her to open up, to divulge.

I'd be happy if she'd move off the floor, for starters. And Nate might be the guy to help her do it. A consequence of Sam's growing up without a father is her vulnerability to men, her lust for their approval. Anything Nate can do to get her back on track is welcome.

He disappears into my bedroom. I don't make it ten seconds before opening the cupboard, shoving aside an ancient bag of flour, and grabbing what's left of the cough syrup. I consume it in one long gulp. When the bottle's empty, I sneak it into the trash.

I feel better and worse at the same time. In a few minutes, my problems will be wrapped in fuzzy force fields, keeping them from penetrating my brain. Until then, I'm exquisitely aware of my failings—

bad decisions upon bad decisions, tracing their roots back to Marina's murder.

How long can I go on blaming my dead sister for the life I lead?

Nate is taking his time with Samantha. I want to intervene, but I don't. Instead, I plop down in front of the TV and feast mindlessly on a murder mystery. It's a familiar tale of greed and betrayal, a husband poisoning his wife for the insurance money. As soft-focus snapshots flash across the screen, portraying the couple in better days, I cycle through a range of emotions: guilt, rage, despair, indifference.

Finally, the medicine kicks in. My mind floats away from me. By the time Samantha and Nate emerge, I'm a hazy version of myself. I watch my daughter detachedly, like she's a character on TV, like I haven't worried myself sick over her every day of her life.

At least she's up and moving around, even if she looks disturbed, compromised. Her eyes have a wild, frightened quality about them.

Sam and Nate exchange glances. "So," says Nate, smiling gently, "things have gotten—how would you say it, Samantha?—somewhat off track?"

"What things?" I ask.

"Do you want to tell her?" Nate asks Sam. "Or should I?"

Samantha's arms are folded over her chest. "No," she mumbles. "You."

Every cell in my body alerts. Nate's magic is about to pay off.

"Okay," says Nate. "I will." He points at the vacant side of the couch. "Why don't you sit down."

Instead of following Nate's suggestion, Sam stares out the window into the darkness. Nate shrugs and takes a seat on the coffee table.

"Is she all right?" I ask.

"It's complicated," says Nate. "Samantha's gotten involved in something—"

"I'm not *involved*," snaps Sam. "Don't say it like that. It makes me sound like a criminal." She continues staring out the window.

Nate shakes his head. "Right. That's not what I meant." He begins again. "Someone close to Samantha is in trouble. He's made poor choices that've caused—"

"Who?" I ask. "Who's close to her?" The condoms flash through my mind.

Sam rolls her eyes. "His name's Jason. Not that you care."

With her fixation on the outdoors, I can't help asking, "Are you waiting for someone?" My heart rate ticks up at the memory of Marina running away. One day things were normal—she was going to school and hanging out with her friends and working her first real job at the bookstore—and then, without warning, she was gone. Soon after, she was dead. My mind has never fully grasped how easy it all was.

"Like I'd have anyone pick me up here," Sam says with a snort.

"Anyway," says Nate, trying to get us back on track, "Samantha's friend is in trouble with some bad people." He taps his foot. "He owes money to a drug dealer. They're trying to collect. That's how Samantha got hurt."

I chuckle frustratedly. "She's protecting the idiot who beat her up?"

Sam whips around. "He never touched me!"

"Give me his name. All of their names. I'm calling the police. We're putting an end to this right now." As soon as the words leave my lips, I know they're wrong; they'll drive my daughter away.

Nate lays a hand on my knee. "There's a misunderstanding, I think. What I said before wasn't quite right. Samantha has corrected the record. She wasn't hurt by Jason; it was these drug guys."

I purse my lips. "So she says." My daughter has every reason to lie if she wants to continue seeing this loser.

Over my dead body.

I demand the names again—let the cops sort the truth from the lies—launching Sam into a frenzy of upset. She's practically hyperventilating when Nate sends us to our separate corners. But this isn't over. I'll get to the bottom of what's going on with Sam. It's my job as her mother. Someday she'll thank me.

CHAPTER 42
LISA

The day after the party, Edward leaves for California—he's speaking at a conference in Anaheim, practicing for a TED Talk a year or two down the road—and the girls go shopping with Ricki. She's pumping them full of junk food and registering them for Christmas gifts at all of the high-end stores within an hour's drive.

After a soak in the Jacuzzi, I spend the morning harvesting the video footage of our little threesome and then wiping it from the system, but not before making a physical copy—a highlights reel of sorts—for the soon-to-be ex-nanny. It's in the TV over our commercial range. The remote control is on the island in front of me.

Ashley stumbles into the kitchen around noon. "Feeling okay?" I ask as she stares into the refrigerator. "You should drink some pickle juice. It'll replenish your electrolytes. You went to town with that cute waiter last night. I thought he was going to have you dancing on the piano." I flip the page of the celebrity-gossip magazine I'm perusing.

"I don't like pickles." She pours a glass of orange juice and chars a slice of bread in the toaster. She's leaning over the sink, nibbling the dry, crispy slab, spilling blackened bits everywhere, when I close the magazine and set it aside.

"We have to talk," I say. Under the remote is a legal pad on which I've worked up her goodbye note. She'll be copying it word for word in her own handwriting.

She takes a few more bites of the toast and throws the rest in the trash. "What's up?" she asks, eyeing me warily.

I laugh to myself. She must have no recollection of what we did together. Her horror will be catastrophic. "Sit."

The island is between us. She circles around the long way, pulls out a stool, edges onto it. "Where is everyone?" she asks, looking around with fresh (though bloodshot) eyes.

"Never mind." I palm the remote and slide the legal pad over to her. "Read this."

She squints at the page. "My contacts are downstairs."

Isn't she full of excuses? "You don't put them in when you wake up?"

"I'm not going anywhere." She groans. "I don't feel good."

It's obvious that she's out of sorts. I beg to differ on her previous statement, though. She'll be a foggy memory by the time my husband returns from the West Coast. "Very well. I'll summarize it for you, then. In front of you is a resignation letter—*your* resignation letter from this job. It states that you've enjoyed your time with us—that's true, isn't it? you've liked fucking my husband and pocketing those expensive gifts?—but you've accepted a missionary assignment in rural Africa"—the idea is genius, if I do say so myself—"and you'll be leaving the country immediately.

"You go on to explain that this work in Burkina Faso—that's where you're headed—reaching out to nomadic desert folk, preaching the Gospel and cultivating faith in Christ, is a calling from God himself. Your spirit soars at the thought of leading so many lost souls to salvation!

"What else?" I tap my chin, thinking. "Oh, yes. I remember. You tell us that the terrain is harsh, the villages remote. There's no cell phone service. The mail is spotty. We won't be able to reach you, even with a Christmas card. You put a little frowny face after that part, by the way. Very sweet. It conveys the turmoil you're feeling about leaving us."

Ashley sits in stunned silence, letting the situation sink in. What I wouldn't give for a peek behind the curtain of those puckered eyebrows into her sad, reeling mind.

I clear my throat. "You wrap things up with an expression of gratitude, calling Edward and me your role models. You claim the girls as your 'heart sisters'—something like that, anyway—and grudgingly leave us with all your love." I sigh. "That's about it, I think. Excellent work. Your writing is quite engaging. The words just leap off the page." I wait for her to respond, but she doesn't. "Any questions?"

Her face is starting to prickle with sweat. "I don't understand."

I pat her hand. "Of course you do. It's right there in black and white—or, well, blue and yellow, ha-ha. You're going to Burkina Faso. You leave at seven fifteen tonight on Turkish Airlines. Nineteen hours in the air with stops in Toronto and Istanbul. You've still got your passport from that long weekend in Acapulco, don't you?" She watched our daughters while Edward and I frolicked in the warm Pacific, sipped tequila (when in Mexico …), and dozed under thatched huts on the terrace of our oceanfront villa. I don't think she was fucking him then, but I could be wrong.

"Yes, but—" Tears well up in her eyes.

"Save the dramatics," I say. "Actions have consequences. You didn't think this whole thing—your infringing on my marriage, right under my nose—would just go away, did you?" I shake my head. "Read your Bible. There's punishment. Atonement. It's the God-given order of things."

She sits up straighter. "You can fire me, but you can't make me go. *He* won't make me go."

"Nobody's making you do anything, sweetie. But pick your poison wisely. You don't want your dirty laundry out there for everyone to see, do you?"

"I'm getting my things." She stands up. "Tell Edward whatever you want."

"Wishful thinking. You made your bed and you'll lie in it. Pack for Africa—you're on a two-year commitment; Edward will have forgotten you by then—or this clip hits computer screens worldwide, with Edward's and my faces blurred, of course." I power on the TV and start the video.

How to describe her reaction? Aghast? Panic-stricken? Mortified? *Speechless* works, I think. *Agog* with a hint of *chastened*. And suddenly, marvelously, *acquiescent*.

She sits back down. "I knew it," she says, her voice shivering. "I knew we shouldn't have—" She makes no mention of my presence in the video, of the things I did to her, which makes me wonder if she's kinkier than I gave her credit for. Maybe she's done this sort of thing before, stone-cold sober.

I rip her goodbye note off the pad and set it aside. "Damn right," I say, sliding a pen across the island. "Now get to work. And be neat about it. I want Edward to absorb every last word."

CHAPTER 43
ROBIN

Thanks to Nate, my daughter and I have settled into an uncomfortable truce. I'm still afraid that if I push her too hard, she'll run off and end up like Marina. So I'm leaving the subject of her thug boyfriend—this Jason—alone for now, in hopes that the relationship dies a natural death. In the meantime, some free therapy might help Samantha value herself more, if only I could get her to go.

"I was thinking," I say as she climbs into the car after school, "that you could start learning to drive." It's the one thing I can offer, the one thing I can *trade*, for her cooperation with the therapist: freedom. And maybe even use of the Caprice, if we can work out a schedule that suits us both.

She squirms around in the passenger seat, shrugging off her backpack. "Seriously?"

I pull away from the curb. "I can start teaching you, little by little. After your birthday, you can get your learner's permit and then ... then your license, eventually." When I hear it like that, I relax. She won't be able to fly solo for a while. By then, maybe the dirtbag will be ancient history.

It's flurrying outside. I can barely see through the blotchy ghosts of snowflakes on the windshield. When I try to pump out the washer fluid, a grinding noise says I'm out of luck.

"That's worse than before," remarks Sam. She's not wrong, either. The wipers have only spread the streaks around.

We go quiet for a while, watching the flakes dance and swirl to their deaths. "I've driven before, you know," Sam says finally.

I hold back the urge to interrogate her. "Are you any good? Because if you are, that's less work for me."

She cracks a smile. My heart opens a bit wider. All I want—all I've *ever* wanted—is for my daughter to be safe and happy. "Meh," she says. "It was last year. We only did it a few times in the cemetery."

We? With whose car? Maybe I don't want to know. "Listen, uh, we've gotta make a stop on the way home, okay?"

"Yeah, whatever."

What I'm about to say must be constructed carefully. I don't want to spook her. "I'm thinking of—" I break off, my mind grappling for the magic phrase that'll unlock her cooperation. "Do you think I need help? Like therapy, I mean? Because of Marina?"

"Probably." She yawns. "Why?"

"When I worked that party last weekend, I met someone—someone who does that kind of thing. She gave me her card."

"Okay."

"She saw me getting stressed. She offered a bunch of free appointments."

"That's weird."

"Not really. It's her business. She helps people."

"Were you drinking?"

"Believe it or not, no," I say. "I was just upset about …" I don't need to finish. She knows what got under my skin.

"It couldn't hurt."

"Will you go with me? I could use the support."

She squints dubiously. "This isn't some lame trick, is it?"

"It's for me," I insist. "For things that've been bugging me since, you know, before you were born."

"You better not be lying."

"I'm not."

"Fine," she says. "I'll go, as long as I don't have other stuff to do. It'd be good if you'd quit drinking."

I thought the same about my mother, but she never made it happen. Now I'm following in her footsteps, to a lesser degree—or so I tell myself.

I think about arguing with Samantha, about defending myself, about bringing up the marijuana baggie in her desk, but it's counterproductive. The promise of driving lessons, combined with the therapy ruse (hell, maybe I *will* spill my guts to the psychiatrist), has gotten me where I want to go for now. Everything else will follow. I just have to be patient.

As we approach New Life—I'd planned on using Scott to tag team Sam about therapy, but the issue is moot—I'm shocked to see that the building is a burnt wreck, a jagged black skeleton looming in the surreal snowfall. "My God."

Sam's head snaps around. "What?"

The Caprice is drifting to the side of the road. I hit the brake and stare past my daughter. "Have you talked to Uncle Scott?" If my brother has followed my sister into the flames, into the grave, my turn can't be far off.

"No."

I haphazardly park the car. "Lock the doors and stay here. I'll be right back." There's a convenience store a hundred yards behind us. Someone there must know what happened.

I jump out of the car and race backward, slipping and sliding as I go. A voice in my head says Scott would've called if he's safe. He must be gravely injured, clinging to life on a ventilator, waiting for a skin graft or whatever else the doctors can do to save him.

The store is rundown and smells of boiled cabbage. "Hey," I say, trying to get the clerk's attention. She's a young girl—late teens, not much older than Samantha—with olive skin, coral lipstick, and a cluster of star tattoos on her temple. "Excuse me. Can I ask you a question?" I insert myself at the counter, in front of a small line of customers. "Do you know what happened to that building"—I gesture at the street—"the one that burned down? Was anyone hurt? Was anyone killed?" My words are coming out in breathless gasps.

Before the girl can answer—*if* she was going to answer, which I somehow doubt (she has an air of defiance about her)—an old man in striped pajamas and moccasin slippers says, "Heard it was electric. Or grease. One of those." He nods in a satisfied way. "Started in the kitchen. Gutted the place real fast."

I can barely stop myself from grabbing the lapels of his pajama top and shaking him. "What about the people? What happened to them?"

"There was an ambulance," he says. "Wasn't anyone in it, though, near as I could tell."

Another man—this one younger, with saggy jeans and a torn camouflage jacket—pipes up. "Some of 'em wasn't there, 'cause they make 'em work and shit."

I'm familiar with the halfway house rules. "My brother lives there. *Lived* there. His name's Scott—Scott Davis. Tall guy. Rugged. Pissed-off look on his face." I scan the crowd for a spark of recognition. "Has anyone seen him?"

Negative responses rumble around me. The clerk cocks her head. "Does he drink Mountain Dew? There's a guy that comes in every night and gets a Mountain Dew and a bag of Fritos—or peanuts. Sometimes he gets those, too."

The Mountain Dew reference throws me—maybe it's a taste my brother picked up in prison—but the Fritos and peanuts I recognize. "That's him."

The clerk: "He was here twenty minutes ago. Bought a lottery ticket and a newspaper."

I lean against the counter and catch my breath. "Did you see where he went?"

"Nope," says the clerk. Then she goes back to ringing up orders like I don't exist.

At least he's alive, I tell myself, pushing away a dark thought: Maybe my brother had a problem at the halfway house that he solved with fire, just like he solved the problem of Marina.

CHAPTER 44
LISA

Once the nanny's on her way to Africa, I turn my energies to more important things, like putting in some face time at work. Even though I've toyed with the idea of giving up my practice, I don't think I could take the boredom, the unyielding restlessness. My mind is a machine, an engine of productivity and accomplishment, churning from task to task with efficient zeal. The two weeks I spent pretending to mourn really took it out of me. I'm in no hurry to repeat the performance.

I park the Hummer at the front door and stride into the office. Jacquelyn has stacked my schedule with the worst of the worst—street urchins with soiled clothes who invariably come up short on cash. I pump twenty through before my stomach starts gnawing. I forgot to eat breakfast, and lunch is about to fall by the wayside, too, unless I send Jacquelyn on a takeout run.

I sift through a stack of menus, searching for something different, something interesting, something that strikes a chord. But it's all the same humdrum mix of sandwich shops and Asian bistros.

Blah.

It occurs to me that Edward and I should buy a restaurant. It'd be fun to have a team of professional chefs at our beck and call, to have our own VIP booth at the hottest new eatery in town.

My reverie is blunted by a knock at my office door. I ignore it. My time is precious. Why doesn't Jacquelyn grasp that?

She knocks again.

I pick up the phone, intending to buzz her desk. But then a third knock brusquely sounds. I've had enough. I march over and whip open the door, my blood curdling with indignation. How dare she impinge on my peace and quiet?

The knocker isn't Jacquelyn. It *is* a woman, though—a familiar one I can't place for a few confounding beats until the detective steps out from behind her.

Detective Luke Jones and his leggy brunette date. Interesting.

"Dr. Hayes?" the woman says, extending a hand. "I'm Detective Mary Samson. I don't think we've been formally introduced." She's traded that bedazzled jumpsuit for a pair of drab olive-green pants and an unfortunate polo shirt over a long-sleeved tee. The faux tan is toned down several notches.

I glance over her shoulder at Jacquelyn, who's wearing an apologetic grimace. Too little, too late. "Oh, hi," I say, keeping things light and casual. "Right, yes. The party." I shake her hand. "Nice to see you again. Come in." To Jacquelyn: "Hold my appointments until we're done."

"Yes, ma'am."

The detectives follow me into the office. Their appearance spells trouble (so much for their questions coming in writing), but I keep my cool. Acting cagey will only heighten their suspicions.

I offer them seats and take my spot behind the desk. "I've been meaning to check in with you about Sophie Gallagher and, well, the awful situation with Dr. Kapoor." I frown and shake my head. Regardless of what I told his widow, I must continue asserting that the doctor was a rapist, a murderer. "But then we had a bit of"—I bite my lip—"a bit of a personal tragedy and ..." They're aware of the miscarriage. It's why they've waited so long to corner me again.

Did Detective Luke bring his horse-toothed partner—in the light of day, she bears a striking resemblance to Seabiscuit—to our anniversary bash for personal reasons, or to give her a glimpse of my private world? What were they hoping to find?

"We were sorry to hear about …" says Detective Luke.

"Thank you. It's been difficult, especially for the children. My husband puts on a good act, a strong front—most men do, don't they?—but he's a wreck underneath. I apologize if he was gruff with you on the telephone. Rest assured, it was nothing to do with you. He's coping in his own way."

"You have a beautiful home," comments Detective Mary—ew, I'll stick to calling her Samson—out of left field.

"I'm glad you enjoyed it." I beam a hostess's smile. "We *do* love having company. It livens up the place. A large home can be quite empty, quite lonely, at times."

Detective Luke uncrosses his legs and crosses them in the other direction. "As you know, we've been trying to get in touch with you to clarify some things we discussed before Dr. Kapoor's untimely death."

Uh-oh. He didn't say suicide. And what's so untimely about a confessed killer taking his own life?

"Mm," I say. "I had assumed as much. I was just too—well, too distraught to speak with anyone. You understand."

"Of course," says Detective Samson. She flips open a pocket notebook and holds a pen at the ready.

Back to Detective Luke. "The thing is, we have new information on the case—the cases. And we'd like to pick your brain. We're still making sense of what you said before, trying to see how it fits into the bigger picture. And certain things aren't adding up."

"Things *I* said?" I chuckle. "I was merely hypothesizing. I hope you didn't take me too seriously. Anything I said wasn't meant as proof of, well, anything, really."

Detective Luke leans forward and trains those luminescent green eyes on me. "When we interview people, we corroborate what they tell us. It lets us know who's being real—who's telling the truth—and who might be putting one over on us."

"That makes sense," I allow.

"But, see, when we checked out what you told us, some of it wasn't holding water."

My face wants to flush. I can feel the blood rising to the surface of my skin. "That's odd," I say, keeping my tone neutral.

"It could be a mistake," says Detective Samson. "Detective Jones might've misunderstood. He could've written something down wrong. So we'd like to double check."

"Whatever you need." I lean back in my chair. "Ask away."

"Let's start with the lead you gave us on the stalker in the Sophie Gallagher case," says Detective Luke.

It's a case now? Officially? "A lead?" I furrow my brow. "I don't remember saying anything about a lead."

Detective Luke: "You said Mrs. Gallagher spoke on the phone to someone about being stalked. The problem is, nobody can verify that—and we've talked to everyone she communicated with in the last six months."

"Maybe they've forgotten," I say. Plain and simple.

Detective Samson's loose curls bounce around her shoulders. "That's possible. Or you could've heard wrong. That would also explain the discrepancy, wouldn't it?"

Does she think I'm brain-dead? As soon as I admit to mishearing, they'll march me down a primrose path to a murder confession. *Multiple* murder confessions. "Mm … no," I insist. "I'm sure I heard correctly. A detail here or there may be askew, but the gist—the essence, the *meat*—of the conversation is accurate." I smile and smooth my skirt across my lap. "It's your job to connect the dots, isn't it? I can't do everything." This may be pushing things too far, but the detectives are wearing on my nerves. What right do they have to pop in here and upend things at a moment's notice?

"What about the truck?" asks Detective Luke, his voice taking on a sharper edge.

I draw a blank. "Pardon me?"

"The red pickup—the one you suggested Mr. Kapoor used to follow Sophie Gallagher."

"Oh. *That* truck. What about it?"

"It was sold months before Sophie Gallagher's death," relays Detective Samson. "The doctor's son didn't own a red pickup—didn't own *any* truck, as a matter of fact—at the time you say..."

I shrug. "I was only trying to help your investigation. If something I said was off base—though I reiterate that I'm reporting events accurately, from my perspective—I apologize. Anyone who knows me knows I'm a people pleaser. My eagerness runs toward overzealousness in matters of law enforcement, I'm afraid. I suppose that's because of my deep admiration for the police department, for the vital public service you provide. Did you know that my husband and I are serious financial boosters of your precinct? We sponsor, gee, *all* of your team-building retreats and a healthy chunk of your ongoing training."

"We're aware of that," says Detective Samson. She scratches a note in her Nancy Drew pad.

Detective Luke redirects us again. "Don't you think it's strange that Mr. Kapoor's suicide note corresponds with many of the questionable details you've provided?"

"Does it? I had no idea." I gaze pensively over their heads. "Maybe I'm on to something. I'm very perceptive, very adroit at judging people, judging situations. You'd do well to hire me as a consultant."

The detectives smirk. At least they're having fun. I'm a good time; ask anyone.

"Let's move on," says Detective Samson, "to Mr. Kapoor's death. Are you aware of anyone who would've wished him harm?"

"Harm?" I frown. "No. Until this—well, this horrible mess with Mrs. Gallagher—I considered him a lovely older gentleman. He was an immigrant, a smart, talented one who rose up from nothing to become a successful, respected doctor. No one would've hurt him. Not that I know of, anyway."

"That's not what the medical examiner says." Detective Samson tilts her head and studies my reaction.

I compose myself before responding. They won't rattle me, as hard as they may try. "I don't understand. My secretary said he hanged himself. I was in the hospital at the time, so I only heard secondhand. I was pretty shaken up, as you'd expect—about the baby and everything else."

Detective Luke clears his throat. "For now, the manner of death has been ruled undetermined, but it's not a suicide."

My mind is spinning. "Really? It sounded pretty conclusive—pretty obvious—that he'd killed himself, according to my secretary's account, that is."

"Nope," says Detective Samson. "The ligature marks—the lines the rope made on his neck—are horizontal. And there's two of 'em."

"So," I say.

Detective Luke finishes the thought: "In a hanging, the ligature mark is an inverted V. And there's only one. See, people don't generally hang themselves twice."

"But they could," I reason, "if the first attempt fails."

"Possibly," allows Detective Luke, "but we've also got substantial neck trauma. That's a hallmark of strangulation."

I screw up my face. "Why are you telling me this? Shouldn't this be confidential? What if this information gets out? What if everyone in town is looking over their shoulder for a crazed strangler?" The idea is comical. I have to clamp my lips together to keep from grinning.

"All the better," says Detective Samson. "We're not releasing these details per se, but anything that brings us closer to a resolution—or, well, two resolutions, since the Gallagher case is still open."

The conversation has assumed a circular logic that may work in my favor. "But if Dr. Kapoor was murdered"—I shudder to convey my discomfort—"then he didn't write the note confessing to hurting Sophie, right?"

"That's our working theory," admits Detective Samson. "We believe Mr. Kapoor was murdered and the note was a red herring, an amateur attempt to throw us off course."

I wonder aloud, "Who would do such a thing?" And to myself: Who is she calling amateur? My brain could tie hers in knots while dancing a jig.

"We'd very much like the answer to that question," says Detective Luke. "And when the DNA from the rope comes back, we'll have it. In the meantime"—he pulls a business card from his shirt pocket and slides it across the desk—"if you remember anything that could assist us, please give us a call."

"There was DNA on the rope?" I ask. "Surely it belongs to the doctor. No one would be stupid enough to do something like that and leave the evidence behind." It's not mine; I wore gloves.

Detective Samson shakes her head. "You'd think so, but you'd be wrong." Her statement hangs in the air, bringing the conversation to an end.

As I walk them out, I make a fuss about changing the locks—there's a killer on the loose, after all—and installing a state-of-the-art security system. Next time they visit, it'll be harder getting into my office than through the TSA line at Philly International.

Once the detectives are gone, I scrawl the scripts for the afternoon swarm—Jacquelyn can dispense them and collect the cash—before locking my office and calling it a day.

My head is buzzing. I drive in tight, overlapping circles, too agitated to go home. A fast-food burger and a pile of fries take the edge off, but only a shopping blitz will clear the nuisance of these investigations from my mind.

By the time I exit the mall with an armload of designer clothes—skirts and blouses and undergarments I didn't bother trying on and don't need in the least—the icy sun is sinking below the horizon.

I'm stuck in traffic at the sixth red light in a row when the sign for Raymore's Service Station pops up in my peripheral vision. I can't say I've noticed the place before—Edward and I have our vehicles serviced at the Jaguar dealership, where you could eat a five-course meal off the gleaming showroom floor—but the flickering neon wrench grabs my eye, jolts my memory. I was supposed to dole out a little street justice to a know-it-all mechanic named Leland or Larry.

The opportunity is irresistible. I cut down a side street and park by a dilapidated fence. The houses behind the service station are dark. I stretch mightily—the Hummer is sized for the Incredible Hulk, not a petite woman like me—for the glove box and retrieve the multitool Edward installs in every vehicle we own. I flick open its sharpest, sleekest knife and lock it in place.

The shadowy parking lot is good cover. I slip around the back of the station to what must be the employee parking area. I feel the hoods of the two vehicles there—a dark-colored SUV and a white sedan. They're both cold.

It's a coin toss as to which car is Leland's. Maybe neither. But I've come this far. I'm going to extract my pound of flesh from someone. It hardly matters whom.

I crouch down by the sedan (the joker who advised my patient to get off drugs would drive such a sensible wreck) and, with steady pressure, carve a groove into the surface of the front passenger tire. I wiggle the knife into the groove and rock it back and forth until the tension releases.

One down, seven to go.

In a matter of minutes, I'm climbing back into the Hummer with renewed buoyancy and a clear mind. Perhaps I'll cross-stitch a pillow with the maxim REVENGE IS A TONIC FOR THE SOUL. It would go nicely with that tufted cobalt-blue sofa.

CHAPTER 45
ROBIN

The day after the fire, my brother resurfaces with a phone call. He's staying at a rundown motel with another parolee while the government scrambles to rehome New Life's displaced residents. The news is relieving to a point. I'm glad that Scott—my only connection to the past, to Marina, to the family we once had—is alive, but what if he started the fire? What if he took our sister to that party years ago and got her drunk? What if he raped her? What if he did it over and over again and then killed her to cover up his crimes? Wouldn't I have noticed more than his peeking at her in the shower?

I shake my head, trying to clear it. Too much speculation has my mind in knots. But what choice do I have? My sister's fate is as much a mystery now as the day she died. If only I could make sense of things, maybe there would be peace for Sam and me—and justice for Marina. It's been far too long.

I'm outside the high school, sitting in my car, shivering as I wait for Sam to thread her way through the throng of bodies. She doesn't know our first therapy appointment is today. When I called the number on that card, the receptionist put me through to the doctor, who remembered me and offered an impromptu visit, a get-to-know-you session to put me and my daughter at ease.

Samantha is a straggler, emerging only when the buses are gone and her friends are off in different directions. "Took you long enough," I snipe as she falls into the passenger seat.

"I was returning stuff to the library." She yanks on the seatbelt, but it just hangs there, limp and unresponsive. "This won't go back in," she says with a huff. "What do you want me to do?"

One thing I've done right is train my daughter to always wear a seatbelt. I'm caught for a moment, but then ... "It's your lucky day." I motion between us. "Switch."

"You want *me* to drive?"

"Uh-huh." I sling open the door. "And hurry up. It's freezing."

I don't have to tell her twice. She swaps places with me and buckles up behind the wheel. We buzz through a pre-trip checklist and I guide her out onto the road. Letting her drive is a risk—she won't be eligible for a permit for months—but I figure it's the lesser of two evils. We're not going far and this peace offering should get her in my corner for therapy.

"Which lane?" Samantha asks, her voice fluttering as we approach a busy intersection.

"Check your mirror—your side mirror, over here—and move to the right. We're turning onto Sycamore." She must be overwhelmed. She hasn't asked where we're going. "Good," I say as she eases up to the stop line. "Nice and smooth. And you remembered your blinker."

My daughter continues impressing me with her agility, her quick thinking, her instincts for evading danger. Only once am I afraid, when a jackass in a bright yellow sports car rockets around us, making the Caprice shake. But even then, I trust my daughter. It's the world I don't trust.

We're in a tree-lined historic district with elegantly restored homes and businesses, which is no surprise after seeing the therapist's estate. I start scanning for building numbers in search of 1304 Chestnut Street.

The even numbers are on the opposite side of the road: 1286, 1290, 1294....

I tell Sam to slow down, signal left, and wait for oncoming traffic to pass. The driveway is narrow. She misjudges the angle, barely clearing the curb and bouncing up over the grass.

The driveway opens up to an ample parking lot that runs alongside the building and continues out back. "Where are we going?" Sam asks. We're running out of road.

"The counselor. Park anywhere." There are plenty of open spaces. In fact, the place looks deserted. I begin to wonder if I've mistaken the appointment time.

Sam noses the Caprice into a spot. Without shifting out of gear, she takes her foot off the brake. We jump forward. She catches herself and corrects the error. "How'd I do?" she asks with a nervous grin.

"Just about perfect." I give her a thumbs-up. "Maybe you can drive home, too."

"Definitely."

"C'mon," I say. "We're running late."

"I've got tons of homework. I'll stay here."

"In this icebox?" I shake my head. "You can do it inside."

Grudgingly, she collects her backpack and follows me. The building is huge and boxy—a Colonial mansion of sorts. I imagine politicians and businessmen of the past crafting fireside deals over snifters of brandy.

As we enter, we're welcomed by a warm, wallpapered foyer and a softly sloping staircase with a ruby-red carpet runner. On the wall above a console table is a directory of businesses. I drag a finger down the list. Dr. L.A. Hayes is in Suite 1 on the first floor. "This way," I say.

Before we get three steps off, the doctor appears in the hall, cementing the impression that the building is deserted. Otherwise, how would she have heard us coming?

"This place is creepy," Sam says under her breath.

The doctor has traded her glittering gown for a fitted gray skirt suit and a pair of black-framed glasses. Her sandy blond hair is bunched in a knot at the nape of her neck. She beams a charming smile and waves us through an empty reception area to a comfortable office. "Please, sit down," she says, when Samantha and I mill about uncertainly.

I feel self-conscious. The doctor is so beautiful, so gracious, so accomplished—everything I might've been if things had turned out differently, if some sick bastard hadn't stolen my sister and sent my family into a tailspin.

I chuckle inwardly. If the doctor could read my thoughts, we'd have a perfect place to start picking at the wounds of my psyche. Then again, we're here for Samantha. I'm an afterthought.

Dr. Hayes spends a few minutes explaining the ground rules of therapy. Sam and I can share whatever we want, and everything is confidential. "Is that acceptable?" she asks. I nod and Samantha shrugs. "Let's begin, then."

The doctor asks a number of questions about how we're eating and sleeping, our energy levels, any unusual stress. She wants to know how we spend our days, what we think about when we're alone, whether we're happy. She has a checklist of statements—over the past two weeks, how often have you been bothered by any of the following problems: little interest or pleasure in doing things; trouble concentrating on things, such as reading the newspaper or watching television, etcetera—that Sam and I are asked to rate on a scale from not at all to nearly every day.

My daughter cooperates in a superficial way, circling not at all for every statement, unwilling to admit the slightest distress. I, on the other hand, toggle between the middle-of-the-road answers—several days and more than one-half the days—reserving my biggest admission, my lone nearly every day response, for feeling bad about yourself or that you are a failure or have let yourself or your family down. The doctor should give me a fat red marker so I can underline the statement and enclose it in a big bull's-eye.

After the preliminaries are done, we move on to the talking portion of the visit. "All right, Robin," Dr. Hayes says, scanning my responses. "Let's start with you. Samantha can jump in anytime, if she has information to add or concerns we should address."

I swallow around a lump in my throat. "Sure." I'm amazed that this rich, powerful woman would spend her time on me or my daughter in the first place. She must have a heart of gold.

"I find it helpful to start at the core of a problem and work outward," the doctor says. "This gives a clearer picture of what's going on. So I'd like you to think about your troubles, your challenges, and whittle them down, as best you can, to their root causes.

"For example, if you fight too much with your husband, ask yourself why that is. If the answer is that you're stressed at work, ask yourself why *that* is. If the answer is that you took a position that's a mismatch for your skills, ask yourself why *that* is. You may find that you're fighting with your husband because a bully pushed you down in second grade."

"I don't have a husband," I point out. "But I see what you mean." The fact is, I don't have to think about the source of my problems. They can all be traced to Marina's murder, to her killer going unpunished, to no one caring—no one putting forth effort—to get justice for the fun, beautiful, witty girl who was a part of me. When Marina was so easily thrown aside, so easily forgotten, the world became an unpredictable place, a place of darkness and peril, a place that would do everything in its power to grind me up like it had her.

I admit to heavy drinking, job hopping, sleeping with vague, faceless men (this is too much for Samantha; she excuses herself for the waiting room). But bringing up Marina is beyond my grasp.

Dr. Hayes has been listening intently, nodding sympathetically, smiling kindly. Every now and then, she says "follow that" or "let's go back to [fill in the blank]." She's easy to talk to, like an old friend, and I find myself opening up to her, letting her see more of me than anyone has in a long time. Exposing the hidden parts of myself, the fractured pieces of the whole, is exhilarating.

Maybe I *will* tell her about Marina, assuming I can find the words to do my sister's memory justice.

When I come up for air, the doctor reaches across the desk and pats my hand. "Great start," she says, eyeing the clock. "We'll pick up from here next time."

I'm immediately deflated. Her attention, her pinpoint focus, has sent a burst of energy racing through me. I tip my head at the door. "I came for Samantha, really. She's a good girl, but she's gotten mixed up with some bad people. A boyfriend, maybe. And drugs."

"That *is* concerning. I should speak to her privately. Can you come tomorrow at four?"

"Sure." What else do I have to do besides hunt for a job?

She pushes her chair back and stands up. "I look forward to it." As I rise to my feet, she slips around the desk and wraps me in a hug. "Don't worry," she breathes in my ear. "I'm with you now. Everything will be all right."

CHAPTER 46
LISA

My first session with the dead girl's sister is an unqualified success. It's eerie seeing her all grown up. It makes me think of what that girl was destined to become, of the dingy road that lay ahead of her. I'm more convinced now than ever that I did her a favor.

In the hour Robin spent pouring her heart out, not a spark of recognition crossed her face. She hasn't the faintest clue what I've done, who I am, how I've shaped her, my impact.

In a way, it's a disappointment. A snub. After the murder, I kept my feelers out, my ear to the pavement. I'd moved on to bigger and better things, but every once in a while, I dipped a toe back in that foul pond. I heard through the grapevine that as soon as Robin could break away, she was in the streets, flipping over rocks, charging down blind alleys, poking sticks in crevices and watching what slithered out. She was convinced that someone had murdered her sister, a conclusion not even the police had drawn, and wasn't going to let the idea go without a fight. Of course, she found nothing—I covered my tracks well—and eventually gave up.

It's tragic, if you think about it. Or maybe *pitiable* is a better word.

I've traveled from the garage to the kitchen without remembering the walk. Ricki is buffing the sink with a soft cloth. A jar of wax sits on the counter nearby. "What's this?" I ask, surprising her. On the edge of the island is a cardboard box, its flaps ripped jaggedly open.

She drops the cloth in the basin and rushes over, grabbing the box with cotton-gloved hands. "Sorry. I was going to get rid of those." She takes a couple of steps away from me. "I'll be right back."

If she's having packages shipped here, it's fine. But they're subject to search and, if the situation warrants, seizure. I let things get away from me with Ashley. It's time to tighten the ship. "Hold on." Ricki is taller than me. I lift onto the balls of my feet, pull back one of the flaps, and peer into the box. Something dark and glossy—a stack of catalogs, perhaps—reflects back at me. I reach in and peel the top one off the stack.

The Christmas calendars from the ob-gyn's office. I'd forgotten about them completely. "Who told you to throw these away?" I ask, transfixed by the image of Edward and me, surrounded by an explosion of snowflakes and poinsettia leaves.

"I just thought ... Mr. Hayes seemed ..."

"Edward's seen these? When did he get home?" I wasn't expecting him until tomorrow.

"A couple of hours ago? I was at the school, picking up—"

"Forget about that. Where's he gone?"

"He didn't say."

I flap the calendar around. "But he said to throw these out?"

"He seemed upset. I thought I should get rid of them."

I don't pay her to think. Still, she's on the right track. Edward's barely over the miscarriage. He's fragile. This sort of thing could jar him into an emotional funk. "Good idea." I jam the calendar back in the box and give it a little tap. "*Sayonara.*"

Ricki disappears. I settle at the island, kick off my shoes, and rub my feet on a fluted column at the edge of the cabinets. I'm pondering the cappuccino machine—usually my energy is unbound, but this afternoon I feel the beginning of a drag—when footsteps pound down the hall. I assume Ricki's forgotten something, but then ...

Edward: "Have you seen the spare keys to the Mercedes?" His voice is brimming with frustration.

I give him a once-over. He's tense, disturbed. Maybe because of the calendars—they've elicited more of a reaction than I predicted—or the loss of his little plaything, Ashley. When I texted him the news about her (she was in the air over the dark Atlantic by then), his response was curt, stunted, the kind of emotional depth one might display over ruining one's third-best pair of pants. But maybe reading her goodbye note for himself had more of a provocative effect. "No," I say to his flustered inquiry. "Why?"

"The Jag's wrecked." He runs a hand through his hair. "I need something else to drive, and since—" The Mercedes used to be his, seven or eight years ago, when the twins were in diapers.

I leap to my feet and throw myself at him. "What happened? Are you all right?" I caress his rough beard—he's managed a record amount of growth since my star turn at the club—and bury my face in his neck.

He pushes me away. "I was on the phone. A kid ran out from behind a car."

Jesus, no. If he wiped out a cherub with missing front teeth and a crooked, kitchen-chair haircut, the media will be salivating. We won't get a moment's peace, and, worse, the authorities will be forced to press charges. When the public finds out we're rich, they'll demand blind justice. Edward could go to jail. His empire could crumble. "You didn't hit him, did you? You didn't *hurt* him."

"Her. It was a girl." He starts rummaging through drawers. "Where the *fuck* are the keys?"

"Edward?"

He stops and stares at me. "What?"

I pull out a stool. "Sit down. I'll get you a gin and tonic."

He takes my advice. While I mix the drink, I press him on the accident. It turns out that he hit one of those ugly blue postal boxes, not a small child. (The child scooted out of the way in the nick of time.) The Jag has premium safety features, so he walked away unscathed. The same cannot be said of his luxury automobile.

"Feeling better?" I ask, once he's drained the glass and his eyes are glazing over. I dig my thumbs into his shoulders, which are solid bricks, and squeeze along the muscles, hoping to relax him, to distract him.

"It was a shit day," he mutters.

"How was the conference?" His performance there may portend our finances for the immediate future.

A groan. "Also shit. I'm going to bed." He stands up suddenly, knocking the gin glass off the island. It smashes against the floor, spraying crystal shards everywhere.

"Wait," I say, tugging his arm. I can't let him curl up and ruminate over the miscarriage, his cratered speech, his vanished blond piece of ass.

Barefoot, I try stepping over the scattering of glass, but a jolt of pain says I've miscalculated. I ignore my throbbing heel and keep on. "I missed you." A sexy pout. "Come upstairs." Without asking, I know he was planning to retreat to the basement. "We'll reconnect." When this isn't enough, I sweeten the pot. "I'm ovulating. I took a test this morning. Don't you want…?"

The tension melts from his face. "Of course I do."

Fifteen minutes later, I'm hot and gooey inside with his seed. As advertised, he drifts off for a nap, during which I dig the splinters out of my foot with a nail file and dab the splotches of blood off the comforter with a soapy, wet cloth. A scalding soak in our jetted bathtub will fry a few of my husband's little swimmers. (The ovulation teaser was a lie, but one can never be too careful.) After I'm clean and refreshed, I slip back into bed and snuggle up to his chest.

"Edward," I whisper, trying to jostle him awake. He gurgles incoherently. "Sweetie, wake up. I need to talk to you."

He rustles closer and threads his fingers into my hair. His eyes ease open. He kisses me on the mouth. "Go on," he says, trailing a thumb across my ear.

"Remember that detective? The one who was giving me a hard time? The one who kept calling?"

"Mm."

"He turned up at my office again with a partner. They were very rude, very abrupt. They seem to think I know something about that patient of mine who died, the woman who went off the road. But I don't—*I don't know a thing!*"

"So tell them that."

"I did, but they won't listen. And now they're asking about my tenant who killed himself."

Edward's confused. With the swirl of grief over the miscarriage, multiple work trips, and the anniversary party, Dr. Kapoor's fate has escaped him. I fill in the gaps of his knowledge with the story I've fed the police. "Ah," he says, "I see. What would you like me to do about it?"

"Make them go away." I dance my fingers around his nipples. "They're barking up the wrong tree. Everything was explained in the doctor's suicide note. You and the chief went on that fishing trip to Key West last year, didn't you? Where you caught the hammerhead sharks? Just explain to him …"

"Will do. Anything else, my love?"

I think about giving him specific instructions, but that might be too suspicious. He should approach the chief on his own terms, in his own words. "No," I say. "You're an angel. This will make things so much easier."

"Consider it done," he says. And I do.

CHAPTER 47
ROBIN

Having nothing to do all day is growing old quick. Despite my laundry list of flaws, I've always worked—until now, until this goddamn recession, until the trouble with Samantha, until my obsession with Marina's murder went off a cliff. I've always taken care of us. But what if I can't anymore? What if none of the jobs I've applied for pan out?

Suddenly, I know how my sister felt when she ran away from home: terrified and alone and desperate, willing to do anything, including sell herself, for a hot meal and a warm bed. I doubt she got either very often. And then she was dead.

I'm scrubbing the inside of the refrigerator with an old towel when an unexpected knock makes me bolt upright, smashing my head on the open freezer door. I feel around in my hair for blood but find none.

"Hang on!" I yell, assuming Lewis is dropping by to chat. Since he got back from Texas, he's asked my advice on everything from soap scents to TV programs, in an effort to make Wanda feel at home. Which would be sweet on its own, but it's even more poignant because Wanda has cancer. (That flowing black hair behind the wheel of Lewis's van was a wig.)

I'm rubbing my head when I open the door. "Nate?"

"Don't sound so excited. Can I come in?" He jostles around an armload of shopping bags. "These are getting heavy."

"Um …" I shrug. "Sure."

He ducks around me and goes inside, depositing the bags on the kitchen table. "Looks like I'm just in time," he says, eyeing the bare fridge.

"What're you doing here?"

He starts taking items out of the bags—bread and milk and ice cream and a bunch of other stuff I didn't ask for. "There's a water main break at the college. They canceled classes. I figured you'd be home."

I close the refrigerator, so he'll stop pitying me. "Oh."

"Are you hungry?"

"No," I say, and it's only a small lie. My body is getting used to starvation. What little food I've been able to keep in the house goes to Sam. I'm thinking of selling my blood if anyone's willing to take it, but I'm not sure it pays enough to justify the drive.

Nate frowns. "You ate lunch already?"

"A banana," I say, "and some cereal." It's a stupid response, but the only one I can come up with on the spot.

"What kind of cereal?"

"Huh?"

"I didn't think you liked cereal."

"How would you know?"

He winces. "Never mind." Without asking, he puts away the groceries. I'm both thankful and insulted. The food will help Sam over this rough spot, but I'm not the charity case he's making me out to be. I'll find a way, no matter how gruesome, to keep my daughter safe and fed.

It creeps up on me that I'm covered in grime. I excuse myself for a shower, knowing Nate will be fantasizing about me—wanting me—while I'm gone. He may be a soft touch, but his sex drive is every bit that of a twenty-eight-year-old.

I make the water as hot as I dare, considering it's winter and our fuel supplies are low. The water stings my face like a thousand tiny bees. I feel myself starting to cry—not much, not dramatically, just enough to know it's happening. Usually I fight the tears, but this time

I give in. I want to get it out of my system here, alone, where no one can see. Especially Nate.

I towel off and slip into a fresh tank top and underwear. I'd planned on wearing the jeans again, but upon further inspection, they're too far gone. I'll have to find something more presentable, since Sam and I have our second therapy appointment today.

Nate catches me in the hallway. He leans against the wall and stares. Goose bumps prickle my skin. I feel a rush of unsteadiness, a deep, insistent craving for beer, liquor, cough syrup—anything that'll blur the rough edges of my life.

"These are dirty." I hold up the jeans. "Be right back."

He follows me to the bedroom. From the corner of my eye, I see him in the mirror, watching me brush the tangles out of my hair. As I'm bending down to open a drawer—my rotation of jeans is exhausted; I'm going to have to dig around for a pair of cargo pants—he says, "You're devastating."

And there's the rub: Nate's a nice guy, a charmer, good-looking (glasses and all), and way out of my league. He should be sampling the twenty-year-old coeds with wide eyes and perfect, glowing skin, not hanging around a single mom who can't get her shit together.

He kisses me, and it's all over. My brain won't fire with his tongue in my mouth. We stumble to bed and soon our clothes are entwined on the floor. I'm expecting the same congenial, athletic, goal-driven exchange we normally have, the friends-with-benefits version (this is our pattern, even when our relationship is on solid ground), which is fine by me. In fact, I prefer the cool, detached version of things, the kind of encounter I might get by hiring a conscientious gigolo.

But this time is different. This time Nate's an explorer and I'm the landscape. He's on me—*in* me—with such intensity, such singularity, that I forget to breathe.

In the aftermath, as we lie there fading in and out, curled against each other like sleepy cats, I realize that this is it: making love, being in love, being owned by—owning—another person.

My stomach heaves. I should've cut Nate loose long ago. I'm not built for picket fences and happily ever afters.

I leave him in bed—he just yawns and rolls over, even though it's the middle of the day—and boil water on the stove for coffee. With the steaming mug cradled in my hands, I slip outside and crunch across the frozen lawn, not sure where I'm headed. All I know is that I must put some distance between me and the sleeping man in my bed.

I pass Lewis's house—he and Wanda have joined a gym and aren't home—and head up the block. The air is icy, sharp. It weighs on my lungs, needles them.

At the stop sign, I have choices: left, right, or straight ahead. Turning back is not an option.

For no particular reason, I take the left and, when the opportunity arises, another—and another and another (the coffee's gone somewhere between the second and third and I'm just toting around the empty mug) until my house comes back into view.

I have to end things with Nate. He's getting too close, insinuating himself where he doesn't belong. It's only a matter of time before he's consumed by my demons.

I won't let that happen.

He's awake, sitting at the kitchen table and reading a newspaper, when I return. I wish for a fleeting moment that things could be different; that I could abandon Marina in the past; that I could get my teaching certificate reinstated (completing a couple of courses should get me over this hump); that Sam, Nate, and I could move somewhere warm and sunny—near an ocean, maybe—and live our lives in tranquil harmony.

Before I get carried away, I slam shut the hopeful window in my mind and brace for a fight. My usual breakup strategy—ignoring a guy until he gets sick of waiting—isn't going to work. Nate's too patient, too understanding. I'm going to have to hurt him.

When I see what he's doing with the newspaper—combing the sparse help wanted ads on my behalf—the fight becomes easier to pick.

He shows me the circled opportunities—he's shooting low: retail, childcare, food service—and I turn immediately cold, distant. I tell him to mind his own business. He's no one. My daughter and I aren't his concern.

I go on, ridiculing his generosity. I say he's a sucker for expending so much time and money on me when I don't return the favor. I call him a martyr. I say he gets off on rescuing hard-luck cases. I say real women—strong, successful ones with standards—intimidate him. I say he's a scared little boy inside. I say his father's right: He needs to grow a pair and stand up for himself. I say I could never love someone as weak and pathetic as him. I make fun of his measly paycheck; his squatting in his parents' condo; his economy car; his bleeding-heart ideals.

First he's confused and then injured. Slowly, he boils to anger. When he comes back at me with some cutting comments of his own—about my self-centeredness, my drinking, my being a quitter (he's still too good-natured to go after my relationship with Sam, even though he knows it's my soft spot)—I feel I've succeeded in pushing him away.

I down a glass of water with shaking hands and wait for him to leave. On the way out, he gets in one last jab, telling me he asked me out as a joke, a dare. He thought he'd try his hand at slumming. This is a lie—his strangled voice gives it away—but he has to save face somehow.

I don't say another word. I just let him go.

CHAPTER 48
LISA

With Edward's pledge to quash the murder investigations in hand, I sail ahead with my therapy practice, particularly the sessions with Robin Davis and her wayward daughter. Now that Robin and I have crossed paths, I must glean what she knows—if she's on to me, if she's smart enough to piece together the puzzle—before deciding whether to kill her, too. No one, not even the original dead girl's sister, is going to topple me from my throne. I've worked too hard getting here.

It's ten after four and Robin has yet to arrive. I tell Jacquelyn she's free to go, but she just laughs and keeps digging through a file box, sorting papers and stapling them for an unknown fate.

As long as she stays out of my way, she can start a three-ring circus for all I care.

At four fifteen, scuffing feet announce Robin's arrival. I pop out to the waiting room. "Come in," I say, waving her and the daughter along.

They take the same seats as before: Robin facing me on the right and Samantha on the left. I scan their appearances, noting puffy rings around Robin's eyes, as if she's been crying. Samantha reminds me of myself at her age: a radiant beauty, barely containable by human flesh.

"Sorry we're late," says Robin.

I brush off her apology and fix my gaze on Samantha. "I thought we could have a private chat today. I got to know your mother pretty well last time, but I'd like to hear things from your perspective."

"She can stay," says Samantha. "It's about her, anyways, right?"

I shoot Robin a cautionary glance. "I think your mother agrees that—"

"Yes," says Robin. She pats Samantha's knee. "I'll wait outside. I've gotta check my phone, anyway, in case any job offers have come in. Say whatever you want to Dr. Hayes. I won't be mad."

Samantha chuckles. "Yeah, sure."

Robin exits, shutting the door behind her. I give Samantha a moment to size me up. "It's good to see you again. How are you feeling about being here?" I ask. "About telling me what's going on at home?"

"Weird. I mean, no offense or whatever, but I don't know you from anyone."

I smile inside. She's my kind of girl: fiery, self-possessed. "That's true. But we have to start somewhere. We can get to know each other a bit today. I'll go first."

"You want to tell me your life story?"

I shake my head. "No. Just a few basic details, so you'll know who you're talking to. That was your complaint, wasn't it? That I'm a stranger?" If she only knew how pivotal I was—I am—to her existence. Samantha wouldn't be here, wouldn't be alive on the planet, if I hadn't shattered her mother's world. I imagine that a distraught Robin was whoring herself around the county at a tender age. Frankly, I'm shocked she only has one kid.

Samantha tucks her legs underneath her. "I guess."

Instead of reciting a condensed biography (I can't reveal anything of consequence, anyway), I wow her with tales of Edward's and my fantastic wealth. She's particularly enamored of our exotic excursions (Belize, Montenegro, French Polynesia), our indoor swimming pool, and our rotating fleet of luxury cars (the amethyst Porsche I jettisoned for the Hummer has her drooling). I paint my husband as a sexy genius, our daughters as well-adjusted achievers, and the family dog as the epitome of his breed. By the time I'm done, she's breathless with admiration. I'm someone to be revered, emulated, trusted with her deepest secrets, her darkest fears.

"Your turn," I say. "How would you describe yourself, your life, your relationship with your mother, your father?"

"My father's dead," she says. "Brain tumor."

Ooh, we're getting to the prickly stuff right off the bat. Fantastic. "How old were you when he died?"

"Don't know. Never met the guy."

I pick through my mind for an appropriate response. From my training, I know I should empathize, but it's unnatural. "That must be painful," I respond, sensing I've hit the mark.

"Not really. It's hard to miss someone you never knew. I haven't even seen a picture."

"Why's that?" I ask, genuinely intrigued. What reason could Robin have for withholding a photograph of the girl's father?

"I thought we were talking about her drinking. She's an alcoholic, you know. Every time we get, like, five bucks, she's at the store buying beer or wine or whatever's cheap."

"She's had a hard life, from what I've heard."

"*She's* had a hard life? What about me? It hasn't been Disneyland, growing up in that broken-down house with all those ghosts. My grandfather killed himself in the living room. Did she tell you that?"

This catches me off guard. Who knew my effect, my taking that girl, would reach so dramatically into another generation? The idea pleases me. "She hasn't said anything about it," I admit. "But we've only had the one session." For now, I'll be a shoulder to cry on for both Robin and Samantha. But something tells me that my best interests lie in pitting them against each other.

"You must know his name," I say, pulling at the missing-father thread. There's something fishy about Robin's secretiveness. I can feel it.

"Donald Johnson," she says. "Or Don—I think they called him that. He worked for the government."

"Don Johnson? From *Miami Vice*?"

Samantha's face puckers. "What's *Miami Vice*?"

I fight a grin. "Just an old TV show. I'm sure it's a coincidence. Do you have your birth certificate? You could check it. It's not the same person, obviously, but it would be good to be more certain about things. A sense of self is hard to form, hard to maintain, if you don't know your history, if you don't know where you come from."

"I'm fine."

I hold up my hands. "Okay. I'm only trying to help you, to help your mother."

"You know what her biggest problem is?"

I shake my head. "Tell me." And make it juicy. Something I can use against her.

"She's an emotional wreck—like she gets these jobs and can't keep them, because her mind's all jumbled up with stuff from the past, stuff about my dead aunt and my screwed-up grandparents and my uncle that just got out of jail."

I'd nearly forgotten about the brother. He wasn't around much in 1985. I can't recall if he even attended the girl's funeral. But he must've, right? "This uncle," I say, "is he involved in your life?"

"Sort of."

"Do you see him regularly?"

I've caught her in the middle of a yawn. She finishes and then blinks numerous times. "Not really. He's on probation. He can only leave the halfway house at certain times."

"What did he do, if you don't mind my asking?"

"For a crime, you mean?"

I nod.

"Drunk driving. He killed someone."

"When was this?" Inwardly, I chastise myself for not keeping better tabs on those I left flailing in my wake. Half the fun of getting away with something is sitting back and marveling at the aftershocks.

"I don't know. I was a little kid. I barely remember—"

"Of course," I say, backing away from this line of inquiry. It's enough to know that Scott Davis is as ruined as his pitiful sister. This girl, though, this Samantha ... there's hope for her yet. Maybe I'll take her under my wing. I could use a pet project. And once I get Robin under my roof, under my watchful eye, Samantha will be easy prey.

I steer the conversation to more mundane territory: school, work—she's an enterprising little thing, running an internet business at her age (more proof we're cut from the same cloth)—boys.

She's reluctant to tell me about her love life. She's not convinced I won't betray her. But I break her resolve by inventing a bad-boy college boyfriend, a nameless guy who dealt in drugs and danger (in reality, *I've* been the one to reckon with in my relationships). I played the Virginia Hill to his Bugsy Siegel—or so I tell her. We got in lots of thrilling scrapes, flirting with disaster at every turn, but always came out on top, always won.

Samantha's compelled to uphold her end of the conversation. She divulges a taboo relationship of her own—a stoner kid who plays the drums and writes sappy poetry. He treats her like a queen. *His* queen. They've been having sex for eight months, at the apartment he shares with an older sister (they're orphans of some sort) and, on a number of occasions, in her own bed.

She cuts a glance at the door. "You can't say anything, right?"

I make a sweeping cross over my heart. "Therapist's honor."

When our time is up, I invite Robin back in and pop the question: Would she be interested in a job as the nanny to a delightful pair of twin girls? It pays six thousand dollars a month—we were only paying Ashley four, but I'm sweetening the pot—and includes a private suite in our mansion.

"Me?" she says.

"And Samantha. Our previous nanny left abruptly for a religious mission. We're having a devil of a time replacing her. She was just so wonderful." I sigh. "So? What do you say? You could start as soon as tomorrow—we'd have a mover come for your things—or as late as next week. Whatever works."

Samantha's eyes dance with dollar signs. "Mom," she pleads, "answer her."

Just when I'm convinced the poor thing is tongue-tied: "Can I think about it?"

What is there to think about? The opportunity of a lifetime just dropped in her lap. Some people ... "Sleep on it," I say. "Talk it over. But get back to me as soon as possible. We're still interviewing candidates." I flash a terse smile.

"Thanks for the offer. I just have to figure out a few things before—"

"By all means," I say. We schedule another session for the next day and conclude.

CHAPTER 49
ROBIN

Our house has never been cleaner—I've got nothing better to do with my nervous energy than spruce things up around here—and I still can't decide whether to accept Dr. Hayes's offer. Like Nate's help, the opportunity seems like a pity handout. The doctor doesn't know me well enough to let me look after her kids. Why would she trust me, anyway, after what I've revealed about myself? After what Sam has probably said about me behind my back?

But the money ...

Six thousand dollars a month would add up fast. Maybe I could just fill in until the doctor finds a replacement. I'm not even sure what a nanny does, especially in a gated compound like that. But it can't be harder than wrangling a classroom full of third graders, can it? In fact, the nanny gig might be good practice, might help me test the teaching waters again. Smart, privileged girls like those must have heaps of challenging homework. A letter of recommendation from a powerful, well-connected doctor couldn't hurt, either.

Even if I wanted to accept the job, moving out of this house is a sticking point for Sam and me. My daughter doesn't want to give up her friends (the twenty-minute drive seems like a world away at her age), and I'm afraid that our home, such as it is, will be overrun by vandals the moment we turn our backs. Too bad Scott's holed up in that scuzzy motel. He'd be the perfect one to stand guard over the ruins of our childhood.

Fate ends up deciding for us. When I go down to the basement to switch over the laundry, Sam's pajama bottoms and graphic tees, which should be wrung out, are floating in a tub of cold water. I figure the decrepit old washer has finally died, but when I pull the light-bulb chain to investigate further, the dusty globe of glass over the laundry area doesn't so much as flicker.

A circuit breaker must've tripped.

The breaker box is on the other side of the basement, behind a mountain of Christmas decorations (we haven't used these since my mother died) and rusty lawn furniture. Luckily it's the kind of bright day that multiplies every particle of light a thousandfold, or I wouldn't be able to cut a path to the electrical panel. As it is, I stub my toe on the leg of a cast-iron chair and scrape my arm on the cracked lid of a plastic tote. The wound feels like it's drawn blood, but not enough to worry about.

Once upon a time, the circuit breaker switches were labeled in our father's perfect penmanship, but the paper diagram has long since curled up, fallen off, and been trampled to bits.

I flip every switch back and forth, listening for sounds of appliances juicing back to life. But no noises are forthcoming.

It hits me that the power has been cut off. We've gotten so many shutoff notices over the years, all of which I've wiggled out of by paying in dribs and drabs, that they're like white noise. I must've missed the last one.

I brush a tangle of hair out of my eyes and head back upstairs. There's no paperwork from the electric company in the entrance by the garage. But when I open the front door, which we barely use, I find the three-day shutoff notice stuck to the inside of the dented aluminum screen door. It's wet and smeared. I leave it and reach for a folded sheet of paper on the threshold.

As I read the notice—it's a list of conditions I must satisfy before the electricity will be restored, including payment in full of the outstanding balance—something inside me collapses. Until now, I'd deluded myself into believing that things would get better, that I'd find a way out of this continual mess. But no matter how fast I run on the treadmill of life, peace, happiness, and security keep slipping through my fingers.

I've only got one choice. And suddenly I'm grateful even for that.

Samantha ditches therapy at the last minute, claiming a migraine. I drop her at the darkened house with instructions to rest until I return, hopefully with a seventy-thousand-dollar-a-year job. With my luck, though, the position has already been filled.

This time when I arrive at the doctor's office, she's with a patient. I take a seat beside the receptionist's desk and wait. I didn't bring anything to read, so I'm just staring at the walls—they're a relaxing shade of beige—and begging the universe to come through for me, just this once. Let the nanny job work out.

A couple of minutes into the silence, the receptionist takes pity on me and strikes up a conversation. "Are you ready for Christmas?" she asks, smiling hopefully.

I stopped answering questions like this honestly a long time ago. "Almost," I say, even though the holidays have barely crossed my mind. "It comes quicker every year, doesn't it?" My daughter has had a lifetime of skimpy Christmases. One more won't tip the scales.

The receptionist—her name is Jacquelyn, I learn—agrees with me. Then she moves on to talking about the weather. A storm is brewing in the long-term forecast. We commiserate about it until the doctor's office door yawns open.

Out limps a man with shoulder-length gray hair and a walrus mustache. He's thin, with a cracked leather jacket and dirty jeans. He reeks of smoke and unidentified chemicals. As he maneuvers through the waiting room, the hitch in his gait softens. He nods at Jacquelyn and keeps trucking out the door.

The doctor's voice makes me jump. "I hope you haven't been waiting long. My last appointment ran over."

"Just a few minutes," I say, following her inside.

As I melt into the chair—it's supple and welcoming, like the hand of God—Dr. Hayes remains standing, staring over my shoulder. "Is Samantha ...?"

I shake my head. "It's just me. Sam has a migraine."

"That's common at her age, for one reason or another: hormones, anxiety, depression, stress. We don't take teenagers seriously enough, I'm afraid. We don't put enough stock in their experiences. I've always said that teenagers will surprise us if we give them the chance." She floats into her seat.

"How old are your daughters again?" I ask.

She laughs. "Eight going on thirty-five. You know how it is."

I've never had therapy before, but Dr. Hayes is so fun and carefree, so open and approachable, that these appointments feel more like lighthearted girl talk than serious counseling. "About the nanny job," I say, pouncing while the mood is right, "is it still available?"

"We're narrowing down the candidates," she says, "unless you've decided to step into the gap. I'm a good judge of people—I have to be, in my line of work—and I have a strong sense that our girls would click with you. Having Samantha around would be a wonderful bonus. It would warm my heart to see our daughters under the same roof, growing and learning together. It's a curse of being an only child, I suppose: I can't stop pining for a busy household, a messy jumble of siblings, a warm body and an open ear only a heartbeat away. That's why I got into this business—to connect with people on a deep, personal level."

I want to tell her that siblings aren't all they're cracked up to be, but then I think of Marina and her words ring true. "I'd like to take it," I say about the job.

"And Samantha?"

I bite my lip. "Honestly, she's not thrilled about moving. All of her friends are in town."

"That's the problem, I'm afraid."

"Pardon me?"

"These so-called friends of Samantha's. They're breaking her down. I don't know how much more she can take. And with the danger of—"

"What danger? Did she say something? What did she say?"

She frowns. "Suffice it to say that Samantha would be safer at our estate, where things are controlled, where access is limited."

"You know who hurt her, don't you? Are they coming back?"

"The biggest risk to Samantha is Samantha. I need to work with her more intensely to get a handle on things."

"She's suicidal? Is that what you mean?" The idea makes a morbid kind of sense.

She reaches across the desk and pats my hand. "I can't explain further without violating my ethics. Trust that I have Samantha's best interests at heart. It's my job to help her—to help both of you—get to a better place."

"Thank you," I say, squeezing her hand. Fate has given me a friend, an angel, someone to walk with me through the darkness and into the light. When she squeezes back, every drop of worry leaves me.

CHAPTER 50
LISA

On Saturday, the moving van arrives with Robin and Samantha's things. I guide the muscle-bound lunks to the downstairs suite, tracking their every move so they don't make off with something valuable, like one of Edward's prized watches. (My husband has a habit of leaving his expensive timepieces lying around the house.)

The movers are in and out in fifteen minutes. Once they're gone, I fiddle around in the kitchen, treating myself to an overdue cappuccino and checking my phone. In the back of my mind, I expect another call from those hapless detectives, but Edward has brought the weight of our fortune, our influence, to bear. It's amazing what folks will overlook when millions of dollars are at stake. Things will remain quiet on the murder front for the foreseeable future.

I *am* still receiving plenty of pick-me-up calls due to the miscarriage, though. When I'm bored, like now—what's taking Robin and Samantha so long? they should've been on the heels of the movers—I scroll through the messages and play back the most ridiculous ones, the ones where the caller (usually a club wife zonked out on pain pills) rails about the unfairness of life and then, in the next breath, declares everything wrought to God's plan. They're amusing in their own way.

Boredom is giving way to annoyance. I don't wait around for anyone; my time is too valuable. But I'm itching to intercept Samantha. She's the most intriguing thing to come my way in a long time. With her, unlike with my own children, I sense the makings of a soul twin, someone whose core being aligns with mine in magnificent and mysterious ways. Of course, Robin might get between us. She seems like the overprotective sort. But if it comes down to it, she can be dealt with, just like I dealt with that girl.

I'm meandering toward the garage—I assume Robin will park her bucket of bolts at the crest of the driveway—dragging my fingernails over the wallpaper (its bumpy texture stimulates my nervous system), when I hear the pitter-patter of Magnum behind me.

Silly dog. He must've been napping in the library, in one of the many doggie beds our interior decorators have hidden around the house.

I spin around and scoop him up, nuzzling him to my face for a prolonged sniff. Forget the scent of a freshly washed baby. A well-groomed dog, especially a silky-haired Yorkie like Magnum, is the fountain of youth.

I continue on, holding my boy close—he loves snuggling up to my chest like a championship football—and daydreaming about future escapades with Samantha. I've always wanted a partner in crime. But until now, no one has measured up; no one has exhibited the raw potential that made me what I am. It's ironic that I should find such resonance with the niece of that girl.

The garage is quiet, but when I buzz open the first bay—*my* bay, where the Hummer's parked—I'm proven right. That clunker of Robin's is idling at the top of the driveway. Both she and Samantha are sitting inside.

I laugh to myself. Ricki must've relayed the instructions for opening the gate but omitted the security codes for the mansion.

I step out of the shadows and wave them inside. They come carrying battered boxes, things too sentimental to trust to the hired lunks. It strikes me that a photograph of that girl is probably in the mix, maybe even a whole album of them.

What have they done to remember her, to memorialize her?

"I forgot you had a dog," says Samantha as we move through the house. "What kind is she?"

"Purebred Yorkshire terrier. His name's Magnum."

"He's beautiful," says Robin. At the sound of her voice, the dog starts growling.

"Hush, baby," I say, gripping him tighter. "These are our new friends, Samantha and Robin. They're going to live here now. Be a good boy and I'll give you some treats." I smile ruefully. "He's only being protective. I promise, he won't bite."

The dog settles somewhat, but he's still grumbling and curling his lip. When we reach the kitchen, I deposit him on the island with a couple of biscuits and escort the ladies to their quarters.

The suite isn't much to my eye—a bedroom, a bathroom, and a living room with a kitchenette—especially when held up against our estate. But the mother and daughter are impressed enough to thank me multiple times for taking a chance on Robin. (Is the woman so inept that I'm her only shot at a paying job? Maybe so, thinking back to that watery Malibu Sunset.)

"I'll let you unpack and then we'll get started. Ricki's ready to show you the ropes," I tell Robin, "and the girls are beside themselves with anticipation. They loved their last nanny like a sister." I put on a sullen, wistful expression. "Oh well. Things change, I suppose. This will be a wonderful opportunity for all of us." I turn to Samantha. "How would you like to join me for some car shopping while your mother's at work? My husband's had an unfortunate accident. We're down a vehicle at the moment. I could use a young person's opinion on the tech gadgetry and whatnot."

Samantha enthusiastically agrees.

"Good," I say. "Meet me in the kitchen in an hour. Both of you."

With Robin occupied for the afternoon, Samantha and I set out for the Jaguar dealership. It's an overcast day with a threat of snow. I take the scenic route, winding over back roads, cruising by farmhouses and open fields, chatting up Samantha on innocent topics like music and TV.

Our conversation is effortless. Still, I steer clear of sticky subjects. We've got all the time in the world to delve into her mother's feeble mental state. Depending on how the chips fall, Robin could end up in a cozy sanatorium (I've never had anyone committed; it sounds fun) or as human compost. Assuming Edward doesn't get any dirty ideas—can I trust him with such a bewitching teenager in the house?—I envision an emotional adoption ceremony at the club next year. Everyone will be racked with joy when we rescue this darling girl so soon after the loss of our own precious child.

Lisa, Edward, Darian, Mavis, and Samantha Hayes. It has a nice ring, doesn't it?

By the time we reach the Jaguar dealership, it's nearing sundown. We're barely out of the Hummer before a plague of salesmen descends. I swat them aside and demand the owner, a golf buddy of Edward's called Royce. But Royce is MIA. I settle for his hippie son, Walden, who's learning the business during his gap year.

I'll teach him a thing or two.

In the waning afternoon light, Walden, Samantha, and I tour the lot, focusing on XKR models. Edward might prefer to custom order his next ride, but he's not here, so my say-so goes. If he doesn't like what I pick, I'll give the car to Samantha and he can start from scratch. Robin will get the Mercedes ASAP, since, God knows, we can't have her shuttling around the girls in that ridiculous jalopy of hers.

"What do you think?" I ask Samantha, wagging a hand between a sporty white coupe and its gray brother.

She nibbles a fingernail. "I like the white. The gray's kinda sad."

I tap the white XKR's fender. "We'll take this for a ride," I tell Walden.

"Okay, yeah." His eyes dart around confusedly.

Is it possible that he's never been on a test ride? "Well, do you have the key?"

Samantha stifles a laugh. She has a natural sense of the absurd, a taste for dark comedy that mirrors—or perhaps complements—my own.

Walden slinks off. When he returns, he insists on chaperoning us. "It's company policy," he says, and I lose what little respect I had for the man.

"Call your father," I demand. "Call Royce. Tell him Dr. Hayes—*Mrs.* Hayes—wants to take a lousy Jag out for a ride without a babysitter." I'm hamming it up, exaggerating my persona to give Samantha a taste of what she can become if she puts her mind to it.

The young Mr. Jaguar folds like a cloth napkin. Better to risk a hundred-thousand-dollar car than look like a fool to Daddy.

I nestle into the driver's seat and Samantha rides shotgun. Soon Walden is a speck in the rearview mirror. We travel only a few blocks before pulling up to a laundromat. "Your turn," I say, grinning.

"Oh, um, I can't. I don't have my permit. You have to be sixteen."

"I know."

"I've only driven a few times. This car is so nice."

"And expensive," I add.

"I'd be way too nervous." She lets out a gushing breath.

"Nonsense," I say. "You want to drive this car. You just don't think you deserve to. Isn't that right?" When she doesn't answer, I up the ante. "I'm your therapist, remember? Part of my job is to push you past your limits, to help you discover parts of yourself that you may be repressing due to—let's say—inadequate self-regard."

We sit in thick silence, darkness creeping over us. "Can I tell you something?" she asks.

My intuition starts tingling. Maybe she's going to confess a lurid crime. Maybe she's more like me than I ever dreamed. "Please. That's what I'm here for."

"I caught him cheating."

I'm aghast. How could anyone betray such an immaculate specimen? "Jason?" Suddenly, we're in our own little melodrama. "What's her name? The girl?" My mind jumps to Ashley. I wonder if she's sunburnt, dehydrated, infested with some dreaded third-world malady. Hookworms, maybe. That'd serve her right.

"It doesn't matter. I broke up with him. I just can't believe I let him use me like that."

"He didn't deserve you," I point out. "Erase him from your mind." I might just erase him from the earth. And no one would blame me, either.

She works up a smile. "I'm trying."

"Good," I say with finality. "Now back to this car. Do you want to take it for a spin? Once my husband gets his hands on it, your chances will be near zero."

Her head bobs up and down. We trade places. I have to coach her on the gear shift, even though the car's an automatic. That relic her mother has had her driving shifts on the column, while the Jag shifts on the center console like a civilized twenty-first-century machine.

Once she settles in, she's a natural behind the wheel—smooth and cool, thanks to my pep talk and continuing guidance. We get lost in chitchat, eventually ending up by the mall. "Turn here," I say, signaling the KFC. I have a sudden craving for the Colonel's mashed potatoes and gravy, which brings me back to my pregnancy days with the twins. For eight and a half months (my little bundles of joy came early), I couldn't get enough of the stuff.

Samantha cuts the turn too wide, causing the Jag to scrape something on my side of the car. At the unexpected crumpling sound, she hits the brakes. I squint out the window. At first I think we've grazed a fence, but the obstacle turns out to be a decorative boulder.

"Keep going," I say. The damage is done. Imagine the look on Walden's face when we return with a ruined car.

Oopsie.

Samantha navigates into a parking spot. "I think I'm done," she says, wiping her hands on her jeans. This is where we differ: I'm not prone to sweaty palms or the nervousness that provokes them.

I touch her shoulder. "That's fine. But don't let a little mishap deter you. Everybody makes mistakes. What separates us from the average person, what makes us better, is that we learn and improve. We don't make the same mistake twice."

She laughs uneasily. "I'll try."

"I know you will."

I take over the wheel. We loop through the drive-through and leave with a bag of hot, steaming food. The potatoes are every bit as salty and gooey as I remember. Samantha's appetite is dulled. She nibbles a biscuit until we return to the dealership.

Walden's silhouette stares at us from the window. He throws on a jacket and heads our way.

"What's gonna happen?" Samantha asks.

I've parked the damaged side of the Jag in the shadows. "Give me your trash." I stuff the paper bag full of garbage and we exit the car.

"So?" says Walden, eyeing Samantha. "How'd you like it?"

I thump the garbage against his chest. "We'll take it for ten percent off the sticker price. Use the discount to fix that nasty gash," I quip, "and have it delivered to our estate as soon as possible. Edward will be waiting."

CHAPTER 51
ROBIN

Our days begin backward now. While Dr. Hayes drives Sam to school, I fuss over the twins, making sure they're pictures of wealth and privilege before whisking them off to Triton Preparatory Academy. The transition is going smoothly enough, despite a sense of unease that clings to me like an ominous perfume.

As out of sync as the morning rituals are, they're also a breath of life. Off-site excursions are frowned upon, except as dictated by the job. So says Ricki, my lifeline to the outside world, my sole confidante. Three days into the job, I'm savoring the slushy snow, the bone-biting cold, the cast of gray that has overtaken every living thing, as I complete my route and return to the compound.

The garage door magically opens when it senses the car. I wonder if this is normal among the rich or if my new boss, the other Dr. Hayes, who's some sort of technology whiz, has invented a prototype system. Either way, it's fantastic.

I've just shut down the car when a form appears in my peripheral vision. My heart skips a beat. I grope for the door locks. But before I can locate them, the form acquires features: a strapping build not unlike my brother's and a bronzed face with a five o'clock shadow.

I've seen Mr. Hayes only from afar as we move opposite each other through the house like repellent magnets. Our paths were bound to cross eventually.

I exit the car. "Good morning," I say, holding my head high and smiling.

His brow crinkles. "Oh, yes. Hello. How are you?" He's staring so intently at my neck, at the tattoo, that the spider starts tap dancing.

Fuck.

I scratch my throat. "I'm well, thank you," I say, too stiff, too formal.

He squeezes my arm as he goes by. "Glad to hear it." Stopping at the driver's door, he says, "I've spoken to Ricki. If I'm not back by two o'clock, she'll pick up the children. My wife promises that the new car will be here tomorrow. I don't know what the holdup is."

"Whatever you need." He's paying me an obscene amount of money to bend myself around, well, anything. I feel a squirmy, unclean sensation in my gut over what I might do for the right price.

"Okay, then," he says. The car door claps shut and he's gone.

With the doctors at work and Samantha, Darian, and Mae at school, the house is quiet. I think about prepping language lessons—according to Ricki, the previous nanny was teaching the children French—but I've still got unpacking to do. I'll work on the lessons when everything is in its place.

In the rush to move houses, Sam and I grabbed only the bare essentials. Among the must-haves are a handful of snapshots of Marina. I scatter them over the frilly comforter—our suite has matching single beds, decorated for Princess Barbie—and sigh.

Where are you, Marina? Who killed you? And why?

I pick up a particular photo—twelve-year-old Marina with a sparkly hula-hoop poised on her hip—and stare into my sister's eyes, hoping for a miracle of ESP. Sometimes I think the photos are wormholes; if I could just link with my dead sister's spirit, my questions would be answered.

I've switched from the hula-hoop shot to an official school portrait—our mother's faded blue handwriting on the back reads "Marina, Age 10"—which I have cupped in front of me, when footsteps sound nearby.

I feel like I've been caught doing something disturbed, something dangerous. I sweep the photos into a pile and stuff them under a pillow.

"Knock knock," comes a woman's voice. "Anyone home?"

"Hang on," I reply, adjusting my vision back to reality.

In the suite's living room, I encounter Ricki. "I like what you've done with the place," she says ironically (we've done nothing but litter the room with empty soda cans and discarded laundry).

"Gee, thanks." I kick a pair of Samantha's leggings under the couch. "Would you like to sit down?"

"Actually," she says, eyeing the door, "I had something else in mind." She pulls a bottle of champagne out from behind her back. "I snuck this away from the party. It's imported. Don't ask me how to pronounce it." She grins. "We've got the house to ourselves. I thought you could share it with me in the Jacuzzi. It'll be our own little welcome wagon."

My heart rate ticks up. I want nothing more than a drink. But I barely know Ricki—might she have ulterior motives? might she be trying to get me fired?—and I'm damn sure every square inch of this place is under surveillance. "Can we...? Won't we get in trouble if...?"

She bursts out laughing. "God, you *are* new." She leans against the wall and studies my neck. "When did you get that?"

The tattoo. Again. "It was a phase." I shrug. "My sister...she..."

While I'm struggling to finish the thought—she overdosed? she was murdered?—Ricki says, "I like it. I've got a few myself." She lowers her voice. "In certain places, if you know what I mean."

It occurs to me that she might be hitting on me—the alcohol, the Jacuzzi, the risqué talk. "I don't have a bathing suit," I say.

"Like that ever stopped anyone." She looks me up and down. "What size are you, a zero? You're so thin." She sounds like a mother hen all of a sudden. Compared to her voluptuous curves, I must appear as a skeleton.

I tell her I'm a size four; it's genetic. Even at her booziest, our mother was as thin and trim as a cover girl.

"One of her bikinis should fit you. She's gained at least ten pounds." She puts a finger to her lips. "Don't tell her I said that, though."

She must mean Dr. Hayes. "That's okay. I've got shorts and a tank top. Just give me a minute to find them." God, do I need that drink.

"Take your time and hurry up. Sometimes Edward only goes out for lunch. Not that he'd care if we use the Jacuzzi. It's *her* you need to worry about."

I tell her to go ahead; I'll catch up in a few minutes.

"Don't be too long." She brandishes the champagne. "I'm real thirsty."

She leaves and I rifle through my adopted dresser. The tank top is easy to find, but the shorts elude me. I end up wearing a mint-green pair of Samantha's running shorts, which are baggy in the ass.

Good enough.

When I reach the pool room, Ricki's already in the Jacuzzi. She's wearing a one-piece swimsuit with an abstract blue-and-black pattern. The champagne is popped and portioned into red Solo cups. Ricki has gotten a head start on me, her cup ringed with fuzzy lilac lip prints.

No worries. I'll blow past her in a heartbeat.

I cringe as my foot meets the frothy water. "Ooh." I let out a breath. "How hot is this?"

She signals a control panel on the edge of the tub. "A hundred and three." She picks up her cup and takes another swig. "The pool guy was here this morning. He turns it up. Lisa likes it at one-oh-one. I always have to turn it back down," she says, rolling her eyes.

I descend the stairs. "Lisa?"

"Mrs. Hayes. *Lisa*. She's worried about aging, drying out her skin and stuff like that." She laughs. "Like it matters. With her money, she could buy a new face and have it sewn on."

A chill skitters up my spine. I don't know if it's from Ricki's macabre comment, the mismatch of water and air temperatures, or something else.

The combination of expensive champagne and massaging water jets in the middle of the day is hypnotic. We drink the whole bottle—Ricki's a champ, but she's no match for me—gossiping about everything from Jaycee Dugard (the California girl who was kidnapped by a pedophile and freed eighteen years later) to Michael Jackson (we both knew it was a drug overdose before the cause of death was released) to the Balloon Boy hoax (some people will do anything for fifteen minutes of fame).

We're relaxing with our eyes closed when Ricki suddenly blurts, "Shit! What time is it?"

I'm on the knife's edge of falling asleep. Still, my eyelids spring open. "I don't know. Why?"

"You're late. I'm late. *Somebody*'s late."

My mind is luxuriously hazy. A few numb seconds slip by before I remember the children—not just that they're due to be picked up from school, but their very existence. "What about Mr. Hayes?"

Ricki sloshes over to the stairs. "You're joking, right? Don't get me wrong—he's okay and everything, at least for a boss—but he's like a TV dad. He pops up when things are shitty at work. That's about it."

We get out of the Jacuzzi and dry off. I'm not remotely drunk, but Ricki thinks I'm too far gone to drive. She asks me to finish cleaning the kitchen—this is where she left off with the housekeeping—while she fills in for me at Triton Prep.

As the new kid on the block, I have no choice but to agree. It's the better deal, anyway, since I can munch on snacks from the fridge while I inspect the kitchen.

I nab a cheese stick and start looking around. At first glance, the place is spotless. Second glance is roughly the same. It takes a special kind of person (one with white gloves and a magnifying glass) to clean up after the filthy rich.

Since everything is already neat and clean—the toaster is sparkling like a rodeo queen, for Christ's sake—the only thing left to do is sanitize. I check under the copper sink, which is buffed to a soft, glowing sheen, for disinfecting wipes.

Bingo.

I wipe down the obvious surfaces first—the counters, the island, the major appliances—and then move on to smaller things like light switches and drawer pulls. I'm running out of real estate when I notice a remote control sticking out of a basket on the wall.

If anything needs disinfecting, it's this petri dish of entertainment. I'm no clean freak, but even I have seen the shows where they take a black light into a hotel room and find what looks like a sloppy crime scene.

As I'm rubbing down the remote, I press the buttons too hard, making the TV jolt on. I glance up and see a tangle of naked bodies before mashing the buttons again and shutting the pornography off. The TV goes dark—thank God—but, simultaneously, a disc spits out, bounces off the counter, and disappears under the refrigerator.

I'm on my hands and knees, sweeping my fingers under the fridge—I've found some grime, finally—for a few seconds before coming out with the disc. When I get on my feet, I'm not alone. "Mr. Hayes," I say, blowing on the disc to remove a speckling of crumbs. "I think this is yours."

CHAPTER 52
LISA

The whole household is eating breakfast together—I've invited Robin and Samantha to join us for Edward's famous pineapple pancakes—when my cell phone rings.

I answer grudgingly. It's the Jaguar dealership. They're trying to deliver the new-and-improved XKR and they can't get through the gate.

I muffle the phone. "Sweetie, your car has arrived. Would you let the deliverymen in? I'll finish up here." The last pancake is within moments of golden-brown perfection.

Edward hands over the spatula and kisses me on the cheek before disappearing down the hall.

"Who wants the last one?" I ask, scanning from my daughters—Mae's plate is empty, while Darian is picking through her stack for pineapple chunks and piling them up on a napkin—to Samantha.

The girls' hands shoot up. "Me, me!" chirps Darian.

Mae withdraws her hand, muttering, "She doesn't even like them."

"Samantha?" I say, tilting my head and smiling.

Robin perks up. "She's had enough. Right, Sam?" She brushes something—a wayward string or a puff of lint—off her daughter's blouse.

"Samantha?" I repeat, ignoring her mother's intrusion.

"That's okay. I'm full." She walks her plate to the sink. "Thanks, though. They were good."

I hover the pancake over Mae's plate before thinking better of the idea and sliding it to Darian. My little spitfire has earned a reward; her sister needs to toughen up. You don't get anywhere in this life by giving up, by giving in. I thought I'd made that clear.

The day unfolds normally until lunchtime, when I leave work and head for Robin's neighborhood. Edward can have his pretty new Jag. I'm expecting a delivery of my own. Only a smashed window and the twist of a doorknob stand between me and the unraveling of Samantha and Robin's blood bond.

As I turn off the main road, I'm struck by a stench of desperation. Dirty, unkempt, vandalized things—from a child's crushed Tonka truck to his father's rust-eaten, spray-paint-tagged Chevy Blazer—fill the neighborhood as far as the eye can see. Among the debris are flashes of what one might call hope: a new porch light or a plant thriving in a tidy bay window.

Checking for unwelcome eyes, I roll up to Robin's house. The recession has hit this street hard; vacancies abound. The few occupied dwellings look like they've survived an apocalypse.

I park in what remains of the driveway of an abandoned dump across the street. If anyone asks, I'm Polly Perkins from AmeriPlex Financial, looking in on one of our delinquent assets.

Sadly, no one emerges to confront me, and my acting skills go untapped. Just for fun, though, I do a little pretend checking of the dump—rattling the doorknobs, peeking in the windows, snapping pictures on my cell phone—before slipping around to Robin's backyard.

In my tote bag are an emergency glass-breaking hammer (the kind nervous Nellies stash in their glove boxes for a watery crash), an airplane pillow (to muffle any unwanted noise), and the smallest pair of bolt cutters I could find (a last-minute addition to my bag of burglary tricks).

I assess the home for weak points. To my dismay, the back door is locked, along with all of the rear-facing windows. I retreat to the east side of the house (the neighboring property is obscured by an overgrown hedge; if anyone lives there, they won't get a good look at me) and try two more windows. One is locked tight and the other has the slightest bit of give. If I were taller, I might be able to get enough leverage to force it open. But I'm stretching as it is, say nothing of how I'd catapult myself inside at such an angle.

I return to the back door—tapping out the glass here seems most efficient—but then it occurs to me to check the bulkhead. It's probably secured inside by a steel latch, but you never know.

With a grunt, I yank on one of the bulkhead door handles—they're held together by a flimsy bicycle chain—and the door pops open a few inches. Marvelous.

I retrieve the bolt cutters, chomp through the chain, and toss the shattered links on the ground. The bulkhead door opens with a squeal. I duck into the dank, cobwebbed stairwell, expecting to be met by a security door. But this obstacle, too, has been removed.

I proceed through the darkened doorway into the cellar itself. I see outlines, mostly, which I navigate around until I find the stairway leading up into the house. The door at the top of the stairs is also unlocked. I push it open and enter the kitchen, which is ramshackle and claustrophobic, though neat and clean.

As much as I'd love to snoop around—I feel like I'm on an archeological dig, unearthing fossils of a time gone by, details from before I set that girl on a path to oblivion—I'm here for a reason. I won't be distracted.

The mail is in a scattered pile on the floor, inside the front door, below an old-school postal slot. The envelope I want is floating on top like a head of foam. It had better be, after I've paid off Robin's credit card (I needed a clean, established account to assume her identity), ordered an official copy of Samantha's birth certificate, and had it rush delivered.

Now here it is.

I rub the creamy envelope between my fingers and slide it into my bag. Then I retrace my steps, making the place look like nothing ever happened, with the exception of that ridiculous bicycle chain.

It's a good thing I came along when I did. The way Robin has been protecting Samantha—and I use the term loosely—she was bound to end up like that girl.

When I return home, I find Robin in the library, curled up in a club chair with a stack of books. In her lap is a legal pad I recognize from the desk by the kitchen—at least that's where I got the one I used for Ashley's resignation letter.

"Oh, good," I say, "you're not busy." Whatever she's doing can wait. My needs take precedence.

She cradles the pad to her chest. "I'm just putting together ideas for—"

"The children, yes," I say, realizing the books are French-language tomes Ashley bought from Amazon by the truckload. "You can do that later. I need you to run an errand."

"Okay," she says, setting the pad aside. "The children aren't due to be—"

"Ricki will handle the afternoon transportation." I shake my head. "Where is she, by the way? I didn't see her when I came in."

Her eyebrows knit together. "At the grocery store?"

"Never mind. I'll text her."

She remarks on my early arrival from work. I tell her that I'm coming down with something, which is untrue but also none of her business.

When I instruct her to rent a U-Haul and drive two hours north to a specialty toy store—Christmas is around the corner, and my little darlings have eyes bigger than their stomachs—and purchase a pair of stuffed, ride-on giraffes, her jaw drops. She doesn't argue with me, though. (Good choice.) She just takes the credit card and goes on her merry, befuddled way.

I fire a barrage of messages at Ricki, redirecting her to Jackman High and then Triton, on my way downstairs to the nanny's suite. With Edward gone—he's returning to himself, finally, after the miscarriage and his little accident—I'll be taking advantage of the alone time to sniff around in Robin's life.

Of all the complications to vex me lately—from Sophie Gallagher to Dr. Kapoor to Ashley—Robin has the most potential for damage, for plucking a load-bearing brick from my tower of lies (that sounds so ugly; I was just claiming my destiny!) and sending the whole brilliant illusion tumbling.

Robin can't be allowed to become suspicious, to sic the authorities on my trail. Not that they'd take such a sorry loser's word for anything. Still, she must be contained. Or eliminated. The latter option has the bonus of serving Samantha up on a silver platter. Where else would she go—certainly not to that ne'er-do-well uncle—but to Edward and me, if her mother were to meet a tragic end?

I'm feeling optimistic—I expect the best and usually get it—as I begin searching Robin's living quarters, digging for anything that might implicate me, anything that suggests she has the slightest inkling of who I am, what I've done to her.

I get through the living room/kitchen free and clear. The bathroom is also bereft of evidence. I should've scoured her house when I had the chance. Who knows what kind of damning proof might be hiding in that rundown time capsule in the deep, dark past.

I tell myself that she has nothing on me. The idea is absurd. She was a child when that girl died. What could she know?

The rationalization holds up until I dump out the top drawer of the nightstand beside Robin's bed. I spread the contents over the Pepto-Bismol-pink comforter—letting Ashley redecorate was a mistake; her tastes would spook a drag queen—and pore over them like they're tea leaves.

Most of the items are frivolous nonsense or useless garbage. The only thing of consequence is a rumpled piece of paper with a list of names on it. There must've been twenty to begin with. After an aggressive crossing-out campaign, only three remain: Nancy Ellis, Carol Blake, and Lisa Thompson.

I've gone by Dr. L.A. (Lisa Abigail) Hayes for a decade now, but still ... you see my problem. There exists somewhere—at the University of Virginia, for starters—a record of my life under the name Lisa Thompson, a trail anybody could follow with the right amount of motivation. I mean, I'm beaming in the front row of our med-school graduation photo, for Pete's sake.

I think briefly of stealing the paper, but it's no use. Robin would've committed the names to memory eons ago. I have two choices: Send her on a wild goose chase—how hard would it be to redirect her toward, say, Nancy Ellis?—or get rid of her. Truth be told, she's turning into a nagging thorn. Samantha and I would be better off without her. It would be a gift to set the girl free of her maternal anchor. Imagine the glittering life she could lead as the beloved eldest daughter of two wealthy doctors.

As I sift through the rest of Robin's things, my mind circles an obvious truth: It's her or me. I didn't think it would come to this—what were the chances of ever seeing that girl's sister again?—but the situation has a certain kind of irony. A dash of poetic justice, if you will. What I did years ago blew a hole in Robin's life. Now it's time to finish the job, to put the wounded animal out of its misery.

The junk goes back in the drawer and the drawer back in the nightstand. I continue poking around—why isn't there a picture of that girl anywhere?—checking in closets and under beds. I hadn't any inclination to search Samantha's things, but then an oddly cascading swath of comforter draws my attention to her bed. I pull back the covers and find, wedged between her mattress and box spring, a gun. A pistol.

I curl my hand around the grip and rest my finger on the trigger. Just when I thought I couldn't get any fonder of Samantha, she surprises me. She might have even more spunk than I did at her age.

Bellissima, my girl. *Bellissima*.

CHAPTER 53
ROBIN

By the time I rent a U-Haul and cross state lines into Ohio—the toy store is just shy of Cleveland, in a little village called Richfield—the weather takes a nasty turn, pelting the truck with sleet and imperiling my journey, not to mention my life. I think about pulling off the road and waiting out the storm, but things might only get worse from here.

I put on the flashers and plant the truck in the slow lane, powering through the last twenty miles with white knuckles and a lump in my throat. The toy-store parking lot is small and angular. I barely get the truck off the road.

A layer of slush coats the ground. I trudge through it with a sigh. As I reach for the shop door, my gaze skims the lettering on the windows—bright, swirly script advertises dolls, games, books, art supplies, antique toys—noting the hours of operation. Except for Sundays, when the shop is dark, the place closes at six o'clock.

It's five forty-something.

I briefly wander the store, which is like a fairytale cottage with twisting aisles and camouflaged nooks and crannies, before stumbling upon the owner. I tell her that I've come for the giraffes. She responds with a blank stare.

"Don't you have a record of the order?" I ask.

She shakes her head. "I'd know if someone'd ordered those." She waves me over to an old-timey cash register, where she flips through a spiral notebook. "We don't keep 'em in stock. I have to get 'em special. See?" She holds up a page of scribbles. "Nothing—or, well, nothing that ain't come in already."

"But I brought a truck," I mutter. "I drove a hundred and thirty miles in the snow."

She tears a sheet out of the notebook and pushes it across the counter. "Give me your information. I'll call the vendor in the morning, if that's what you want." She peers at me with milky gray eyes. "Is that what you want?"

I'm paralyzed. Should I call Dr. Hayes and ask for guidance? It *is* her money. "What about delivery? Can you guarantee them by Christmas?" I can't go back empty-handed; I'll look like a fool. I slap down the doctor's Amex card and cock my head.

"That depends," she says, fingering the card, "on where you want 'em delivered."

I recite the address. She marks it down and consults another notebook. "That shouldn't be a problem."

I tell her to write up the order. The giraffes are $1,289 (each) plus a $200 delivery fee (each). I feel like I'm spending Monopoly money, signing for $3,000 worth of stuffed animals.

With the paperwork jammed in my pocket, I grab a lollipop from a teapot by the cash register and unwrap it on my way out the door. As I'm exiting the parking lot, the lights go out in the little toy shop.

Dr. Hayes doesn't flinch when I show up after a nail-biting return trip without the giraffes. "*C'est la vie*," she says, tucking the Amex card back in her wallet.

"What should I do with these?" I ask, unfolding the receipt and delivery contract. "The lady—the owner of the shop—said they'll be here by Christmas. She wrote it down right here."

"Ask Ricki. She must have a folder or a shoebox or something."

I was hoping for a pat on the back or at least a thank-you. After all, I could've died for those stupid, overpriced toys. I consider saying as much, calling her out on the insanity of the request, but then she reaches into her purse and comes out with a fat stack of cash.

My heart flutters. "Do you need anything else?" I ask. "I should check on the children—unless they've gone to bed already."

"Stay a minute." She gestures at an ottoman. "I have terrific news."

I sit.

"It's about Samantha." She beams a triumphant grin. "We've had a breakthrough. Something you'll be happy to hear."

Suddenly, the money is irrelevant. "What? What is it?"

"She's broken up with that ne'er-do-well, that miscreant."

"Jason?" His name tastes like acid in my mouth. Even though Sam denies his responsibility for her injuries, I have nowhere else to direct my rage (these drug thugs are as easy to pin down as Jell-O). If Jason hadn't gotten mixed up with them in the first place, my daughter's spirit (and much more) wouldn't have been broken.

The loser can rot in hell.

Dr. Hayes nods. "I knew my methods would work, but the results were faster than expected."

I'm overwhelmed by gratitude. She's given my daughter back to me. "Thank you so much. Can I hug you?" She holds out her arms and I collapse into them. As she rubs my back, I continue murmuring thank-yous into the hollow of her neck.

"Do one thing for me," she says. "Keep this between us. Samantha can't know I've told you. It'll break her trust in me, her trust in the process. We don't want that happening, right?"

I sit up and brush tears from my eyes. "Right." In the span of a few short weeks, she's done what I didn't think possible. She's the savior my daughter needs—the savior *I* need—in more ways than one.

It's teetering on ten o'clock when I finish with the children and head downstairs to check on Sam. With our dueling schedules (I'm tied up with nanny duties in the evenings when she's free), I'm seeing less of my daughter than ever. But at least she's safe. That's the important thing. And if what Dr. Hayes says is true, I can breathe easy. In fact, life is looking pretty rosy.

I'm wondering about that pile of cash—it looked more like the proceeds of a bank robbery than walking-around money—as I pad down the hall toward our suite. But before I can get there, a crackle of voices catches my ear. It's probably the TV in Mr. Hayes's office, which is at the opposite end of the basement. Between him and us are a game room, a movie theater, a home brewery, a gym, a laundry facility, and an array of lesser-defined spaces.

Something about those voices—or one of them, anyway—is too familiar. It resonates in my nervous system, setting off a cascade of vague panic.

The living room of our suite is empty, as are the bedroom and bathroom. Of course, it was Samantha's voice—not the words, specifically, but the cadence, the timbre.

I whirl around and take off down the hall. In a matter of seconds, I'm hammering on Mr. Hayes's office door. If I'm wrong about him, about his being holed up with my daughter (why can't these pervs keep their hands to themselves?), God help me. And if I'm not, God help *him*.

The door opens with excruciating slowness. "Yes?" he says, his eyes twinkling with mischief.

"Is Samantha—?" I begin, then stumble over my words. "My daughter … I thought I heard …" I weave sideways and peer around him, but the room is pooled in shadows.

He throws the door open wide. "Come in. We're just playing a little basketball. Your Samantha is quite good."

I step past him. The room is lit by amber wall sconces. Across from a huge, cluttered desk are a circus-themed pinball machine and an arcade-style basketball game. Samantha is swishing one ball after another.

I hang back and wait.

Mr. Hayes studies my daughter's form.

The game has a buzzing countdown clock. When Sam's time runs out, she spins around, grinning, her cheeks flushed. Upon spotting me, her face falls like an underbaked cake.

"It's late," I say. "You need to get some rest for school." I tip my head at the door. "Come on. Let's leave Mr. Hayes alone to—"

He cuts in. "She's no bother. Truly. She's welcome anytime." He chuckles. "I could use a little friendly competition. It gets the creative juices flowing. And *she* won't let me win, unlike everyone at the office."

Isn't that cozy, a grown man and a child becoming best buds? "Sam," I say, when her feet remain glued in place, "please."

She sends a beseeching glance at Mr. Hayes, but he just shrugs. "She's the boss," he says, winking. "We'll continue this another time."

Like hell they will. What happened to Marina was a travesty but a predictable one. Hookers, even young, beautiful ones from decent, middle-class families, risk death with every trick they turn. But no millionaire porn king is going to get his hooks in my Samantha. I'll make sure of it, even if it costs me this job.

CHAPTER 54
LISA

I thought about giving Samantha the birth certificate last night while her mother was in Timbuktu sniffing out those ludicrous giraffes. But Edward came home in a mood and Ricki's pot roast burned and I was bone tired by 9 P.M. (breaking and entering really takes it out of you!). So I decided to let the news marinate overnight.

This morning, Samantha and I are taking the show on the road. "I thought we'd do something different today," I say as the gate closes behind us. "How does that sound?"

"Like what?"

She's supposed to be heading to school and I'm due at work. But I've told Jacquelyn to backload my appointments. I'll deal with the pill fiends this afternoon. Until then, I'm as free as a summer breeze.

Hmm. What do teenagers like to do? "We could go into the city," I offer. "Visit a museum—the Andy Warhol or the Carnegie Museum of Art." She's a fledgling artist, so this should appeal. "There are many excellent restaurants, too, of course."

"Seriously?"

"Why not?"

"Somebody will have to call the school," she points out. "Mom will freak out if I just disappear. She's sensitive because of, you know, what happened to my aunt. And the stuff with Jason."

I never tire of hearing how I've affected those in my orbit. It's satisfying, knowing I've made a difference; I've done something impactful. And if I can bring Samantha around to my way of thinking, my way of *being*, my reach will multiply exponentially. "Go ahead," I urge. "Make the call. You sound enough like your mother." I motion at my purse. "You can look up the number on my phone."

She's quick to take my advice. After a few moments of familiarizing herself with the phone, she puts in a smooth, practiced performance as Robin. Her tone, her diction, even her facial expressions are so spot-on they almost make me weep.

In my wildest dreams, I never imagined finding such a fitting protégé. And what is a master without her student, anyway? Less than, I'd say. But not anymore. To use a shopworn cliché: She completes me.

A key has been turned in a lock and my spirit is vibrating with possibilities. I can barely contain myself, my exuberance, as we venture on past the high school, past my office, and out of town.

The museums are a solid thirty miles away. We fill the drive with talk of books and movies—she's a crime buff, which only sweetens the pot—until, out of nowhere, she brings up Sophie Gallagher.

My mind does a double take. Have I let something slip?

"It was around here, I think," she says, gesturing at the trees.

The girl is so entrancing that only now do I notice that we're on Route 9. I could feign ignorance—"Sophie who?"—or regale her with the sordid tale of Sophie's and my entanglement. But I opt for a middle ground. "The accident, you mean?" I say innocently enough.

"They can't prove it. There was no reason." She keeps a laser focus on the woods. "Why would she just go off the road like that? It doesn't make sense."

"You're right," I say, "except—"

"What?"

A grin splits my face. "Can you keep a secret?"

"You know something?"

I nod. "She was a patient of mine."

"Oh my God, really? I just got chills." She pushes up her sleeve. "See? Goose bumps."

"I'm not at liberty to say much," I claim, "but Sophie Gallagher's death was no accident. In fact, the police have been at my office a number of times, collecting evidence."

"What did they say?" She leans in. "What did *you* say?"

"I told them about her husband. He's a piece of work. Cheated on her left and right. He had a big, fat insurance policy."

"No way." Her hand claps over her mouth.

"There was also a stalker. He killed himself and left a confession note. The authorities are following up on it as we speak."

"It's the stalker," she declares. "It's gotta be, right? I mean, why would someone confess if they didn't do it?" She puts her feet on the dash and ponders the idea, her lips twisting in a delightful, evocative sort of way.

Fate has bestowed upon me a second self, a host organism into which I may plant my seed and watch it bloom, a vessel—and a divine, shimmering one at that—to bear my essence forward in time. Even if I were to be struck down by a nasty disease or fell victim to a tragic accident, a black kernel of my making would survive in Samantha.

I turn the conversation away from Sophie—some topics are too close to home—and toward her love life. With this Jason out of the way, she must be shopping for a new boyfriend.

As predicted, she has prospects in her sights. "There's this guy in my calculus class. He's really smart"—she laughs—"obviously. But he's funny, too."

A sense of humor is overrated. The brains, though ... those can be valuable. Look at what I've done with Edward. "Smart is good," I say. "How tall is he?" Tall men outearn their punier counterparts. They're also catnip to the ladies, which is a double-edged sword. Ideally one could have her cake and eat it too without defending it against every Tanya, Dixie, and Harriet.

"Taller than me." She shrugs. "I don't know—six feet, maybe. His eyes ..."

"Let me guess: crystal blue?"

"Uh-uh. Brown. But they've got these little gold specks in 'em."

Fixating on such details is a sign of immaturity. (What can those specks do for her, anyway?) But she's young. With a little training, she'll be looking past such nonsense in no time. "Interesting," I say. I can't recommend the boy one way or another, so I turn the conversation again, this time to art.

The rest of the drive evaporates as Samantha gushes about balance and composition, movement and rhythm, positive and negative space. As we close in on the city, I make her choose between the Warhol and the Carnegie. We don't have time for both.

"Mm," she says, her face wrinkling in contemplation, "that's so hard."

"Flip a coin?"

"No, no. Gimme a second. They're both good, I bet. I just know I'm gonna regret not picking whichever one—"

"We can come back, you know. Think of this as a preview. We'll make a day of it next time—hire a car and driver, reserve the best table at one of those glass restaurants overlooking the city. Maybe for your birthday …"

"The Warhol," she says. "The Carnegie seems bigger. Or broader or whatever. It'll take too long. You'll be dragging me out of there by my hair."

Her logic is unassailable. We drop the Hummer in a garage and get busy taking in the soup cans and self-portraits, the Marilyns and Maos, the skulls and guns and electric chairs (our Andy had quite the death fetish!).

To describe Samantha as elated would be missing the point. She *is* that, of course—though *enraptured* may be a better word, the way she blinks dreamily and speaks in rambling, out-of-breath jags—but there's also quiet gratitude bubbling from her pores. I've opened the world to her. I've seen her in ways her mother never has, in ways *no one* has. I've honored her core truth, the creative impulse that makes her Samantha and not some random girl drifting toward nothingness, courting a life of mediocrity and worse.

She's special. So am I. We're of the same tribe. In her own way—a brush of my arm, a soulful glance, murmurs of heartfelt appreciation—she acknowledges the connectedness I've known all along.

As we conclude our pop-art tour, peacefulness settles over me. The feeling lasts straight through lunch, which we consume in an intimate (read: small, wood-paneled, softly lit) tap room of a historic downtown hotel, in whose lavish ballrooms Edward and I have attended our fair share of charity events. (A luau-themed benefit stands out for Penelope Anne's drunken hula dancing.)

I've abandoned my Angus burger—my tummy's queasy—but Samantha plows ahead, finishing hers and licking the juices from her fingers.

"How about dessert?" I ask with an encouraging smile. An apple tart à la mode or a hunk of triple-chocolate layer cake will console her when the bad news hits, when the truth about her lying mother comes to light.

She takes me up on the offer. To humor her, I order a second slice of cake and pick at it with the tines of a fork—a few drops of frosting are all I can handle—before removing the envelope from my purse. "So," I say, "I have something to show you."

With a quizzical look, she replies, "Okay." She carves off another chunk of cake and lifts it to her mouth.

I remove the birth certificate and set it down, still folded, beside my silverware. "It's up to you if you want to read this," I say, tapping the paper, "but I've pulled some strings and gotten a copy of your birth certificate. The story you'd been given seemed ... well, it seemed suspect. I thought you deserved to know the truth."

"Has my mother seen—? How did you get—?"

"I have connections," I say vaguely. "It's public record—vital statistics and whatnot."

She takes a gulp of water and wipes her mouth with the back of her hand. "You wouldn't be showing me that unless something's wrong."

Of course, she's right. But I downplay the idea. "Don't think of it that way," I say. Just then, the waiter shows up to refill our water glasses. I shake my head and he cuts to another table. "Information is neither good nor bad; it's what you do with the information that matters. Wouldn't you rather have accurate 'bad' information than inaccurate 'good' information?"

She shrugs.

"Let's say you have a disease. An ugly one. Cancer or something else life-threatening." I swirl a finger around on the birth certificate, tracing an invisible figure eight. "Let's also say that this disease can be cured if it's caught early, if it's aggressively treated."

"Yeah," she mumbles.

"You'd want to know about it as soon as possible, right? Even though it's bad news? Even though it could kill you?"

She holds out her hand. "Just give it to me."

That's more like it. "I'm sorry if this hurts," I say, sliding the paper across the table. "I'm sure your mother had her reasons."

CHAPTER 55
ROBIN

In the morning rush, I almost miss the envelope of cash taped to our suite door. Sixteen crisp hundreds, days ahead of schedule.

The bills are new. They stick together. I count them twice and then crumple them before shoving them in my jeans and heading upstairs.

Samantha spent the night in one of the guest bedrooms—the modern black-and-white room adjoining the children's suite. When I try to peek in on her, she's in the shower. She barely said two words to me last night before disappearing to study.

I can't wait around. The children must be gotten ready for school. I'll catch Sam on her way out the door or, worst-case scenario, later this afternoon.

The twins' room is a study in purple—plum floor pillows, lavender bedspreads, fluffy mauve throw rugs, a sparkling violet chandelier—offset by creamy white armchairs and wrapped in silver wallpaper. Even though I'm the adult, I'm out of my league in the space. I don't belong amid the luxury these kids take for granted.

Still, I have a job to do. I knock softly and swing open the door, expecting to find the children stalling for time. A favorite trick of theirs is staring dead-eyed at social media sites while ignoring me and everything else in the real world.

My first surprise is that Mae is dressed in her school uniform—a plaid jumper, knee socks, and a green cardigan with Triton Prep's coat of arms on the sleeve—and her hair is combed into neat pigtails. "You're ready early," I say as she straightens her sweater in front of the mirror, lining up the halves and threading the buttons through their holes. "Great job." I look around for Darian but see nothing but a rumpled bed. "Where's your sister?"

Mae shrugs. "Sleeping prob'ly."

I laugh, thinking she's being funny, but as I wander toward Darian's bed, I see a foot sticking out from under the covers.

I haven't been here long, but a pattern is already emerging: On alternate days, the twins take turns hassling me. Yesterday, Mae "accidentally" dumped her yogurt on the floor when I gave her the strawberry instead of the vanilla she wanted. Today Darian's making me earn my money.

No one said this was going to be easy.

If the foot were Samantha's, I'd tickle it. But something tells me that the Hayeses wouldn't appreciate this tactic being used on their daughter. "Good morning," I say, peeling the bedspread away from Darian's face. Her skin is mottled. When her eyes drift open, they're glassy and unfocused. "What's the matter? Are you sick?" It's a rhetorical question. Anyone would know the child is under the weather.

I press my palm to her forehead. It's warm, not hot. Maybe she's just dehydrated. I duck into the bathroom and come back with a glass of water. I set it on the nightstand and help her sit up. "Drink, sweetheart," I say, lifting the glass to her mouth.

From across the room, Mae watches curiously.

I get a few ounces of water into Darian before she pushes the glass away and sinks back into the pillows. A tug on my shirt surprises me. "Pshew," I blurt, catching Mae's silhouette. "Don't sneak up on people."

A ghost of a smile crosses Mae's lips. "What's wrong with her?"

I run my fingers through my hair. "I don't know. A bug, maybe? It's nothing to worry about. Her temperature's normal." Or normal enough—though I should ask Dr. Hayes what she wants me to do. For all I know, these millionaires run to the hospital every time they stub a toe.

Mae collects her backpack and exits the room. I tell Darian to stay put—she won't be going to school in her condition—until I come back and check on her. She murmurs something unintelligible and clutches the sheets to her throat.

By the time I reach the kitchen, Mae's perched on a stool, eating a vanilla yogurt. I laugh to myself. These girls get what they want, one way or another. I thought Darian was the more demanding of the two, but Mae's giving her a run for her money.

Not only is Sam among the missing, but I haven't seen either of the doctors today. I linger in front of the sink, staring out the window at a pair of crows. For a parklike estate bordering protected wilderness (signs near the entrance gate ward off hunters, snowmobilers, etcetera), precious few animals are around outdoors. The indoor ones are inanimate—a stuffed trophy wolf in the game room; gargoyle statues sprinkled around the bookcases; rugs with dragons and snakes and birds of prey—except that yappy little dog.

The crows sense my watching and take flight. As I turn back toward the kitchen, Ricki is arriving.

Thank God.

I tell her about Darian. She says the Hayeses aren't sensitive. A trip to the doctor is overkill. "Can you check on her while I'm gone, then?" I ask. The drive to Triton Prep is thirty-five minutes each way.

Ricki agrees and I finish up with Mae. She's got a test today on dividing fractions, and I'm giving her some last-minute tips. When I'm satisfied she'll ace the test, we bundle up and go on our way.

Darian sleeps until eleven o'clock and then awakes miraculously recovered, leading me to question the validity of her illness. "What's one-sixth divided by one-third?" I ask, peering over her shoulder as she opens her laptop in front of the huge plasma TV in the great room.

She ignores me and tunes the TV to *Wizards of Waverly Place*.

"Are you supposed to be watching that?" I ask. The kids on the show look like teenagers and no one has briefed me on the household media policy.

"One times three is three. Six times one is six. Three-sixths reduces to one-half," she recites robotically.

True enough. One-sixth divided by one-third is one-half.

"Very good." If she missed school on purpose, it wasn't because of the test. "How about lunch? I'll make grilled cheese sandwiches."

"I want egg salad."

"Coming right up," I say, even though it'll take me a while to boil, cool, and peel the eggs. I leave her with the electronics and get to work. When the sandwiches are done, I convince her to eat with me in the kitchen. She fights the idea halfheartedly, but there's a lull in her TV lineup and she eventually complies.

Ricki joins us for lunch before taking off for a cleaning-supplies run. Once the dishes are in the dishwasher, the island is wiped down, and the floor is swept, I suggest a board game.

"I don't like games," says Darian, wrinkling her nose.

What kid doesn't like games? She must be trying to get a rise out of me. "We could do word puzzles, then," I say. Along with the French manuals, the former nanny has left stacks of crosswords, word searches, and hangman games.

"Nah."

When I was a teacher, this passive-aggressive behavior might've earned her a timeout. But the lines are blurred now. Who's in charge? I have more than a sneaking suspicion that if I displease the children, I'll be fired. In a twisted way, *they* have the power; *I* work for *them*. "What *would* you like to do?" She's worn me down with little effort. Then again, life gave her a running start. I've been swimming against the tide for as long as I can remember.

"Dress up."

I know my marching orders when I hear them. Still ... "Really?" Darian's beyond her years intellectually—now I know what Dr. Hayes meant when she said the girls were "eight going on thirty-five"—but she retains a playful innocence, a beguiling mischievousness.

"Mm-hmm."

I follow her down the hall. She's pulsing with energy, so much so that she's hopping and skipping and bumping into walls. When she zings past her suite—I'm picturing a Louis Vuitton trunk stuffed with feather boas and tiaras in the back of her walk-in closet—I assume she's overshot her mark.

"Where are you going?" Soon we're at the door of the master suite. "Your father might be—"

"Uh-uh," she says, flinging open the door. "He's in New York." She disappears inside.

I take a deep breath and follow her. The enormous room is every bit as opulent and elegant as I'd imagined. Particularly striking is a blue couch on the far wall that looks like it belongs in a Danish palace. I'm also floored by the massive bed. A baker's dozen of me could fit on the embroidered silver-and-gold bedcover.

This must be what heaven looks like. Marina would love it. For a moment, I allow myself to believe that my sister lives on somewhere pleasant and safe—mystical and exotic (just like her)—for the vastness of eternity.

"What're you doing?" I ask, trailing Darian into an adjoining room, which turns out to be a shoe closet. Before I can stop her, she snatches a pair of bejeweled suede boots from an eye-level shelf (luckily much of the footwear is over her head and out of reach), kicks off her unicorn slippers, and flops down on the floor, jamming her bare, undersized feet into the boots without undoing the zippers. "I don't think your mother would want—"

"She loves playing dress up. We do it all the time."

My hands go to my hips. "Your mother lets you put on her things?"

Darian's chin toggles up and down. "We pretend it's a fashion show. My mother was in a beauty contest, you know. She won the blue ribbon."

Don't they award ribbons to farm animals and crowns to pageant queens? As for Dr. Hayes's astounding beauty … well, that's a given. "Let me help you," I say, grasping Darian's arm and steadying her as she wobbles onto her feet.

She gets off a few wrenching steps, wincing as her ankles fold over. The closet is carpeted, but if she makes it to the hardwood floor, I'll have two catastrophes on my hands, the damaged boots (those jewels are bound to pop off any second now) and the gouges in that flawless floor.

Ain't gonna happen.

I throw her over my shoulder and rush her to the bed. Breathing hard from the effort, I deposit her on the mattress with her legs dangling over the side.

"What'd you do that for?" she asks, her eyes wide and blinking.

I get down on my knees, unzip the boots, and tug them off. "These are ugly." I make a face. "You should be wearing something prettier, don't you think?"

She bites her lip and shrugs.

I jog to the closet and come back with a pair of emerald-green ballet flats with puffy bows on the toes. (I can't imagine the doctor wearing these. They're goofy and floppy, and she's a paragon of elegance.)

Darian reluctantly lets me put the ballet shoes on her. They're too big, but her feet are sticky with sweat, helping them stay in place.

"Green's my favorite color," she says, kicking her feet up and down, watching the bows flutter. The scissor kicks last for a few minutes before she grows bored and launches herself off the bed.

As Darian spins and leaps toward an adjacent room—the master suite is the hub of a wheel, spokes reaching out in multiple directions—my cell phone rings. I wiggle it out of my pocket and check the caller ID.

Nate.

My heart clenches. It took everything I had to hurt him, to banish him for his own good. But things have changed. I'm not the needy basket case I was. He doesn't have to rescue me anymore. Maybe we can try again.

Impulsively, I answer the call. Nate offers a lame pretext for contacting me—something about a receipt that fell out of his wallet at my house—before asking how I've been, inquiring about Sam and our whereabouts. (I assume he's been by the house and noticed we're gone.)

I wander to the couch and sit down, turning away from the bedroom in favor of the panoramic view outside. As I gaze over the rolling hills, I update him on my good fortune. He's thrilled to hear about the job but less enthusiastic about our living situation. ("Do they really need you twenty-four hours a day?") When I tell him about Samantha's change of heart, about her dumping the loser boyfriend, he says, "She's a good kid. I knew she'd do the right thing."

We talk awhile longer about mundane stuff—his students, my brother (in a series of sporadic texts, Scott has kept me up to date on his relocation saga, which still has him living in a hotel but a nicer one than he started with), and even Tiger Woods's strange middle-of-the-night car crash.

I'm wrapped up in the conversation; I lose track of time. Darian could be halfway to Tijuana by now. Actually, I've forgotten her altogether when she comes tromping along with that little dog clutched to her chest.

As she approaches, the dog starts yelping and squirming and paddling his paws. In the process, his nails slash her arm. She screeches and tosses him to the floor. He lands at my feet and scrambles around, nipping at my ankles.

"Sorry," I tell Nate, shielding the phone, "but I've gotta go." I don't wait for his answer before ending the call.

I shoo away the dog and invite Darian, who's draped in jewelry (she must've raided her mother's stash while I was preoccupied), onto the couch so I can evaluate her injuries. But her hand is clamped over her arm, protecting the spot in question, and she just shakes her head when I encourage her to show me the damage.

"C'mon," I prod, "let me look." I start prying her fingers away from her arm. She continues to whimper, but it's an act now. She's playing up for sympathy. "Shh," I coo, "it's okay." The dog has scratched her pretty good—there are two scrapes on the underside of her forearm, one of which is leaking blood—but she'll be fine with a little hydrogen peroxide and antibiotic ointment.

I'm about to break the good news and maybe even throw in a trip to the ice cream shop on the way to pick up Mae, when the nest of necklaces around her throat catches my eye. She must have on twenty intertwined layers of pearls and diamonds, rubies and onyxes, silver and gold. Peeking out from this storm of jewels is something that stops my heart: a burnt-orange pendant, a square citrine that so closely resembles Marina's beloved treasure that my blood runs cold.

CHAPTER 56
LISA

Edward arrives home from New York, from a meeting with one of his manufacturing partners, in the dead of night and then absconds again for the weekend (something about a "supply-chain issue" in Brazil), leaving me at loose ends. Never fear, though. I'm capable of amusing myself.

Saturday belongs to leisurely swims in the natatorium with Samantha—she's still reeling from Robin's betrayal and lost in a funk over the identity of her bio dad—and an obscene amount of retail therapy via the internet. I didn't keep track, but a ballpark figure on Samantha's and my little shopping spree, which includes several matching outfits, would be fifteen grand. Or twenty. Actually, not so obscene for someone of my means.

When Sunday rolls around, I spirit Samantha away to one of my favorite hotels, where we order a smorgasbord of spa treatments—Swedish massages, lavender-chamomile facials, full-body sea-salt exfoliations, mani-pedis, the works.

After we've sunk into a euphoric haze, I buzz room service for a couple of dry-aged steaks, a basket of fries, and a round of mimosas. It takes no convincing for Samantha to imbibe. From our therapy sessions, I know she's experimented with a variety of drugs but has never come close to addiction. Like me, she values control and stops short of the point of no return.

Smart girl.

With Robin under the gun preparing Darian and Mae for their midterms—Triton has a long history of torturing students in the lead-up to winter break—Samantha and I are in no hurry. We sprawl out on the bed with an old Hitchcock movie on TV as a backdrop for our conversation.

"Have you talked to your mother about the birth certificate?" I finally get around to asking.

"What for?"

"She owes you an explanation, don't you think?"

"She probably doesn't know who my father is."

"Come again." The guy's name is typed in that slim little box: Chuck Dalton.

"She's a drunk—like a minor one that can be, you know, sort of normal—but then she goes on these … these …" Samantha shakes her head. "I've seen her go off the deep end so many times. I bet she was passed out when she got pregnant with me. She probably just picked a name out of a hat and stuck it on the birth certificate."

I waffle between agreeing with her and insisting on Chuck's legitimacy. If he *is* real, he might try to exert his dominion over her. And I can't have that. "You've got every right to be angry," I settle for saying. Hopefully the revelation that her mother has lied to her will sow discord, will bring Samantha under my power.

When she snuggles up to me in that lush hotel robe and drifts off to sleep with her hair splashed across my shoulder, I consider the experiment a ringing success.

I'm padding out of the master bathroom, swaddled in a towel, when I catch Edward whispering on the phone. He's at the far end of the bedroom, past the sofa and bank of windows, sitting rigidly in a fauteuil armchair circa 1735. He doesn't notice me until I'm within arm's reach, close enough to hear the bubbling of a woman's voice on the other end of the line.

Here we go again. Whom is my husband fucking now? I'm not the jealous sort, but his pubescent behavior is getting tiresome.

"All right, then," he says. "We'll speak more about that later. Goodbye." He hangs up and sets the phone on a side table. I eye it, wondering if he's dumb enough to leave it unguarded around me. Through our entire relationship, I've never felt the need to check up on him. What he does between the sheets with some money-grubbing twat means nothing to me. But the sneaking around, the lying, the attempts to outmaneuver me—those are insults to my intelligence, ones I don't intend to abide.

"Who was that?" I ask, opening the towel and shimmying it across my back, giving him a bounce-and-jiggle show.

He stares at a painting over the bed, a woodland scene of nymphs and fairies and hobgoblins, and ignores my exhibitionism. "Just work," he replies vaguely.

I bend over and dry my legs from ankle to thigh. Then I shed the towel and lean in for a kiss, expecting an explosion of desire. He should be driving his tongue down my throat and parting my legs with his sandpaper fingers. Instead, his lips flop against mine like a mechanical fish.

Disgusting.

I shoot him an inquisitive look—I know a rat when I smell one—as I pivot for the closet. I slip inside and get dressed, losing ten minutes to the search for a skinny silver belt that complements my gray tweed skirt. I'm poking the prong through the middle belt hole—I've pouched out in the tummy, which could explain Edward's lackluster response—when my husband raps on the closet door. "Will you be much longer?"

I strut out, looking like one of the Robert Palmer Girls—high cheekbones, slicked-back hair, toned legs—minus the glossy red lips and the guitar. "What is it?" I ask, modulating my tone. He can't be allowed to detect my displeasure, my creeping suspicions about him.

He's at the fossil of a dresser he insists on keeping—it's an heirloom, to hear him tell it—even though we have ample closet space and the thing clashes with my continental décor. The drawers are pulled out haphazardly, as if they've been tossed by a hurried thief. "Have you seen my ties?" he asks, pointing at the shallow top drawer. "They were right here."

"Did you check the closet?" His work wardrobe is arranged by our human wonder, Ricki.

"Not those ones. The ones the kids gave me."

My eyebrows pinch together. I can't recall our daughters having ever bought him a necktie, though Ashley or another nanny could be behind the gift.

"Ellen's kids," he clarifies, "Jane and Tommy. Last year for my birthday…"

"Those garish novelty ties with the little creatures on them?" The ones I blindfolded the good doctor with before strangling him? "I have no earthly idea. What would you want with those ugly things?"

"We're doing a white-elephant exchange at the office. It was Lorraine's idea." His right-hand girl. My husband is a scatterbrain with details. If he didn't have Lorraine—or an equivalent substitute—the money train would grind to a halt. "She wants something to wrap up by today."

"You're the boss," I say, playing to his ego. "Shouldn't you contribute something better than a couple of hideous ties?"

"It's a joke." He grins. "The real prize is a Toyota Prius."

How environmentally conscious of him. "Just stop by Walmart or somewhere." That'll be a shock to his system! "You can get one of those Rudolph sweaters with the blinking nose."

"You really don't know what happened to them?"

"Sorry," I say.

He straightens the dresser drawers and jimmies them back into place. "By the way," he says, as I'm turning to leave, "I need the Hummer. You can take my car to work."

I stop dead. "For what?" He sure is acting peculiar. First the hushed phone call and then the quest for those ridiculous ties and now this?

"We're moving offices. Reconfiguring teams and reorganizing for greater synergy." He locks his hands together to demonstrate the concept.

Who does he think I am, one of his airheaded concubines? "And my car is going to schlep around a bunch of filing cabinets?"

"I'm more concerned about the computer equipment. With all the proprietary information—"

I've heard enough. "The keys are on the hook. Have someone vacuum it when you're done. Those monitors are dust magnets."

"Will do." He nods. "Anything else, darling?"

If he's offering ... "I'm holding tension in my neck. Can you schedule Lyubo for seven o'clock? And, oh, some Thai food would be wonderful. Order from that new place on Pike Street and have Ricki pick it up."

"Done and done."

CHAPTER 57
ROBIN

I took the necklace. I couldn't help it. It reminds me of Marina. It isn't hers, of course—how would it have ended up in the jewelry collection of a wealthy doctor who can afford things not even my starry-eyed sister could've dreamed of?—but then why does it have such a pull, such gravity? It's like Marina is reaching out from the grave and saying, "Look here, dummy. Look here and you'll find the answer to my death."

I wish it were that easy.

Still, the necklace haunts me. Over the weekend, I keep it with me at all times, even wearing it to bed in hopes of drawing Marina into my dreams. But she's as elusive as ever.

If Sam were around, she'd give me hell. She's sick of my fixation. Plus, if I get fired from this job, she might disown me. She's having the time of her life with Dr. Hayes, testing the waters of a world I couldn't give her in a thousand lifetimes. I'm happy for her, as long as she stays grounded, as long as she doesn't forget me. I owe Dr. Hayes the leeway to do what's best for my daughter, even if that means seeing less of Sam for a while. The doctor has worked miracles already; I can't wait to see what she does next.

It's only noon and I've finished putting together the study aids I'll use with the children this week. Which leaves a couple of hours before they must be picked up from school.

I meander from the library, where I've been bent over a stack of textbooks all morning, to the kitchen, stretching my neck and kneading my thumb into a tender spot behind my ear. The house is empty. (Again, Ricki's dashed off on a vital errand.) In front of the refrigerator, I let out a howling yawn. I open the fridge, searching for something caffeinated, something sugary. Downstairs is a bag of M&M's, but the walk's too far and I'm in a lazy mood. The Hayeses won't mind if I sneak a bottle of orange juice or a slice of pie—Ricki makes a mean key lime—since Ricki will just replace it tomorrow.

A can of Coke kills two birds with one stone. I crack it open and take a long gulp.

The chat with Nate the other day was cleansing. Despite our bumpy road, he means something to me. He's been so dependable—so selfless—that I can't shake him from my heart. And why should I? The way I'm reinventing myself—the job, the money, the progress with Samantha—might just make me worthy of him.

My phone is in my pocket. I take it out, mulling over the idea of messaging him. Maybe I could meet him for coffee before picking up the girls.

After rolling around the idea—and checking for missed calls (negative)—I decide to wait. A polite phone call, which we've already had, is a good first step. There's no sense pushing things in a direction they're not ready to go. I don't want to ruin our chances at the first glimmer of hope.

I *will* call Scott, though. I've been meaning to catch up with him. "Hey," I say when he answers, "it's me."

"Hi." A loud grinding noise fills his end of the line.

"Are you at work?"

"Yeah. What's up?"

"Just checking in. Have you taken your lunch break?"

He coughs for a solid twenty seconds. "Nah. We're off schedule. The trucks are late 'cause of—"

I steal a sip of Coke. "They're not letting you eat lunch?"

"Did you want something? I only answered 'cause I thought Sam …"

"If I bring sandwiches, can you get ten minutes off? I have a few things to tell you."

"When?"

I glance at the microwave. The clock reads 12:18. "Between one and one fifteen?"

"Ten minutes," he agrees. "That's all I got." A brief pause. "And no turkey."

Our mother made thousands of turkey sandwiches in her life. We kids ate most of them. For all I know, the prison menu was also turkey-based, which would've been Scott's own personal hell. "I remember," I say, chuckling. "See you soon."

I can't find my brother, even after pulling the Mercedes up to a big industrial building that looks like an airplane hangar. I roll down the window and shout at a barrel-chested guy in a hardhat. He's leaning a broom against a pallet rack and squinting—my voice hasn't carried over the symphony of mechanical noises—when Scott drifts around the side of the building.

I wave off the janitor and unlock the passenger door. Scott hesitates before deciding that, yes, his screw-up of a sister *has* just rolled up in a newish luxury car. He gets in, shaking his head. "Do I even want to know?"

"Actually, yes," I reply, grabbing the bag of food and thrusting it at him. "Ham and salami. Take your pick." I've also brought a couple of Yoo-hoos, for old times' sake—our father used to load a case of the chocolaty stuff into our station wagon each summer for the trip to camp—and a bag of chips.

Scott takes the chips and starts shoveling them down. "Where are we going?" he asks when I make the turn off the lumberyard road.

"Not far." In a matter of seconds, we coast into the parking lot of a strip mall. I bring us to rest in front of a pet store, which somehow seems preferable to a tanning salon, a bank, and a sporting-goods store.

"So," says Scott, surveying the Mercedes, "explain."

I run through the series of events that led to my working for the Hayeses.

He's as dumbfounded as I am. "The lady just hired you to watch her kids? She moved you into her mansion? You're driving *this*?"

"It's a little crazy."

"I'd say." He holds out the chip bag. I take it and finish them off. He licks his fingers and moves on to the sandwiches.

"It was a godsend, really, the timing of it," I say.

"Yeah?"

"We were flat broke. Well, you know how it is." I let out a gentle sigh. Things are better now. That old life can't touch me anymore. "The electricity was cut off. We were up the creek without—"

"How's Sam like it?"

"Oh, God, she loves it. Dr. Hayes takes her everywhere. She treats Samantha more like her own daughter than … than her own daughters." I laugh, even though it hurts—*because* it hurts. If being snubbed is the price I have to pay for Sam's success, her happiness, so be it.

Scott spends a couple of minutes updating me on the housing saga, which is poised to turn a corner. The government has finally found him a stable place to stay, if halfway houses count as stable. He'll be settled in by the end of next week.

"That's great. Looks like we're both moving on."

His sandwich is about gone. "You gonna eat this?" he asks about the other one.

I tell him that the chips are plenty; I'm not hungry. The Hayeses have enough food to last through a nuclear holocaust. Plus, I've got something to talk to him about, and it shouldn't be done on a full stomach.

"Listen," I say, "I need your opinion."

His eyes roll: What now?

"Remember that necklace of Marina's? The one I had before? The one I sold?"

"Unfortunately."

I'm trying to give him a chance, but if he doesn't stop trashing our sister, it's going to be the end of us. "She wore another necklace, too. It had a brownish orange stone. It's called a citrine."

He shrugs.

"Did you ever see her with that one?"

"That was—shit, Robin—twenty-five years ago," he says, rubbing his temple. "I gotta get back to work."

"Would you recognize it? If I showed it to you, would you be able to tell if it was the same—?"

"I doubt it."

I reach into the neck of my shirt and expose the pendant. It floats over my henley like a bobber on the night sea. "Here," I say, twirling the chain around and unclasping it. I cup the necklace in my hand. "Tell me if you've seen this before, if it's one of the necklaces Marina used to wear when ..."

My brother pokes the chain around my palm like it's a carcass he's stumbled upon in the woods. "Could be," he says. "I don't know."

"That's the best you can do?"

"What do you want? I didn't pick the damn thing out. I didn't get a box and wrap it up and stick a pretty little bow on it." He releases a tense breath. "Can we go now?"

Scott's an ass, but he's given me an idea. There *is* someone who'd recognize the necklace with certainty. And I know just where to find him.

As usual, Triton Prep is mobbed with nannies, most of them young and foreign, all of them in expensive luxury cars.

I'm late. I join the line of vehicles along the tree-lined edge of campus and creep toward the main entrance as other cars clear out. Finally, I spot the twins. By the time I reach them, they're irritated from the wait. They get in the car grumbling.

I ask about the social studies midterm. Hopefully they made me proud. One thing that could secure my future, in this job or elsewhere, is current proof—in the form of stellar test scores—of my teaching abilities.

"It was easy," declares Mae.

Darian takes the sentiment a step further, insisting she got everything right, including the bonus questions.

A wave of relief crashes over me. I'm not worthless, after all. I've done something meaningful. I've helped these children succeed. It's true what they say: A job well done is its own reward.

Despite the continued grousing—Darian has demanded to know the reason for my lateness, which makes me laugh—I'm feeling upbeat as I plot a course for home.

I've never driven from Triton Prep to the old neighborhood. My instincts are slow to kick in. But eventually we're cruising by familiar sights: the beauty school where Sam and I get our hair cut; my regular gas station; the Dunkin' Donuts where I lost my virginity (back then, it was the home of a pimply-faced science fiction geek with a working single mom and a squeaky twin bed).

"Where are we?" asks Mae as we coast to a stop in front of Lewis's house.

I hadn't thought of how to explain the detour to the kids. "My friend lives here," I say. "I'm checking on him, seeing if he needs anything."

Darian's nose wrinkles. "Why?"

"He's old. He had an operation. He can't get around as good as he used to."

Mae whispers, "As *well*."

"That's right, Mae," I say. "He can't get around as *well* as he used to."

Mae beams and Darian shoots her a biting look.

I tell the children I'll be back in a few minutes, but as I reach for the door handle, I have second thoughts about leaving them in the car. You never know what kind of lunatic might be drifting through this neighborhood. "Actually, change of plans. Everyone out."

Single file, we traipse up the strip of driveway between Lewis's house and his van. Before I have a chance to knock, the screen door flies open and Lewis leans out. "Oh, Robin. I thought you were the deliveryman. Wanda's ordered new drapes for the living room. They'll be arriving any minute now." His gaze falls on the children. "Won't you come in?"

We take him up on the offer. The house is warm inside—stuffy, even—and cozy. In fact, it feels downright tiny now that I'm used to the lofty ceilings and gaping rooms of the Hayeses' mansion. By the looks of the children—they're huddled together in the middle of the kitchen, as if the walls might eat them—they're even more claustrophobic than I am.

I ask about Wanda. Lewis says she's in the bedroom, watching *Oprah*. "Damn near broke her heart when that woman announced the end of her show. She won't miss a minute of it now; she wants to see every last episode."

I felt the same way about *The Facts of Life*. Those girls were my sisters after Marina died.

I explain briefly about the nanny job. Lewis ushers us into the living room and puts the TV on Cartoon Network. Then he sets out a plate of Oreos. The girls are perched on the edge of the couch, nibbling over the glass coffee table, when Lewis and I slip back into the kitchen. I don't waste any time. I pull out the necklace and dangle it in front of him.

His eyes grow wide. "Where did ...?" he says, trapping the pendant in his fist and bringing it closer. He shakes his head. "The first one was, well, a miracle after all these years. But now ... now you've brought ..."

"Was this Georgette's?" If so, Marina was a thief. But I may be on the verge of finding her killer.

"Yes," he says, sounding astonished, "I believe it was."

"Are you sure?"

"Sure enough." He frowns. "I'm sorry about your sister. I didn't want to be the one to tell you."

"It's okay," I say. "Do you have a picture of Georgette wearing this necklace? I have to be a hundred percent sure."

He holds up a finger. "Wait right here." He takes the necklace and disappears down the hall.

I drag a chair away from the table and collapse into it, cartoon noises fluttering around the edges of my mind. My blood pounds out a question, *the* question: Did Edward kill Marina?

A few moments later, Lewis returns, clutching a framed photo—a Glamour Shot, it looks like—of Georgette. The glass is dusty; he smears away the particles with his thumb. Georgette looks so healthy, with full cheeks and even fuller hair, that sadness wells up inside me. I push it down and compare the photograph to the necklace. There's no doubt that the two pieces of jewelry are similar, but the photographer has focused on Georgette's sparkling eyes and not the gemstone resting between the upturned collars of her denim shirt.

I coax the necklace out of Lewis's hand and study it, going back and forth between the real thing and the out-of-focus image. "Do you have any other pictures?" I ask. "Something clearer? And closer up? This is beautiful—I forgot how kind Georgette's eyes were—but I can't tell if..."

Lewis leans against the counter, staring at the photograph. "I'm afraid not," he says. "None better than this. Unless—"

"Unless what?"

"Unless you want to see the catalog. It'll take a while to find. You could make a cup of coffee."

"Catalog?"

"The one I ordered the necklaces out of."

My face twists with disbelief. "You still have it?"

"No promises. Don't get your hopes up," he says. "But yes—I think I do."

"Please."

I'm already too jittery, so I skip the coffee and pace the linoleum, checking on the twins twice. They're angels of the highest order, suddenly.

True to his word, Lewis comes back with the proof. The necklace is a match. I make an excuse not to relinquish it (I envision slipping it back into Dr. Hayes's jewelry cabinet while I work out what to do next), and Lewis doesn't push it.

Finally, after all these years, I have an answer. And his name is Edward Hayes.

CHAPTER 58
LISA

Edward is hilarious, flailing around like a chicken with its head cut off, searching for his phone. He's a fool to have taken his eyes off it around me—was that middle-of-the-night Devil Dog really worth it?—now that he's tripped my sensors, now that he's landed under my watchful gaze.

It's all I can do to stop from blowing coffee out my nose as he rips apart the kitchen with a scarlet face and sweat beading on his hairline. If anyone should know better than to cross me, it's my dear husband.

"You haven't seen it?" he asks for the hundredth time. "Anywhere?" He slaps a hand on the island and exhales violently.

Maybe what's on the phone is even more telling, more valuable, than I suspect. "What about the bathrooms?" I say, making a little joke. I've sunk the phone in a jar of cotton balls in the master bath. "Have you checked all of them?"

Edward scowls. "If you find it, don't touch it. Entering the wrong passcode too many times erases everything. I've been lax in backing it up and—" He breaks off as Samantha appears. "Spread the word," he says, cycling a hand through the air. He drops a kiss on my temple and wishes Samantha a good day before cursing the clock and rushing off.

Samantha opens the refrigerator and peers inside. "The word about what?"

"Oh, nothing," I say, dabbing at the corners of my mouth with a napkin. "Ricki made sticky buns. They're in the basket by the stove." I suck a gob of icing off my thumb.

"Is that what smells so good?" Samantha pulls back the checkered cloth and serves herself the largest pastry of the bunch, which does my heart good. Maybe once her mother's gone—and probably my husband, too (Edward's star is fading fast)—I'll ship the girls off to boarding school and it'll just be Samantha and me. Imagine the fun we'll have then....

I leave Samantha to her breakfast and return to the master bath. I lock myself inside, intending to remove the battery from Edward's phone. But the case is factory sealed and impenetrable. Keeping the phone turned off will prevent Edward or one of his techie minions from tracking it and, hence, me.

During the morning ride, Samantha and I forgo our usual chat in favor of a CD she wants me to hear. My opinions weigh heavily on her now, a fact that tickles my soul.

The music is not to my taste—some sort of indie folk rock with a melancholy vibe—but I tell her to turn it up, anyway. She curls up in the passenger seat, rests her head on the window, and stares into the distance, probably thinking about her cheating ex or her derelict father.

The moment she hits the sidewalk in front of Jackman High, I turn off the music. The melodies are too nostalgic. The secret of my success, my power, is never regretting, never looking back. And why should I? Everything I have, everything I've become, is a result of my shrewd decision-making. Really, I should teach a course.

When I arrive at the office, the door is locked and it's dark inside. Where's Jacquelyn? She should've been here an hour ago.

I rummage through my purse for the key. Eventually, my fingers strike gold. I slip the key in the lock and let myself in.

Jacquelyn's desk is a chaotic muddle. I pick through the mess, looking for a note of explanation. With my luck, she got hit by a train and

I'll be stuck managing all of the appointments today. Not that she does much; not that I can't handle it. I'm just not in the mood.

There's no sign of any communication meant for me. I turn on my heel, intending to do some online research there must be a way to crack into Edward's phone without wiping it clean—before the first client drifts in. But then my coat brushes a pile of papers, sending them floating to the floor. I don't bother crouching down to retrieve them. It's not my job and, more importantly, something else has caught my eye: on Jacquelyn's desk, a business card from Detective Luke Jones. I recognize the police logo.

I pinch the card and slide it out of its hiding place. The face looks predictable enough, but when I flip it over, the back is inscribed with a date and time. Which can only mean one thing: Jacquelyn's been meeting with detectives behind my back.

Briefly, I seethe, my mind taking a dark turn—I picture Jacquelyn's head underwater, my hands locked around her throat, squeezing tightly—before realizing that, try as she might, my little Benedict Arnold doesn't have the goods to so much as dent my armor. I'm far too meticulous to be brought down by the likes of her. In fact, maybe Jacquelyn's blathering is a good thing; maybe her crackpot theories and addled observations will have the cops running on hamster wheels for the foreseeable future.

Aaah. That's better. Nothing to worry about, after all. I toss the appointment card on the floor, step over it, and proceed into my office.

According to the internet, Edward's phone can't be hacked. I can either guess his password in the allotted number of tries, summon a tech guru from the dark web, or—and this is a long shot—rekindle a relationship with an Israeli national named Eitan whose bell I used to ring between anatomy class and lunch in my university days. It wouldn't surprise me if Eitan is in the intelligence biz. He had a talent for spy games and a brilliant ease with computers. Maybe he's a founding father of that shadowy hacker collective, Anonymous.

I'm at my desk, staring at Edward's phone, which is nothing more than a paperweight at the moment—I won't be turning it on until I have a solution to my little dilemma—when Jacquelyn bursts in with a winded apology. The water heater in her apartment broke, and the maintenance guy took an hour vacuuming up the deluge.

I care about this why? "Fine," I say. "Just make up the time this afternoon." I pay her for forty hours; she needs to work them.

She agrees and scuttles off. Ten minutes later, my first client arrives. She's a fresh face, a young woman with spiky blond hair and a series of unattractive piercings.

Freak. Not that I haven't seen my fair share—and much worse than her, actually—of questionable people in this line of work. Still, must these gremlins mutilate themselves to prove a point, to distinguish themselves from the crowd? I mean, look at me. I'm anything but ordinary. And I'm as pristine as the day I was born, except for a couple of facial tweaks to quell any suspicions about that girl and a high-end dye job that demands retouching every twenty days. Oh, and an itty-bitty shoulder tattoo that hardly bears mentioning.

I ask the woman for her paperwork. She hands over the stack and waits, gazing out the window as I evaluate her worthiness. Not of the pills—I couldn't care less where these pharmaceutical wonders end up—but of my trust, my complicity. One wrong move could send me away for a long time, and I'm not about to let that happen.

As I scan the checklist of symptoms, my radar starts twitching. She's ticked boxes that don't jibe, like a test taker working a pattern, trying to beat the house at its own game. Which would be fine for the SAT or some other trivial rite of passage, but not here. Not in my realm. Not with my world hanging in the balance.

I lob a few introductory questions about work, family, school, etcetera, which she answers in a rehearsed manner. (She's a receptionist at a car dealer. Never married. Community college dropout.) Other things are suspicious about her, too, like her stiff posture and, come to think of it, the gunslinger stance she bore upon entering my office. You can take the cop out of the uniform, but you can't take the uniform out of the cop. She's used to wearing a bulky belt of accessories—radio, handcuffs, baton, flashlight—and it shows. Kudos to whoever tapped her for undercover work, though. The piercings and her overall shabby appearance would've fooled a lesser mind.

"You're feeling restless and also sleeping excessively?" I ask, verifying her illogic.

She leans forward in the chair. "I can't get my head straight since my brother killed himself."

I'm taken aback. "Oh," I say, reconsidering my conclusions. If she *is* with the police, she's flirting with entrapment. She can't feed me lies and then fault me for prescribing an appropriate remedy. My lawyers would have a field day with her in court. The police department would be a laughingstock.

I probe the dead-brother angle further—she holds up, but I still sense deceit—and decide that, cop or no cop, she's not worth the risk. I trot out some homework exercises—journaling, meditation, that sort of thing—and blow her off.

Clutching the instructions, she says, "What about medicine? Can't you give me something for—?"

I purse my lips and shake my head. "Sorry, this isn't *Let's Make a Deal*. If, in my judgment, you'd benefit from pharmaceutical intervention, we'll go down that path. But let's start with self-reflection, behavior modification—the tried-and-true pillars of therapy. Too many people want a quick fix. A pill isn't necessarily the answer to your problems. It can do more harm than good."

The woman is crestfallen, but she doesn't press the issue. As she leaves, her hips once again braced under the weight of that phantom police belt, I know I'm right. She's a mole, a plant. Someone—Detective Luke or maybe even the feds—sent her in to expose me. But for now, she's failed. I've won.

The idea is cold comfort. With the investigations into Sophie Gallagher and Dr. Kapoor simmering away on the back burner (I'm not delusional enough to think they've been dropped altogether), the constant threat of being recognized by Robin (keeping your enemies close has its drawbacks), and Edward's suddenly strange behavior (the sooner I unlock his phone the better), I'm feeling a bit suffocated, a bit like the walls are closing in.

Maybe it's time to get rid of Robin. That would take one stressor off my plate. Or Edward. It's hard to say which could do me more harm.

I yawn and buzz Jacquelyn. Almost immediately, my next client—the former school principal—comes loping in. I pluck the prescription pad off my desk and start writing.

CHAPTER 59
ROBIN

It's a good thing Samantha's holed up in that suite near the children, because I'm getting drunker by the minute, combing through Marina's case, searching for a connection to Edward Hayes. That sliver of proof must be in here somewhere.

I chug the last of my seventh or eighth beer and immediately crack open another, my mind failing to surrender to the haze.

Part of me knows the quest is doomed. If Edward killed Marina, he got away with it for a reason. He was smart enough to cover his tracks. No amount of detective work is going to expose clues that don't exist. The police failed miserably. Thinking about the evidence they could've collected if they'd given my sister the benefit of the doubt, if they'd seen her as more than just a dead hooker, taps a volcano of rage in me that refuses to stay dormant.

If I could find my gun, things would be easy. I'd storm into Edward's office and demand a confession, point-blank. It makes me sick to think that this man—this *killer*—has so callously taken my sister and then gone on to live a charmed life. And who's to say he hasn't killed others along the way? People like him—demons in human form—don't change.

A vision of Samantha swims into my mind. She was in Edward's office the other night. And she's been acting strange—keeping her distance and mentally checking out (I couldn't even get her to help me spend that fat first paycheck). What if this monster—this make-believe family man, this pillar of the community—is grooming my daughter as his next victim?

My heart thumps and my head swirls. I don't have my gun, but I *do* have the switchblade. The question is whether I have the guts to stab someone to death. Because once I start, I can't stop until the job's done. The threat must be fully subdued, permanently neutralized. Edward can't come back to hurt me or anyone else ever again.

My brain sloshes around in my skull. I scoop the evidence—the jumble of notes and maps and pictures and articles—into a pile and cram it back in the box.

I wish I had two things: Marina's grimy purse and her partially melted identification card, both of which were found near her blackened corpse. I could shove them in Edward's face and study his reaction. Maybe his shifty eyes would be proof of my suspicions; maybe his hollow denials would propel me to act.

As for the necklace, I haven't found the right time to slip it back into Dr. Hayes's collection. For now, it remains mine. I reach for my throat and roll the chain around between my fingers. It's alive with Marina's spirit, which tells me in a mute language—a wavelength of pain—to end the animal who took my sister, to kill her killer.

The switchblade is hidden in the toe of a boot. I sweep my hand under the bed and come out with an old tennis shoe. On the second attempt, I try harder, latching on to one of the boots. I drag it out, only to find that it's the wrong one: no knife.

A blast of dizziness hits me. I lean sideways, using the bed for support. The beer has finally kicked in. I let a few woozy moments pass before proceeding.

Boot number two is more fruitful. I'm once again in possession of the knife. I'm staggering to my feet when the door flies open and Samantha bursts in. She's been gone so much lately that her appearance shocks me, frightens me. My whole body quivers.

"What're you doing?" she screams, her eyes flashing with disgust. "Everyone's looking for you, and you're … you're …"

I collapse onto the bed. "I'm not drunk."

"Yeah, right." She grabs a tote bag and starts snatching up beer cans and tossing them inside. "You can't do this. You've gotta stop. Talk to Lisa. She'll help you."

My mouth is Silly Putty. I garble out, "Who's Lisa?" Suddenly, I'm sweating like it's Death Valley on the Fourth of July.

"Urrh," growls Samantha, "you can't be serious."

She hasn't noticed the knife. While her back is turned, I nudge it under the bed. "I don't feel good," I say, curling up and shutting my eyes.

"Big surprise. What do you want me to tell them?"

"Who?"

"You're supposed to be teaching a lesson, remember?" A long, deep sigh. "Which one is it?"

"The books," I mumble. "Everything's in"—I gulp back a well of vomit—"it's in the study."

"The library, you mean?"

I can only nod.

"Whatever. I'll figure it out." I hear her move into the bathroom and then return. "You look horrible. If you have to puke, do it in here."

My eyes crack open. I see the blurry outline of a trash can. My eyes shut down again. I want to thank my daughter for stepping into my shoes, for taking care of me, but all that comes out of my numb, bubble-wrapped lips is a groan.

From the sound of the door clicking shut, I know Samantha has gone.

Before Marina's murder, I never had nightmares—or if I did, I didn't remember them. But throughout my teenage years, my dreams were stalked by an unknown predator, a pulsing mass of evil with hot breath and sharp claws (I could feel them trailing down my neck when I awoke in an icy sweat), reptile skin, and vacant, glowing eyes.

The creature had no name—no identity—and frequently shifted forms. Sometimes it was a boy from school—an acquaintance of an acquaintance—talking to me in the lunchroom before its skin peeled off in bloody strips to reveal its deadly core.

Other times the creature was my brother or the neighbor (sorry, Lewis) or a clerk at the corner store. One thing never changed, though: The creature thirsted to show me what it had done to my sister. It longed to take me kicking and screaming to the cold, dark pit of the earth.

What scared me more than the imagery was the smell, a rotting funk that bloomed in my nostrils, sending fingers of death coiling into my brain. That scent is strong tonight as I slip through the veil of consciousness into a liquid netherworld.

Like most dreams—or most of mine, anyway—I'm dropped in the middle of things, reeling to make sense of my surroundings.

I'm indoors. It's dark and smoky. Glowing red cigarettes cluster like fireflies, tracing patterns in the air as their owners' hands gesticulate. There's music—greatest hits from the eighties, stuff Marina used to listen to at night on her boom box while she painted her nails and practiced putting on makeup.

I'm alone. I can't tell if I'm a participant in the dream or just an observer. I might be a floating speck of dust or a spider or a ghost. My mind is a blank videotape, spooled in loopy circles, ready to record.

I start moving—gliding in a nonhuman way, as if on an invisible conveyor belt—among small groups of people, their conversations flickering in and out like rabbit-eared TVs in a storm. Each time I try to focus on someone, their face melts and I can't make sense of the features.

I'm looking for someone, but I don't know whom.

Forward is the only direction, the only option. Behind me the room is disappearing in a black void.

I keep going, down a crooked, narrow hallway. The floor is warped and spongy. A buzzing sound clouds my head. I come upon door after door. All are locked. I feel lost and confused. I want to ask someone what I'm doing here, who I'm trying to find, but there's nobody around.

A soft yellow light radiates in the distance. I have the sense that it's a fire—an inviting one, like at a ski lodge on a snowy winter's day. But the hallway stretches to the horizon.

Why is it still so hazy? I'm already starting to forget that roomful of smoking gnats.

I put my lips together and blow, parting the fog and bringing the beacon of hope closer. I do it again and again. The distance collapses. Now I'm standing at the threshold of a stately reception room with a domed glass ceiling. Rays of sun pierce the dome and dapple the glossy oak floor. The only object in the room, dead center, is a blood-red fainting couch.

Everything goes eerily silent. "I've been waiting for you," whispers a man's voice. "It took you so long to come."

I crane my neck, peering around, searching for the source of the voice. Is it talking to me?

"Yes," the man says, as if answering my thoughts, "you're the one, Marina. Now let us dance."

I'm not Marina and yet somehow I am. My sister and I are sharing a soul for a blip of time. "I don't see you," I say, squinting.

The next time I blink, the room is full of people—men in tailcoats and white bowties, women in ball gowns and evening gloves. They're waltzing in tight spirals, turning against one another and making the whole room spin.

Over a crying carnival of music, the man's voice says, "I'm still waiting."

When I step forward, my perspective shifts. I'm at the top of a grand staircase, surveying the merriment below. Slowly, I descend.

At the bottom of the stairs, apart from the mesmerized dancers (they're chalk-eyed and mechanical, like carousel horses), stands an attractive young man. He's impeccably dressed, even more so than his peers. He holds out his hand. "At last," he says, smiling.

"Who are you?"

He doesn't answer. He just sweeps me into his arms and begins twirling us in triple time. I follow his movements unconsciously, like a tail chasing a kite, my skirt inflating like a hot air balloon.

We dance until I'm breathless and giddy. "That's enough," I tell him. "I need to rest."

He leads me to the fainting couch and helps me recline. Around us, the party churns on.

"Who are you?" I ask again.

He stares into my eyes. "Don't you recognize me?"

"I don't even recognize myself," I say with a laugh. Am I Robin or am I Marina?

"Think," he says, leaning closer.

My head twitches back and forth. "I don't know."

"Sleep, then," he says, frowning. He smoothes a clump of hair away from my forehead. "Maybe you'll remember tomorrow."

I tell him that I can't sleep with this commotion, this revelry (what are we celebrating, anyway?)—and now a distant rumble of thunder.

His fingers crawl up my arm. He coaxes the glove away from my elbow and wiggles it down to my wrist, where it bunches like a silk handcuff. He reaches into the breast of his jacket. "This will help," he says, withdrawing a syringe. Before I can stop him, he uncaps the needle with his teeth—his mouth is suddenly clownish and menacing—and jams it into my arm.

The dancers spin faster. The music crescendos. Edward spits out the cap and grins.

Edward.

He's put a needle in my arm, in *Marina's* arm. He's trying to kill us. He's *already* killed her.

His face is clear and recognizable for a moment—he's aged two decades in the turn of a page—before my whole body starts prickling with fire. "Why?" I gurgle, but soon the couch is erupting in flames and Edward is receding into the smoky swirl of dancers.

I want to follow him, but I can't. My flesh—*Marina's* flesh—is disintegrating, and all we can do is burn.

CHAPTER 60
LISA

I'm determined to get to the bottom of Edward's secret phone calls. Like they say about cockroaches, for every one you see, there are a thousand you don't. But first I must slog through another day of work. Without Sophie Gallagher and Dr. Kapoor around, my practice is becoming stale. Who's left to entertain me, to challenge me? Certainly not that wishy-washy stick-in-the-mud, Jacquelyn. She's as much fun as a wet sock.

I don't know how long I can hold out before stowing away to Bora Bora and reinventing myself as a hot American travel guide. A change of identity might be in order soon, anyway, depending on how the murder chips fall. Just think of all the international businessmen I could charm under a coconut tree or unravel in a lagoon bungalow. With any luck, I could coast into a royal wedding—I've always pictured myself on a jewel-encrusted throne—and end up running, say, an up-and-coming European principality.

The fantasy carries me from the parking lot to the office with a dreamy smile.

Jacquelyn's on time today. In fact, when I enter the office, she's finishing up paperwork—photocopying the lease and collecting the deposit—with the new tenant, a real estate agent who's striking out on her own.

It would be rude not to introduce myself. And I'm curious about the kind of person who would be eager to occupy the site of a gruesome suicide. Perhaps someone of my ilk? "Hello," I say, interrupting Jacquelyn's prepared speech. "I'm Dr. Lisa Hayes." I stick out my hand. "I own the building."

The tenant has just stepped out of an '80s primetime soap opera: wavy dandelion-yellow hair, a shiny magenta dress with puffy sleeves, and brassy gold-tassel earrings.

Yee-haw.

She grabs my hand and starts pumping away. "Oh, yes. I know who you are. My husband's a lawyer at Clark, Benson, and Hale."

This means nothing to me.

"He worked on one of your patent cases—or, well, your husband's case, I guess it'd be. He's not really a patent attorney, but it was a big case." She gives a hiccupping laugh. "Of course, you know that."

I extricate my hand. "Nice to meet you," I say with a cold smile. "Welcome aboard."

As my gaze flits over Jacquelyn, she makes a dodgy move to slide something out of view, batting over a bottle of root beer and bathing half of her desk, including the aforementioned paperwork, in a sticky, sopping mess.

Typical.

While the tenant paws through her purse for a napkin, I take my leave, but not without jotting a mental note about Jacquelyn's skittishness. Like Edward, she's not herself; her nerves are rattled. If she's done anything to betray me—that detective's appointment card comes rushing back to mind—a little twitch will be the least of her worries.

As I cross the threshold of my office, Jacquelyn ceases to exist. She's the thing you went looking for in another room and forgot about after stepping through the doorway.

I shed my coat and situate myself at my desk with Edward's phone. According to the clock, the workday begins in twenty minutes—maybe more, if the addicts are dragging.

What are the chances that I can break into Edward's phone before the first prescription demands writing?

I've given up on soliciting a criminal from the dark web, and the search for Eitan hit a predictable wall (as hard as I tried, I couldn't remember his last name). So the job falls to me. Which is comforting, in a way. I'm a problem solver. I get things done. Why should this be any different?

Before I turn on the phone, I retrieve a legal pad from my desk and flip to a new page. The passcode is four digits; this much I know.

I must think of as many significant number combinations and sentimental four-letter words as possible and then whittle them down to the most likely suspects.

I tap my fingers on the desk, trying to jog my mind. What does my husband like? What moves him? If I had to admit a flaw, it would be a diminished capacity to put myself in other people's shoes.

Edward likes fast cars, particularly Jaguars. I grab a pen and write JAGS on the pad in big block letters.

Other possibilities: GOLF (the only "sport" my husband still plays); DUKE (his college-football obsession); the METS (or is it the JETS? one of those underdog New York teams he hopelessly roots for); AC/DC (the band, not the electrical current); INXS (the band, not the way my husband likes his women); BEER; CRAB (of the giant-crustacean-leg variety); TACO (what he'd eat for dinner every night if he were poor).

So far, the list is off to a good start. I add his sister's name—FAWN (the only one that fits the pattern)—and his med-school roommate, CASH (this packs a double wallop, money being one of Edward's primary life goals).

Now for the numbers. I note the four-digit month-day combination of the twins' birthday and, separately, their birth year. I do the same for my birthday—the one Edward knows about, anyway—and for Edward's.

What else?

The year Edward graduated from high school (1987); and college (1991); and medical school (1995).

I'm tempted to veer into pop-culture quicksand—imagine the reams of paper I'd fill with references to TV shows and movie stars—but I rein myself in.

I stare at the list, feeling like something's missing. But then—duh!—it hits me: our wedding anniversary. I add these digits, too, and stop to ponder.

Ten tries. That's all I have to get this right. Otherwise the phone will be wiped clean and not only will I remain in the dark about my husband's activities, but his business may suffer, too.

I nix the food items and all of the sports references except DUKE (I can see Edward tapping out this particular sequence). The names of his baby sister and old roomie are long shots, so they also bite the dust. I can't bear to part with any of the bands, but they'll be secondary to significant dates like birthdays and anniversaries (Edward's nothing if not sentimental).

I've narrowed down the list to sixteen contenders. I check the clock. The trickle of addicts will begin in T-minus eight minutes.

I pick up the phone and depress the power button, then slide to unlock. Up pops the passcode screen. I stare at those four little boxes for half a heartbeat before entering the numbers for DUKE—3853—and getting an error message: WRONG PASSCODE, TRY AGAIN.

I make a tally mark on the pad and then try the girls' birthday.

WRONG PASSCODE, TRY AGAIN.

Another tally mark.

Next I type 2001, the girls' birth year.

WRONG PASSCODE, TRY AGAIN.

Tally mark number three.

With only seven tries left, I've got to get surgical. Out go two of the three bands (I'll keep AC/DC in my pocket, just in case) and Edward's birthday and birth year (if he's dumb enough to use something so obvious, God help us all).

Our anniversary is tugging at me. I punch in the numbers.

WRONG PASSCODE, TRY AGAIN.

Tally mark.

If he hasn't used our anniversary *day*, then our anniversary *year* is a safe no. I cross it off the list.

My supposed birthday is up next.

WRONG PASSCODE, TRY AGAIN.

Tally mark five.

Bye-bye 1970, my supposed birth year.

I'm waffling between Edward's various graduations when a glaring omission occurs to me: LISA.

Of course.

My thumbs fly over the keys. Instead of the familiar error message, the home screen glistens into view.

Edward's a busy boy. There are numerous unanswered phone calls, unseen text messages, and languishing emails, all having arrived since yesterday.

If I had sleeves—my crushed-velvet blouse has only a flutter of fabric at the shoulders—I'd roll them up. Instead, I grab my desk phone and dial Jacquelyn.

"Yes?" she says with a huffy sigh. I imagine she's drip-drying that lease page by page.

"Hold my first appointment. Something's come up. I'll be busy for a while."

"Until when?"

"Until I'm not."

"All right. But people are getting restless. You've been gone a lot lately."

"And your point is?"

"Nothing. Never mind."

"I thought so."

I drop the receiver in the cradle and go back to Edward's phone. The calls are the logical place to start. They're the least numerous and I caught him hushing a verbal exchange. The potential trove of written betrayal is too vast to contemplate. (If he hasn't hooked up with twenty or thirty tramps at work over the years, I'll eat a fried rat dipped in bat guano.)

The call log tells a story of nose-to-the-grindstone dedication. My husband is the glue holding together a multimillion-dollar empire; everything goes through him. Still, all work and no play ...

I scroll through the log, looking for the day and time of that suspicious call. When I find it—Monday at 7:03 A.M.—the number is unfamiliar. The call lasted six minutes and forty-two seconds. I was in the shower for most of it.

Sneaky Edward.

I search back a few weeks and find that Edward has been in contact with this mysterious number on nine other occasions.

It's time for my husband to check in with his secret friend.

I tap the number and wait while the call rings through. After a subtle click, a woman's voice comes on the line. "You've reached Detective Samson. Leave a message and I'll get back to you." *Beep.*

My eyes glaze over. It crosses my mind that my husband is fucking the detective. I mean, I can't help but notice that he's trading calls with the leggy brunette and not her ruggedly handsome partner. Maybe she made a move on him at our anniversary party.

I'm about to hang up—there's no sense leaving a message and incriminating myself—when the phone starts ringing.

I back out of the original call and let the new one go to voicemail. Then I scan the text messages for the detective's number.

Jackpot.

What I find is worse than any two-bit affair. Edward's helping the police finger me for Sophie Gallagher's murder. He's provided my car—the real reason for his taking the Hummer—for tire-track analysis. When the authorities compare the Hummer's tires to the skid marks at the scene, they're likely to get a match. In fact, they've probably already gotten one.

So what? That doesn't prove anything but the Hummer's presence on Route 9. A murder charge is still in the foggy distance, where, if I have anything to say about it, it'll stay.

Finding this information is a blessing in disguise. My mission has jolted into focus: Kill Robin Davis—she could tie me to that girl and unravel my world from the ground up—and then patch the holes in my relationship with Edward. In the unlikely event that Edward can't be swayed—have detectives so easily poisoned him against me?—I'll run.

Samantha and I will run, I tell myself, which makes all the difference. I can feel the wind at our backs already.

CHAPTER 61
ROBIN

I take an extra long shower, letting the water boil over my face and batter Marina's necklace (it's become a grotesque part of me, like a parasitic twin), trying to shake off the dream. I don't want to believe that a man like Edward—someone with class and intelligence and an idyllic family life—is capable of anything sinister, much less the murder of an innocent young girl (whatever mistakes my sister made, she didn't deserve to die; she didn't deserve to burn).

But then … that's the trick, isn't it? Playing normal? Appearing harmless? Putting people at ease? Getting them to lower their defenses so you can strike?

I need to cry, to get this ugliness out of me, but the tears won't come. Screaming would serve the same purpose—relief valves take many forms, I've learned over the years—but as big as this mansion is, there's nowhere safe. Especially now.

My old fallback comes to the rescue. When Sam collected those empty cans, she left the rest of the beer behind. I'm not usually a morning drinker—or at least not a before-breakfast drinker—but one can is nothing.

I throw on some clothes, run a brush through my hair, and fish around inside the jagged opening of the cardboard box for a beer. All twelve ounces are sloshing around in my stomach when Samantha slips into the suite.

"Thank God," she says, "you're awake."

"Why wouldn't I be?" She makes it sound like I should be gurgling in a pool of vomit.

She plunks down on her unmade bed and starts rifling through her nightstand. "No reason."

"Pretty sweater," I say, noticing the striped turtleneck she's wearing. "Where'd you get it?"

Her eyes roll back. "Where do you think?"

I don't like this version of my daughter. Maybe Dr. Hayes can do something about Sam's attitude. Of course, I don't know how much help she'll be if I target her husband, if I get him arrested. It's a fantasy, probably, to think the police will investigate him after all these years with so little proof. Getting justice will fall to me. So will dispensing punishment. "Is something wrong?" I ask. "What are you looking for?"

Her fist jerks out of the drawer. "Found 'em," she says, gripping a set of purple earbuds. She stuffs them in her pants and stares through me. "Actually, yeah. Something *is* wrong." An airless pause. "Who's Chuck Dalton?"

My brain seizes up.

"You put him on my birth certificate."

"Who told you that?"

"Jesus, Mom." She groans. "Just stop, okay? I have a copy."

I figured this day would come. But why now, when I'm tangled up in Marina's murder? When I'm a hair's breadth away from catching her killer?

I lean against the wall. "What do you want to know?"

"Who is he?"

"A guy."

"No, really?"

"This is a bad time, Samantha. I've gotta—"

"Don't even." She shakes her head. "Don't you even dare say that. You owe me an answer. You didn't care about your job last night, did you? I was the one that took care of everything while you were passed out drunk."

My daughter has never been so cutthroat, so determined. Her eyes are fiery and menacing. I feel like I have no choice but to provide the bare-bones information about her father. Maybe the news will help her come to terms with herself, give her a stronger foothold in the world. I just hope she isn't torn up by the truth. She's taken enough beatings, physically and emotionally, to last a lifetime. "We met at a bowling alley. He was sort of a jerk—whooping and hollering, being obnoxious and acting like a fool."

Samantha's frozen. I'm tempted to shake her to see if she's still breathing.

"My friends were bugging his friends—zinging insults back and forth, that sort of thing." I wish I could remember more, but the details are hazy. So much has happened since then. "I thought there was going to be a fight, because things were getting out of hand. But then he, Chuck—I didn't know his name yet, though—and his friends just left. We finished our game and turned in our shoes and went outside."

"That sounds like BS," Samantha mutters. "You better not be lying."

I hold up my hands. "I swear, this is it. I would've told you sooner, but—"

"Whatever." She twirls her arm through the air. "Just keep going."

"When we got outside, Chuck's friends were gone. He was alone in the rain, smoking a cigarette. Only a sliver of sun was out; it was just about dark."

The next part is even fuzzier. "I don't know how he ended up in our car. My friend Janine—she was this girl from college I'd only hung out with a few times—was driving her dad's SUV. Someone must've offered him a ride. Maybe it was Janine."

I continue explaining that Chuck and I sat squashed together in the back, our thighs rubbing. He offered me a swig of bourbon he had stashed in his coat (in reality, it was a puff off a joint, but I don't want to admit this to Sam for obvious reasons). I drank (smoked) a little with him that night and when we dropped him off—he lived in a huge stone house with fairytale vines and turrets—he gave me his number. We got together a few times. Alone. Things got physical.

"Okay, okay," says Sam. "TMI."

It's not like I was going to give her a play-by-play. "So, obviously, that's when I got pregnant."

"And?"

"And what?"

My daughter sits up straighter, braces herself. "What did he say?"

I don't want to hurt her, but another lie would be worse than the truth. I fight a rush of tears—not for me (I wasn't in love with the guy) but for Samantha. She didn't deserve to be written off like that. "He was young," I say, trying to soften the blow. "We both were. It was overwhelming."

"Was he there at all? Was he interested? Did he come to the hospital when I was born?"

I pull in a breath and shake my head. "He moved," I say, leaving out the part where he tried to pay me two thousand dollars to get an abortion. He was barely eighteen. I've always wondered if his parents were involved in the bribe. "I think his father got relocated. They were gone before …"

Samantha stares past me. "What about later?"

She must be nursing dreams of a father-daughter reunion, casting me as the villain who stood in their way. Even though it would make her hate me, I wish it were true. "Sorry," I say. I'm tempted to regurgitate the cliché things people say in these situations—it's his loss; you're better off without him—but no words are up to the task. So I wrap my daughter in a hug. "I love you, Sam," I whisper into her hair. "You're the light of my life. Don't ever forget that."

My daughter is invincible. She's had to be to coexist with my demons. But she's also a wounded child. She curls up in my arms and weeps. I pat her back, barely staving off my own outburst of grief.

After a few minutes, she pulls away and dries her eyes. "It's late," she says, collecting herself and heading for the door.

"Are you all right?" I can feel my face pinching into a frown. I make an effort to relax the muscles around my eyes.

She nods and swallows hard, and I know not to ask anything more.

Belatedly, I follow Samantha to the kitchen. Dr. Hayes is sipping coffee and flipping through a magazine. Are my eyes playing tricks on me? She's wearing the same sweater as Sam.

The doctor glances up from her magazine and laughs. "Great minds think alike," she crows, gesturing at Samantha. "I guess we should've coordinated—or, well, *un*coordinated, ha-ha."

Why do they have the same sweater? The question hangs uncomfortably in my mind before being swept away by the appearance of Edward. It's the first time I've seen him since the dream.

The nightmare.

My mouth goes dry; my pulse quickens; my palms start to sweat.

He wishes everyone a good morning, like nothing's wrong, like he hasn't slaughtered my sister. A shocking idea dawns on me: Maybe he doesn't remember killing Marina. Maybe the crime was so long ago and so trivial (in his mind) that it's faded away like an old bruise.

I'm here to remind him.

Dr. Hayes flaps the magazine shut and waits for Sam to unwrap a granola bar. They take off down the hall like two striped peas in a pod. I feel a pang of jealousy watching them, but then I remember everything the doctor has done for my daughter and my hurt feelings evaporate.

I'm due to check on the children, but I linger in the kitchen, pretending to tidy up. This isn't my job—Ricki will pop up any minute now and put my cleaning skills to shame—but Edward hardly notices. He's staring blankly, hauntedly (I could swear he's reliving Marina's murder), into a bowl of mushy cereal. He lifts a spoonful to his mouth and swallows it down.

I think about the switchblade, about how it's in my back pocket, about how easy it would be to slice his throat and watch him bleed out on his fancy marble floor. Or maybe I'll threaten his children, make him feel the anguish—the guilt, the powerlessness—of fearing a loved one harmed.

No. It's not in me to hurt those girls, no matter what their father has done. I'll find another way to settle the score.

I've just tucked away Dr. Hayes's magazine (the address label says Ricki Cole, so it's a transplant), when Edward clears his throat. "Can I ask you something, Robin? It *is* Robin, isn't it?"

"That's right." I've been here for the better part of a month, and he barely knows my name? How can he be so careless with his children? Not that I'm one to talk.

"Please," he says, nodding at a stool, "sit down." The hairs on my neck stand up. Guardedly, I take a seat. He studies me, his gaze a sort of detached molestation. "How are you adjusting? Is everything as you expected?" He chuckles. "I hope the girls aren't too much of a handful. They've got fire in their bellies, those two. You can count on it."

I don't know what he wants me to say, and, anyway, I'm at a loss for words. "They're spirited," I reply.

"They get that from their mother. I was the shy kid, the nerd. But Lisa ..."

I can hardly stand making small talk with the man who killed my sister. Yet I comment on the doctor, "She's very outgoing."

"That she is. I can't tell you the number of charity events and parties she's arranged over the years." A heavy pause, then a new subject: "Has she helped you—in therapy, I mean? My wife talks so little of her work. I always wonder what she's up to. I know she must be doing a lot of good for people. But that kind of thing is hard to quantify." He stares into the cereal again.

What is he looking for?

"She's been wonderful with Samantha," I say without pause. I feel like I'm counseling him, like he's come to me for guidance. (Is there a problem in his marriage?) Or maybe he's laying the groundwork to hit on me.

A darker explanation of his interest in me is that he *hasn't* forgotten Marina. Maybe I remind him of her. Maybe he's recognized me.

I glance down the hall. Where's Ricki? Will anyone hear me if I scream?

"You're different," he tells me. "Very down-to-earth. Accessible."

The only thing he'll be accessing of mine is the razor-sharp blade in my pocket.

"With Lisa, it's more ... *complicated*. Sometimes I don't feel like I know her at all. There's something in her that defies ..." He shakes his head. "Have you noticed that? That she's remote? That you can't draw a bead on her?"

I fidget with a pen, clicking it on and off and wondering if Edward is really talking about himself. Maybe *he's* the one hiding something. "I find her very warm and welcoming," I say.

He cocks his head and smirks, the same clownish grin from the dream. "Do you?"

"Mm."

"See, now that surprises me. Don't get me wrong; my wife is amazing. But she doesn't quite wear her heart on her sleeve."

I lift off the stool. "I really should be—"

"Yes, of course. Thanks for humoring me. Sometimes you can be too close to something—or some*one*—to see it clearly."

I don't know what he's trying to pull—he's painting himself as some kind of philosopher—but my view of him is static-free. I just have to figure out what to do about it. "No problem," I say, maintaining our cordial façade. As I turn to leave, I sense him staring at my ass, but I ignore the assault and keep going.

His time is up. And soon I'll have him in a position to prove it.

CHAPTER 62
LISA

Edward is doing cartwheels over getting his phone back. I wasted no time reporting that it had crept into my purse—darn those rascally kids!—only to be found when I was rummaging around for a breath mint. Fifteen minutes later, he was at my office with his hand out. He's so giddy, in fact, that before work this morning, he crawled on top of me, forced my legs apart, and had his way. Which makes me wonder if his fascination with a certain horse-faced detective has run its course. In any event, my husband isn't ready to turn me over to the authorities just yet. So back to the grind I go. ...

As usual, the workday drags. We've been picking up clients here and there—that undercover cop hasn't returned, but plenty of tweakers have mushroomed up in her place—to keep the practice flush with cash. Which is good, because there's no telling when I might need to raid my safe-deposit boxes, stuff a suitcase with hundred-dollar bills, and hightail it to a foreign locale—the Principality of Andorra, perhaps—that doesn't have an extradition treaty with the United States.

Before I can jet off anywhere, though, I must deal with Robin. It's a shame we'll be in the market for another nanny so soon.

I finish with my last client and close up shop. Normally, I'd pick up Samantha on my way home, but she's staying after school to sign up for the crew of the spring musical. Which leaves me free to meander.

I'm halfway home when a craving for those gooey mashed potatoes and gravy strikes. The KFC is a few blocks west. I cut sharply across two lanes of traffic and position myself for a left turn. Oddly, the car behind me—a nondescript little sedan—mimics my movements.

Is someone following me? With Edward's recent shenanigans and that undercover cop in the mix, anything's possible.

Better safe than sorry.

When the light turns green, I spurt through the intersection and make a hard left, ending up on the back side of a used-car dealership. I check my rearview mirror, and, sure enough, the sedan has made the same abrupt turn.

Interesting.

I travel a number of blocks—the car's still behind me—and start evasive maneuvers: S-turns, backtracking, imprudent speed. Through it all, the car persists.

Screw it. I'm hungry. If my secret admirer gets his kicks from watching me eat, it's his lucky day.

The next time KFC comes into view, I swing in. The sedan just keeps rolling by. I wonder briefly if Edward has hired a private detective to spy on me but quickly dismiss the idea. Cooperating with the authorities is one thing—my husband is a Boy Scout; I should've known he'd roll over—but launching his own inquiry? He's got nothing to gain and everything to lose if his wife ends up being anything but the hot, successful psychiatrist he's paraded around town for a decade.

The sun is setting earlier and earlier. It's blinking below the horizon as I exit the drive-through with a steaming container of mashed potatoes and gravy. Although the potatoes resemble wallpaper paste, I scarf them down with unbound zeal. Then, with a gurgling tummy, I head for home.

When I enter the kitchen, Edward and Ricki are huddled around the island. I can tell by their body language—by the way he pokes her, by how she throws her head back and laughs—that they're having great fun.

I'm here to kill their good time.

They must hear me coming, because their heads snap around in unison. "Perfect timing," says Edward, waving me over. When I get within spitting distance, I see that my husband and the housekeeper are admiring photos from the anniversary party. "The photographer's assistant dropped these off ten minutes ago."

"Did she?" I say.

"He," says Edward.

Ricki reaches for one of the albums—the photos are printed in hardcover books, which are strewn across the island—and flips through it. "This is my favorite," she says, running a spiky red fingernail across a picture of our darling twins, who are nose-to-nose in their pearls and chiffon, giving each other Eskimo kisses.

Edward begs to differ. He singles out a shot of me alone. It's a close-up portrait with a wash of blurry lights in the background. My head is ringed by a glowing halo and that collar of sunflowers dazzles like a meteor shower.

If nothing else, the man has good taste.

"Here's the order form," says Ricki, sliding a stack of papers my way.

I squeeze in between her and Edward. After mining the books for a suitable family portrait, I settle on one of the four of us abreast. Edward's smile is crooked and Mae looks like she's holding in gas, but Darian and I are impeccable. "Is there a pen?" I ask.

Ricki ducks over to a drawer and comes back with a marker. "Here you go."

I make a swirly bull's-eye around the proof in question. "How big is that painting in the great room?"

Edward: "The Marsden?"

Like I know the artist's name. "I'll take your word for it."

"Three by five?" Feet, he means. I guess it isn't life-size, after all.

I scrawl out an order for a huge canvas—the sooner that wretched caricature is replaced the better—and then peck my husband on the cheek. "Feel free to order two of everything," I tell Ricki. "And these books"—I shake my head—"they're too flimsy. Tell the photographer to spring for something better. I'm sure he can find an upscale supplier."

"No problem," says Ricki. And with that, I excuse myself for a shower.

Samantha and I are establishing a routine with our after-dinner swims. She's a water bug like me and grabs every opportunity for a relaxing dip. Already, she's forgotten where she came from; she's shed her roots like a snake sheds its skin. Which will make it that much easier to get over the loss of her mother. Give me a month with her in Fiji—soaking in the hot springs; floating in the turquoise lagoons; sipping tropical drinks by the fire at sunset—and she'll be born again. Robin will be a halcyon memory.

We've done our laps—it's therapeutic to get the blood pumping—and retreated to the shallow end of the pool, where we're floating on our backs like beautiful corpses. I last only a few minutes in this meditative state—the quiet and stillness conflict with my electric brain—before nudging Samantha. "Let's warm up," I say, nodding at the Jacuzzi. Beyond the towering windows, snowflakes flutter against a bruised sky.

Samantha corkscrews through the water like a dizzy fish. I catch myself laughing in earnest. The reaction is a surprise. I can't remember the last time anything—any*one*—tickled my soul with such precision (probably never). Whatever it takes, I must have this girl for my own.

As usual, the Jacuzzi is overheated. I ask Samantha to lower the temperature, which she does with ease. We nestle into the contoured seats. "You're a wonderful swimmer," I say, paying her a compliment she richly deserves. If we keep up our routine, she'll be as good as me soon. "Who taught you?" It can't be that flaky mother of hers—I'm counting on it—or her runaway father. The jailbird uncle is a possibility, depending on when she learned.

"The YMCA."

"Oh," I say, a smile creeping across my lips, "so your mother didn't ...?"

She shakes her head. "Nope."

I need more information than that, I'm afraid. "Doesn't she know how to swim?" I make a show of looking around. "I haven't seen her down here since you moved in." A not-so-innocent observation. "Most of the workers can't wait to take advantage of all this."

Samantha's glistening shoulders rise. "My grandparents took her to the lake every summer. She's told me the stories a million times. My uncle was a really good swimmer. My aunt, too. Mom just wasn't into it. The gene skipped her or something."

"Wasn't she in class with you? I assumed it was one of those Mommy and Me things."

"Uh-uh. I was in second grade. Those are for, like, toddlers."

"So you've never been swimming together?" I'm beating a dead horse, but my plan hinges on this detail.

"Nope," she says again.

"Isn't that a shame." I lean back, shut my eyes, and let the warmth overtake me. Soon I've had too much of a good thing. The heat has blossomed in my stomach like a noxious organism.

I inform Samantha that I'm not feeling well. She's as sweet as pie, helping me to the bathroom. In a flash, I'm down on my knees, hugging the toilet. As I start to retch, she scoops the hair away from my neck, holding it up like a bridal train (how many times has she done this for her drunken mother?).

After a few ugly minutes, I'm as good as new. I dab my mouth with a tissue and splash cool water on my face. When I suggest dessert—Ricki has whipped up a batch of sugar cookies and a pumpkin cheesecake—Samantha flinches. "Are you sure you're okay? I can get Mr. Hayes." She holds up a finger. "It'll just take a second."

"Never mind," I tell her. "Girls like us bounce back." Which is what she'll have to do once her mother's gone. I might as well model the process.

I take off, leading the charge for the kitchen. With an admiring smile, she follows along.

CHAPTER 63
ROBIN

I'm in a darkened theater with the twins, impatiently waiting for the movie—*The Princess and the Frog*—to get underway. The previews are an ear-splitting bore. Still, the longer they drag on, the harder and faster my heart beats.

I'm no good at lying. Yet here I am, risking everything for the truth about Marina.

The previews fade away. I wait until the children are engrossed in the story before checking my phone—it's five after three; Scott will be waiting—and making up my mind.

I turn to my left, where Mae's nibbling from a sack of popcorn, and whisper, "I'm going to the bathroom."

Mae registers my statement with a vague nod.

I lean to my right—the children are strategically divided, a technique left over from my teaching days—and repeat myself.

Darian raises an eyebrow. She's too inquisitive, too on the ball. I insisted on the children using the restroom before the movie, and now I'm ducking out at an inconvenient time.

I bump past Darian and sail for the exit. On my way through the lobby, I don't give the bathrooms a second glance. My nerves are raw, at the surface, like a fresh burn.

Outside, the cold air is a relief. My breath comes out in clouds of silver vapor. *Puff, puff, puff.*

The Mercedes is across the parking lot, in a row of beat-up cars that look like they belong to the teenage movie-theater employees. As I hustle toward it, I make out a shadowy form in the passenger seat.

Good. Scott let himself in.

"About friggin' time," he says as I drop into the driver's seat. He blows hot air on his hands and rubs them together. "I'm freezin' my balls off."

Charming. I'm no Delicate Daisy, but save the genital references for the prison crowd.

I don't bother making apologies. The quicker we get this over with the better. If the girls come looking for me, I'm done. The investigation will crumble through my fingers. And I can't let that happen now, when I can taste the end. "I know who killed Marina. I need your help getting him."

Scott snort-chuckles. "You don't quit, do you?"

I turn on the car and blast the heat at my face. "Good thing. Or he would've gotten away with it, would've *kept* getting away with it."

"So you're smarter than the police?" He shakes his head. "Shit, Robin, I ain't one to stick up for—" He stares across the parking lot at a group of kids, one of whom is a dead ringer for Amy Lawrence, the girl he killed. I wonder if he sees her ghost like I see Marina's.

"The police didn't do a damn thing," I say, "and you know it."

His gaze follows the kids until they disappear inside. "Maybe not." He jams the heel of his hand into his eye. "Cause they didn't have to. It was an open and shut case. She OD'd."

My teeth set up to grind. "Are you going to help me, or not?"

"Do what? Chase an imaginary—?"

"We don't have to chase him; I know exactly where he is."

"Where's that?"

I dig into my pocket for Marina's necklace. "Remember this? Marina had it when she ran away from home."

My brother's face is flat, expressionless. Our father would be proud.

I keep going, explaining about Edward—the kitchen porno; his fraternizing with Samantha behind closed doors; the Glamour Shot of Georgette wearing the necklace.

"Marina stole it?" he says. "That sounds right."

I check the clock. Five minutes have already slipped by. "Listen, I don't have time for this. You're gonna have to trust me. Edward's the guy. He did this. He took our sister away. Don't you want to do anything about it?"

"Like what? You've got no proof."

"Then help me get it."

"What if you're wrong?"

I shake the necklace around. "I'm not."

Scott's foot starts tapping. "Where's Sam?"

"Out driving. Dr. Hayes is giving her lessons."

"Get her out of there—out of that house—and we'll talk."

"We're talking now."

"You think this guy is dangerous, and you're letting her stay where he can get to her?"

"It's not like that. I'm there all the time. And Dr. Hayes is involved, too. I don't think he'd be able to …" I groan. "Where would she go, anyway? It's not like you can take her."

"How about home?"

"No electricity."

"Turn it back on. You're making the big bucks now, right?"

"Not for long." The job of a lifetime is about to go up in smoke. "Just help me get to the bottom of what Edward knows. You won't have to do much. I've got it all worked out. After that, I promise it'll be over. Things will go back to the way they were before—"

"You'll let it go?" He scowls. "I ain't gettin' arrested for this shit."

"Don't worry. You won't." We lock eyes—I never realized how much his baby browns resemble our mother's—and the deal solidifies. "I'll text you the details," I tell him. Then I turn off the car, remind him to lock up, and rush back to the girls. As I settle in between them, I feel a twinge of angst—a spiky flutter in my chest that lingers a beat too long—over what I'm about to do. But it's not my fault; Edward brought this on himself. I have no reason to feel guilty.

The whiff of a resolution makes my nerves sing. I promised we'd get him, Marina. And now it begins.

Some extra prep time would've been nice, but when the stars align, you grab the opportunity with both hands.

Samantha and Dr. Hayes are off on another Sunday expedition (my daughter will have toured every art museum in the state before long), while Edward's holed up in his office down the hall.

I'm on the hook to watch the children—our weekends center on enrichment activities: private music lessons; ice skating and gymnastics; a rotating menu of country-club events—but Ricki has agreed to sub for me in exchange for my tutoring her son for the SATs.

The mansion is empty, except for Edward and me. I could confront him now, but I don't want the episode recorded (I've made a game of spotting video cameras, and they're even more numerous than I suspected), in case things take a bad turn, in case I have to hurt him.

Hopefully it won't come to that. Hopefully he'll tell the truth. Hopefully he has a conscience rattling around in that gigantic brain of his.

Another reason to move the interaction to a secondary location is privacy. A team of interior designers is due any minute now to deck out the mansion for Christmas.

I scan the suite, checking for things I might need. If I could find my gun, I'd holster it as insurance. But it's gotten away from me. At least I have the knife. And my cell phone. And my brother in the wings for backup.

It's our childhood all over again—Scott protecting me from bus-stop bullies. If only that had been the worst of it.

I pull out my phone and text Scott: 20 minutes. He's become adept at defying the halfway house rules since the new management took over. This outing and the meetup yesterday won't even blip the radar.

The return text is blunt: yup.

As I exit the suite, I shoot a glance down the hall. Edward's door is still shut. It has been all day. I just hope I can lure him out of there. I hope he takes the bait. It wasn't easy thinking up a ruse, and I'm not sure I've nailed it.

I cleanse the negative thoughts from my mind and head for the garage. The cemetery is fifteen minutes away, and I don't want to leave Scott hanging.

For this time of year, the day is sunny and warm. I coast through the iron gates of Franklin Hills Memorial in the Hayeses' Mercedes, sickeningly aware of the fact that I'm driving my sister's murderer's car to her grave. What choice do I have? The Caprice was hauled off to a junkyard the day after Samantha and I moved in. (It was leaking oil on the pristine driveway.) And it wouldn't have worked in my plan, anyway.

The cemetery is big—maybe a hundred acres—and our family plots are at the back, along the river. Before our father shot himself, he bought enough eternal-resting space for all of us, though I have no intention of rotting here in a neat little row. I doubt Scott does, either.

Speaking of my brother, he's hiking along up ahead with his hands stuffed in his pockets. I pull over and let him in. Stoically, we drive on, passing the occasional mourner with a flag or a wreath or a potted plant—time's running out to embellish graves for the holidays—and a trickle of exercise fanatics, who don't mind their cardio with a side of death.

As we approach the patch of grass where the bones of our family lie, I take pains to avoid Amy Lawrence's grave. Her picture on the headstone is too bright and happy and alive. I doubt my brother can handle it.

The car crawls to a stop. "You sure about this?" Scott asks, eyeing a grove of trees in the distance.

I motion at a baton-style flashlight in the backseat. "Take it, just in case." My brother will get involved as a last resort, if something goes wrong, if Edward shows his true colors.

He twists around and grabs the flashlight. "Ain't this overkill?"

"It was the best I could do. Sorry."

"You want me to stay?"

"Nah. You'll just make me nervous." An audience is the last thing I need.

He slips out of the car and fades into the landscape.

I inhale sharply and dial Edward's number. It's for emergencies only, particularly emergencies with the children. By the third ring, waves of prickly heat are rolling through me.

Pick up, dammit. I haven't come this far to give up now. You owe me this. You owe me closure.

The fates are listening. On the fourth ring, Edward answers. I blurt out my fabricated story: I'm at the cemetery (true), visiting a relative's grave (somewhat true), and I locked the keys in the car (soon-to-be true, if he agrees to rescue me). I'm also sick (a stomach bug, to complicate things), and I can't wait for the auto club to show up and spring the locks.

He suggests Ricki. I say she's off somewhere with the children (again, true). He pauses for a few moments, like he's mulling over alternatives, then abruptly changes course, asking for my location. I break out in a cold sweat, but I manage to pass along the information. He says he'll be here ASAP.

The phone clicks off. A feeling of dread falls over me. I should be happy, but I'm paralyzed by the thought that this will all be over soon, that I'll have to say goodbye to Marina for real, for good. In a strange way, keeping the investigation alive has kept my sister alive, too. I don't want to let her go.

After a few blank minutes—my brain is having trouble firing up—I realize that I should be prepping the digital recorder and staging the car to match my story. I wedge my phone into my jeans, toss the keys on the passenger seat, and slip the recorder into my shirt pocket. Then I lock up and meander along the edge of the grass, glancing from the stand of trees where my brother is camouflaged to the river.

Straight ahead is Marina's grave. I shudder at the sight of it, at its barrenness, its cold finality. I don't come here often. It's too mind-bending, seeing the proof of my sister's death. Even our father's gory suicide makes more sense.

Feeling dizzy—breathless—I pause before my sister's headstone and say a prayer, on the chance that I'm wrong about the existence of God. I ask Him to reveal the truth and finally put the mystery of Marina's demise to rest.

Amen.

I've reached an uneasy peace when a vehicle comes rolling up behind me. I assume it's Edward and click on the recorder. But when I turn around, the Jaguar is a MINI Cooper and there's not a millionaire in sight.

False alarm.

The MINI creeps by and keeps going. Dodging islands of snow, I tiptoe up on the grass and make eye contact with my brother. He's wearing a mask of bleak resignation. I know in my gut that this is my last shot. Scott won't follow me any farther down this rabbit hole. And I'm too burnt out to go it alone.

Maybe Sam will pick up the mantle. The thought leaves me torn. Should I give up on Marina or sacrifice my daughter to the hunt for my sister's killer?

It's a close call but an easy one: Samantha will be free of this macabre anchor, even if I die without getting justice. Still, the opportunity remains to bring this disturbing chapter to a close. And here comes the devil.

As the Jaguar approaches, my mouth goes dry and my stomach drops. This is my one chance to get Edward to confess. I'd better do it right.

The Jaguar pulls ahead of the Mercedes, stopping in front of the graves of Marjorie Jean and Francis Alvin Washington. Dark clouds blot out the sun.

I expect Edward to get out of the car, but he doesn't. So I go to him. I'm standing at the driver's door for a few chilly seconds—I should've worn a coat; the cloud cover has caught me off guard—before the window slides down. "Hello there," he says, flashing a piranha smile. His eyes are hollow, reptilian. "I believe you're looking for this." He plucks a key out of the console.

"Thank you," I say, purposely not reaching for the key, which he's dangling like a poisoned carrot. I stagger and bump into the car. "I'm not feeling very good. I hope it's not the flu."

He eyes the Mercedes in the rearview mirror. "Will you be able to drive? I would've brought someone along—the house is overrun with elves at the moment—if I'd known you'd need a chauffeur."

"Some fresh air will help, I think. I should walk." I gesture weakly at the graves. "Walk it off, I mean."

I take a couple of wobbly steps, drawing him out of the car. He's still gripping the key, but he's no longer trying to force it on me. He offers his arm for support. I don't want to take it—his touch makes my skin crawl—but keeping him close is my best option. So I let him help, throwing my weight into it, exaggerating my dependence on him.

By a stroke of luck, he steers me in the direction of our family plots. I rack my brain for what I'm going to say when we meet my sister. But it's hard to think when I'm so repulsed by him. "Can we stop?" I ask, locking my feet to the ground between Marina and Mom. "I'd like to say a few words."

He releases me. "Please, go ahead." But he doesn't seem to be focusing on the graves. He's staring at the river, where crows have begun screeching in alarm.

There must be a hawk nearby.

I murmur the Serenity Prayer—our mother adopted this as a mantra after Marina's death, and it brought her comfort—and then tell my sister that I miss her, that I love her, that the world isn't the same without her.

"Marina?" says Edward, studying the tombstone. "That's an unusual name. Beautiful and"—he shakes his head—"where have I heard that before?"

I sense the recorder vibrating in my pocket. "It's an old family name from our mother's side. When she was twelve, she picked it for her firstborn daughter. She gave it to my sister twelve years later."

Edward grimaces. "I know that name from somewhere."

It's as bad as I thought: He killed her and forgot. "You're about the same age," I say. "Maybe you met her. Did you grow up around here?"

He laughs. "I can count the girls I knew in high school on two fingers. I was president of the chess club. I didn't have a girlfriend until college." He goes quiet, somber. "Kathleen D'Angelo. She fell off a balcony and—"

If his story is true, how did he cross paths with Marina's street crowd? The facts don't add up. "She died?"

A faraway look washes over him. "I'm afraid so." After a heavy pause, he adds, "Thank goodness for Lisa. She did so much to help me through that time. We hadn't known each other very long, but she stepped in and handled everything. I was a walking zombie, to put it mildly. She carted me from place to place—the florist, shopping for funeral clothes, the wake—with the patience of a saint. I've never forgotten that."

I want him to keep talking; maybe he'll slip up and mention my sister. I limit my response to: "Mm."

"Without Lisa, I might've dropped out of college when Kathleen died. There didn't seem to be a point anymore. But Lisa had lost a friend a few years earlier—to a drug overdose, I think it was. And a fire. A cigarette caught something ... well, I don't know the details. I only know that Lisa was so brave, the way she pulled herself together and went on with her life. It inspired me to do the same."

His words are like an avalanche. I'm left suffocating in a cloud of confusion. "Lisa Thompson?" I murmur, the name coming off my lips before I can stop it.

Edward's eyes narrow. "Pardon me?"

I gulp down a lump in my throat. "Never mind," I say, biting back the urge to grill him about his wife. How would she know that story—*Marina's* story—unless she'd been there, unless she'd participated in my sister's death? *Dr. Hayes is the other set of lipstick prints at the crime scene.* The idea is too bizarre for my mind to process—could a respected doctor have once been a streetwalker alongside Marina?—and yet somehow I know it's true.

After a thousand dead ends and wrong turns, I've landed at the threshold of an answer—only it's not the answer I expected. Or is it? In the back of my mind, I've always wondered if one of Marina's so-called friends did her in.

"Ready?" asks Edward after a respectful silence.

I breathe slowly, deeply. "Yes," I say, reckoning with what I must do next, "I think I am."

CHAPTER 64
LISA

I couldn't decide whether to eliminate Robin before or after Christmas—each option has its pluses and minuses—but then Edward mentioned offhandedly, like he was adding toothpaste to a shopping list (as if!), that he'd been to that girl's grave. Marina Davis's grave. Just as nonchalantly, I prodded him for more details, in an effort to gauge how close Robin is to putting together the puzzle.

The answer? *Too* close. My timeline has taken a quantum leap forward. It's a shame, too, because I'm feeling rather rundown and uninspired. I would've preferred squeezing in a mini vacation—to Palm Beach, perhaps, where the temperature nudges eighty degrees, even this time of year—before putting myself through the wringer again. Truth be told, taking down Dr. Kapoor was a challenge (rope burns? really?) and I imagine Robin will be more of the same. But when duty calls ...

The good news is that once Robin's dead, the delicious work of consoling Samantha will begin. It puts a pep in my step, thinking of how entwined we'll become, like creeping fingers of wisteria on a garden trellis. If I have my way, you won't be able to tell us apart.

Tonight the club is throwing its annual Christmas extravaganza. For once, I've persuaded Edward to go. Ricki is happy to tag along. Samantha will be tied up with costume designing—preparations for the spring musical are already underway—until 10 P.M. and probably later, if the kids hit Denny's on the way home. (I slipped Samantha five crisp hundreds to make it a sure thing.)

Which leaves Robin and me. I'm flipping through a Rolodex of excuses in my mind to justify our staying behind. Once I have her alone, things will go off without a hitch: a relaxed dinner (I've had Ricki whip up a batch of my mother's famous spaghetti and meatballs); drinks in the natatorium (Robin's choice: blue Hawaiians or piña coladas); and, while I'm doubled over in the bathroom with cramps (or so I'll tell first responders), a slip-and-fall accident, leading to a tragic drowning. I'll pull her out of the water and administer CPR, but it'll be too late.

I've got it: Christmas presents. It falls within the nanny's job description to wrap gifts for the children.

I find Robin in the library, scanning through some book or another. At the clack of my heels, she looks up. "Is it time?"

She must be reading my mind. "Yes," I say, tittering on the inside at the double meaning of her question (if she only knew!), "Edward and the girls are preparing to go."

She jumps to her feet. "I didn't realize it was so late."

I lay a hand on her arm. "No need to rush. I can use you here tonight. We'll have to trust Edward and Ricki to handle things at the club."

Her brow creases. "You're not going?"

"Gosh, no. I've been to a hundred of those things. They get old after a while." I sigh. "They're for the children, anyway. While they're out, we can get a jumpstart on things and wrap the presents." My face takes on an impish pout. "You don't mind, do you?"

She glances around. "It'll just be us? Everyone else is—?"

"Gone?" They will be soon enough. "Not yet. I'll be seeing them off in a few minutes. I thought you could join me for dinner before we get to work."

Her eyes dance with excitement. What a weak, attention-starved little thing. "Sure." She scoops a bunch of note cards into a pile. "Just give me a few minutes to organize, and I'll meet you in the kitchen?"

"Actually, take half an hour." I smile warmly. "That'll allow me to see the children off." Among other things. I want everything *just so* for the big reveal. My mind is crackling at the prospect of tying up loose ends and gaining power over Samantha. I'd say it's nothing personal, but with Robin, there's an element of familiarity, a simmering contempt (a grain of that girl survives in her, one I mean to stamp out like an errant centipede).

On cue, Edward and Ricki round up the children. They're flummoxed by my absence—Ricki's eyebrow notches at the news that Robin will stay behind to assist me, and Edward lobs a last-ditch plea for my attendance ("The girls will miss you terribly. Won't you, girls?")—but the holiday hustle has them shackled by the ankles. They have no choice but to shuffle along.

I stand inside the garage, waving as the Hummer's taillights float down the driveway.

Next up are the security cameras. I disconnected them yesterday while the decorators were milling about—good lies thrive on coincidence; I'll tell anyone who asks that the workers pulled the plugs while illuminating our nativity display—and now I must be sure Edward hasn't gone behind me and corrected the "error."

Another win in my column: The cameras are still dark. Fantastic.

A night like this calls for an eruptive plume of flowers (three dozen blue irises, jammed in one of the many crystal vases Edward has gifted me over the years), soft jazz (Vince Guaraldi's *Autumn Leaves* will do the trick), and the golden blur of candlelight on our faces.

The stage is set in the dining room. (Why waste such a dramatic space? The ceiling is frescoed with puffs of silvery clouds.) And I'm ready for action.

I catch Robin on her way to the kitchen. "I hope you're hungry," I say, joining her. "There's a huge pot of spaghetti and meatballs and warm Italian bread."

"Sounds delicious."

"You'll love it. It's an old family recipe." It dawns on me that I could've laced her food with a lesser-known poison, something coroners don't test for. But that would've involved a meticulous research process, and I don't have time. No, the drowning accident will do nicely. And with a lush as the victim, no one will bat an eye.

Robin assumes we'll be eating at the island and goes into the cupboard for place settings, but I tell her the chore's already done. We just have to tote the food around the corner and voilà—dinner is served!

She slips her hands into a pair of oven mitts and, with a trivet tucked under her arm, grasps the pot.

I cradle the cutting board, keeping it level so the bread doesn't slide off.

The atmosphere in the dining room is spot-on: the candles, the music, the waterfall of bluish purple blossoms. I've even arranged an apéritif—Campari on the rocks in Baccarat crystal tumblers. I can't imagine Robin has been treated better by anyone on earth, much less the assortment of forest trolls she's invited into her bed. If you think about it, I'm a fairy godmother of sorts, rescuing her and Samantha from harm's way, showing them a life they couldn't have envisioned in their wildest dreams. But all good things must end. Truth be told, I'm the faintest bit maudlin over her story's premature close.

The table is mahogany, the dependable workhorse of fine furniture, and grossly oversized. With only two of us dining (Robin and I are grouped together at one end), the surface is vacant and lopsided. The asymmetry is unavoidable, I suppose. Still, it chafes me.

Robin isn't bothered in the least. In fact, the flowers are working their magic. "These are"—she cups a blossom to her face and inhales—"so pretty. Blue's my favorite color."

"Is it? I saw them in a shop window and, on a lark, pulled over and bought a bunch—or, well, three bunches." Nothing about tonight is accidental, but everything must appear so.

"And the candles? They're lovely, too, by the way. But why …?"

"I enjoy their warmth. Don't you?"

"Yes, yes—of course."

"Who says we can't indulge ourselves? Let's use the good china and drink the good wine, whether the men are around or not." I motion at the glasses. "Speaking of which, I thought we might whet our appetites with some Campari. Have you had it before?" I reach for mine and take a sip.

"I think so," she says, eyeing hers.

I'm not surprised. Campari is common enough. With her alcohol predilection, she would've encountered it somewhere along the line. "Go ahead," I say. "You're off duty. Think of this as a girls' night in."

She lifts the glass to her lips, admiring the way the candlelight dances off the faceted crystal. "Mmm," she says, making a little face, "it's good."

I pick up a small knife with a mother-of-pearl handle—a holdover from Edward's bachelor days, gifted to him by one of his sisters—and poke at the bread. A serrated blade would've been better, but this darling piece of cutlery has special occasion written all over it. "Can I get you a slice?" I ask. "We have whipped herb butter." Ricki keeps topping herself in the kitchen.

Robin studies the knife like she knows I'm dangerous. But I've chosen a watery mishap as her swan song, not a dull blade to the heart. "That would be nice," she says, sliding her plate over to catch the hunk of bread I've sawed off.

To put her at ease, I turn over the knife. As her fingers brush mine, an invisible current sparks between us, setting my skin ablaze.

She dips the knife in the ramekin and butters the fluffy white surface of the bread; meanwhile, the Campari slithers down my throat like a liquid organism.

As she eats, I watch her neck—particularly that ridiculous tattoo—undulate with every swallow. The spider isn't crawling, exactly. She's quivering or perhaps shuddering, the difference being one of degree. Maybe she—the spider, I mean—knows what's about to happen.

I'm pondering the creaminess of Robin's skin under that befouling of ink when the glint of a gold chain catches my eye. My gaze follows it down over her blouse like the dotted line of a treasure map. But instead of an X-marks-the-spot, I find a square citrine pendant. It's a coincidence, probably. She doesn't have the gall to steal from me right under my nose. Yet the message is clear: I've acted not a moment too soon.

I reach for the lid of the pot. "Shall we?"

CHAPTER 65
ROBIN

The necklace is a test. It dawned on me at the last moment, in the half hour she gave me to prepare, that I could use it as bait. If she's who I think she is—if she stole this pendant from my sister all those years ago—she'll react to the sight of it; she'll give herself away.

As she sips her Campari, I finger the necklace, hoping to draw her eye. At the same time, I'm spooling back in my mind, trying to match her face to that ratty old Polaroid. It's an impossible task. I never met Lisa Thompson. I've only stared at her blurry image for most of my life and wondered: Where are you? What do you know? Did you kill my sister? Why, why, why?

When the lid comes off the pot, I'm enveloped by a cloud of sentimental memories—memories of family dinners clustered around the kitchen table (our mother was a better than average cook; her specialties included shepherd's pie, fried chicken, and, ironically enough, spaghetti and meatballs), of stories swapped in heightened voices (Marina was always good for an entertaining yarn), of feeling safe (as long as something hadn't set off our father), connected, invincible—until it all fell apart.

Lisa spoons out the meal. I haven't finished the bread—my appetite is nil—so I take a while getting around to the main course. "What's the matter?" she asks with a frown. I catch her staring at the necklace. "Don't you like it?"

"Sure," I say. "I'm sure I will." I take a bite to appease her.

"More Campari?" she asks, tipping the bottle over my glass.

My mind fights itself about the liquor. I should stay sober to confront her, to keep control of the situation, but another shot might give me the courage to plow ahead. "Thanks." I dose myself in one long gulp.

We pick at our food, pushing nests of pasta and crumbling meatballs around our plates like fussy children. "It seems neither of us is hungry," she comments amusedly.

Setting down my fork, I say, "I guess not."

"Perhaps we'll have time for a soak, then. I'm tempted to skip the presents—I can bring in outside help to do the wrapping—and extend our little diversion. It'd be nice to get to know each other better, don't you think? You've been here for a while and we've hardly had any time alone."

I agree to cut dinner short and meet her in the pool room. Before we go, she breaks off two flower blossoms—one for her and one for me—and suggests tucking them in our hair. I feel silly, but I go along, placing the burst of petals behind my ear. Whatever it takes to get her to open up, to admit what she's done, and, more importantly, to explain why.

No answer will be good enough, because it won't bring Marina back. But if she reveals anything substantial, anything worth investigating further—I have fantasies of a notarized murder confession, but I'm not holding my breath—I'll call in an anonymous tip to the police. They'll take the information more seriously coming from Joan Q. Public than from a disgruntled sister with an axe to grind.

Ten minutes after abandoning the meal, we reconvene by the pool. Lisa has beaten me here, which makes little sense unless she had that shimmering turquoise bathing suit and that gauzy multi-colored kimono waiting. She's at the poolside kitchen, mixing drinks. The same music that was playing in the dining room—an instrumental piano composition with a rainy-day vibe—has followed us here.

"Piña colada or blue Hawaiian?" she asks. Chilled Hurricane glasses are at the ready. A bottle of Caribbean rum, the same brand my mother used to drink, and other assorted ingredients (pineapple juice, coconut cream, blue Curaçao) are standing by.

Something at the far end of the room catches my eye. Stuffed in the corner by a row of lounge chairs is an imposing shadow. My mind jolts to the familiar nightmare, to the demonic lizard beast that's stalked me since Marina died. I know the monster isn't real, but it's so present—so *relevant*—that I can taste its rotting flesh.

I need this to be done, the quest to end. One way or another. Lisa or me.

I opt for the blue Hawaiian. While she prepares it, I wander toward the shadow. Slowly, it acquires a form. The neck gives it away: a giraffe. Two giraffes, actually, from that toy shop in the middle of nowhere.

How are the children going to ride those? They'll need ladders just to climb aboard.

I don't hear her coming—she's barefoot and graceful, imperceptible over the tinkling piano tune—but suddenly she's at my side. "Here we go!" She thrusts the drink into my hand and raises her glass. It's filled with the same electric-blue liquid as mine. "Cheers!" she says, crashing our glasses together.

My glass is slick and frosty. I lose my grip. The drink pinwheels for the pool, glancing the tile surround. The stem snaps off and swirls around our feet while the curvy body plunges into the water and sinks out of view.

"Sorry!" I gasp. "It was wet. I didn't mean to ..." As I bend down for the jagged stem, the blossom falls out of my hair and wilts in the puddle of Curaçao.

"No," Lisa says, pulling me back, "that's sharp. You'll cut yourself." She steers me away from the accident, away from the mess. "Take mine," she says, passing me the other drink. "You've lost your flower, too." She plucks the bloom out of her hair and slides it into mine. "There," she says, fluffing the petals. "That's better."

This isn't how the night's supposed to go. I should be grilling her about Marina. About the drugs. The fire. Yet I thank her again, because the time hasn't arrived for such a brutal exchange. It's coming, though. The words are turning over in my mind, arranging themselves in a coherent order. Soon they'll have nowhere to go, nothing to do but fill the air with a lifetime of unanswered questions.

We pause at the mouth of the Jacuzzi, me in my jean shorts (I needed somewhere to stash the knife) and flowy tank top, her in that tropical kimono. "Please," she says, motioning for me to enter first.

I set down the drink and undress—I've scrounged up an old bathing suit of Samantha's that roughly fits—folding the tank and shorts and placing them in a pile nearby.

Lisa slips the kimono down over her tawny shoulders—her skin has a natural glow, even with Christmas on the doorstep—and drops it in a heap.

Like last time, when Ricki and I played hooky, I shock at the heat of the water. Lisa carries my drink down the steps, stealing a sip on the way. Then, for the third or fourth time this hour, she fills my hand with alcohol.

I might as well drink it. My tolerance is sky high. If she's trying to incapacitate me, she's got a long, steep climb.

We soak for five minutes in silence, the music washing over us in soft waves, the pool lights bouncing—dancing, shimmering—on the walls like the reflections of a disco ball. It's a life of peace, pleasure, satisfaction—one she doesn't deserve. Not after what she's taken from me.

I drain the glass. As I'm returning it to the tile surround, Lisa says, "That's a beautiful necklace."

My heart rate ticks up. I touch the stone. "It was my sister's," I say.

"The one who died?"

I push out a nod. "It reminds me of her. I like to keep it close." I'm sick with the knowledge that I've spoken of my sister to her killer.

"What was her name again?"

She's playing with me, pressing my buttons, hoping for an emotional outburst. I won't give her the satisfaction. "Marina," I say. "Her name was Marina."

She smiles faintly. "Oh, yes. That's right." A pause. "If you feel like talking, I'm here to listen. It must've been hard, losing someone so young, so vibrant. Those kinds of tragedies haunt people."

"It was," I say. "But what I really want are answers."

We're side by side, speaking crossways. "I bet you do."

The words are a slap in the face. I stumble for a reply.

She goes on: "It's human nature to solve riddles, to make sense of the senseless, to bring order to chaos—or try to, anyway. But some things aren't meant to be understood. They don't happen for a reason, beyond a rudimentary impulse, that is. Do we ask why the mountain lion preys on the sheep? Not really. Not *seriously*. Because the sheep are weak and the lion must feed."

"No offense, but you don't know anything about my sister. She was different. Better. She was smart, inventive, bold. She could take care of herself. She wasn't a pushover. She made mistakes, getting involved with shady people and"—I gulp down a knot in my throat—"selling herself."

"You make it sound like she was a victim. Like prostitution was someone else's idea. Like they tricked her into it. But isn't it possible that she went into sex work as a choice? For the money? The power? Perhaps she had a harem of her own, taking a cut of the proceeds and keeping her hands clean, relatively speaking."

My mind tumbles. "She was a pimp—or a madam or whatever?" Imagining my sister as a hooker was shattering enough, but to think she'd hurt other girls—other confused kids with nowhere else to turn—that she'd put them in danger for money? The idea is devastating. What if Lisa was one of those girls? What if Marina prostituted her? Could I blame her for wanting my sister dead, then?

Marina's entrepreneurial streak ran deep, but that kind of sick manipulation doesn't seem possible.

Lisa's lips curl into a grin. "Hypothetically speaking, the shoe fits, doesn't it?"

"I wouldn't know."

"Or perhaps you don't want to know," she muses. "Perhaps you can't stand to admit that your sister wasn't the naïve ingénue you've made her out to be."

I should introduce Lisa to Scott. And Lewis. They'd agree with her about Marina, I'm afraid. Have I been trying to avenge a fiction?

I need another drink. I glance across the room at the bar. "Do you mind?" I ask, snatching up the empty glass and sloshing for the steps.

She chuckles. "Knock yourself out."

I'm gone and back in a few short minutes. The drink—I've doubled the liquor and skipped the ice—goes down easy. Practice makes perfect, as they say.

We fall into a lull, each awaiting what the other might say next. She has a clue, I think, that I'm on to her, that I've recognized her as the Lisa Thompson from Marina's sordid past. Actually, it's like she wants me to know, like she wants to bare her secrets, like she wants to tell me what she did to my sister, how she killed her—or at least how she covered up after the fact. Which is my cue to grease the wheels. "I have a confession," I say, my voice struggling against a tremor, my pulse bumping in my throat. I unclasp the necklace and hold it out.

She meets my eye with cold, steely glee. "Yes?"

"I hadn't seen this in twenty years, until Darian took it out of your jewelry cabinet."

She removes the necklace from my hand. "It looked familiar. It could've been a coincidence—I was giving you the benefit of the doubt—but I thought that, yes, it was possible you'd stolen it."

"*I* stole it?" *She's* the thief, even if my sister came by the necklace dishonestly. (I'm holding out hope that Georgette gave Marina the necklace. Lewis did say he and Georgette thought of Marina as a daughter.)

She drapes the necklace around her throat. The pendant settles in the valley of her cleavage. "I think we can drop the false outrage," she says.

Her callousness—her flippancy—is getting under my skin. "I took it, yeah," I say. "I took it *back*." She cocks her head and studies me. My stomach turns over. I reach for the pile of clothes and finger the knife. "But it wasn't yours to begin with. It was my sister's."

"What's the old adage? Possession is nine-tenths of the law?" She throws back her head and laughs.

My mind goes blank. Before I know it, I'm gripping the knife. My thumb slides across the trigger and the blade shoots out.

"Whoa, now," says Lisa, putting up her hands. "Let's not do anything rash, anything we might regret. We've got Samantha to think of."

"Tell the truth," I say. "All of it. Everything you know. And this will be over." I shake my head. "I'm tired; I'm just *so tired*."

She taps her chin thoughtfully. "Where to begin?"

"That stuff," I say, motioning with the knife, "about Marina being … about her making the other girls …" I let out a pained noise. "Did she do that?"

"You should be proud. Your sister had a head for business. She made a lot of money."

On second thought, maybe I don't want to know. "Were you one of …?"

"Me?" She cackles. "Lord, no. Can you imagine?"

"What were you, then? Friends?"

"Something like that."

"Partners?"

"In a way."

"Were you there when she died?"

"Can I plead the Fifth?"

Reflexively, I lunge at her. At the same time, she glides toward the stairs. In a matter of seconds, she's splashing up onto the pool deck.

Still clutching the knife, I surge after her, my muscles lighting up with adrenaline.

She could keep running—the exit's clear—but instead, she stops by the deep end of the pool.

I corral her between the knife and the water. A step backward and she'll be taking a plunge. Forward is the tapered point of the switchblade. "I'm not screwing around," I gasp. "Just ... just stay where you are and start talking. No bullshit, either. I want the truth, so help me God." An exhausted sigh. "Who killed Marina?"

Her mouth twists devilishly. "Nobody." She sweeps her fingers over her chest. "Cross my heart."

"It was an accident? She took too much of ... whatever it was?" She stares through me with blank, impenetrable eyes. "She didn't kill herself, right?" I can live with anything but the knowledge that Marina left us on purpose.

"What makes you think your sister is dead?"

Every hair on my body stands up. "Don't—don't toy with me." I shake the knife around. If she's not careful, I'll do something crazy, something only one of us will live to regret.

She frowns. "It's disappointing, actually. On some level, I was rooting for you to figure it out."

In the roped-off depths of my mind, a sinister memory stirs. But I can't wrestle it into the light.

"Admittedly, the family resemblance is thin," she says, looking me up and down. "But with the girls ..."

My ears buzz. An oily pool of nausea spreads through my gut. I start to tremble. "What?"

She gives a crooked little smile. "I get why you wouldn't recognize *me*: a nip here, a tuck there. Hair dye. Colored lenses." She reaches up and removes a contact from her eye, her iris shifting from warm honey to rich, chocolaty brown. "Not to mention two decades of refinement."

My body goes slack. The knife drifts down to my side and hangs there, suspended in my limp hand. I float above the scene, above the pool, in a bubble of muffled thoughts and thick, distorted perceptions.

"Samantha, though," she says, her voice reaching me as a whisper, "has some of my features—the nose, especially—wouldn't you agree? And the twins have your complexion. Or Mom's complexion. Her side of the family is practically translucent."

My mind is cracking into two equal but contradictory parts. My sister is dead; I know this for a fact. Yet this creature before me, this silver-tongued minx—suddenly, I believe in fairytales, mythology, resurrection—has bottled Marina's spirit and is wearing it like an intoxicating perfume. "But ... but ..." I stammer, unable to pluck a thread of cohesion from my mind, "... Dad saw ... he identified the body."

"I'm sure he did. My plan wouldn't have worked otherwise."

Shaking my head, I say, "Stop. Just stop. You're confusing me." Her name is Lisa Thompson and she killed Marina. Or she knows who did. Everything else is a trick, a distraction, a ploy to throw me off course.

"It's really quite simple," she says. "This was before DNA, mind you. And I'd never had any dental work. You must remember my avoidance of the dental chair. That tub of lard with the greasy nose and the armpit stains, poking his sausage fingers around in my mouth? Thanks but no thanks."

"Dr. Goldstein?"

"See, I'd forgotten his name." She grins. "Goldstein. Yes, that's him. He's dead now, I assume."

A snake slithers up my spine. "Marina could've told you those things."

"Lots of things *could've* happened. We're talking about what *did* happen. Aren't you glad, finally, to know the truth? I thought you'd take it better. I thought you'd be happy. The sisterly bond is very strong—at least ours was. You must've missed me."

I don't know who—or what—this thing is, but she's not my sister; she's not Marina. I materialize again in my body and tighten my grip on the knife. "No," I say. "I don't believe you."

"That's to be expected," she remarks. "Your thoughts—in this case, about my supposed death—aren't matching reality. The quickest way to fix things is to accept what I'm telling you."

"No," I repeat, the word running on a loop in my mind: *no no no no no no no.*

"Well, then ... gee, I don't know what I can say to convince you. I guess I could tell you about Lisa Thompson. About how we could've passed as sisters—it was dumb luck, really, that I found such a suitable stand-in—about our matching tattoos." She picks me over with those different-colored eyes. "Did anyone ever show you the photo? I sent one home before the fire to get it on record. With no other way of identifying me—the body was pretty crispy, after all—the tattoo was my only shot. It worked like a charm, as they say." She lets out a happy, purring breath. "Want to see it? I'm surprised you haven't noticed it before." She twists sideways, revealing a small inked butterfly on the back of her shoulder. It's faded with time, like the web on my neck, which immediately starts tingling. "Excuse the cliché," she says. "I was young. And to be fair, I liked butterflies long before they were tramp-stamp chic. Mine's on the classier side, though, don't you think?"

My lips are frozen, my mind numb.

She takes advantage of the situation, confessing to overdosing Lisa Thompson, strategically burning the body, sprinkling her—Marina's—possessions around the crime scene, and vanishing in the mist with a new identity.

"But ... why?"

"You people," she says. "I knew you wouldn't let it rest—you wouldn't go on—without closure, without an ending, without a body. So I gave you one. If you think about it, the blood's on your hands. All I wanted was a fresh start, a life of my own, an adventure. That never would've happened under the suburban cloud you call a family." She sneers. "I mean, look in the mirror. And then look at me. It goes without saying, but I'll say it anyway: There's no contest. Can you imagine how disgustingly average I would've ended up?"

If this is my sister, she's better off dead. "They'll dig up the bones," I mutter, "and test them. You'll go to jail. Prison." *Or I could end it here*, I think, only half convinced that this shape-shifter is Marina and not Lisa. Her whole story could be a bluff. Instinctively, I raise the knife. A call to 911—I only need to reach the phone on the other side of the room and jab out the numbers—would get the ball rolling.

"That's where you're wrong." She grabs my knife-wielding arm. Instead of pushing me away, she pulls me toward her. I lose my balance and, in a tangle of limbs, we fall into the water.

The knife gets away from me. As I bob around, struggling to get my footing—the water's over my head, I quickly realize—she clutches a fistful of Samantha's bathing suit and pulls me under.

I'm a weak swimmer. Marina would know that. But I'm a fighter, too.

I kick and flail, trying to land a blow somewhere vital—that turquoise bathing suit is a welcome target—but the water slows me down, blunts my movements. The connections I make are superficial and impotent. If I don't calm down, if I don't conserve my energy—my oxygen—I'm going to have to inhale; I'm going to have to open my lungs and let the water in.

My sister is strong and focused. For every bit of progress I make—I break the surface for a fraction of a second and gulp a small breath—she redoubles her efforts, using any means necessary (choking, hair pulling, eye gouging, a knee to the abdomen that comes excruciatingly close to triggering my cough reflex) to destroy me.

Samantha needs me; I can't die here.

With a swift, wrenching turn, I disrupt her grip and splash away. As I'm throwing my arm over the side of the pool, blindly grasping for something to hold on to—there's nothing but that slick tile—I become aware of a high-pitched barking sound. My wheezing breath is met by Magnum's snarling face. Still, I hurl my other arm onto the pool deck and try pushing myself out of the water. But before I can plant a knee, my hair is yanked back and I splash down again.

The barking continues along with the attack, but it's faraway and muted like a half-forgotten dream. Soon I don't hear it anymore.

The next round of fighting is choppier. My sister is getting tired. Yet I can't separate myself from her for more than a second at a time. I slash, kick, bite—at least twice, my teeth find her flesh—and, in between, steal precious sips of air.

Just when I think I might beat her, I might leave this pool and this mansion and this twisted version of my sister behind forever, Marina gets a second wind. My stamina fades as she claws up my back, stuffs my shoulders down with all her weight, and submerges me for what might be the last time.

I hadn't appreciated the water until now—its sweet, lulling rhythm, like the rocking of a baby's cradle. My body relaxes. A comforting tranquility envelops me and a thought tiptoes across my mind: This wouldn't be such a bad place to die. The water is seductive in a weightless, cajoling sort of way.

A screaming voice—Samantha's voice—breaks my delusion. She's pleading with us, emitting the sort of shrill, panicked commands—"No! Stop! Don't!"—that I would've launched at the scumbag who hurt her if I'd had the chance.

My sister tightens her grip.

I dig deep for an extra ounce of determination and strain against the force of her will. I've made little headway when an explosion sounds. The piercing noise and juddering vibrations swell my eardrums and play my spine like a saxophone.

Marina lets go.

With my whole body rattling, I gulp my first breath in far too long. Choking and coughing, I paddle lopsidedly for the edge of the pool. When I'm able to look around—my vision has a cloudy, surreal cast—I see that one of the windows is blown out and pebbles of glass are scattered around the poolside kitchen. On the opposite side of the room is Samantha, my .38-caliber pistol clutched in her hands. Before I can stop her, she zeroes in on the water, on Marina, and pulls the trigger.

CHAPTER 66
MARINA

The bullet misses me entirely. My niece is many things, most of them sparkling and admirable, but a crack shot at a moving target in a vast, dim room isn't one of them. Or maybe the water deflected the bullet just enough to save me. Either way, I emerge from the pool unscathed after a suitable waiting period (no sense giving Samantha a second chance to take me out on dry land).

By the time I'm shivering into a towel—the influx of cold air from that broken window has my teeth chattering—Robin and Samantha are gone. And the situation has gotten stickier. I never would've confessed my identity if I'd known my sister would live to tell about it.

But will she—tattle, I mean? It's a natural impulse to spill the beans on such a juicy secret. (If you could've seen the look on her face when I got it across that I'm alive. It was worth the decades of waiting.) But if she exposes me, I could have Samantha arrested. I'd never do such a thing to the only being alive who shares my unique potential, my shining inner light. But Robin doesn't know that.

I have to speak with my sister—and pronto.

Leaving the chilled natatorium behind, I rush to the great room, where I last had my phone. I assume Robin and Samantha have fled the estate. Maybe they're en route to the police. Maybe my sister is dumb enough to feed that darling daughter of hers to the wolves.

Not if I have anything to say about it.

The phone is on a small copper table by the fire. I sink into the chocolate suede armchair, the thought briefly registering that I'm wet and the fabric will stain. Oh well. Just one more thing that'll need replacing due to this little fiasco.

I find Robin's name in my contacts and tap the phone icon. The call lands in her voicemail. "Hi, Robin. It's Lisa," I say, keeping up the façade. "Everything's fine. I didn't want you to worry." I pause, considering what I can say without giving anything away. "Nobody's hurt and the window will be fixed as soon as I get hold of the contractor. A day or two, at the outside. No need to involve Edward; he's busier than a one-armed paper hanger." I laugh lightheartedly. "So, yes, business as usual here. The girls are looking forward to spending the holidays with you and Samantha." Hint, hint: Get back here and help me cover up this mess. "Let me know if there's anything I can do to make your Christmas merrier. See you soon. Bye-bye."

As long as Robin can read between the lines, she'll get the message: Samantha's attempt on my life—as well as mine on Robin's—will be swept under the rug in an oopsie-daisy quid pro quo. I'll keep her secret if she'll keep mine, including the all-important identity question. The way I see it, my baby sister has little choice.

The next morning, Ricki launches an inquisition at breakfast when Robin and Samantha don't show up. To explain their absence, I fudge a story about a death in the family. Now watch them waltz in and make a liar out of me.

Edward's gulping down scrambled eggs like he's one of those competitive eaters. He takes a momentary breath. "Your nose," he says, waving the egg-speckled fork around, "is it swollen?"

Robin landed one good blow, resulting in the damage he's noticed. "I don't think so." I've spackled on enough makeup to resurface the moon.

He shrugs. "My mistake."

Ricki finishes washing the frying pan and sets it in the dish drainer. "Do we know when the window in the natatorium's being fixed? I'd like to get the girls down there this afternoon for a swim."

"Two o'clock," I say firmly. I made the call first thing this morning. "It won't take long." God knows I'm paying enough to erase this little blunder.

"You really didn't hear anything?" Edward asks.

I push back my stool and stand up. "Why don't you check the video cameras?" I suggest, pecking him on the cheek as I breeze by. I titter on the inside, knowing the security system is disabled and will show nothing. "My money's on a bunch of drunken yahoos poaching deer."

"This close to the house? I can't imagine—"

"Just a hunch. Feel free to investigate further." I've cleaned up all the evidence I could find: the broken Hurricane glass, the pool of Curaçao, the sopping iris bloom, that ridiculous switchblade (did she really think I'd lie down and let her stab me?), Robin's left-behind clothes (no one can know we were in the natatorium when the window broke), and the bullet. Or one of them, anyway. Where the first one went is anyone's guess. I wasn't exactly paying attention when my niece shot out that skyscraper of glass. (Kudos to Samantha for taking charge, though. I love a girl with moxie!)

"I just might do that," remarks Edward. And on that note, I march off down the hall.

As I coast down the sloping driveway, I tick through a mental list of things I must do, top among them a heart-to-heart with my baby sister. If I know Robin, she's on a bender somewhere—a pay-by-the-hour motel with a liquor store next door, maybe—and poor Samantha is along for the ride.

I wonder what Robin has told Samantha about me, if she's spilled the family secret, if she's let on about my murderous past. Something tells me she hasn't; she's overprotective to a fault. Which will break in my favor once I get hold of Samantha again. I'll be able to put my life, even the unsavory parts, in context. I'll be able to make her see that everything I've done was for the best. My success is the proof in the pudding.

I roll through the gate and, after waiting for an unusual burst of traffic to clear, make my normal right turn. The Hummer skips a beat, grasping for traction on a slick spot of road. But it recovers quickly and soon I'm cruising along with the radio on (a classic-rock station, playing Queen's *Somebody to Love*), the heater blazing—Old Man Winter has kicked autumn in the teeth—and my mind wandering.

The murder plot has fizzled, but maybe there's another way to get rid of Robin—or at least shut her up indefinitely. I can't have her telling Edward that I'm not Lisa Thompson; I'm not the woman he thinks he married. The fallout would be extreme. Not that I don't have a plan B. I'll triumph one way or another. I just prefer things on my own terms.

I'm lost in thought, mulling over potential strategies—would Robin leave the country on the next flight to, say, New Zealand, if I deposit a million or two in a Swiss bank account in her name?—and weighing possible interception points (I must find her ASAP and bring her around to my way of thinking), when the howl of police sirens cuts through my fog of concentration. I glance in the rearview mirror and see flashing lights. Three cop cars, minimum.

To the shoulder of the road I go, expecting the cruisers to shoot by. But they fall in line behind me. Except the last one; it pulls parallel to the Hummer and edges ahead, cocking its wheels and blocking me in.

My stomach burbles. Either I've broken some mundane traffic law or my sister has gone rogue. Without any proof, though, can the cops even question me? I'll see what our lawyers have to say about that.

I shift the Hummer out of gear and silence the radio. *Speeding*, I tell myself. *You must've had a lead foot. Just grin and bear it, and you'll be on your way in no time.*

When I roll down the window, a blast of cold air rushes inside. I brace against it and put on an innocent smile. In the side mirror, a gang of tiny uniformed officers strides my way. I hang my head out the window and chirp, "Is something wrong, gentlemen? I hope I wasn't going too fast."

This time the problem won't go away with a little sweet talk. Even assault charges against Robin are wishful thinking. To my chagrin, I'm informed—rather gruffly, I might add—that I'm under arrest for killing Dr. Aarush Kapoor.

The brutes pat me down and read me my rights and even cuff me before stuffing me into the back of a squad car and leaving me to rot while they verbally blow each other for a job well done.

When I'm finished with them, they won't have jobs at all. Let's see how high and mighty they are then.

CHAPTER 67
ROBIN

Sam and I race away from the mansion, not knowing if Marina is dead or alive. When we end up on Nate's doorstep, I'm as surprised as anyone. We could've gone lots of places, but nowhere feels safe. Everywhere I look (billboards on the highway; behind the wheel of the minivan beside us; crossing the road under a hazy streetlight) is my sister's grinning face.

I didn't believe it at first—part of me will *never* believe—but the truth is starting to sink in. The girl I knew as Marina, the sister I adored for ten magical, carefree years (I was too young then to grasp our dysfunctional family dynamics; those realizations came later), has morphed into something evil, something empty, something cold. Or maybe the trick is the other way around. Maybe the fun-loving dazzler had a black heart all along.

My mind is tangled. From Nate's stoop, I glance back at the car, making sure Sam is staying put (affirmative), and then ball up my fist and pound on the door. It takes Nate a while to answer. When he does, he's barefoot, shirtless, dressed in a pair of lounge pants and wearing a confused, eyebrows-pinched-together frown. "Robin?" he asks, holding the door open only a crack. "What're you—?"

I try pushing the door open wider, but he resists. "Sorry. I didn't know where else to …" I swallow hard. "We're in trouble. Sam and me.

There was a shooting." I can't believe the words coming out of my mouth. "Can we—?"

Nate squints into the parking lot. "Samantha's here?"

"In the car. On the other side of—"

"Is everyone okay?"

A strangled laugh bursts out of my throat. "Physically? Yeah, I guess, but …"

He glances over his shoulder, back into the condo. "Listen, uh, someone's here. You'll have to give me a minute to clear the place out. Can you wait in the car with Sam?"

I'm powerless to argue. I just slink back through the parking lot and bide my time with my shaken daughter—we're both too stunned for conversation—until Nate's door opens again and a pretty young redhead ducks out. I expect her to continue on alone, but Nate appears, in a hoodie and sneakers, and escorts her to a small SUV. They share a brief kiss before she gets in the vehicle, starts it up, and leaves.

My shock over Nate's relationship fades fast—what did I expect him to do, pine for me forever?—considering the trouble Samantha and I are in. The consequences of my daughter's actions are crashing on me like a tidal wave—she could be charged with murder; she could go to prison—when Nate taps on my window.

Sam is in a daze. We usher her into Nate's condo. The three of us gather around the table in the corner of the living room. "So?" says Nate, his eyes flashing with concern.

I reach into my waistband for the gun and set it down between a textbook and a coffee mug. "We need to get rid of this."

Nate shakes his head. "That's empty, right?"

"Mm-hmm." The leftover bullets are in the Mercedes. They'll have to be disposed of, too.

Sam has bitten her thumbnail down to the quick. I move her hand away from her mouth.

Nate requests a recap of the night's events, which I provide to the best of my ability. I can't say who's more shocked, him or Samantha.

"Aunt Marina?" says Sam, wide-eyed.

"You don't know if she was hit?" Nate asks, ignoring the headline: *My murdered sister is back from the dead.*

I draw a deep breath and let it out. "She didn't seem to be moving," I say, dragging my fingers through my hair. "But it was dark, and we ran out of there pretty fast. She could've survived, I think, even if Sam shot her."

"I didn't mean to. You know that, right? I just wanted to get her off you."

"It's okay, honey," I say, patting Sam's leg. "You did the right thing."

"We should watch the news," says Nate. He jumps up and turns on the TV, even though it's only eight thirty. "This is big enough that it'll be on every channel."

A thought dawns on me. I focus on my daughter, trying to see into her mind. "You did the right thing," I repeat. "But why did you have my gun?"

"I needed it."

Nate: "For protection? From Jason's friends? From the guys who …?"

Sam sighs. "Jason had nothing to do with it—not that it matters now, anyway. We broke up a while ago."

I'm not following. "Nothing to do with what?"

"The stuff that was happening. The money. The pot. Not being able to pay those creeps."

Marina is washed from my mind. I nudge my daughter to explain further.

"I messed up," Sam says. "I got a bunch of orders for jackets and bags and stuff, but I didn't have enough money for supplies. I couldn't ask you—we're always broke—so I thought it would be okay, just for a little while, to help these girls sell some, you know, pot around school. I bought the fabric and paint and rivets and stuff with the money. I was gonna put it back when I finished the orders and got paid, but then the three biggest ones canceled and …"

"*You're* the drug dealer? Not Jason?" Honest to God, I can't take any more surprises tonight.

"I barely did anything!" Samantha yelps. "You know how much those girls sell all the time? Like thousands of dollars' worth. I only sold a little for a few weeks. Six or seven hundred bucks. That's it."

"And that makes it okay?"

"I didn't say that."

Nate has sunk back in his chair. He looks overwhelmed. I bet he's thanking his lucky stars that he'll be rid of us soon.

"I still don't get it," I say. "Who beat you up? And what were you doing with the gun?"

Samantha shrugs. "I just wanted to scare them. It was working, too."

"The girls?"

She nods.

"*They* did that to you?"

"There were five of 'em. Five against one."

"Oh, Sam." I lean over and pull her into a hug. "You should've told me."

"I know."

After a brief silence, Nate says, "What are we going to do about that?" The gun. Possibly the murder weapon.

In a sick way, I hope Samantha did kill Marina. Then I can keep the happy, golden memories of my sister and discard the monster she's become.

"Do you have gloves?" I ask. "And a cloth?"

Nate disappears and comes back with a pair of lightweight gardening gloves and a hand towel. I put on the gloves and meticulously wipe down the muzzle, the barrel, the trigger, the grip, and everything in between, trying to expunge any fingerprints. It's a blessing that I bought the thing off the internet in a don't-ask, don't-tell situation. Any records on it won't link up to me.

"That's as good as it gets," I say, wrapping the gun in the towel.

I summon Nate to the kitchen, leaving Sam in the living room with the TV. She doesn't need to hear how we're going to smooth this over. She's in too deep already.

Nate and I are on the same page: Chuck the .38 in a nearby body of water. By the time anyone finds it, hopefully Mother Nature will have done her damage.

Once the plan is settled—we'll take Nate's Honda, in case the cops are looking for the Mercedes, and stick to back roads—Nate finds a blanket and pillow for Samantha. We leave her with instructions to keep the door locked and stay off electronics. For the time being, we're invisible.

The night is black and cold. Nate and I travel for miles in search of a fishing hole his father used to take him to as a kid. He thinks he knows where it is, somewhere past a greasy spoon called Deena's Eats, just before a horse paddock and a big gray barn. But everything looks the same in the dark and we quickly become lost.

Nate has lent me a jacket. I hug it to my body and suggest something more immediate, something we've passed at least twice in the last few miles: a well. Sneaking onto someone's property to get rid of the gun is a risk—they could shoot us or sic attack dogs on us or just call the cops and get us caught red-handed—but it would be done fast. And a random hole in the ground seems more discreet, more undetectable, than taking our chances with a flowing current. With my luck, a guy out walking his dog would find the gun washed ashore tomorrow. And then where would Samantha and I be?

"I don't think so," Nate says, peering at a stretch of farmland. "But you gave me an idea." He swings into a closed auto-glass shop and turns us around.

Once we give up looking for the fishing spot, Nate gets his bearings and backtracks toward town. We've reached the college district where I used to slosh coffee for coeds and he still preaches the gospel of Darwin. He cuts down a side road and stops.

"What are we doing?" I ask.

He holds out his hand. "Give me the gun. The bullets, too."

I'm relieved to see that he's wearing gloves. I don't argue. I just turn over the gun and everything else and pray for a miracle.

"Sit tight," says Nate. He leaves the car running and starts off down the block. Just before the road turns a corner, he peers around—a couple of buildings have lights on, but there's no one, not even another car, on the street—and bends down by the curb.

A lightning bolt hits me: He's slipping the whole incriminating lot down a storm drain. Sometimes the simplest ideas are best. As the saying goes—out of sight, out of mind. Hopefully the evidence stays that way.

When we get back to the condo, Samantha's fast asleep. Nate gives me his bed, which is rumpled and musky with sex. I feel a little aching twinge at the idea of him with another woman, but in a bittersweet way, I'm happy for him, too. He deserves a better life than any he could've had with me.

I don't expect to be able to sleep with the problems swirling through my mind—Samantha, Marina, another job down the drain—but my body mercifully overrides my brain, and I collapse in a dreamless slumber. Soon Sam's perched on the side of the bed, rustling me awake. "C'mon. It's late."

I glance at where the alarm clock should be—I've napped here a dozen times in Nate's arms—but it's relocated to the other side of the bed, on a shabby-chic stand with curved feminine legs and dusty-rose paint. This must be the girlfriend's addition. She's testing the waters of living together. Maybe they've even made plans. Seeing this, I'm surprised she left so willingly last night. I wonder what Nate told her about me. Nothing flattering, probably, if he told her anything at all.

The clock reads 11:07. I feel like I've slept for a week. "In a minute," I say, shooing Samantha away.

Eventually, I drag myself out of bed. I'm scuffing along the carpeted hallway, heading for the bathroom, when Samantha yelps, "Oh my God! Oh my God!"

My reflex is to run. As I round the corner of the living room, I catch Sam and Nate huddled around the TV. On the screen is a BREAKING NEWS alert, alongside a picture of Dr. Lisa Hayes—the same picture from that business card she slipped me.

The word *homicide* pops out.

Oh, shit. Here we go. I hold my breath and press closer, so I can read the squirmy ticker at the bottom of the screen. What is our fate?

Instead of implicating Sam, the stream of words targets Lisa. Marina. My brain stutters and resets.

The news that my sister is alive falls by the wayside as I realize that she—whoever she is, whatever name she's attached herself to—has been arrested. The victim is someone I've never heard of. Another doctor. Maybe a professional rival. Or just some poor, unlucky soul who's had the misfortune of crossing Marina's path.

If the charges are true, Marina has killed again. But this time she got caught. Which gives me faith, for the first time in a long time, that the universe is just. That actions have consequences. That the rest of us aren't just spitting in the wind trying to do right. Because even with the mistakes I've made—and I've made plenty—I never set out to hurt anyone. That's the difference between my sister and me.

CHAPTER 68
MARINA

By the time we reach the jail, news crews are poised to catch my anguished reaction. And I swear I can hear helicopters whirring overhead. But instead of cowering or putting on a deer-in-the-headlights act, I raise my chin and smile brightly as the gun-toting chimpanzees haul me inside.

The booking process, though meant to be dehumanizing—most people find the cavity search traumatic and humiliating, I suppose—is a trivial annoyance. The mug shot and fingerprints; the stripping of personal property; the blood draw, under the guise of protecting my jailers and fellow inmates from disease; even the jeering and preening are routine (these civil-servant types relish the opportunity to taunt and crow).

As soon as the formalities are done, I ask to speak with my lawyer. I have a particular fellow in mind, a cigar-chomping Greek with offices in New York and Philly, who's known for his clairvoyant jury-selection techniques, and, if worse comes to worst (it won't; I'll be long gone before then), his brash, confrontational—and let's not forget winning!—courtroom style.

When my request is granted, I'm almost annoyed. Part of me wants a reason to argue. But getting out of here ASAP outweighs any petty squabbles. I'll be laughing all the way back to the mansion while the guards snap on fresh gloves and order another crack whore to bend over and spread 'em.

Even with Mr. Spiros on the job, I'm held overnight. But bright and early the next morning, the preliminary arraignment gets underway. I sit politely, astutely, soaking in the scene. Somewhere in the back of my mind, I've always known it would come to this. The flurry of activity gives me a pleasant shiver.

The hearing starts with a reading of the charges. I bristle as if the suggestion of violence is stomach-turning. The magistrate asks a bunch of silly questions about my criminal history (none that they know of), my ties to the community (longstanding and deep), and my employment (solid, respectable, lucrative).

I've been warned that getting out of jail pretrial is a long shot when accused of a violent felony. (Whatever happened to innocent until proven guilty?) But my attorney is brilliant. He paints me as Little Bo-Peep and offers to keep me under house arrest. Electronic monitoring will assure my angelic behavior and appearance at future proceedings. Beyond that, my passport will be surrendered, erasing my ability to flee the country, wink-wink.

It's a slam dunk, as they say. Short of getting the case tossed out of court—a girl can dream, can't she?—Mr. Spiros's job was to get me released with the fewest possible conditions for the least sum. I'd say $3 million (the doctor *is* dead, after all) and a pesky ankle bracelet, which will soon be moot, hit the mark.

Leaving court, Edward and I—and a phalanx of lawyers (Mr. Spiros is the top dog among many)—are met with a media firestorm. It's fun, in a way, being the shiny, new toy everyone wants to play with. Sadly, though, I'm feeling nauseated and crampy (jail food! egads!), so proclaiming my innocence for a wall of TV cameras will have to wait.

My husband sweeps me into an idling van with tinted windows; meanwhile, Mr. Spiros strides up to a microphone on the courthouse steps and begins shaping public opinion.

We travel in silence for a while, Edward behind the wheel, obsessively checking the rearview mirror. A few photographers and journalists have broken free of the pack and are tailing us, but most have stayed behind to swallow the drivel our lawyers are spooning out. "You must be tired," Edward says finally.

"Yes. The jail is woefully ill-equipped. And freezing. We should think about funding an improvement project, when all of this is said and done."

"Are you crazy? We'll be lucky to have ... to have *anything* left after ..." He shakes his head. "My business will be bankrupt. The negative press alone ..."

He's being dramatic. Hospitals aren't going to stop ordering his doohickeys because of anything I've done. Still, I roil at the accusation. "If you hadn't gone behind my back, if you hadn't helped the police frame me for something I didn't do, we wouldn't be in this spot."

"This is *my* fault?"

"Isn't it?"

"I want a divorce. Not now, obviously. That wouldn't be good for anyone, especially the children. But after you're cleared—*if* you're cleared—I'll have the papers drawn up. What do you want?" From the estate, he means.

Everything, of course. And then some.

I laugh. I can't help it. Does he know how ridiculous he sounds? "A husband who doesn't ass fuck the maid would be nice." I don't mean Ricki. She's the only one whose pants he hasn't invaded. She must be too old for him. Or she turned him down.

"You did it, didn't you?" he says, sounding aghast. "You killed him." A bloated pause. "Why?"

I'd love to clue him in on my activities, just to see the look on his face. And I'm tempted to do it, since I won't be sticking around for the fallout. But he could be recording me—I wouldn't put it past him to be schilling for the police, still—and confessing to murder on tape is a rookie move. "I didn't kill anyone. The doctor took his own life. And you're part of the conspiracy against me. My own husband!"

"How did Bart's DNA get on the rope, then?"

Bart. Ellen's husband. The carwash manager. "Excuse me?"

Edward informs me that detectives have been in touch with my in-laws. "So?" he says. "How did it get there?"

"Innocently, I'm sure. Or the police planted it." Sowing doubt about law enforcement can only work in my favor.

"Jane said you were over there—at the house, in the garage—snooping around."

"Sounds like someone's putting words in poor little Janie's mouth."

"The rope came up missing afterward. Since when do you visit my relatives, anyway? Never that I can remember."

"They've arrested me on the word of a twelve-year-old?"

"She's fourteen."

"Well, she's very flat-chested."

"They've got Bart's DNA. He's never been near your office, let alone had contact with this ... this murdered doctor."

"It was a suicide," I stubbornly insist.

"Can you explain that?" Edward shakes his head. "How his DNA got on the murder weapon?"

A thought occurs to me: Why was Bart's DNA on file with the police? They didn't just pick him out of thin air. There must've been a hit in the database. Maybe I can make my brother-in-law into Suspect Numero Uno.

I ask Edward about Bart's crimes, but he pleads ignorance. I probe him for more information, for everything he knows. His status as an informant must be worth something.

"I was trying to help," he says. "Jesus Christ. I wanted to clear your name."

"That's admirable," I say. "I do appreciate it. But it appears you've played into their hands. You should've come to me. I would've told you what to do."

"That's enough. Let's change the subject. We're almost home, and I don't want the girls upset. They don't need to hear any of this."

"You're right," I say. "We must spare the children." And I might just spare them by taking them with me on my escape. Depending on whether I can spirit away Samantha, I might need the company. And the cover. A woman traveling alone could raise suspicions, but a woman with child garners immediate trust and goodwill, a fact I'm banking on to turn the page on Dr. Lisa Hayes and recast myself as … as …

I'm lost in thought, pondering new identities—I've always wanted to give Cheryl a try; I could be Cheryl Anderson or Cheryl Young or, for a twist, Sheryl Green—as the gate clatters shut behind us, thwarting the media and leaving Edward and me alone.

CHAPTER 69
ROBIN

As soon as I learn of Marina's arrest, I go scrambling back through the Mercedes for my phone. I find it wedged under the seat. A message is waiting from her. When I play it, I'm knocked over by the familiarity of her voice. How could I have been so blind?

I pull in a breath and call Scott. It's time he knew the truth.

My brother's phone just rings and rings. I get a canned message saying his voicemail isn't set up.

Nate's helping Sam forage through the cupboards for the makings of lunch. He won't mind if I disappear for half an hour, will he? I should ask him, but I don't. He's been so good already, putting himself at risk for my problems. I can't bear to grovel for yet another favor.

The lumberyard is a quick ten minutes away. Still, I'm worried that I'm being followed or tracked by software in the car. Marina was set on getting rid of me. I doubt she'd give up so easily, especially now that I know everything. Now that I could expose her as a fraud. Now that I could implicate her in the murder of Lisa Thompson—a scheming, premeditated murder that's slipped through the cracks for a quarter of a century.

It's time for my sister to pay up.

Tracking down Scott proves harder than usual. After three different workers give up looking for him, he comes wandering out of a patch of trees by the road.

"What're you doing here?" he asks, strutting up beside me.

He hasn't seen the news. Or he hasn't made the connection. "I need to talk to you." I can't mention Marina, or he'll roll his eyes. He's had enough of our sister to last a lifetime. "Is there somewhere we can go?"

"Around here?" He takes a sweeping view of the lumberyard. "Not really."

"What about lunch?" It's been our go-to escape before. Maybe today is no different.

"They're having a catered thing in the break room," he tells me. "For morale or whatever." He shrugs.

I move toward the Mercedes. "Can you skip it? This won't take long."

"I ain't got time—"

"Fine." I pull out my phone and bring up Marina's message. "Listen to this and tell me what you hear, *who* you hear." I put the phone on speaker and play the voicemail.

A few words in, his facial muscles tighten. "What the hell is that?"

Until this second, I'd been hoping I was wrong, hoping Lisa Thompson was diabolical enough to assume Marina's identity and fool me. "You hear it, don't you?"

"Why does that sound like …?" He grabs my arm. We end up in the Mercedes, watching his coworkers crisscross the yard in a dance of productivity.

There's no easy way to say it. "She's alive," I inform him. He just sits there, dumbfounded. "You know my boss, the psychiatrist? Dr. Lisa Hayes?"

"Yeah."

I explain about "Lisa" being Marina, about the murder and the stolen identity, about her trying to drown me, about the shooting, about Marina killing again, about her being arrested.

My brother is blinking in rapid, sporadic bursts. "What the fuck?"

"Watch the news. It's a big story. She's pretty well-known as this doctor."

He stares at the trees. "She's been here all along? Right around the corner? Laughing at us?"

I can't believe it either. "I guess so."

"What did the cops say?"

"Huh?"

"The cops. When you told them."

I shake my head. "She's already in jail. And I can't prove anything. It'd be my word against hers."

"So?"

He's right. I have to do something. I have to bring our sister's evil deeds to light. But can't I have a moment to breathe, to think, to make my daughter's world safe again before opening that wound? "I will," I say. "I'll tell them." If they dig up Marina's grave, they'll have the beginnings of another murder case.

"I'll go with you," offers Scott. "Just say the word."

"Thanks. It means a lot." I make eye contact with him. We're both hollowed out. Drained. But we'll recover from this. We've survived too much to give up now.

On the way back to Nate's, I call Ricki. Edward might be a better choice, but I don't know his level of involvement in Marina's schemes. I can't trust him. Even Ricki is a crap shoot, but I have to get rid of this car before I'm sucked any further into my sister's tornado of pain.

Ricki answers with stress in her voice. "Hello?"

"It's me. Robin."

"Where are you?" she snaps. "All hell's breaking loose. The phone's been ringing off the hook and you're supposed to be—"

"I'm done. I'm not coming back. You should leave, too." I groan. "It's only going to get worse." If I know Marina—and now, after everything, I think I do—she'll dig in for a fight. She'll take anyone and everyone down with her to prove a point, to make them suffer. And yet somehow she'll come out smelling like a rose. She'll step over the bodies, flick the dust off her shoulders, rebrand herself, and thrive.

I hope I'm wrong. I hope she gets what she has coming. But history predicts otherwise.

"This is insane," says Ricki. "How can they arrest her for murder? I've been keeping the kids busy, but eventually they're going to find out."

"Let them," I say. "Let them see what their mother is." The truth will serve them better than a sick, distorted fantasy. I should know.

"You think she did it?"

"Don't you?"

"No." I imagine her shaking that glossy black head of hair. "I can't see how."

It's a lost cause, trying to make someone see what they won't. Deep in our psyches, we're programmed to fool ourselves. Ricki's smarter than most, though. She'll come around eventually. Until then ... "Just pay attention," I say. "And be careful. Don't let your guard down." My sister is toxic. Malignant. Her ability to infect others is endless.

"What should I tell them?"

"Whatever you want. I'm leaving the car at the bus station—the one on State Street. The keys will be in the glove box. They should send someone for it soon."

"Is Sam okay? Are you guys going to be—?"

"We'll be fine," I say, even though I haven't thought past this very minute. "Can I call you in a few weeks, when things settle down? Sam will want her stuff back. Maybe you can box it up and ..."

"Sure. Whatever you need." I'm about to thank her when she says, "Shit, Edward's here. I gotta go." The call abruptly clicks off.

I feel like laughing in a frustrated, exhausted sort of way. But I can't. And I can't cry, either. So I turn up the radio and roll down the windows—the cold air is a refreshing jolt—and let the road hypnotize me until the bus station pops into view.

Nate's condo is only a few blocks away. The walk will do me good.

I park the Mercedes at the farthest spot from the station entrance. After tossing the keys in the glove box, I lock up and stride away, determined not to look back. Too much of my life has been lived in the rearview mirror already.

My resolve holds until I cross the first intersection. As a fresh batch of cars gets the green light and goes whizzing by, my head turns. It's a reflex, a reaction etched in my bones. I don't know what I'm expecting to see. Maybe the twelve- or thirteen-year-old Marina—the fun, happy-go-lucky girl I've been grieving for so long, the figment of my imagination—leaning against the car with her legs crossed and a playful smile on her lips, waving me back to her.

I shake my head and turn the corner. Nate and Sam will be looking for me. They'll be worried. And I don't want to cause them any more pain.

CHAPTER 70
MARINA

Edward and I arrive home to find the mansion silent and grim, the holiday decorations evoking a surreal, apocalyptic mood instead of the intended warmth and cheer.

This Christmas will be hard for the Hayeses, I'm afraid, especially the children. I could stick around for a few more days and give them a happy memory to cling to, but at what cost? The only thing that matters now is my freedom, my survival.

"Don't go far," says Edward as I roam toward the library. "The lawyers will be here soon."

I peer over my shoulder at him. "For what?" They've already gotten me out of jail. And a trial is months—possibly years—away. Or maybe never, unless they try me in absentia.

"To strategize a defense. Don't you want to know what they have against you?"

"What could they have? I didn't do anything. I'm innocent." As much as I loathe him, as much as I'd like to rock his world with the truth (he'd crumble like an ancient ruin at the first whiff of my authentic self), it's in my best interests to maintain the façade, repeat the lie, escape with my hide intact.

I linger in the hallway outside the library, waiting for Edward's footsteps to fade. When the coast is clear, I beeline for a row of bookshelves by the windows. From the top shelf I remove a brightly painted box Edward and I picked up in our travels across Indonesia. In Bali, if memory serves.

I slide back the carved lid and reveal a hiding spot the size of a brick. In this cubby are two disposable cell phones, programmed with the numbers of thugs I can summon for help in disappearing; a rubber-banded stack of false ID cards and documents (Canada has five or six versions of me on the books); and a set of keys to my very own safe house in the Great White North. (Andorra will have to wait until traffickers are lined up to smuggle me out of North America.)

I get a happy little rush at my resourcefulness, at knowing I'm going to win. My planning—some might say *plotting*—is about to pay off.

The materials slip into my purse and go along to the nearest bathroom. I tug a chair away from the vanity and sit down, not a moment too soon. I've been feeling under the weather, but now, suddenly, the vague malaise (a touch of nausea and lightheadedness; a low-grade fever) has blossomed into a wave of left-sided pelvic pain.

Is it time for my period? I click back through my mind, trying to remember where I am in my cycle, but end up perplexed. I've been too busy to make notes on a calendar. The pain feels like menstrual cramps run amok.

I check for blood. Sure enough, the toilet paper comes back splotched reddish brown. I clean up and take a series of controlled breaths. But the pain, which has a pulsing quality like a heartbeat, just hammers on.

Pain pills. Opiates. I need something to dull my senses until things level off. I must have a bottle of Vicodin around here somewhere. Which reminds me: I should pack a travel pharmacy for the road. It's not like I can stop off for a prescription refill along the way.

When I double back to the kitchen, I expect to find Edward hanging around, awaiting the swarm of lawyers. But he's vanished to his office, or so I assume.

I rummage through the pill cabinet—it's stuffed with children's cold medicine and gummy vitamins—eventually locating a vial of

Percocet. I swallow three pills and tuck the rest in my purse. I'm about to disappear—the wheels must be thrust into motion ASAP for my middle-of-the-night escape—when the security intercom chirps.

Dammit.

Mr. Spiros and his minions have arrived. I give them the gate code and proceed to the garage, where I unlock the entry door. At the top of the driveway, I greet them.

My defenders slog inside, muttering and breathing hard (there's not a man under forty in the bunch—or a woman, for that matter), hauling soft leather briefcases and rolling file carts along behind them.

Has my case generated so much useless paper already? I shudder to think of the mountain of dead trees we'd be buried under if the whole truth came out.

As I'm leading the throng into the dining room, Edward appears by the kitchen. He's lost his humble court suit for something even more lowbrow: sweatpants and a grease-stained undershirt. Which will instill confidence in my high-priced legal team, I'm sure. Then again, who cares? Our meeting is an exercise in theater, a drama of distraction until I can make my getaway.

I catch Edward's eye and wave him over. The Percocet is working to a degree—there's a nice, hazy blur around everything—but still, intermittent jabs of pain are breaking through. "Please handle this," I say, gesturing at the dining room. "I'm feeling quite ill."

He checks my face. What does he see? Ghostly paleness or flushed cheeks or something else? "You must've picked up a virus in jail," he says, sounding softer. Repentant. I almost want to stick around and fight the charge to prove that I can win him over again. Who does he think he is, trying to stand up to me? And asking for a divorce? I don't think so. "Just sit in," he says. "And listen." He pushes a dangling clump of hair away from my eyes. "There will be questions only you can answer. If it's too much, we'll pick up again tomorrow."

"All right." I might as well play my part for a bit longer.

Edward goes to the kitchen and returns hugging an armload of water bottles and clutching two big bags of potato chips. While the lawyers sip and crunch, they dissect the information they've received thus far, which amounts to a load of circumstantial conjecture. My DNA has been found nowhere. Not the rope or the computer or the suicide note or even those fugly ties of Edward's, which someone dug out of the dumpster and—here's the baffling part—provided to the police.

It's agreed that the case against me is weak. The prosecution's best "evidence" is the testimony of that mousy, pink-eyed secretary, who places me at the crime scene. But it's not enough to overcome reasonable doubt, or so my lawyers believe.

As the discussion rolls on, I learn that police are eager to pin Sophie's murder on me, too. But the case won't hang together. It's nearly impossible to get a medical examiner to rule a car accident as a homicide, unless the victim was dead before the car was, say, pushed off a cliff. Sophie was very much alive when her BMW went to its wooded grave, so the Hummer's tire tracks are irrelevant.

My mind jumps to Robin. If I'd had a few more minutes with her in the pool, I could've taken her out of the equation. Truth be told, my baby sister is the biggest stumbling block to holding on to the life I've spent decades building. Then again, thirst for a new adventure is bubbling in my veins.

A twisting stab in my belly interrupts the beginning of a daydream. I feel hot, sweaty, faint. After a rushed apology, I excuse myself. I must call my underworld contact now, before it gets any later, and lie down for a few hours before launching my plan.

CHAPTER 71
ROBIN

Part of me wants to leave Nate and Sam sleeping, slip out of the condo, and hop a bus to the courthouse. Seeing my sister again, showing her that I'm still here—she hasn't broken me—might help me pound the last nail into the coffin of our relationship. But Marina has taken enough from me already, and I can't help thinking that she'd view my presence as proof of her continued influence, her everlasting power over me.

I have to shake her. Staying away is the first step. The next will be a phone call to the police. Maybe the exhumation of my sister's coffin. A long overdue trial.

In Nate's kitchen, I'm heating a mug of water in the microwave, watching it spin around and around, thinking of Lisa Thompson, the doe-eyed girl in the picture from Marina's purse, the one I'd suspected of knowing something integral, of holding the key to the mystery of Marina. It turns out that I was right in a strange, convoluted way. But the realization is no comfort.

I wonder if Lisa's parents are alive, if they're decent people or disturbed monsters, if I'd be able to tell the difference.

The microwave beeps. I remove the mug and sink a teabag in the water. Coffee would be better, but I can't find any. And I won't wake up Nate to ask.

My appetite's still fragile, but a fruit cup seems palatable. If nothing else, it'll stop my stomach from growling.

I'm curled up on the couch, nibbling chunks of peaches and pears, staring at the dark TV. I'd turn it on for company, but I don't want to make any noise, or, worse, be confronted by my sister's grinning face.

As I sip the tea, a sunrise glow brightens the sliding glass door beside me. Soon Nate comes wandering along with bed hair and squinty eyes. "How long have you been up?" he asks, dropping onto the couch.

My shoulders rise. "Half an hour?" It's a white lie. I've been awake most of the night, tossing and turning, staring at the walls and wondering where my life is headed next, which jagged bits I can cobble together to form a future, whether my efforts will be enough to give Samantha the childhood she deserves before it's too late.

Nate yawns, rubs his eyes, looks me over. "You feeling okay?"

I catch myself biting my lip. "Yeah," I say, straightening out my mouth.

He glances down the hallway and then back at me. "So, uh, should we talk about ...?"

"No," I say, thinking he wants to discuss Marina. Can't he leave the twisted mess alone? There's nothing to be learned from my sister's lengthy crime spree. She's a sick, deranged—I would say *person*, but the term is above her—*entity*, wrapped in a shiny, enticing cover. The Ted Bundy of her own warped world.

"It just started," says Nate. "Nothing was going on while you and I were ..."

Oh. He's talking about his girlfriend. "You don't have to explain. It's fine. More than fine." My throat tightens. "I'm happy for you."

He nods almost apologetically. "Thanks."

We sit in heartbreaking silence—the kind that comes from letting go of something meaningful but knowing it's the right choice, the *only* choice—for a few minutes, bathed in the orange light of dawn. I think about telling him that I love him. I want him to know how much I appreciate him, what he means to me. But it's too selfish. It would confuse things. And I'm done ruining him.

Nate speaks first. "If you and Sam need to stay for a while, it's okay. Cindy's cool. She understands that—"

"Thanks," I say. "But we have to go home." The way forward is through the past. We might as well get started.

Nate, Sam, and I share a last meal together at a sandwich shop near the café. It's bittersweet, but we keep things light and casual. The subject of Marina is banned until I can get my mind around what she's done.

After lunch, Nate drives us home. I thank him and hop out of the car, anxious to avoid an emotional scene. Sam takes a minute to catch up. I'm turning for the house when I realize I'm still wearing Nate's jacket.

I spin around. He's just reversed out of the driveway. I chase him, stripping off the jacket and waving it in the air. He stops and rolls down the window. "I almost forgot," I say, pushing the jacket at him with a huff. Better to cut the last tie now than leave something hanging.

He looks vaguely let down, like he'd planned on coming back for it, like he knows *this is it*. He slides the jacket over to the passenger seat and looks me dead in the eyes. "Listen, um, I have to say one more thing." A long pause. "You're better than you think you are, okay? Remember that." He cups his hand around my head and pulls me toward him, landing a tender kiss on my cheek.

Struggling to keep my voice steady, I whisper, "Bye, Nate. Thanks for everything." I break away and go inside. What's done is done. Maybe sometime down the road, we can be friends. But I can't worry about that now.

The house is as we left it: dark and dingy. A stale smell fouls the air.

Samantha has shut herself away in her room. As bad as Marina was—*is*—readjusting to this life, a life of struggle and disappointment, is going to be hard, especially for my daughter. All I can do is love her and hope for the best.

I go around opening shades and windows. Without electricity, we'll need the natural light. (I have the money to turn the power back on, but it might take a day or two.) And cleansing the air is a must. I'm about to inspect the refrigerator—I can't remember if I purged the food, which might explain the smell—when a voice catches me off guard.

"I hope I'm not intruding," Lewis says, shuffling down the hall.

"Oh, hi. Come in." Usually he knocks, even this far into our friendship. But maybe age is catching up with him. Maybe he's becoming forgetful.

He stops for a breath, just inside the kitchen. "I saw the activity—the car in the driveway and whatnot—and thought I'd check on you." He cranes his neck. "Is Samantha here? I swear I saw her slip in."

I cut a glance at Sam's room. "She's taking a nap. It's been a long couple of days." I'm overcome by a wave of exhaustion. "Sit down." I start to offer him coffee but realize I can't make any. How did people live without electricity? "Can I get you a snack?" There must be something left in the cupboards.

Lewis pats his belly. "Thanks anyway, but I just ate. Wanda's a whiz in the kitchen. I've gained nine pounds since she moved in." He chuckles. "You should sample her fried plantains. They're out of this world."

"That would be nice." Anything from a warm stove is appealing right now.

Lewis scowls at the open windows. "Are you trying to build an igloo in here, or what?"

I explain about the power being cut off. "You don't have an extra bed, do you? Just for a few days?" The least I can do is get my daughter out of this icebox.

"I knew it was dark over here, but I assumed you'd left it that way on purpose, because you were working out at the doctor's place." He eases into a chair.

"I would've done that if it hadn't been shut off first," I say.

"You and Samantha are welcome anytime. Actually, Wanda would love the company. She's lonely up here, I'm afraid, rambling around the house with me. Did I tell you she has eight children?"

"Uh-uh."

"Well, she does. And thirteen grandchildren," he announces proudly. There's a spark in his eyes that I haven't seen since he was a much younger man, since before Georgette died.

"Wow." Family hasn't worked out so well for me. I can't imagine a brood in the double digits. Speaking of family... "Have you been watching the news?" It's a dumb question. He lives by the weather forecast. "Have you seen the arrest? The big murder case against...?"

"Don't tell me that's the woman you work for."

"That's not all." I tell him about Marina being alive—not the whole story (it's too much to get into now), but the broad outline: She faked her death and stole another girl's identity.

He shakes his head. "When you think you've heard everything, something like this comes along and takes your breath away." He stares past me, his face clouding over like he's lost in thought, like he's remembering my sister in more innocent times, like he's replaying the tape of our lives and looking for signs of trouble.

He won't find much. Certainly nothing to suggest a serial killer in the making. If everyone who lied or stole turned out to be a cold-blooded murderer, the world would be a scary place. And maybe it is. Maybe we just never bothered noticing.

CHAPTER 72
MARINA

I rest until the mansion is quiet and everyone who doesn't belong is gone. My belly pain has only intensified, bringing with it cold sweats and profound exhaustion. On top of everything else, my nervous system has chosen to surrender to anxiety, a feeling of impending doom invading my cells like a flesh-eating bacterium.

Despite my ragged shape, I stumble out of bed and splash water on my face. To look at me, you wouldn't know anything was wrong. My skin, ghostly as it may be, is flawless. In the elaborate Venetian mirror, I'm as beautiful as ever. Eternally so. Forget the Venus de Milo. *I should be immortalized in marble for the whole world to see.*

Perhaps someday. But first I must finish things here.

Edward is sleeping in his office, so the master suite is mine, which makes the limited packing I'm doing—traveling light, remaining nimble, will be the secret of my success—that much easier. In ten minutes, I've got the essentials tucked in a Prada tote. The cell phones and fake IDs join stacks of cash in my Gucci hobo bag.

I check the clock. It's quarter 'til midnight. My ride is due at 3 A.M. on the western edge of our property, at a dormant apple orchard. Surely the police will be watching the main gate. Even the frontage on the eastern side is likely under surveillance. (The courts don't just release an accused killer and expect her to behave, do they?) But chances are slim that they've surrounded all hundred acres, since there's no easy through road from east to west. At most, patrols will occasionally cruise by. And I'm slick enough to outfox them.

After popping another Percocet, I prowl through the house and put my bags on deck by the kitchen. The western hike, which is equivalent to multiple football fields, will take a while in the dark. I have an hour and a half to tie up loose ends here before I must be on my way.

Edward is my first order of business. Unless he's incapacitated, he could raise the alarm against me too soon. I could be caught before escaping the jurisdiction.

Better safe than sorry.

I head downstairs and lurk outside his office. The door is ajar. I weigh the merits of sneaking inside. If he's awake, my chance will be blown.

Straining my ears, I pick up a faint snore, the kind one might expect from a congested Labrador retriever. Hallelujah. He's conked out solid. I get a thrill at being right. Again. Always.

As I proceed into the office, I straighten up—it's amazing what a confidence boost will do for one's posture—but the cramps surge again, doubling me back over. This period had better be an anomaly. Another monthly visit like this will have me running to the gynecologist for a hysterectomy. Rip the whole works out and be done with it.

My husband's office is dim and predictably messy. He's never outgrown dorm life—just look at those silly arcade games—never buried the nerdy dreamer he was for the powerful, self-made man he's become. If you ask me, that'll be his downfall: holding on to the past, becoming skeletonized, lethargic. The name of the game is change. Adapt or die, I'm always saying.

Back to business.

The crushed Rohypnol, aka the date-rape drug, is in a plastic baggie in my pants. If I know Edward, he has a tumbler of something—scotch or cognac or vodka—within arm's reach, so he can roll over and wet his whistle in his sleep.

I float past his desk, peering ahead at the assemblage of furniture. When we built this house, I urged him to add an extra wing for his workspace. But he prefers a cozy cave where he can disengage from the world.

Not so fast.

As usual, my husband is collapsed on the chaise lounge. On the coffee table are an empty beer mug and a half-gone bottle of Maker's Mark.

Could my luck be any better?

I waste no time sprinkling the powder in the bottom of the mug and filling it with bourbon. It's hard to say if the combination could kill him. Probably so. But that's not my intent, not my problem. I just need him out of commission until I cross the border. After that he can do whatever the hell he wants.

As quietly as possible, I reset the stage—he must be able to swing a sleep-dead arm into the mug's vicinity—and tiptoe back through the tulips.

Time is ticking down. I make a final pass through the house, looking for small objects I might stash in my pockets—some of my high-end jewelry comes into play here—chugging on a bottle of Pepto-Bismol the whole way. I'm starting to think that on top of the violent period, I've come down with an intestinal parasite. Or a foodborne illness. Because something sure is twisting my guts in knots.

One thing I haven't made up my mind about is the children. Circumstances have forced my hand with Samantha. Grudgingly, I'll leave her behind. But who knows how things will play out. Maybe she'll end up in Andorra or another intriguing locale with me when all is said and done. God knows Robin isn't equipped to handle such a feisty young woman. On the other hand, my door is always open to the niece who was tailor-made to follow my lead.

Darian and Mae are tucked in their matching canopy beds. They've been kept in the dark about Mommy's Little Problem. As I linger in the doorway, deciding whether or not to steal them away from Edward—it'd serve him right to wake up to an empty house, assuming he wakes up at all—a clammy sweat breaks out on my face, and my stomach heaves.

I'm going to be sick. The nearest bathroom is in the children's suite. I dash inside, barely getting the toilet seat up before a river of hot, pungent liquid evacuates my throat.

I vomit a number of times, blindly balling up toilet paper and mopping my eyes, my nose (an explosion of acid is stinging my nostrils), my mouth, my chin.

Fuck me. This is not the time for such bullshit.

The bout of illness lasts roughly five minutes. When it's over, I scrub my face, swish some mouthwash around, and puff my lungs full of air, letting it out slowly, settling my nerves.

The children will stay. If they were older, I'd take them along. They could be useful. But eight-year-olds are dead weight.

Time is getting away from me. I leave the children without a second thought and head back to the library. There's one last thing I must do before vanishing forever.

I'm steps away from my destination when Magnum comes bounding down the hall. Out of habit, I wait for him. He slips around me and charges into the library, heading straight for the huge wrapped canvas that arrived while I was in jail.

"Easy, boy," I say. He's on his hind legs, spinning in excited circles. You'd think the canvas was a hunk of aged prosciutto.

I tear the glossy beige paper away from the frame and there we are: Lisa, Edward, Darian, and Mavis Hayes, immortalized with our sparkling shoes and glowing complexions. The quintessential American family on steroids. It's enough to make one weep with joy.

Not for long.

By the windows is a kidney-shaped desk Edward bought on a whim at a garage sale. It's cornflower blue and doesn't match anything in the house, but I keep it around as a reminder of his foolishness.

The desk has three drawers—a scalloped one over the kneehole and deep, rectangular ones on either side. I grab the dangling brass pull of the left-hand drawer and tug it open. A pair of scissors practically levitates into my hand. Before I can close the dozen steps between the desk and the canvas, my pelvis swells with pain and my vision grows spotty.

I've never fainted, but I've faked it a number of times. How anyone can give in to the abyss—relinquish control of their consciousness—is beyond me. Still, I'm perilously close to passing out. My eyesight has tunneled down to a thin stream of color and light. The rest is blackness.

I get down on the floor, on my knees. Falling from a standing position would ruin me—shattered wrist, anyone?—but if I crawl to the canvas (this doesn't bode well for my getaway hike), maybe I can stay awake. Alert. Alive.

The tactic works. My pants are a bit dusty—if I was planning on sticking around, I'd have a word with Ricki about her subpar floor cleaning—but otherwise, I'm no worse for wear. No worse than a prisoner of war with a gutful of ulcers, that is.

Sigh.

I'm kneeling in front of the canvas—from this angle, the Hayeses are larger than life—with the scissors clutched in my hand and Magnum poking around beside me. I open the blades and jab one into the picture above Dr. Lisa Hayes's ear. The canvas is sturdier than it looks. Cutting around Lisa's hairline takes real, sustained effort. I barely have the strength. Never fear, though. I'm nothing if not persistent. Soon Lisa's face is carved away, leaving a yawning hole in its place. A haunting effect, if I do say so myself.

I fold up the face and slide it into my pocket. I'm about to abandon the scissors when it occurs to me to do something about the dog. I can't leave him here to rot with these people, can I? He's *my* dog. He'll be lost without me. He'll die of a broken heart within the week.

I do have the scissors. I could put him out of his misery now. Really, it's the humane thing to do. "Here, boy," I say, patting my leg. He doesn't know any better than to obey.

CHAPTER 73
ROBIN

The power will be back on at our place tomorrow, but until then, my daughter and I are staying with Lewis. The timeout will be a good distraction, and I'm glad for the chance to get to know Wanda. She's been somewhat of a ghost, caught only in passing, side-eye glimpses.

Sam is ahead of me, climbing the steps of Lewis's porch. She knocks, announcing our presence, and then, without waiting for an answer, lets herself in. I flash back to Marina—to the entitlement she displayed, stealing those necklaces from Georgette when Georgette was already overpaying her for the chores—to her nonchalance as she crossed this very threshold. She knew that she wouldn't be caught, that she had everyone fooled, that even if someone got wise, she'd squirm out of trouble one way or another. She was too beautiful, too charming, for anyone to stay mad at for long.

That was our mistake: letting her get away with things time and again. It taught her to just keep pushing.

Lewis greets us and takes our bags. It's barely five o'clock, but the kitchen is already bursting with delicious smells: tomato, garlic, onion, pepper. Wanda's at the stove, stirring a meat mixture around a large skillet. The counters are dusted with flour, and bowls and utensils clog the sink.

"Hi," I say, giving a small wave.

Wanda is focused. I don't think she's heard me. But then she turns around and holds out her arms. "Welcome, ladies," she says, scooping me into a hug with the spatula clutched in her hand.

Sam murmurs a hello and tries to sidestep, but Wanda is quicker—or at least more determined. She hauls my daughter into her arms. "You didn't think you'd get away so easy, did you?" She laughs. "Good to see you, *mija*."

Noticing that Wanda could use help, I jump in and clear the sink. Once the dishwasher is loaded, I wipe down the counter. "Is there anything else I can do?" I ask, tucking the sponge in beside a bottle of soap.

Lewis has reappeared. He's loitering in the doorway of the living room. Samantha claims a seat at the kitchen table. "I'm surprised she let you do *that*," Lewis chimes in. "I haven't been able to rinse a fork for a month."

"Sounds like a good problem to have," I quip.

"You know," says Wanda, planting a hand on her hip, "these empanadas won't stuff themselves." She nods at Sam. "Would you mind helping? The filling has to cool for a few minutes, but then we can—" She pulls the pan off the stove.

"Sure," says Sam.

As Sam and Wanda finish making dinner, Lewis and I drift into the living room. The news is on. I don't want to see Marina. I ask him to turn off the TV, and he does. "I've spoken to Wanda," he says, stretching out in his recliner, "and we want you and Samantha to stay through Christmas."

I shake my head. "The power will be back tomorrow. You guys have done too much already."

"Nonsense! I promised your mother I'd look after you. I hate seeing what's happened to you kids." He pauses thoughtfully. "Have you made peace with it?" I tell him that I haven't. How can I accept Marina's double life, her lies, the trail of bodies? It's despicable. "Give it time," he says, "and open your heart. The only one you'll hurt by holding a grudge is yourself."

It's sound advice. And maybe someday, when Marina has been in prison for a long time, when she's faded into a craggy shell of her former self, when her hair is bristly and gray, her teeth loose and rotted, every last drop of beauty wrung out of her—maybe then, when she's living her own personal hell, when she's powerless and broken, I can begin to let it go. But not now.

I don't say any of this to Lewis; I just change the subject. "How's Wanda? Is her health okay?" I've been so tied up with my own problems that I haven't bothered to find out what kind of cancer Wanda has, the prognosis, and how the whole thing is affecting Lewis. After losing Georgette to the same ruthless disease, he must be having painful flashbacks of his own.

"They took the breasts six months ago, back in Texas," he says. "And a bunch of those armpit lymph nodes, too." He softly shakes his head. "The chemo ended just before I drove down there. We waited for everything to run its course. She's got an excellent oncologist in Pittsburgh—a woman doctor who's had breast cancer herself. She relates to the patients very well, as you'd expect."

"That's great," I say with a bittersweet smile. He's braver than I am, signing up for such a battle for a second time around.

After a short pause, Lewis asks what I plan to do next. The question is heavy and mind-numbing: Where *do* I go from here?

"I'd like to get away," I say. "Sam and me. To somewhere beautiful. Somewhere warm, with a beach. We need to regroup. Reset. And after that ... who knows? Go back to teaching, maybe—if they'll let me." Not around here, though. I can't travel these ghost-filled streets for the rest of my life, looking over my shoulder.

"Have you thought about leasing your house?"

I snort-chuckle. "Who'd want to rent that dump?"

"Wanda's daughter, for one. She's been looking at apartments in the area. If you think *your* house is bad, you should see the pigpens on Craigslist."

"She's moving here?"

"Mm-hmm. As soon as she can find a place. It'd be nice for her to get something furnished, so she doesn't have to hire a big truck."

"Oh." The idea is shocking, but also perfect. I could rent out the house, delaying the sale until my head is screwed on straight and the real estate market rebounds. In the meantime, the income would be a nice cushion to start Samantha and me off in our new life.

"Did I tell you that Corinne's a computer programmer—or a software engineer? I forget which," says Lewis. "Anyway, she's got two job offers. Can you believe that?"

With the economy in the toilet, it's impressive news. "And you think she'd want to rent our house?"

Lewis's head rocks up and down. "I guarantee it."

The empanadas are every bit as tasty as they smelled. After dinner, Sam and I take over the kitchen, earning our keep by tidying up. Lewis and Wanda watch *Wheel of Fortune* and then invite us to play a game of Scrabble, which they win by two hundred points. (The glint in Lewis's eye should've told us we were being hustled.) It's the kind of mellow family evening I've yearned for since Marina took off, since she snatched our hearts and stomped them to bits so long ago.

By nine o'clock, Lewis and Wanda are in bed. Samantha makes use of the desktop computer in what looks like a combination home gym/sewing room, while I sip wine in the dim kitchen and consider what to do about Marina.

I have to expose her. It's the only way. If she hadn't killed Lisa Thompson, things would be murkier. I could've argued that she'd be punished enough for the murder of this doctor (I'm still wondering what he did to incur her wrath), assuming she's convicted. Revealing her as a fraud would only feed the fires of revenge. Speaking out would be vindictive and self-serving.

But what about Lisa's family? Don't they deserve to know what happened? Shouldn't they get a shot at justice, even if it's delayed?

I think so.

I'm two glasses into Lewis's merlot when my thoughts start coming together. Quietly, I search the house for a pen and paper, finding both in a slant-top mahogany box.

With a fresh glass of wine, I set up at the kitchen table. The words spill out of the pen.

To Whom It May Concern:

My name is Robin Davis. My sister, Marina Davis, went missing in 1985, when she was sixteen. (The incident should be in police records, if they've survived.) She lived from place to place—my family never could catch up with her—and sold herself, and possibly others, on the streets for money and/or drugs. A body thought to be hers was found burnt in the basement of a crack house.

For more than two decades, I believed that my sister was dead, that her bones were buried in Franklin Hills Memorial Cemetery beside our mother and father. But I've recently learned different. I now know that my sister is alive. She killed a teenage prostitute named Lisa Thompson and stole her identity. She went on to become a doctor—a psychiatrist, of all things—and marry a wealthy inventor named Edward Hayes.

Lisa Hayes, the same woman charged with murdering a Jackman doctor, is my sister, Marina Davis. She's confessed this to me, and I have every reason to believe her.

I'm writing to ask for your help in bringing my sister to justice and, more importantly, providing a measure of peace and closure to Lisa Thompson's family. They deserve to finally know the truth.

If you have further questions—and I assume you will—please contact me at 412-260-1927. I'm ready to help in any way that I can.

Sincerely Yours,
Robin Davis

Relief floods through me—just getting the words down on paper is cathartic—as I fold the page and set it aside. In the morning, I'll borrow an envelope and stamp from Lewis and look up the address of the police station. Once the letter is on its way, floating through the mail with people's car payments and medical bills, I'll rest easier, knowing I've done the right thing, knowing I've started the ball rolling toward the truth. It's the only thing I can hold on to now that my hopes for Marina, for catching her killer, are dead.

CHAPTER 74
MARINA

Instead of sending Magnum off on a cloud to doggie heaven, I end up with a bunch of nasty bite wounds on my forearm and a nagging feeling of frustration that will shadow me on my escape.

The wounds should be cleaned more thoroughly, but I only have time for antibiotic ointment and a patchwork of Band-Aids. It's a contest now which ailment will bring me down, an infection or this godawful period. Or perhaps a Percocet overdose.

If I had to pick, I'd take the pills. I gobble down three more in a pained haze. A trip to the hospital may get wedged into my itinerary if something doesn't break soon, if the pressure in my abdomen doesn't subside.

After removing that pesky ankle bracelet (that pearl-handled knife does more than butter bread!), donning my goose-down parka with the oversized, fur-trimmed hood, and retrieving my bags, I cast a final, satisfied look around the mansion—I've accomplished so much; it really is astounding—and then slip out a seldom-used door behind the pantry.

The night is cloudy. Frigid. Silent. My boots make crackling sounds as they punch through the crust of frozen snow and sink into the powder beneath. I'm lucky winter isn't further along. Luckier still that my husband went through a redneck phase when the children were young and bought a fleet of ATVs and snowmobiles. Over the course of six or seven months—his attention waned when golfing weather came back around—we covered every square inch of the estate, including the vast wooded areas, atop those rugged little vehicles, experience that'll serve me well tonight.

Sadly, the ATVs are long gone. But I'm certain enough that I know the trails, that I've memorized the landscape deep down, to leave the compass behind. God knows I'm too compromised to operate the thing, anyway. Better to rely on instinct and intuition, to trust my gut. It's never steered me wrong before.

The land around the mansion is clear, and the going is easy—or easy enough, even for someone in my condition. I wait until I cross the tree line before digging through my bag for one of those silly headlamps coal miners use. My night vision is better than most—maybe I was an owl in a former life, ha-ha—but with the moon obscured and the forest surrounding me, I'll need a helping hand to stay on course.

With a sardonic chuckle, I strap on the headlamp. I can only imagine how ludicrous I look. The things one will do to shirk a murder charge...

I check my watch. It's 2:12. I have plenty of time, if not energy, to zigzag through the woods and pop out on the other side, at the spot where my getaway driver will be waiting.

I click the headlamp to its brightest setting (even if the estate is being watched, no one will see me in this clump of trees) and start up again, each step echoing through my body like the aftershocks of a grenade. A lesser woman would fall to her knees, buckle under the pain, beg for mercy. But not me. I'm tougher than quantum physics and twice as fun.

I soldier on, scouring the ground for tree roots and debris—the last thing I need is a trip-and-fall injury to add to my growing list of maladies—until the trail forks off in multiple directions. I stop briefly in a small clearing. If memory serves, the forks farthest left and right lead back to the mansion. Of the branches ahead, one goes to the apple orchard and the other to a pond on the outskirts of our property.

Eenie, meenie...

Just kidding. I know which path to take: meenie.

I hoist the bags back up onto my shoulder and proceed. Soon I'm in the thick of the cold, black forest, my teeth chattering and my bones aching. I'm nauseated and sweaty. Something sharp—a knitting needle hammered by an angry nun or a gap-toothed prison matron—spikes through my abdomen again and again and again.

The pain is too much. I hunch over in the trailside brush and relinquish my stomach contents. All I've lost is the Percocet and a few teaspoons of stomach acid. Still, the act of vomiting quells the pain, if not the pressure, and allows me to trudge on with burning nostrils and tears streaking down my face.

Time drags. I stay focused on the trail, beaming that ridiculous headlamp along the forest floor until another choice demands making.

At this point, I'm less sure of where to go. I don't remember how the wood divides. If I take the wrong path, I'll miss my connection. And then what? I can't exactly hitch a ride in the middle of the night with my face on every TV for a hundred miles, with this raging sickness and this comically dog-bitten arm, with this tote of cash, with … with …

If I had a coin, I'd flip it. Instead, I draw a breath and slowly exhale. Something tells me to take the middle path. With my memory failing, it's a guess, a hunch. But I have a feeling it's a good one.

I forge ahead. The trail extends forever. I've been wobbling along for twenty minutes, stopping here and there to brace myself against a tree—lightheadedness has become Enemy Number One—when a finger of doubt taps me on the shoulder.

Have I chosen the wrong path? Shouldn't I be at the orchard by now?

Shaking off the thought, I double down. A quarter mile on, my bet is rewarded. The trail becomes gradually less forested and spills out at the back of what is normally a large dirt parking lot, which is now covered with snow.

Believe it or not, I'm early. It's 2:50. Ten minutes 'til blastoff.

Mentally patting myself on the back, I find a shielded spot to wait among some unkempt bushes. The vegetation is good cover and will buffer the wind, which has intensified to a guttural howl.

I turn off the headlamp and make myself as comfortable as possible on the cold, wet ground. Having a long waterproof jacket is a bit of engineered luck. Fighting nausea and dizziness, clammy sweats and unrelenting cramps, I hug the jacket around me and watch the clock tick down.

Nine minutes.

Eight.

Seven.

Six.

Five.

Four.

Three.

Two.

One.

The parking lot remains dark and vacant. An ominous feeling falls over me. Where the hell is Jasper? Probably nailing a stripper in the bathroom of an underground gambling den or passed out in a puddle of his own piss. By the name alone—Jasper? does it get any more trailer trash than that?—I should've known not to trust him. You'd think twenty grand, with the promise of another ten once we cross the border, would be enough to lure a rat out of his hole. But you'd be wrong.

I can't afford to be wrong. Not now. Not ever.

A seed of rage grows in me until a whole garden of revenge has taken root. Jasper's head is on the chopping block if he doesn't materialize in the next two minutes. What I did to Sophie Gallagher and Dr. Kapoor will pale in comparison to what I'll pay someone to do to him.

Cross me once ...

I dig through the hobo bag for my primary burner phone. My contact is a dirty cop who's built a retirement career as an outlaw.

The phone just rings and rings. Eventually, a robotic voice dashes what little hope I have of holding someone—anyone—accountable. I forgo leaving a message. For all I know, even my thuggish friends are in league with the police. I can't have my voice recorded asking for a getaway van.

The one time I don't have a backup plan, things go straight to shit. Now I'm in a bigger mess than ever. My only choice is to hike back to the house and start planning again tomorrow, once I've gotten some sleep. In fact, this might be a blessing in disguise. With this period spiraling out of control, there's a good chance that I'll need surgery. A dilation and curettage. Scrape my uterus clean and be done with it.

To prove the point, blood gushes between my legs. Without a bathroom, there's nothing I can do but ignore the situation and slog home.

The bright spot in this infuriating saga is that I'll get to see the results of my handiwork; I'll be around to witness the effects of the roofies on my dear, clueless husband. If I took it too far—he could be in a coma or worse—another murder charge will be breathing down my neck.

Oh well. Nothing comes without risk. I've done what was required. I've protected myself, my interests. Who can blame me for that?

I illuminate the headlamp and double back into the forest. The going is worse than before, the night reaching a whole new level of blackness. The beam, which is bouncy and dim, balks at the challenge.

My body is balking, too. Every fifty yards, I must pause and regroup. But leaning against trees is fast becoming moot. If I don't get horizontal—or, better yet, upside down (the tingling in my head says my brain is starving for oxygen)—I'm going to faint.

There's a first time for everything, though I wouldn't have chosen such an inconvenient locale to test the experience.

With the same determination I've applied to everything in life, I drive forward. The first fork in the trail confuses me only briefly. I veer right and keep going. I've just caught a second wind when the headlamp sputters and abruptly shuts off.

As pathetic as my field of view was before—that hazy four-foot cone of light wasn't exactly cutting it—I've gone down to nothing. Less than nothing, in a way, since my eyes were adjusted to the headlamp and are now blind.

This little blunder of an escape is working my last nerve.

I pull off the headlamp and hurl it into the woods. Dropping to my knees, I fumble through my bag for the Percocet. Three more pills go down dry. (Water would've been a key item to pack, but who would've thought things would go so stunningly wrong? Certainly not me.)

Within a few minutes of taking the pills, I'm far more impaired than from previous doses. The solution is clear: sleep. Even a short nap might dull my symptoms. If that doesn't work, I'll have to wait until daybreak to hike the hell out of here.

Once again, the jacket comes to my rescue. I curl my legs up inside and lay my head, shrouded by that furry hood, on the lumpy bags and shut my eyes.

I don't sleep. I'm not built that way, even with the drugs flowing through me. My mind is too active, too alive. It paces like a caged tiger.

In lieu of sleep, my brain plays a game of retribution. It's fun cooking up punishments for those who've wronged me. And the list just keeps growing. Maybe I could get them all in one place for a pretend giveaway—people love an expensive freebie—and then ... *kaboom!*

Ah, see. Now that's better. Fantasizing has hushed my brain. On second thought, I might be able to nap.

I can't say for how long I drift off. Maybe five minutes, maybe an hour. But I'm awakened by excruciating cramps, the quality of which is new and concerning. Previous bouts were pulsing, stabbing, jabbing, etcetera, but now I have a terrible ripping feeling, like my insides are coming apart.

I poke my head out of the hood and find that it's started snowing outside. Big, icy, cotton-ball flakes. I try to sit up, but my abdomen is tight, swollen, tender. Behind the pain is a bottomless pit of nausea. I fall back down, my ears ringing, my pulse racing, my face dappled with sweat. I can't get enough air. I'm suffocating.

Is this what a panic attack feels like? I've heard them described in my practice, but until now they were academic abstractions. Now I see what all the fuss is about.

It's easy to convince myself that the problem is in my head, that I've succumbed to fear, emotion, anxiety—these are not my wheelhouses, but a dying brain will grasp at any straw—that I'm not hemorrhaging internally like every speck of my medical training suggests.

The jig is up.

I've got to call Edward and have him send help, pronto. Consequences be damned. The worst-case scenario is that the authorities send me back to jail, which is better than the alternative.

I fish one of the phones out of my bag, but then ... I don't know Edward's number. It's not programmed into the burner phones. We have a landline, too, but I'd only be guessing at the number.

Fuck fuck fuck fuck fuck.

I'm on one elbow, swaying back and forth. My head hurts and my vision is clouded, blotchy. Snow is piling up on my coat.

In a flash of clarity, I remember the number of the landline. The phone screen shimmies and hiccups as I punch the buttons. It's ringing! My God, it's ringing! If I can just ... if I can just stay awake long enough to ...

The answering machine picks up. Edward must be roofied into next week. "It's me. Answer the phone. *Please.*" My mind is starting down a long, dark tunnel. "Help," I croak. "*Help me.*"

The pull of nothingness is too strong. I black out. Everything ceases.

Sometime later, I revive slightly—enough to sense the phone in my hand and consider calling 911. But the effort is like lifting the Empire State Building. Impossible. I don't have the energy to even try.

Soon the darkness comes again. This time I surrender.

CHAPTER 75
ROBIN

After a restful night of sleep at Lewis's, Sam and I go home and wait for the power to be restored. Around noon, the appliances chirp back to life. Leaning into Sam's room, I say, "You can take a shower now." We left Lewis's with morning breath and bed hair.

Speaking of beds …

My daughter is sprawled out on her unmade bed (some things never change), reading a book. "You can have it. I'm gonna walk to the library."

"It's cold out. You're walking that far?" The library is a mile and a half away.

Samantha sits up. When I look at her eyes—those thoughtful, brooding eyes—I see Marina. And Scott. A legacy of pain and destruction. But a spark of hope, too. Because something tells me that no matter what fate has planned, we still have choices. Marina may have been born with a black mark on her soul (I'm fast becoming a believer in nature over nurture), but she could've erased it. Or painted over it with every color in the rainbow. She could've looked in the mirror and decided to change. She didn't, of course. She took the easy road. And we're all paying the price.

"How else am I gonna get there?" asks Sam, shrugging.

She's right. We don't have a car, a situation I need to remedy ASAP. Winter in Pennsylvania is no time or place for traveling on foot. "Bundle up," I say, "and take your phone." It flashes through my mind to ask Lewis to drive her, but I don't want to impose on him any more than we already have.

Sam stands up. I'm shocked by her height. She's been taller than me for a year now, but suddenly she's shot up another two inches. "I know, Mom," she says, shoving her feet into a pair of boots Marina must've bought (I don't recognize them and they look like a designer brand).

Once Sam has set off for the library, I head down to the basement—the shower can wait; I'll be dirtier after this, anyway—and haul out the tote of photo albums and memorabilia. A grid of silver duct tape sits loosely on top, creating a tic-tac-toe pattern.

I remove the lid and stare at the shadowy collection of artifacts—albums, yes, but also loose pictures (Mom only got so far in organizing our childhoods before the stroke), shoved in with report-card envelopes, award ribbons, paper snowflakes, macaroni necklaces, and other sentimental things she thought we'd want to reminisce over one day.

I laugh. I can't help it. Of all the endings I imagined for Marina's story—if this is, in fact, the end; if she gets convicted and put away forever—it never crossed my mind that *she* was the monster, that *she* was the one we should've locked our doors against, that *she* was the one we should've checked for under our beds.

Scott is only a phone call away. I could ask him if he wants any of these things, but I have a feeling I know the answer. Of everyone, he saw through our sister best. He knew the darkness she was capable of.

Everything here must go, along with the sad, drooping altar upstairs. If I had a fireplace, I'd burn it. Ashes to ashes. Clean the slate and move on.

I empty the tote into a trash bin and then lug the bin up to my bedroom. In go the notes and maps and internet printouts, the spreadsheets and index cards and newspaper clippings, and all of the remaining pictures but one: the spotty, out-of-focus, disintegrating Polaroid of Lisa and Marina. The moth and the spider. Sadly, the tattoo was wishful thinking. If only I could've frozen Marina in ink, if only I could've kept her two-dimensional and harmless.

My neck itches. I ignore it and tie up the trash. Outside, the bag drops into the garbage can with a thud.

The nearest mailbox is two blocks away. Writing the letter to the police was easy, but sending it—laying my sister's sins bare for everyone to see—is harder. It's the last hurdle, though. And then I can get on with my life. (I don't plan on hanging around for Marina's trial—at least not this one. If prosecutors need me to testify in the future about Lisa Thompson, I'll cross that bridge when I come to it.)

The walk takes longer than it should. I'm moving in slow motion. When I reach the mailbox, it opens with a metallic shriek. Holding my breath, I release the envelope, turn quickly, and stride away.

By the next afternoon, the bareness of our cupboards is setting in. Samantha and I can only eat so many peanut butter and graham cracker sandwiches before our bodies start rejecting them.

I knock on Lewis's door and let myself in. "It's just me," I say, scanning the kitchen. The van's in the driveway, so someone must be home.

Lewis's head pokes out of the living room. "Be with you in a minute," he says, breathing hard. "I'm trying to Swiffer this darn ceiling fan."

I think about offering to help, but I don't want to overstep. It's good for him to do things while he still can. (I learned this lesson with Mom in the nursing home.) When people start feeling useless, they tend to give up on life. I'd like Lewis to stick around for as long as possible. He's one of those stabilizing forces, like gravity or the ocean tides.

A few minutes later, he appears, wielding the mop. It's covered in tendrils of dust. He removes the dirty cloth and throws it in the trash. "Phew," he says, leaning the mop against the refrigerator, "I sure could use a drink."

I'm near the faucet, half staring outside—it's a chilly blue day—and half admiring a pretty sun catcher in the window.

I turn on the tap and fill a tumbler for Lewis and one for me. We sit at the table and chat. He wants to know what brings me by. I don't bother dancing around the subject: I need a ride to the grocery store and, if possible, to look for a car. The buy-here, pay-here place by the mall should have something in my price range.

"You know," Lewis says, "I've been thinking of selling the van. I'd let her go cheap. She's got some wear and tear, mind you."

"First you find a tenant for my house and now you want to sell me your car?" I shake my head and laugh. "How much?" The truth is, I'd like to see him driving something newer. And a van might be perfect for Sam and me on our escape.

His eyebrows pinch together. "Six hundred? No, no," he says, backtracking, "I just put in a new air filter. Six twenty-five."

"Well, the price is right. Can I think about it?"

"Sure thing. The offer stands for twenty-four hours. After that, we'll have to renegotiate."

I smile. "It's a deal."

The grocery store is foreign. I've barely shopped in months. Still, I load a cart with basics like bread and milk and cinnamon doughnuts (one of Sam's favorites), leaving Lewis to browse on his own (he mentioned needing gumdrops and thyroid medicine).

I'm in front of the freezer case, staring at bags of broccoli, trying to think of what I could make with them—some of the energy I used to devote to searching for Marina's killer could go toward learning to cook—when my cell phone rings. I assume it's Sam, calling to add something to the list. "What's up?" I answer.

The voice on the other end of the line isn't my daughter. "Sorry to bother you," says Ricki, "but something crazy is ..." She sighs. "I just had to tell somebody."

"Tell me what?"

"The police are crawling all over the estate. Lisa was missing this morning, and Edward's ..."

"She's gone?" I ask, a shiver racing through me. Marina has done it again, slipped through the cracks and slithered off to wreak havoc on some other innocent souls. If I'm convinced of anything, it's that my sister will never change. She's corrupted deep down, where sunlight can't reach.

"She's dead."

"Dead?" My mind skips like a scratched record: *dead dead dead dead dead dead dead*. "Are you sure?"

"They found her in the woods. Frozen. Trying to get away." Ricki gulps. "And Edward's in the hospital. He was passed out when I got here. I couldn't wake him up. The paramedics were talking about suicide. I can't believe he'd try to kill himself, even with the arrest and—"

"You're sure she's dead?"

"They took her out in a body bag. I saw them loading it in the ambulance. She made it pretty far. One of the dogs tracked her to the orchard."

I'm overcome with fear and apprehension—not because Marina is dead, but because she might not be. I've been here before, and it was all a lie. What if she's playing us again? A whisper at the back of my mind says evil like her won't die so easily, so quickly, so completely.

I blurt out a few stammering sentences before Lewis comes wheeling around the corner with a shopping cart of his own. I wish Ricki luck and hang up.

Lewis pulls up beside me. "Is everything all right? You look like you've seen a ghost."

I stare into his cart: Ritz crackers, mouthwash, tomato soup, gumdrops, hot sausage. "Is it that obvious?"

He'll find out about Marina soon enough. I might as well give him a heads-up. The only story bigger than a local doctor arrested for murder is the same woman found dead in the woods.

On the ride home, I fill him in. He's surprised but not surprised, which sums up my reaction, too. I've spent most of my life believing my sister was gone, and now she is. My world is back in its familiar, uneasy balance. The only difference now is that I can stop searching for Marina's killer.

Dr. Lisa Hayes's funeral is two days after Christmas, in a cathedral in Philadelphia. Part of me wants to go, but burying Marina again is too much for my chapped emotions. I watch the scene unfold on TV with morbid interest—I'm half expecting my sister to spring out of that rose-draped casket like a stripper from a bachelor-party cake—as curious strangers clog the street for a glimpse of the murderer in repose.

I have yet to hear from detectives. Maybe they've written me off as a nut or closed the file on Marina's crimes because of her death. Which is fine by me, except for the problem of Lisa Thompson. What if her family is still looking for her? I can't move forward with that injustice hanging over my head.

Lisa Thompson is one thing—she's been dead for a long time, and there's only so much I can do for her survivors—but Edward is something else. Despite the suicide attempt (like Ricki, I have a hard time believing he'd try to kill himself), he's on the steps of the cathedral, hand-in-hand with his daughters, stone-faced in grief. My conscience says I have to tell him about Lisa. About Marina. The whole twisted truth.

Three more days go by. I sign a six-month lease with Corinne—she's accepted a systems-analyst job with a government-contracting firm (something to do with nuclear submarines) that starts mid-January—and agree to Lewis's price on the van. Samantha and I will be on the road by the New Year. The timing feels right, a natural dividing line in the sand.

On the morning of the thirty-first, I call Edward. He's flustered for a moment—in truth, I think he's forgotten me—but then he agrees to a meeting. I pick the place, a diner on the river where, as children, Marina and I sat across from each other, slurping root-beer floats, watching the current dance, and dreaming about the future.

I wanted to be a journalist. She wanted to be a pilot—a helicopter pilot, if I'm remembering right. We'd team up and charge into danger, into disaster, getting the story and getting out by the skin of our teeth, maybe even saving an injured child or a stranded puppy along the way.

Whatever happened to those dreams? Whatever happened to those girls?

I'm too anxious for the meeting, too anxious to get this last detail out of the way, so I arrive early and hang around in the van until it gets too cold—my breath is fogging up the windows—and then head inside, taking a familiar booth.

I've ordered coffee and a glass of water. The thought of food is nauseating. The waitress comes by a third time, trying to sell me on a piece of blueberry pie. I'm politely declining when Edward's Jaguar coasts up to the curb.

Just a few more minutes, I tell myself, *and it'll all be done.*

Edward enters looking younger, like a poison has been cleansed from his blood. He sits down opposite me. We exchange greetings. "I assume you've heard," he says after a brief pause.

"Yes. It's hard to believe."

He shakes his head. "I didn't even know she was pregnant."

"She was pregnant?" I hear myself repeating.

"They thought it was an overdose. She had a bottle of pills in her bag. But it was an ectopic pregnancy. It ruptured."

"Oh." I sip the water. "Ricki said … well, she must not've known."

He waves the waitress over and asks for a glass of milk and a slice of carrot cake. Then he turns back to me. "Was there something you wanted? Do we owe you money? I don't carry cash, but I can have my assistant send you a check."

"No, nothing like that." I reach into my purse for the Polaroid and slide it across the table. "Look at this and tell me what you see."

He lifts the photo to his face and studies it. "I've never seen her so young. There was a fire. Her parents died and all of the photographs were destroyed. She had a really hard road afterward." He eyes me suspiciously. "Where did you get this? God, she looks like Darian, doesn't she?" It's a strange comment, since the girls are twins. Then again, that devilish charm of Marina's does flow stronger through Darian than Mae.

Before we proceed, I need to be sure of one thing. "You're talking about the girl on the left, right? That's Lisa? You recognize her?" Of course, my sister is on the left; the *real* Lisa Thompson is on the right. The last sliver of doubt in me is pulling for the impossible, aching for him to exonerate Marina of these terrible crimes.

The milk appears along with the cake. Edward thanks the waitress. "She's hard to mistake," he says. "There's no one quite like her, is there?"

I gulp a breath. "Listen, I have to tell you something. And I'm not sure how you're going to react." He probably thinks I'm about to confess to stealing the picture. If only it were that simple. "I know something about Lisa, about her past, that's ... that's ..." Words escape me. "It's bad," I say after a few beats. "And I need your help."

He stops with the fork poised over the cake. "Okay."

Everything in me wants to run away—not just for my sake, but for Edward and the children. They didn't ask to be ensnared in my sister's web of lies. But Lisa Thompson's family is my priority now. For them, I'll speak the truth.

A nor'easter is forecasted two days out, but Sam and I are blessed with a window of clear weather for our New Year's departure. If we make it south of Washington, D.C. by tonight, we'll have sunshine all the way to Fort Lauderdale. We've decided that the beach-bum life suits us, at least for the time being. Where we'll end up is anyone's guess. Probably back in Jackman, when the lease on our house—and that steady drip of money—runs out. Or maybe Wanda's daughter will fall in love with the place and Sam and I will chart a whole new course into the future.

The van is idling in the driveway. "Is that everything?" I ask Sam as she lugs an overstuffed backpack down the front steps. We can only take the bare necessities, since we'll be sleeping in the van and showering at campgrounds and the like.

Sam tilts her head at the house. "Double check. We can't come back, right?"

This adventure already feels like a solid break, a full stop and a ninety-degree turn from our previous lives. Some might say we're running away, but I beg to differ. We're getting the perspective we need to heal. And aren't we entitled to that?

I make a bittersweet reckoning of what we're leaving behind: furniture and dishes and a lifetime of family memories, most of them stained by my sister's disappearance. In a strange way, we had it better when we thought Marina was the victim, when we could lay claim to the moral outrage of survivors. Now we're limbs of a poisoned tree.

I'm glad my sister is dead. She doesn't belong among the beating hearts, with those of us who are trying to do well, trying to do good.

My purse is on the counter. I grab it and lock the house.

Sam is waiting in the van. I hold up a finger and continue on to Lewis's. I'm about to slip the house keys through his mail slot—he's keeping them for Corinne—when the door opens.

I'm expecting Lewis (in truth, I'm avoiding him because I don't want to melt into tears), but it's Wanda. She's holding a grease-stained paper bag. "A little something for the road," she says, smiling.

I take the bag and peek inside. "They smell yummy," I say, sniffing the fog of cinnamon and sugar. "What are they?" They look like small discs of fried dough.

"Sopapillas. I make them for my kids' birthdays. My grandkids', too."

I thank her and turn over the keys. She passes along a message from Lewis about the van's power-steering fluid—it might need to be topped off along the way—and wishes us safe travels.

Getting out of the neighborhood is hard. Part of me wants to turn back. But a bigger part craves privacy, anonymity, a fresh start. I can't find those here, and neither can Sam.

We keep going. Every mile on the highway is easier. Still, the past trails us like an iron chain. By the time we reach Georgia, though, most of the links have broken apart and scattered.

Florida greets us with sunshine and shimmering waves of heat. A downpour is gathering in the distance. *There's always another storm*, I remind myself. *Always*. But the worst is behind us. And the best is yet to come. I have to believe that. And so I do.

EPILOGUE

Two weeks into our Florida excursion, Samantha and I have found our groove. We walk the beach in the morning, collecting shells and sea glass and little bits of pottery before the sun starts broiling. Afternoons are spent indoors, browsing quirky shops and sometimes escaping to the mall. Evenings are for campfires and lawn games—my daughter throws a mean horseshoe, I've come to learn—with our fellow wandering souls.

We're in the middle of a cornhole tournament (Sam and I are up against another mother-daughter team from Ohio) when my cell phone rings. My turn is coming up. I almost don't answer, but then I do. When I hear Edward's voice, I step away from the game, cover my ear—kids are raising hell at the volleyball court, and I can barely hear through the phone's lousy speaker—and start walking along the rutted dirt road toward the van.

I climb in and shut the door. "Sorry," I say. "I can hear you now."

What Edward says next shocks me. I don't know why. I should've known that with his resources, he'd find Lisa Thompson's survivors. I just didn't expect him to do it so fast. I spent most of my life searching for Marina's killer, and look where it got me.

He tells me that Lisa Thompson's parents are dead. It's a gut punch, finding out they went without knowing, with a gnawing question in their hearts. She has two brothers and a sister who are still living, though. Edward's preparing to contact them through his attorneys and break the news. "On that note," he says, "we may need to exhume the body."

"Sure," I say. "Whatever I can do to help."

We talk about the police, about what their involvement should be. Edward has contacts within law enforcement who can put the case on a discreet track, so the whole world doesn't have to witness Marina's crimes. It's a relief that justice can be done without harming the twins any further. There's nothing to be gained from dragging Marina's name through the mud now.

The conversation has run its course, but neither of us hangs up. We just listen to each other breathe. "It's late," says Edward eventually. "I should get the children their baths." With Marina gone, he's taking a more active role. I count that as a win.

"Keep in touch. I'd like to know how the girls are doing."

He laughs. "Well, you *are* their aunt."

The remark is strange, but comforting, too. I've lost so much family. It's nice to have found some for a change.

We wish each other well and say goodnight. I'm about to flip the phone shut and get back to Sam when I notice a missed call from Lewis.

My heart starts racing. I'm still geared for worst-case scenarios. (With someone Lewis's age, any call could be *the* call.) I doubt that'll ever change. But I talk myself down and listen to the message. A package has arrived for me at home. I can't imagine what it is.

I check the time. It's eight o'clock. Lewis should still be up. "Hi," I say when he answers, "I just saw your message. I must've been busy—"

"Think nothing of it. I didn't know if you'd want this box opened. It came by courier this afternoon. Corinne brought it over. I figured maybe it was important."

"Courier?"

"I thought that was strange myself. Hence the phone call. So?"

"Who's it from?"

"Um, the handwriting's atrocious. I really couldn't say."

"But it's addressed to me?"

"Near as I can tell."

I shrug. "Go ahead and open it." As long as it's not a bomb, we're in the clear.

"Will do." While he shuffles through the house, looking for a pocketknife or a pair of scissors (or so I imagine), Sam pops up outside the van. She makes a pouty face, which means we've lost the cornhole match.

I roll down the window and tell her to grab the chocolate bars and marshmallows from the cooler. Losers supply the ingredients for our nightly round of s'mores.

Sam disappears and Lewis comes back on the line. "Let's see." He huffs through opening the box. "I don't ..."

"What is it?"

His voice is suddenly scratchy. "Is this for me?"

"What is it?" I repeat.

"The necklace. Georgette's necklace. It's beautiful."

The citrine. When I asked Edward to look for it, I didn't think he'd take it seriously. Finding Lisa Thompson's family was the brass ring. But he's come through for Lewis, too. With a happy little pain in my heart, I say, "You're right. It *is* beautiful. Just like her." I don't have the words for how I feel. Not long ago, my life was a puzzle with missing pieces and others jammed in the wrong spots. Now everything is where it belongs. It feels good. It feels right.

"Thank you," says Lewis.

"You're welcome." I close my eyes and smile through the tears.

ABOUT THE AUTHOR

NINA GRANT loves all things twisted, darkly funny, and a bit vulgar. As a sociology undergrad, she was drawn to the study of deviant behavior. Her favorite stories have unpredictable characters who violate social norms. She's enthralled by true-crime mysteries and often finds herself feeling sad that *Dateline* is a rerun. When she's not writing, Nina enjoys the beaches and forests of Maine, where she can be found working through kinks in a plotline or snapping pictures of moonrises and native birds. Nina is also a trivia fanatic—her lifelong ambition is to be a clue on *Jeopardy!*—and the proud rescuer of a silver tabby named Stella. Connect with Nina at:

Website:
https://www.ninagrantbooks.com/

Facebook:
https://tinyurl.com/mr25bhvx

Goodreads:
https://tinyurl.com/y9k544n5

Printed in Great Britain
by Amazon